FEAR OF THE GUN

FEAR
OF
THE GUN

A tale set in the New Mexico & Arizona Territories: 1849 - 1884

JOHN GERTS

John Streg Publishing

Acknowledgments

Cover art: John Gerts
Contributing Editors: Steve Gerts, Paul Gerts, Marda Gerts, Margretta Dumas

Research: John Gerts

Thanks to Terry Gerts, my life mentor.
Thanks to my wife, Margretta, who is my inspiration, my love, my life.

Printed in the United States of America
First Printing, 2022

ISBN 978-1-7326034-3-1

John Streg Publishing

Lorenzo's Luck

Hanna's Hope

PART ONE

1 |Shepherd of the Mountain

Eighteen days west of Albuquerque and a thousand feet higher, Lorenzo checked his Bowie knife on his right hip. *Still in its scabbard.*

Pain shot up his leg every other step during the trudge-a-long as if someone kept sticking the point of his Missouri toothpick deep into his left thigh three inches above the back of his knee. The shrapnel from the explosion that flattened him in the Battle of the Sacramento River north of Chihuahua in February '47 caused a hitch in his every other step. Lorenzo had taken the brunt of a howitzer lob as he tackled Daniel Martensen, saving his friend's life.

He didn't dwell on his battle injury. Walking to Alta California, across the New Mexico territory, had not been part of his plan. He cursed the loss of his saddle and horse. The three queens he held at the Cantina del Canon saloon in Albuquerque should have been a sure bet. Lorenzo's luck continued to hound him, all bad.

Lorenzo Brennan considered himself an excellent poker player. During a conversation with anyone downing tequila, the gambler would reveal the amount of money he had won in his travels. A typical gambler, he declined to mention his losses. Lorenzo exchanged his horse and saddle for eight dollars from the pot, canceling his game debt. He would need to be careful (not gamble) until he made it to San Francisco and the gold field.

On the day of the three queens, Lorenzo listened to two ranch hands on the way to California from El Paso. Coming out of the saloon, he watched a covered wagon pass him with the words "Gold Rush" painted on the canvas. Perhaps Lorenzo could swing his luck back to the positive side. He followed the wagon out of town.

In the months following his discharge from the Maine Militia, Lorenzo became a rounder: working the circuit of saloons, brothels, and gambling halls in the southeast New Mexican territory. In February '48, the war ended with the Treaty of Guadalupe Hidalgo; whatever that was, Lorenzo didn't care.

Lorenzo and Daniel Martensen volunteered to accompany Captain Smith out of Fort Preble, Portland, Maine, in '46. The company marched along Cumberland Road and proceeded up the Missouri River by steamboat to Fort Leavenworth, Kansas. They drove supply wagons along the Santa Fe trail, joining Colonel Doniphan's army on a march into Mexico. The two friends traveled together, scouting Indians and learning soldiering during the 2,500-mile trip to the war front. Battle-weary by the time of their discharge eighteen months later, Lorenzo at the time told Daniel he would not return to Maine. Instead, he tasted the whores available in Texas and New Mexico, living poor, moving between poker games. Daniel traveled back to his wife and child in Portland.

After months of reckless behavior, Lorenzo became tired of the prostitutes. He never seemed to win enough to afford the pretty girl, settling for more tequila and the leftover fille de joie. Thus, Lorenzo avoided "the calamity."

A good poker player needs a hook, an advantage. Lorenzo, tall and skinny, had a bit of a vacant look about him. At times, the look matched the man. Affable in the extreme, the gambler made friends everywhere, thus making it harder and harder as he roamed to find poker neophytes to beat.

Walking toward the sunset, he stayed focused on getting to the Sacramento valley, ignoring his leg. The horseless traveler was motivated by dreams of men panning gold nuggets in freezing ankle-deep California mountain streams. Suppose he had gotten wind of the strike four months ago. He could have taken Cooke's Wagon Road west out of El Paso Norte through Tucson to San Diego and Los Angeles and on up the Missions Trail to San Francisco. Gold would already be filling his pockets. It would take a month to get back down to Cooke's Road. The Old Spanish Trail and the Armijo route north of his present location would take him through snow-buried mountain passes he had no business trying alone. Lorenzo had scouted with Daniel from Fort Leavenworth, Kansas, down to Santa Fe and beyond, and then down the Rio Grande in Mexico. He recognized the western Indian tribes on sight. By heading due west along Indian trails to the Great Basin Desert and along the Colorado River to Lake Bigler, California, Lorenzo figured to miss the worst of the long winter. Then he lost his horse on a sure bet.

February of '49 had been unseasonably warm throughout the mountains Lorenzo trekked. Tonight, though, looked like the start of a cold snap. Lorenzo's bad luck ran true, the temperature dropping into the high twenties. Wearing his long dark-grey canvas duster and wide-brimmed hat pulled down on his forehead, he unrolled the bedroll he carried and wrapped the wool blanket around his shoulders, looking all the time for suitable shelter along the trail. Snow nearly buried the path. A clearing up ahead would have to do. He planned to lean boughs from a pinyon pine against a branch, crawl out of the wind and build a fire; hopefully, his fingers weren't too numb to start one.

When he reached the clearing, he saw the light across the valley up in the foothills, and Lorenzo decided to head for it. Perhaps he would find a friendly neighbor. Yes, a cabin and an outbuilding. A pen next to the barn held a herd of sheep. All seemed quiet, yet a dog inside the house began barking a warning when he stepped on the covered porch. A woman's voice soothed the dog to quiet. Lorenzo hesitated. Surely his gruff appearance arriving out of nowhere in the dark would scare the shit out of the woman, her husband, and the dog. In the wilderness, Lorenzo feared a shoot first and asked questions later attitude might greet his knock on the door. He could see the light streaming from underneath the door.

The blanket wrapped around him; Lorenzo lay down facing the door, curled into a ball. Warmth streamed from beneath the door and warmed his hands. He figured the time: *after midnight*. In the light of day, he could explain himself. If the snow stopped, he would move on before the cabin's inhabitants woke. Another long day. He slept.

***

The cabin's two glass windows were frosted over. Chris Sandler's mule-drawn wagon had packed his wife's essential living requests in a four-month round trip to Denver after roofing their cabin.

Glass windows topped Rachel Sandler's list as they planned the cabin and a wood-fueled cook stove. When her mother died, Hanna Sandler was ten years old. She eased her father's sorrow by taking over all her mother's house chores and helping Chris with the sheep and garden duties. Hanna grew up fast and lonely. Now twenty-six, she had missed any prospects for marriage or a family.

Her mother married a gentile. In ten rapid growth years, Rachel imprinted on Hanna her important Jewish beliefs: strength in education and knowledge, treating people with dignity and respect, and the importance of making the world a better place. The other Jewish traditions Rachel left in the move west with her soul mate Chris Sandler.

The Sandlers built the cabin in the foothills east of the San Francisco Mountain Peaks; the sun soon lightened the morning sky. In the afternoon, the sun sets early behind the mountain, shortening the daylight hours in the cabin.

After flinging off the covers, Hanna stoked the fire in the stove, adding a log to start. She dressed and opened the cabin door to let Bandit out. The dog leaped over Lorenzo, still asleep in front of the door.

Melting snow dripped off the roof line on the bright cloudless day. Smiling, Hanna glanced down as Lorenzo stirred.

Lorenzo, eyes widening, grabbed the porch post and pulled his rangy frame upright, rubbing his eyes and slapping himself awake. Hanna, too, couldn't speak. Lorenzo began to stammer, "I most deeply apologize for my trespass on your porch, Madam. I arrived late last night and did not wish to disturb your family unduly." Bandit jumped back on the porch, sniffing the tall traveler. Lorenzo let Bandit lick the back of his hands, forming a friendship, "I received warmth from your fire from underneath the door; it might have saved me from frostbite. I had planned to be off before you or your husband stirred."

Lorenzo stepped off the porch, moving away toward the valley and the Indian trail he meant to follow. "I'm sorry to have bothered you, Madam."

Hanna shook her head, thinking she must be dreaming. As Lorenzo stood, she had to raise her head as he towered over her. Her father's height of five feet nine inches made this man seem like a giant in comparison. Broad-shouldered but skinny. He looked like no man she had ever met, limiting her perception of men.

Lorenzo walked fifteen feet before Hanna found her voice. “Sir! Oh, Sir, you must be hungry. I have flapjacks planned for breakfast.”

“No, ma’am, I wouldn’t think of putting you out. This porch saved my life, though; thanks again,” said Lorenzo. He noted a beautiful woman in the doorway with the sheepdog beside her. The woman possessed black hair, all skewed and frizzy. She was shapely through the chest and thin-waisted. Not beautiful, but nearly so, and capable, Lorenzo guessed. If she asked him again, he would turn back.

“Why don’t you leave after breakfast,” Hanna said, “I’m making flapjacks. You might as well get a good start on your journey.”

“OK,” he said, “If you want to check with your husband and he agrees, I’m sure I could eat at least six pancakes.”

“I’m the one that makes the flapjacks, and I’m the one who says who eats ’em,” Hanna replied, “Besides, I don’t have a husband, and my father is off looking for gold. That’s Bandit. Seems to like you.”

“I’m on my way there myself, ma’am,” Lorenzo said.

Hanna indicated a seat at the table to Lorenzo. She went behind the curtain that separated her bedroom from her father’s bed and the rest of the cabin. Lorenzo heard the sound of her hairbrush pulling through her nighttime tangles. When she returned to the kitchen, Hanna had curled her hair in a bun on the back of her head, held up by an ivory stick pin. Hanna’s neck appeared lean and long to Lorenzo, soft; he would bet. *Yep, beautiful.*

The stove fire felt right to Hanna, so she stirred and spread the coals. Her cast iron griddle would be ready in a couple.

Hanna cracked two eggs, flour, baking soda, powder, and a dash of salt into a wooden bowl. She retrieved the goat's milk from yesterday evening's milking, stirred, and poured four discs on the griddle. Lorenzo ate all four while Hanna poured more batter. When Hanna brought the second batch to the table, Lorenzo stood and introduced himself.

Hanna brushed flour from her hand and offered her name. Lorenzo urged Hanna to sit and eat the second batch while he made the next round. Hanna didn't think the tall man would look comfortable in a kitchen but didn't wish to seem impolite, so she let him make the subsequent two batches. Besides, she didn't want him to leave. The pancakes, smothered in honey, turned out as well as Hanna's attempts.

The couple took turns at the stove until they both had their fill. Hanna set a second cup of steaming coffee in front of Lorenzo. "Your father has a head start on me," he said, "I bet he's fishing nuggets from between his toes already."

"That would be a miracle," said Hanna, "father promised to give it a year. That means I'll be on my own for spring shearing."

Every minute Lorenzo spent chatting with Hanna, the less he wanted to leave. *Sure, she has rough hands, but she's yearning for something.*

"Where are you from, Lorenzo?" asked Hanna as she cleared the table and set the kettle back on the stove to heat dishwater. The man had manners but a northern accent.

"Way up in Maine, but I haven't been there since '46."

"We shepherded our starter herd here from Albuquerque," Hanna commented. "Two Churro rams and two ewes. Now we're at thirty-two sheep in all. We have all the grazing land we might want. The water from a spring up on the mountain to the west runs by the back of our cabin. That seems like a miracle in hand to me."

"Your father sounds like a man of action, Hanna," said Lorenzo, "I kind of have that kernel in me as well."

Dishes done, Lorenzo retrieved his hat and slicker, heading for the door.

"Would you care to see our herd, Mr. Brennan? I must send the sheep to our upper pasture for the day."

Lorenzo did not wish to seem impolite in his haste for gold, "That does interest me, Hanna. Does Bandit lend a hand?"

"You watch. Bandit, time to go to work," Hanna said.

Lorenzo and Hanna walked sixty feet to the barn. The snow from the previous night mostly melted, Bandit herding them in circles the whole way. At the shed, they passed an outhouse. Lorenzo turned back toward the outhouse.

"I need to use your barn privy, Hanna. Do you mind?" said Lorenzo.

Hanna shook her head, and Lorenzo hurried into the outhouse. Fifteen minutes later, he emerged, pale, with a slight shake, "I don't know what has come on to me. I must have picked up something from someone at the trading post where I stopped. I better move on down the trail."

"You look night and day different than at breakfast," she countered, "you look like you could fall over at your next step."

What the hell is happening? Lorenzo thought. He felt like hell. "Sorry," he said and abruptly returned to the outhouse.

Hanna had little worldly experience, but her mother had made sure she could read all thirty-six books on the shelf in the cabin. *Cholera,* Hanna thought. The man could die in days or weeks. Sorrow entered her heart. In twenty minutes, when Lorenzo emerged again from the outhouse, looking even more pale and gaunt., Hanna had made up her mind. Lorenzo nearly fell over as he sat down, leaning against a tree for support.

"You won't make it down the trail," Hanna said, "I'll set up your bedroll on some hay in the grain barn, close to the barn privy."

"Hanna," said Lorenzo, "too dangerous; I do not want you sickened."

"Nonsense," she said, "I can't turn you out now against my mother's religion. I'll make broth, set up clean water next to your bed, and look in on you on the hour. I'll stick close to the cabin and use the necessary there. Give me five minutes."

When she returned, Lorenzo had thrown up pancakes five steps from where he had sat down and returned to the outhouse, uncomprehending what else could come from his body. Hanna assisted the tall man to the bed she had devised in the barn and then rushed for a bucket in case he threw up again. Next, she hoisted a bucket of clean water from the stream and set it down with a ladle next to Lorenzo's new home.

Leaving Lorenzo to struggle, Hanna went to the cabin and made a salted mutton stew. When she returned to Lorenzo's side, he had passed out.

She slapped him awake, "Mr. Brennan, you must keep drinking water and eat as much of the stew as possible. Take small bites often and sip water. I'll check on you after the sheep move up the mountain. Promise me you'll do as I say?"

Lorenzo looked like death but managed to nod. Hanna had done what she could. *It will be up to him and God.*

***

For the next seven days, Hanna did nothing but deal with Lorenzo except to herd the sheep to pasture and milk the goats. Lorenzo made it to the barn privy on his own accord, but in between bouts, he sometimes became delirious, yelling to an imaginary friend named Daniel to get down and stay down.

With encouragement, he would take sips of water. Like it or not, Hanna forced stew broth down Lorenzo three times an hour, all day, all night. His fever broke after four days. So weak he could barely walk, Lorenzo figured he might survive. He knew of so many that didn't.

Hanna had heard stories of thousands dying in a single city. Her fastidious mother often quoted Deuteronomy verses on cleanliness and the separation of clean water and outhouse waste. Upon inquiry, Lorenzo spoke of a small trading post he had stopped at five days before reaching the sheep farm. Hanna believed the mountain's miracle spring brought Lorenzo back to life.

Lorenzo recovered, regaining his appetite. In the fourth week, he helped with light chores around the cabin and barn and began to absorb the tasks involved in the sheep farming business from Hanna. Watching and collaborating with Bandit amazed and delighted the tall man. Hanna's day-long smile aided his recovery.

For his part, the raven-haired beauty occupied his thoughts, supplanting gold nuggets with a dream of the softness of Hanna's neck, lake-blue eyes, and dimpled cheeks. *What could she see in me?* He began to work even harder on the chores around the farm, suggesting repairs and improvements he could complete within his skill set.

Hanna appreciated the industrious man keeping her company. Sometimes she could not tell what he thought of her, the sheep, or the farm. He hadn't mentioned the gold fields since that first day. Would he be gone when he regained all his strength, weight, and dreams of riches? He looked a little empty. Not dumb, she guessed, but not exceptionally smart either.

She knew Lorenzo possessed the qualities of a good man, considerate, kind, and respectful of her and Bandit. At times she contemplated Lorenzo holding her in those long arms, kissing her while she tousled his mop of hair.

Lorenzo prepared to leave in the first week of April, wrapping his bedroll and checking and cleaning his rifle. Over breakfast, he broached the subject of his departure, "I guess it's time for me to stop taking advantage of your hospitality."

"You are leaving then?" she asked, sitting hard opposite Lorenzo at the table.

"I thought," she stammered but couldn't think how to continue.

Lorenzo tried to read her manner, searching her words for hidden meaning, "You have done so much, saved me for sure."

"You have given back and then some, Lorenzo," she said.

Scared as he had been during the Battle of the Sacramento River, the woman across the table terrified Lorenzo ten times more than the lancers, the bayonets, or the cannon volleys. Summoning his battle courage, he choked out, "Could I stay? Would you have me?"

Tears dropped to the table from Hanna's swelling eyes as she smiled, "Could you stay? Will you stay, Lorenzo? Do you love me?"

"I guess I do," said Lorenzo, standing, circling the table, and lifting Hanna from the chair into his arms, "I do love you. You are everything I need." He felt the warmth of her, her strong frontier arms. *Gold, be gone.*

2 |Blue Sky

From that day, even when it rained, Lorenzo envisioned a blue sky beyond the whistling Ponderosa Pine treetops surrounding the farm clearing. Recovering from Cholera sharpened his focus. He respected the sturdy cabin, ignored the constant bleating of the sheep, and stepped lightly with his come-a-long leg among the rocky terrain, letting his boots sink in the lush high meadow where the stock grazed. The view down the mountain to the verdant valley spreading south took his breath, as did the curly-haired running Bandit streaking black and white as he circled a miscreant ewe. Hanna, skirts swishing while carrying the sloshing water bucket, thrilled him with imagined nighttime possibilities.

A week later, Hanna laid shearing tools on a barn table.

"We've waited long enough, Lorenzo," she began, "will you help with the shearing?"

"Never even seen it done, darlin," said Lorenzo, "show me how, and I'll give it a try."

As Lorenzo cleaned and scraped the barn floor, Hanna set up the shearing run fence uprights into the steel bases permanently set in the ground. The posts formed two lines a single sheep's width from the corral to the barn.

Hanna affixed braces to hold fence rails to each post. Lorenzo helped Hanna attach rails on the brackets to complete the run. He fastened the sheep-holding yokes by dragging two shearing frames to the run. Hanna showed Lorenzo how to sharpen the shears for the rest of the day. Bandit and Lorenzo brought the flock down off the mountain to the pen. Hanna would start the shearing process in two days, barring rain, after the sheep went a day without eating.

On the morning of the second day, after an early breakfast, Hanna signaled Bandit to cut out one ewe and force it down the shearing run while Lorenzo held up the slide gate.

Hanna took hold of the ewe and flipped it over to shear the belly. She spent an hour shearing, talking through the steps, and asking questions. The process looked intricate to Lorenzo, requiring considerable skill. The next sheep Bandit sent through Hanna sheared in fifteen minutes, intimidating him beyond nervousness. Hanna slowed down again for the third shearing. She handed the shearing scissors to the tall, trepidatious Lorenzo for the fourth ewe. His hands seemed to have ten thumbs. He knew the sharp scissors could slice through wool, skin, and bone. Sweat dripped down his back. He couldn't do it, and he looked up at Hanna.

"Go ahead; the first is the worst. I'll talk you through," said Hanna.

Lorenzo couldn't speak. The farm of his youth produced corn and alfalfa, milking cows, three horses, and vegetables. The tall man's eyes pleaded with Hanna, but she stared back until he shrugged and tried it. His disastrous first fleece looked pitiful next to Hanna's work.

Hanna laughed, "See? Not the end of the world." She leaned over the shearing stand, hugged Lorenzo, and offered a kiss. She took the shears and spent ten minutes shearing Lorenzo's sheep to its summer coat. Then she gave the scissors back to Lorenzo. "Try it again, Lorenzo, a bit closer this time. Just remember to protect her teats with your other hand."

Bandit barked, anxious to herd the next victim to Lorenzo's station while Hanna held the slide gate. Lorenzo took a deep breath, thankful Hanna hadn't lost faith in him, and tried again. He did a little better.

The couple sheared half the sheep before Hanna started for the cabin to fix supper, instructing Lorenzo on the cleanup and temporary storage of the wool fleeces.

After Lorenzo and Hanna finished shearing the rest of the herd the next day, fleece cleaning began. First, the couple clipped out the tag from the back legs and butt and threw it into a separate pile, too dirty to attempt cleaning. Then they piled the fleeces, shorn in one piece from neck to haunch, next to the scouring tub.

Lorenzo built a fire beneath the spit holding the hot water pot. While he tended the fire and transferred clean water to the scrubbing tub, Hanna stirred, sloshed, and kneaded the grease and shit out. The first of four cleaning rinses. Lorenzo spread rows of washed shearings to dry in the spring breeze and shade of the barn. Ten days later, both working in tandem, clean, dry, fluffy wool filled the barn loft.

Two hours each day, the couple broke away from the wool tasks to till, plant, and mind the garden in the dell. They planted beets, potatoes, carrots, beans, lettuce, onions, sweet potatoes, squash, and turnips. A garden section for herbs and spices held parsley, mint, thyme, and oregano.

Wild huckleberries, elderberries, saskatoons, and strawberries grew on the mountain among the pines. Lorenzo would collect a year's supply of honey soon. In the spring, they would boil maple syrup. Lorenzo's new lifestyle balanced food production for sustenance with wool production for profit, and he maintained the land and structures for Hanna's peace of mind.

Bandit slept outdoors in the spring, summer, and fall to guard the garden and the sheep.

Lorenzo built two more winter sheep huts this year for the expanding herd. The ewes had so far produced five lambs. Hanna surmised she would add three or four to her stock while slaughtering two rams for their table.

Hanna transformed the fleece into wool fabric bolts for sale to the mercantiles in Albuquerque and Santa Fe. Her trademark patterns involved weaving cloth from huckleberry died fleece with the natural grey and whites shorn from her flock. Her cloth stockpile from last year's shearing occupied shelves in the corner of the cabin.

For the two weeks of fleece staining, Lorenzo teased Hanna about her blue hands and arms, addressing her as the purple forest monster haunting his bed.

While Lorenzo herded sheep and tended the garden, Hanna carded the wool. Late fall and all winter, she would spin the yarn, weave the textiles for sale, and make blankets and clothes for Lorenzo and Hanna's use. As far as Hanna knew, her great-grandmother from Germany had passed the loom and spinning wheel down to her mother, who had treasured them during the trip west.

Sweat and smiles marked the passing of summer days. Lorenzo adapted to bathing in the freezing spring-fed pool up the mountain a short distance from the cabin. Hanna always commented on his cleanliness as she invited him into bed. Needless to say, Lorenzo took a bath a day.

By late May, Hanna knew she was with child. Three weeks later, being the frank and forthright daughter of a stalwart Jewish tradition, she informed her common-law husband of their impending family expansion.

After Hanna washed and boiled the dinner dishes, she asked Lorenzo to sit opposite her at the table, "Lorenzo, I'm pregnant."

Lorenzo's expression didn't change except for slightly widening his eyes. *Vacant!* Hanna thought, "I want us to be married," she concluded.

"I'm not much for churches, Hanna," said Lorenzo, "I have confessed a comfort for saloons, but church makes no sense to me."

"I have gathered as much, Lorenzo, and that is OK. You have accepted me and my Jewish background without hesitation. I love you more for your honesty.

"My mother practiced little of her religion after moving west to our mountain, but she did pass on one tradition that I think could apply to our situation. I have drawn up a marriage Ketubah. If you read it and sign it, we will be married in my eyes."

Suddenly nervous and stunned, Lorenzo read the short paragraph Hanna had smartly written on one of the precious sheets of parchment she kept for making bills of sale. Lorenzo's full name graced the top of the section in large letters. The paragraph stated that he would promise to provide Hanna with food, clothing, and conjugal rights, inseparable from marriage. It included a guarantee that Lorenzo would pay half of everything he owned in the event of divorce and give inheritance rights to his heirs in case he died before Hanna.

Lorenzo cocked his head and read the document a second time. He wasn't sure he understood what he read, the promise of food, clothing, and conjugal rights. That must mean keeping up his ardor in bed, a pleasure, not a chore. He loved Hanna. He took the pen and signed in the space beneath the paragraph.

Hanna took the paper and signed beneath the second paragraph, which promised to honor Lorenzo with an equal commitment. Then she entered the bedroom and returned with a ring, placing it on the table before Lorenzo.

"This is my mother's wedding ring," she said, "I'll wear it now that we are married."

The simple gold band, only a little more than a sixteenth inch wide, fit Hanna's finger, and Lorenzo admired it.

"Wait," he said, "you're pregnant?"

***

As the months peeled away, Lorenzo became increasingly nervous, trying harder each day not to show his state of mind in front of Hanna.

What did he know about babies, children, and birth? He did know one thing. The birth process could be dangerous. The nearest town, Albuquerque, twelve days away by horse, would be their best bet. They could travel there when Hanna approached her due date, but that might mean two months away from the garden, the sheep, and the cabin.

In October, Hanna, due in the middle of December, decided she and Lorenzo could not wait any longer for her father's return. The couple packed their mule with their trade goods. Hanna made a list of the yearly supplies of foodstuff and dry goods she needed, including linen to make clouts for the baby. In one of the saddle bags, she tucked a letter to her father, inquiring as to his health and success in the gold mines of Alta California. Their plan hinged on Lorenzo finding a midwife willing to travel to their mountain and help with her delivery.

Before mounting Shady, their white-maned, charcoal-colored horse, Lorenzo turned back to his wife, a sudden stab of pain in the center of his stomach, "Give me a kiss and a hug, Hanna," he said, "A hug that will last me till I get back. I miss you already."

"Go on with you now, Lorenzo; I'll be fine. I'll be here doing all the work, so hurry."

"Listen, Hanna," Lorenzo choked, "You are the prettiest woman on this or any mountain. I'll return like a jackrabbit, so keep the bed warm." He gathered the mule's reins and mounted Shady. As the sun broke over the pines in the east, the horse threaded the forest trail down the mountain.

***

The rider leading the burdened mule heard the murmur of people's voices as they went about their daily business in Albuquerque. Traveling Romero St., these first voices other than Hanna's that he had heard in over nine months sounded like a choir singing. Lorenzo stepped down from Shady in front of Rosenstein's Dry Goods store on Plaza Street. He shook his legs to stimulate blood circulation, recalling how he hated riding a horse. Back in Maine, he had grown up just outside of Portland and didn't ride a horse more than three times until he joined the Maine Militia. On this trip, Lorenzo had pushed himself and Shady for thirty miles a day to get to the city in nine days instead of eleven. He hoped to return to the trail after one day of heaven-sent hotel sleep.

Hanna had directed Lorenzo to try Simon Rosenstein's store and reference her mother's name, Rachel Sandler.

Behind the counter, a man about the height of Hanna engaged a young woman in conversation. Mr. Rosenstein wore his thinning hair plastered with a pomade close to his scalp. His thin mustache never moved. His business suit sported a gold and black vest encompassing his considerable girth. A watch chain dangled from the right front pocket.

Lorenzo looked the worse for wear after traveling the Indian trails for so long without the opportunity to bathe.

"Good afternoon, sir," said the proprietor, looking up from his conversation with the young lady, "How may we help you on this fine fall day."

"My name is Lorenzo Brennan, Sir," said Lorenzo, "I understand you knew my wife's mother, Rachel Sandler, now deceased, and her husband, Chris Sandler. I have brought our stock of textiles woven by my wife Hanna to trade for supplies."

Simon smiled and shook Lorenzo's hand, "Very pleased to meet you, Mr. Brennan," said Mr. Rosenstein. "My name is Simon Rosenstein, and this is my daughter, Rebecca. Rachel and Chris have been our vendors for eight years. I recall that Rachel passed on eight years back, and Hanna took over as business manager for Chris's ranch. That girl knew how to barter, let me tell you."

"I believe you, Mr. Rosenstein," said Lorenzo, "for being so pretty, she sure is capable."

Rosenstein laughed, "How is Chris? How is the ranch doing?"

"I have not met Chris Sandler," Lorenzo said, "He left the ranch in Hanna's hands and took off during the gold rush. Hanna's herd is up to thirty-four sheep, four goats, and fifteen chickens. Shady, our horse, and Buster out there carry the goods."

"Mr. Brennan, if you unpack your mule and lay your goods on the counter, we'll see what we can negotiate."

"Mr. Rosenstein," Lorenzo said, "before I forget, I have a letter addressed to Chris Sandler from Hanna. Do you have a post office in Albuquerque?"

"No, I'm afraid not. Still two years away. We'll see when the railroad reaches us. There is a mailbox in the plaza, and the postman collects the mail every couple of weeks. If you write my address under Hanna's return address, I will hold any correspondence from Chris Sandler until your next visit."

Lorenzo worked out the barter to his satisfaction. He suspected that Hanna would have done better, but he did his best. Rosenstein took the list and pulled all the dry goods on Hanna's list. Pocketing the cash portion of the barter, Lorenzo asked for the nearest grocery, and Simon directed him around the corner of the block.

"My other purpose in Albuquerque, Mr. Rosenstein," said Lorenzo, "is to inquire as to a midwife to assist Hanna in the birth of our first child. Someone to assist with the baby and my wife for several months."

"Mm," murmured Simon, tapping his forehead in thought, "that is quite an appeal. Just how far west is your ranch, Mr. Brennan?"

"Ten days," said Lorenzo.

"Mm, I doubt you will find anyone willing to venture that far off the Santa Fe trail, Mr. Brennan. Indians around here, you know, are unpredictable."

"The Sandlers and I are on good terms with the Hopi and Navajo along the way. When we meet on the trail, I offer to trade our blue patterned blanket with one of their Navajo patterned blankets, and we're all smiles."

"I'm afraid I have no thoughts on the matter, Lorenzo," said Simon, "Perhaps inquire with Señora Vasquez at the Palace."

The young lady hurried over to Simon. "I'd be willing to go, Father."

"No," Mr. Rosenstein said, "of course not, much too young!"

Rebecca addressed Lorenzo, "I am sixteen, Mr. Brennan," she said, "I assisted my older sister Mary in the birth of my nephew Jacob just three months ago." Rebecca turned to her father, "You know I'm capable, Father, and Hanna needs help. She has always been kind and helpful to me when she visits."

Simon Rosenstein, exasperated, shifted the responsibility, "Your mother may have something to say about it," he said, but Simon knew he had been outmaneuvered.

Lorenzo suggested that the two travelers would head out in the morning if Rebecca's mother agreed. He offered Rebecca generous compensation for her efforts, eliciting a smile from Mr. Rosenstein. That settled the matter.

At the general store in the next block, Lorenzo loaded the mule's saddle bags with food. His grocery list included a firkin of wheat flour, a sack of rice, and a tall four-inch square tin of sugar.

He had enough money for dinner and a night's stay at Señora Vasquez's Palace, a two-story adobe inn that could take in five guests; dinner and breakfast were included for seventy-five cents. Lorenzo set all his purchases in the corner of his room, ready for packing in the morning. As he walked past the parlor to tend to his horse and mule, Señora Vasquez signaled that dinner would be prepared in ten minutes. Lorenzo led Shady and Buster to the stable, paying the handler for the night's feed, hay, and stalls.

After Lorenzo sat at the dinner table, another man clomped in and sat in the opposing chair.

"Antoine Leroux's my name, sir," he said, reaching across the table with a hand extended for a shake.

"Lorenzo Brennan. Glad to meet you," replied Lorenzo.

Lorenzo had served with the Maine Militia in the Mexican/American war under Captain Smith of the Maine Militia. Captain Smith reported to Colonel Alexander W. Doniphan, commander of the First Regiment Mounted Missouri Volunteers. The Missourians had come away from their backwoods homes and farms dressed in buckskins. They fought Mexicans as if angry bears had attacked their families.

A rough bunch, they gave no quarter to any man but followed Colonel Doniphan as if Jesus whispered in his ear.

Antoine Leroux's hair lay in soft, voluminous curls on his shoulders. His beard looked clean and combed as well. The odor of animal fat rose off the man's buckskins, filling the cabin. His attire was not overly soiled. His mustache covered his mouth, but his penetrating eyes revealed the cleverness of an educated man. He spoke fluent Spanish with Señora Vasquez. Lorenzo guessed he knew French as well.

For a mountain man, Antoine seemed more social and educated than the lone wolves Lorenzo had met in the war.

"I hail from Taos," said Leroux, "I'm on my way back north with a wagon load of supplies tomorrow."

"I will load up my mule and head west tomorrow as well," said Lorenzo, "I help manage a sheep ranch up in the San Francisco Peaks with my wife, Hanna."

Antoine, impressed, said, "I have trapped through there. Been a while, but beautiful country. What's your spread like?"

"We have thirty-four sheep, a log cabin built by my father-in-law, two barns, and winter sheep houses. It is beautiful. The stream in the back of the cabin flows year-round, and we have a pasture up the mountain and down in the valley."

Vasquez came out of the kitchen carrying two plates with beans, rice, and shredded pork. She returned to the kitchen and brought a plate of cornbread and a pitcher of maple syrup.

Both men devoured their food. Vasquez snatched the empty plates and left to fill them again, returning moments later.

Leroux finished his second plate and set down his knife and fork, "I've got over two hundred sheep up in Taos," Leroux said. He described his ranch to Lorenzo. Stating the particulars as if the two men both operated small homesteads.

They exchanged war records. Lorenzo reviewed the Battle of the Sacramento River, and Antoine told of scouting for the

Mormon Battalion under the direction of Philip St. George Cooke in his drive to reach San Diego from Santa Fe. Cooke's Wagon Road is the southern artery across the territory between the two towns.

Lorenzo spoke of the small Maine Militia group traveling the Cumberland Road to St. Louis and Fort Leavenworth, down to Santa Fe, and into Mexico. Antoine described the breadth of his travels. His trapper, explorer, and guide skills had already reached legendary proportions.

"What say we continue over at the saloon," offered Leroux.

"A whistle wetter sounds marvelous to me," answered Lorenzo.

The evening began to blur for Lorenzo after the second Cactus Wine (tequila and peyote tea.) He spotted a faro table in the corner of the saloon and, after his third drink, lost sight of his resolve never to gamble again. Antoine and Lorenzo, now boozing buddies, played the table, Antoine winning, Lorenzo losing. When Lorenzo bet his last nickel, he asked his newfound friend Antoine Leroux for a loan. Antoine, shorter than Lorenzo by four inches but with a frame solid as a buffalo, refused and tried to talk Lorenzo into coffee and bed.

Lorenzo suddenly remembered his promise to himself not to lose money gambling. He became morose, describing Hanna to Antoine as a steadfast, strong, and beautiful frontier woman he genuinely loved and wished not to disappoint.

He begged Antoine for a small stake.

Antoine Leroux drew his right arm back, smashing Lorenzo on his left cheek with his gloved right hand, sending him spinning to the floor. He helped Lorenzo up and led the dazed luckless man back to Señora Vasquez's Palace, at which point Lorenzo passed out on the bed in his room.

In the morning, Lorenzo woke with a sore purple cheek and a twenty-pound headache. Pulling himself together, he entered the dining room, sat down, put his elbows on the table, and held his head in his hands. He asked Señora Vasquez for coffee. Lorenzo checked his pockets. *Not a dime to my name. Just like the last time I left Albuquerque.*

Señora brought a bowl of rice and the leftover pork from the previous evening. Thinking about the long ride ahead, Lorenzo choked down every bite and asked for a third cup of coffee.

Señora brought the coffee and placed an envelope next to his bowl.

"Antoine left this for you. He said to tell you he felt bad hitting you last night and hoped you could both still be friends."

Lorenzo opened the envelope. Money spilled out along with a note. It read:

> ***Lorenzo, I doubt you remember, but you had the good sense to turn over half of your money to me before we went to the faro table last night. I am returning it. Go home to Hanna. You are the unluckiest gambler I have ever met. Antoine Leroux, fellow shepherd.***

With equal hope and shame, Lorenzo retrieved Buster and Shady from the stables, packed and tied down all the purchases and his bedroll, and led the animals to Rosenstein's Dry Goods. He met Rebecca Rosenstein standing on the porch of her father's store. She held the reins of her sorrel pony. A round leather pouch behind her saddle housed her spare clothes and unmentionables. Her bedroll looked to include one of Hanna's rolled wool blankets, and Rebecca tucked in a slicker between the bag and cantle. She wore a brown suede split riding skirt and a floral-patterned calico blouse. With her hair pinned up and tucked into a broad-brimmed sun hat and sporting a red bandanna around her neck, Rebecca looked the part of a cowboy in chaps.

Lorenzo mounted Shady and began pulling a ladened Buster toward the trailhead west. Rebecca nimbly mounted her pony to assure Lorenzo of her determination to ride the distance to the San Francisco Peaks. Her trail partner noted her comfort on the horse. He hoped his luck in finding Rebecca would counter, in Hanna's eyes, the money lost at the faro table.

3 |White Massacre

On October 31st, '49, a soldier surrounded by a whirlwind of dust skidded to a stop in front of the home of Antoine Leroux. The sergeant had ridden hard from the Army post in town to the Leroux hacienda three miles north of the community of Taos. Near a corral and the barn, men shepherded twenty sheep into two farm wagons, ready to travel north to Denver slaughter. Sergeant Robles spotted Leroux helping among his crew and approached. Antoine walked around the wagon to face the soldier.

The soldier saluted Antoine, "Sergeant Roble at your service, Mr. Leroux. I have been sent by Captain William Grier of Fort Fernando de Taos to accompany you back to town."

"Hold on, Sergeant," said Leroux, "I just returned from Albuquerque with supplies. Tomorrow I'm off to Denver with a load of sheep."

Leroux let his words sink in a moment, "In other words, I'm not available." Antoine turned back toward the wagon.

Sergeant Roble manhandled Leroux's shoulder and turned him back around.

"I am ordered not to take 'No' for an answer," Roble said through a clenched jaw. "This is urgent, and the captain needs your tracking skills. A band of Jicarilla Apache and Utes has kidnapped a white woman and child. The Colonel ordered Captain Grier and the 1st calvary to find and rescue the woman and child and their negro slave."

Antoine shot back, "I find that hard to believe. We haven't had any problems with those Indians. I'll get my gear and horse and head to town with you; I want to hear the whole story."

***

Antoine knocked, and he and Sergeant Roble entered the captain's office. Grier and Robert Fisher, a friend of Antoine's and a fellow tracker, paused in their study of the New Mexico territorial map to greet the newcomers.

"Thank you for coming, Antoine," said the captain, "You and Robert are acquainted, I believe."

"Yup," said Leroux, "Now what's this hogwash about a Ute, Jicarilla ambush."

Dressed in buckskins like Antoine's, Robert Fisher raised his hands, shrugging, "Let's just say civility went out the window when a group of greenhorns pushed too hard."

"Let's stick to the facts, Robert," said Captain Grier, "I have the report right here."

Grier picked up the written account off his desk for reference.

"Four days ago," he said, "James White, a merchant with established mercantile businesses in Santa Fe and El Paso, traveled west of Kansas City with thirteen wagons of supplies. He had joined Aubrey's ten-strong wagon train."

"François Xavier Aubry?" Antoine interrupted, "He's a respectable wagonmaster, minds his p's and q's with the Indians."

"That's just it," Grier continued, "After the wagon train finished traveling through Ute hunting grounds and figuring the dangerous part of the trip over, Aubry called for the caravan to camp.

"White got an itch to move on, deciding to separate from Aubry and the wagon train and advance to Santa Fe alone. The fool salesman brought along his wife Ann, baby daughter Virginia, a negro nursemaid, a servant named Bushman, two Mexicans, and a German called Lawberger. Aubrey's wagonmaster, William Calloway, led the small group for two days in two carriages, pausing near Point of Rocks, between Rock Creek and the Whetstone Branch.

"On October 24, a band of Jicarilla Apache and Utes approached the group asking for presents."

Fisher interrupted, "Standard practice shouldn't have been a problem."

"White and the other men drove the Indians away from the camp," said Grier, "but the band returned to ask again, receiving the same response.

"The third time the Apaches and Utes returned, they attacked. According to the report, an Apache shot Calloway through the chest and Lawberger through the neck. The two Mexicans fell nearby as White defended his family, dying from eight bullet and lance wounds. White's servant, Mr. Bushman, died as well.

"A party of New Mexican buffalo hunters happened on the scene. While the hunters ransacked the carriages, the Indians attacked again, killing one hunter and wounding his young son. The buffalo hunters retreated and moved on. The injured boy played possum until the Jicarilla Apaches, and Utes left, crawling back to Point of Rocks and finding help.

"News of sightings of a white woman and child among a band of Jicarilla Apaches and Utes reached the army post at Las Vegas. Captain Judd ordered Sergeant Swartwout and twenty men to negotiate an exchange for the white woman. The small troop found the wreckage and buried the dead.

"When Aubry's wagon train arrived in Santa Fe, he received the news from Point of Rocks and Sergeant Swartwout and sent this report to me. His reputation being at stake, he has offered a $1,000 reward for the return of Mrs. White and the baby, who he noted as missing and not among the dead.

"There you have it. Experienced mountain men will ensure the success of our mission. Dick Wootton, Jesus Silva, and Tom Tobin have agreed to help. Antoine, you will be my chief scout. I need trackers. I have organized a joint force consisting of forty-two men of the 1st Dragoons and forty mounted New Mexican Volunteers under Captain Jose M. Valdez. We'll also take along pack mules with supplies and a battery of 6-pounders. We will rescue the kidnapped woman and ensure the Utes, Apaches, and all other tribes think twice about molesting Americans on the Santa Fe trail," Grier concluded.

"That kind of talk will surely result in the slaughter of a white woman," Antoine said, with an acknowledging nod from Fisher.

"Let's go, then," said Leroux, resigned, "get it over."

"Rayado is less than three days away. I also want to recruit Kit Carson to help on this mission," Grier said.

Antoine snorted, "Up to you. You've got trackers. Fisher, Wootton, me, and the others, but in the country that includes mountains, rocks, plains, and desert, the more trackers, the better. We're losing daylight; the trail is a week old."

"Sergeant Robles," Grier ordered, "assemble the men. Be ready to march in thirty minutes."

4 |Guarding the Sheep

Bandit whined at Hanna, nudging her skirt until she awoke slumped in a chair on the front porch. A three-quarter moon rose above the Ponderosa pines, so even though her fire in front of the cabin had died, she could easily see the barn and corral. The sheep shifted and bumped, crowding together in a corner by the barn.

Hanna adjusted the furs and blankets thrown over the chair, sat up, and scratched Bandit behind his ears as he laid his head on her lap. Lorenzo had left twenty days ago. Conservatively, Hanna figured to guard the corral for four more nights.

The wolf had shown up the night before. Bandit had charged off the porch barking, waking Hanna. She came out of the cabin carrying Lorenzo's rifle in her nightshirt. Cloudy conditions had made it impossible for her to see much in the direction of the barn. She heard the snarls of wolves and sensed Bandit trying to herd the wolf away from the sheep. She called him back three times before he returned, trotting around her, waiting for a signal to work the wolf or wolves.

Hanna had told Bandit to sit and lay down as she cocked the rifle and fired, shooting over sheep's heads. She heard a board of wood splinter on the barn. At least she had hit something. The sheep quieted, and so did Bandit and the sheep. The wolf had left. Hanna spent the rest of the night sitting on the edge of the porch, leaning against the loaded gun. The wolf returned sometime later. The rifle scared him off again. In the early morning, Hanna picked out three pairs of eyes as wolves skirted the corral. She fired the gun and sent Bandit out to chase the wolves away, recalling him before he crossed the distance from the cabin to the corral and barns.

Tonight, she remained dressed and on guard. Before taking up her post in the chair on the porch, she had set up a second chair tipped on its side a few feet off the porch. She had practiced leveling and steadying the rifle across the legs of the chair.

Suddenly, Bandit's ears shot up, erect. He scampered eight feet off the porch and stopped, turning his head back to Hanna, awaiting orders. Hanna swished off the porch and kneeled behind the overturned chair, taking up her shooting position, cocking the rifle. She caught sight of the wolf approaching the corral from the right. If she hurried, she could shoot before the wolf came close to the herd huddled at the barn.

Hanna's father had drilled her on the importance of taking a sure shot, not a hurried shot. She took three deep breaths, steadying her nerves and the rifle, and squeezed the trigger. A screeching howl erupted from the wolf as it crawled off, able only to use its front legs. Hanna's shot had shattered the wolf's hips.

The rifle's kick in the kneeling position knocked Hanna back to the ground. She couldn't see over her tummy. In Hanna's excitement, the baby thumped inside her, kicking hard. Hanna rolled over, returned to the porch, and reloaded the rifle. A minute later, she returned to the tipped-over chair, kneeling, ready for a second wolf approach. The continuous screaming of the wounded wolf diminished either from exhaustion or distance.

A half-hour later, Hanna returned to the relative comfort of the chair on the porch. The baby in her womb had calmed down as her nerves eased; the gun cradled on her lap beneath her extended belly.

5 |Needle In a Desert Snowstorm

Captain Grier led the 1st dragoons, the group of trackers, the volunteers, and mules through the Sangre de Cristo Mountains along the Taos Canyon. All parties reached Agua Fria on the high mesa in a day. The next morning, after crossing the flatland, the army company followed the Agua Fria creek and the Rayado creek to reach Rayado late on the third night out from Taos.

Captain Grier, Leroux, and Fisher hunted down Christopher Carson at the home of Lucien Maxwell. Grier explained the mission to Carson, describing the general area where the attack on the wagons occurred.

"The Whetstone branch near Point of Rocks, you say," said Carson, "We'll have to start from there to pick up the band's trail."

"That's the plan," said Leroux, "we'll pick up the Cimarron and push like hell to get to the kill site tomorrow."

That's when it began to snow.

Captain Grier's army troops came upon the wagon wreckage and graves on the second day of pushing the horses and men. Most of the party and all the horses stayed back while the group of trackers crawled around the site, brushing three inches of snow from their path and looking for signs. Tom Tobin came across the trail left by the Ute, Jicarilla Apaches, hours later. The Indians were heading southwest, not north. The surviving injured boy had been fooled. The Indians headed north to trick the boy and circled back to the rest of the band traveling on the trail Tobin found. Daylight hadn't faded when Kit discovered the first Indian campsite and Virginia White's little rocking chair covered with snow. Leroux and Carson pushed Grier to follow the trail until dusk. The trackers spread out and stopped every fifty feet, sweeping away the deepening snow to verify the track.

When the troop came to the Canadian River on the morrow, Fisher signaled Leroux and Carson.

"They are following the river south now," said Fisher, "We'll make suitable time for a while, I bet."

Leroux shrugged, "They may get tricky. Tracks along the river here. Well-traveled. I hope we don't lose them in the mix."

Two days later, the trackers reported to Captain Grier that the trail had vanished. They needed to backtrack and look for signs off their path. Grier decided to camp at the present location and let the trackers work the area.

It took two days to pick up the trail. The trackers assumed that the Indians had not crossed the river. They divided the land on the east side of the river into sections and assigned two trackers for each segment to pick along the trail for signs. Fisher and Tobin stayed within fifteen feet of the river, Leroux and Wootton worked between fifteen and thirty feet, and Carson and Jesus Silva even farther out.

On the second day of the careful search, mostly on hands and knees, Fisher found a torn piece of cloth sticking out from beneath a rock. The scent of perfume on the fabric, faint to anyone but an experienced and capable tracker, suggested a white woman. The trackers revised their sections, widening their radius from the center point of the found bit of cloth.

Encouraged by several moccasin footprints in an area of soft soil below seven inches of snow three hundred yards from the river, the trackers visualized a line perpendicular to the river. The line aligned the rock with the cloth and the footprints; the trackers moved forward. In three hours, Antoine found an Indian campsite. The mountain men concluded the Indian band had broken from the river to throw off pursuers.

Robert Fisher drew the short straw and returned to the Canadian river to report to Captain Grier. Kit Carson continued tracking to the east, and Antoine Leroux was a reference point for the troops.

At dusk, Antoine lit a signal fire that guided the army to his location. Kit Carson showed up mid-morning the next day. He and Jesus had followed sign as far as Whetstone creek, whereupon the Ute and Apache group turned south again, the tracks evident.

The entire company pushed forward along the creek bank, the trackers scouting three hours ahead to avoid missing any signs or allowing the horses to obscure the trail. Two long days later, the trackers, now working in ten inches of snow, again ran out of tracks and signs. Antoine and Kit crossed the river, hoping to pick up indications on the other side of the creek, while Fisher, Wootton, Tobin, and Silva searched in a radius west of where the Indian tracks vanished. The two trackers on the east side of the creek admitted defeat in half a day and returned to camp, joining the other trackers in a sweep of the land to the west.

Intermittent snow plagued Grier as he urged the mountain men, trackers, and troops forward. Knowing that the snow must be slowing the Indian band's progress, Leroux and the trackers redoubled their efforts. The company traveled a punishing forty miles that day. Grier decided to encamp in a grove of nearby cottonwoods to rest his horses and men for the final push forward. Leroux suggested he and Wootton climb Tucumcari Butte (rising one thousand feet above the prairie) to try and locate the Ute, Jicarilla Apache camp.

When the two scouts reached the top of the mountain, Leroux scanned the landscape for the Indian camp or travel route. Wootton pointed south.

"Ravens, Antoine," he said, "flying in circles to the south. They are interested in dead animal carcasses in the Indian camp."

Antoine focused his spyglass on the cottonwood copse below the birds. He could see movement. Then he spotted teepees.

"We're close enough to set up a parley for first thing in the morning," said the lead tracker, "Let's get back and report to Grier."

Jesus Silva and Tom Tobin returned from their scouting efforts, having located the Indian encampment. Grier ordered the company forward on a trot. He kept pace until the company reached hills above the Apache and Ute teepees interspersed in the cottonwoods along the Canadian River.

Carson, far in advance, could see that the troops had alerted the Apaches, who were breaking camp in a hurry. As he galloped forward, he called back to the men to follow him.

At that moment, Leroux and Wootton rode up to Grier. Antoine dismounted and grabbed the reins of Captain Grier's horse. "Where are your senses, Captain," said Leroux, "You've ridden up close to their camp at full strength. We got to parley a trade for the woman."

The captain dismounted, boiling.

Kit Carson rode up to the captain as well, furious, dismounting. "Why are you waiting? We've lost our advantage." Carson planted his feet shoulder-width apart, stretched his diminutive five-foot one-and-a-half-inch height, puffed his chest, snarled, and poked Captain Grier. The six-foot captain never budged.

"No, Kit," Grier said, ignoring the affront, "Leroux suggests a parley. We'll try to get the woman out first. Antoine, Kit, Sergeant Robles, and Sergeant Fincham ride forward with me. Sergeant Robles, carry the white flag."

Carson threw up his hands, "This is nuts!" he said, turning to his friend, Antoine, who couldn't have disagreed more.

"Captain, send the troops and volunteers back a quarter mile to show a peaceful intent," Leroux suggested.

"The company will stay where they are, ready to charge," said Captain Grier, "Let's go."

Five riders cantered forward. The captain reined in his horse one hundred yards from a line of Indians. Behind that line, the rest of the band scurried to bring down their teepees and gather their children and belongings.

Captain Grier began walking his horse toward the camp. His small party stayed close. Suddenly, the white woman, easily recognizable despite mud caking her blond hair, broke through the Indian line and ran toward the white flag.

"Captain, something's wrong with her; she's barely able to walk, let alone run," said Fincham, "We need to gather her up."

The woman looked wretched. Her feet were swollen and blistered from forced marches since her capture.

The Apache line had not moved.

"Get down, woman," Antoine said, "Lie flat. Give us a chance to get to you."

"Fool woman," Kit agreed, "Hurry, woman, run, run!" he shouted. The party mounted and set their horses at a run to try and reach the screaming white woman. She hobbled twenty more feet, then pitched forward as Leroux had suggested. An arrow in her back had ended her escape.

Kit Carson reached her first, dismounted, and turned the dead woman over. The arrowhead peeked out of her breast, dribbling blood. Knife cuts and dried blood peppered Ann

White's face, arms, and legs. Her swollen bare feet were encased in dirt-cake boots.

Rifle shots and arrows from the Indian camp momentarily stunned the men standing over Ann White. Recovering, the men began to mount their horses. Captain Grier spun to the ground, wounded.

Kit Carson had enough. He leaped on his horse and began frantically waving to the troops on the hill to charge. Sergeants Fincham and Robles scooped up Captain Grier, threw him across his horse's saddle, mounted their horses, and ran Grier's horse back to the command tent.

Antoine and Kit charged the Indian line with the dragoons and volunteers now only twenty yards back.

A roar erupted from the line of soldiers on the hill as they descended on the Indian encampment, scattering Apache and Ute men, women, and children as they attempted to escape. With the trees offering cover to the Indians, the battle turned into one-on-one exchanges between mounted soldiers and running warriors weaving in between the trees. Fisher shot one warrior as he swam the river. Twenty-five Indians outdistanced the pursuing soldiers on their fresh horses and quickly dispersed, melting into the woods. Indians pursued by soldiers and militia volunteers died from saber slashes or pistol shots, women and children included. The chastisement that Captain Grier intended was conducted in the extreme.

When it ended, the scouts gathered in Captain Grier's tent. The captain sat in a chair, showing off the smashed bullet that struck him in the breast. The bullet hit his suspender buckle and deflected its course into his gauntlets tucked into his coat pocket. He, therefore, avoided significant injury.

"Gentlemen," he said, "we did not save Ann White. We have no idea of the whereabouts of her daughter, Virginia. However, our casualties and injuries are minimal. The Ute and Apache tribes will hear talk of the skirmish on the Canadian River. My report on the matter will praise our trackers. No one could imagine we could follow this band in calf-high snow for two hundred miles.

"My report will include Fisher's excellent shot of the Apache swimming the river. As to the rest," Grier paused, looking at each man surrounding him in the tent, "the weather is turning sour again, and the snow is blinding. The bones of the dead Ute and Jicarilla Apache can rot beneath the snow for all I care. Prepare the company for immediate travel to Taos."

On the return trip to Taos, the blizzard continued to push against the troops, and men suffered terribly. Grier's black servant died in the storm. On November 24, the men staggered into Captain Judd's camp at Las Vegas, New Mexico, where Kit Carson left the command for Rayado. The rest of the troops continued to Taos, arriving on November 29th.

"Juana, Juana," shouted Antoine, roving from room to room to locate his wife.

Juana came running in from the wellhead. Antoine's booming voice reverberated throughout the house.

"Ma chéri, I missed you," he said, catching her up and spinning her around. "I missed you terribly."

"Merde," said Juana, using her favorite French word in her limited French vocabulary, "I don't believe that for an instant. You and your adventures."

"Perhaps you are right, ma chéri," he said, "but I sure enjoy coming home to you." Dusk had settled on the hacienda. Antoine took Juana by the hand, leading her to the bedroom.

6 |Hanna's Mettle

Lorenzo and Rebecca arrived at the cabin the morning after Hanna crippled the wolf. Hanna sobbed in Lorenzo's arms, releasing the stress of keeping her herd of sheep safe. Lorenzo hugged her so tight that Hanna didn't notice Rebecca in the doorway petting Bandit.

Minutes later, Hanna dried her eyes and hugged Rebecca.

Hanna and Rebecca chatted, reviewing family stories from Albuquerque. Then Hanna hugged her husband again, whispering, "Thank you for bringing Rebecca, Husband."

"She has experience with her sister," said Lorenzo, "I believe you can count on her. I will help as well, Hanna. Please tell me what you need when the time comes."

"I have been having practice pains since you left for Albuquerque," Hanna told them both.

Lorenzo stayed out of the way, tending the sheep and crops for the next week and a half. Rebecca and Hanna worked on pickling and drying vegetables, pulling the potatoes and carrots for the root cellar, and preparing a quantity of deer jerky.

All three worked on the preparations for childbirth. Hanna smiled whenever she caught Lorenzo rubbing his hands together or kneading the circulation in his thighs. No one spoke of the actual birthing process, dangerous as it would be to Hanna and the baby.

Rebecca had instructed Lorenzo to cut away the front of one of the straight-back chairs to form the birthing station. Old wool covers graced the floor close to the stove, the birthing chair centered on the blankets, ready. Pots for hot water, a bucket with a ladle for water drinks, and plenty of wool and linen rags sat on the table near the chair.

To Rebecca's recollection, every detail looked complete and ready. Frontier women matured out of necessity. Hanna as well took the inevitable in stride. The two women did not have long to wait. Hanna's water broke during dinner. Rebecca helped her clean up, and Lorenzo helped her move to the birthing station.

Hanna, in the chair, petticoats bunched at her knees, progressed in labor next to the warm stove. As the tightening intervals shortened, the pain of each increased. Hours passed, and Hanna accepted a leather belt to bite on as she fought the pain. Rebecca sat on the blankets before Hanna, only checking Hanna's bottom every half hour to not appear anxious. The baby would emerge when ready; Rebecca had no control over it.

Lorenzo stood behind the chair, rubbing Hanna's shoulders and back, cooling her forehead with a water-dipped cloth. As the hours of tension crawled on, Lorenzo pulled up a chair but maintained the massages. His neck was stiff. His stomach never released the knot. His knees locked awkwardly behind the birthing chair.

Hanna bit through the leather belt in three places in twelve hours before Rebecca declared a sighting of the top of the baby's head.

"Now, Hanna," she said, "You can push the baby out."

Hanna spat out the belt and screamed, bathed in sweat, exhausted. She slumped when the pain eased a moment. Terrified, Lorenzo looked at Rebecca, pleading with his eyes for news of his wife.

"Wake up, Hanna, Hanna, Hanna, get ready, Hanna, again. Now, push, push.

"Yes, push, keep pushing."

Hanna screamed again. Lorenzo swallowed the bile in his throat, terrified that his wife's strength would give out.

The baby boy slithered out, and Rebecca wiped away the blood and mucus. Lorenzo came around the birthing chair and pleaded a wan smile out of his wife.

An hour later, with both mother and baby boy cleaned up, the cord tied off and cut, and the afterbirth discarded, Hanna truly did smile at Lorenzo. Her face was peppered with popped blood vessels resembling freckles, and her husband beamed and relaxed. Inwardly, he worried that the danger wasn't entirely over.

Hanna knew. She felt sore but OK, the bleeding minimal. Baby Jeremiah, tentative at her breast, warmly wrapped, opened his eyes for a moment and tried to suck again. Jeremiah Joseph Brennan was born on November 17th, 1849. On the same day, Anna White died next to the Canadian River. The same day the 1st Dragoons abandoned the search for Anna's baby girl, Virginia, five hundred fifty miles east of Hanna and Lorenzo's cabin.

***

For the first six months, Lorenzo personified the naive father. He paced the cabin with a faraway look, trying not to get in Hanna's way, willing himself not to cover his ears at the constant crying.

Lorenzo tried to imagine when the child could walk behind him in the woods, play poker, or work with Bandit as a miniature shepherd. He loved his new son, devoting every spare moment to the baby, providing him with wooden toys, berries from the woods to eat, and fetching his blanket when Hanna asked. That never wore off.

Hanna announced her second pregnancy on New Year's Day, '51. She predicted a new baby would arrive in late September or early October. Lorenzo knew about complicated pregnancies, but Jeremiah's arrival was still a fresh memory. The distraction of Hanna's rounding belly and her morning sickness did not find much sympathy from Lorenzo. He concentrated on the little boy taking his first shaky steps. Lorenzo didn't want to miss a moment of his son's progress.

Another child, a boy, would help around the ranch. If a girl, Hanna would dote on her, and Lorenzo could concentrate on Jeremiah's boy skills, hunting, tracking, and wrestling.

In late March, while herding his sheep back from pasture, Lorenzo met a fur trapper passing through the valley, leading a horse stacked high with traps and furs. Lorenzo asked the mountain man to stay for dinner. The man stunk up the cabin, appreciated the lamb chops Hanna served for supper, and offered news of the world away from the San Francisco Peaks.

Hanna and Lorenzo listened to anecdotes of more settlers heading their way, disrupting the trapper's territory. The beaver hunter had met a family clearing timber just two days' walk east of the cabin. In their fifties, the parents had three sons in their late teens and two girls interspersed in age with the boys.

Mr. Sandreen spoke through his beard, speckled with dried grease, of a new fort eight days ride east from the peaks and west of Santa Fe. The trading post at the garrison would be more convenient than traveling to Albuquerque or Santa Fe for supplies. The thinning beaver population had forced the trapper to travel further northwest in the Ponderosa Pine Forest and widen the radius of his traps.

Lorenzo felt the want in his chest as the man related the doings and changes in the territory. He had given up his wanderlust nature to settle with Hanna. His growing boy, the expanding herd, and the improvements Hanna had suggested to the ranch gave Lorenzo a sense of accomplishment. He missed some aspects of his former life, the tales of his card prowess, and the laughs around a poker table. The drinking. On balance, he felt lucky. Yet the sameness of the ranch routine contributed to an itch somewhere in the middle of his back that he couldn't, wouldn't scratch.

Hanna, the pragmatist, viewed her second pregnancy with confidence and eagerness. She always saw the glasses on the dinner table as half full of the best-tasting spring water in the world. Her husband never put off the demanding work of the farm; he never raised a hand or a loud voice to her. Lorenzo loved her every day and told her so with a kiss every night. She had never known life away from the cabin. Her cocoon world was comprised of her mountain, her man, her child, and her sheep.

Hanna had firmly admonished Lorenzo when he returned from Albuquerque with Rebecca, confessing to the money lost at the farro table.

"Well, a lesson learned, right?" she said. "You just lost half of our profits on our year's work."

"Hanna, I am a fool," pleaded Lorenzo, "I had hoped to buy you a dress from Rosenstein's, or a pretty stick pin, or…."

"What would I do with any of that," Hanna interrupted, "I just needed you home to shoot the damn wolf."

"I know, Hanna, I know. I will never lose money playing poker ever again," said Lorenzo.

"You will never play poker again, husband, for the sake of our marriage."

"I promise!"

"Good," Hanna said in a softer voice, "If there is something you need to buy soon, think again. I will spend the money you brought home until you have worked off your loss. Agreed?"

"Of course," said Lorenzo, "I agree."

***

Summertime on the mountain settled into an uncomplicated rhythm. Shepherding for Lorenzo and baby Jeremiah's play time, garden weeding, and ranch repair. For Hanna, the dyeing, carding, and wool weaving took her mind off the child growing inside her. She decided from the mild kicks against her side that this next baby might be a gentle soul, whether boy or girl. The flock count had reached sixty-two. Hanna discussed the trip to Rosenstein's Dry Goods because they had skipped a year due to Jeremiah's age. Hanna wanted to wait a month or six weeks after this next birth to travel as a family. That way, Lorenzo's gambling would not be a temptation or a problem. They still had not decided whether Lorenzo would fetch Rebecca again or travel to the new fort and seek a midwife there.

During the weekly discussion on September 13th, '51, Bandit jumped up, hearing a strange sound; the knock on their cabin door was so rare it startled the dog and humans alike. Jeremiah woke up crying.

Lorenzo opened the door, his left hand on the barrel of his loaded rifle leaning vertically in a cubby above Jeremiah's reach.

In the doorway stood Antoine Leroux, rifle cradled across his folded arms. Lorenzo recognized him, hidden behind his foot-long full beard. His hair, wavey black with gray streaks at the man's sideburns and running back over his ears.

"Hanna," Lorenzo gasped, "This here is Leroux, the man I told you about who saved our last dimes in Albuquerque just before Jeremiah's arrival."

"Bonjour, Madame Brennan," said Antoine, "I suspected this cabin might be yours, Lorenzo, from your description. The light in the window led me right here from the trail."

"Please, Mr. Leroux, Antoine, isn't it?" said Hanna, "My name is Hanna. Have you eaten? I have a stew that is still warm on the stove. Would you have a bowl?"

"Never turn down a cabin-cooked meal," Antoine said. "My fire cooking on the trail barely qualifies as sustenance."

As Hanna retrieved a bowl of stew, Lorenzo invited the mountain man to sit at the table, clearing Hanna's knitting and retrieving a spoon for his guest. Leroux brought forth his hunting knife and set it on the table in case anything in the stew needed cutting.

Hanna left the table, returning with Jeremiah in her arms, wide awake, wide-eyed. Lorenzo pulled the boy from Hanna's arms and sat down at the table with him on his lap. "Jeremiah, this man's name is Antoine."

"B… Bear," said Jeremiah.

Antoine laughed, "Call me Bear, young man," he said, "Been called worse names."

"What brings you to Antelope Springs, Antoine?" Lorenzo said.

"Antelope Springs?" said Antoine, "That's one of the reasons. How did you come up with that name?"

"That is what Trapper Sandreen called our ranch," explained Lorenzo. "The first time he stopped at our spring, an Antelope jumped the creek before him. Gored him with one of his eight points as he flew by."

Leroux's grin widened, "Maybe tomorrow we could trek up along the creek," he said, "I may be able to convince the survey crew to come through here. You know water is God's hope for settlers in this territory.

"Brad Sandreen, eh, haven't seen him in four years. Anti-social, you might say. A good trapper, although the pickings are sure slimmer these days."

"Survey," said Hanna, taking Jeremiah back and carrying him to his crib. "What does that mean?"

"I apologize, Hanna," Antoine continued, "I work for Captain Lorenzo Sitgreaves. He's in charge of an expedition surveying a path to San Diego. He's with the Corps of Topographical Engineers, a branch of the army planning the construction of roads, railroads, and lighthouses."

"That sounds impressive," said Lorenzo.

Antoine continued, "Sitgreaves' crew is under the protection of thirty soldiers commanded by Major Henry Kendricks. Over eighty mules carry tents, tools, surveying equipment, ammunition, provisions, and water tanks. A group of nature enthusiasts has come along to collect samples and artists to draw landscapes and record the terrain. Samuel Woodhouse, a naturalist, heads that group and serves as the expedition's physician. Yes, we are pretty well set. However, we have slaughtered twenty-eight of the forty sheep we herded this far. Salted meat from here on."

Lorenzo recalled exchanging army experiences with Antoine when they first met in Albuquerque. Leroux had talked about scouting for an expedition at the start of the Mexican war in '46. Antoine guided the Mormon Battalion on a road-building trek from Santa Fe to California along the thirty-third parallel near the border with Mexico.

"So, you're leading this group due west from Albuquerque to San Diego?" Lorenzo interjected.

“That would be true if Sitgreaves would listen. We should be able to shorten the trip to California via a route along the thirty-fifth parallel,” said Antoine.

“From Albuquerque to here is a pretty straight trail, isn’t it, Lorenzo,” Hanna said.

“True enough,” said Lorenzo, “Not wide enough for wagons, maybe.”

Antoine shrugged, “The problem is Sitgreaves keeps thinking river travel is the answer. His orders are clear but not realistic.

“We started following the Zuni river to the southwest, shrinking this time of year and a dry riverbed in winter.

“Then, at the confluence of the Little Colorado river, we followed that river northwest. It took me two weeks to convince the commander that the Little Colorado River would lead him into the deepest, most extended, and most dangerous canyon west of the Appalachians.

“By the time I changed his mind, we were north of the San Francisco Peaks, and Sitgreaves decided to survey a route around the north of your mountain.”

“That is unfortunate,” said Lorenzo, “The path overland through our valley south of the mountain is just not that difficult.”

“Not only that,” said Antoine, “but there’s the spring. This excursion is a side trip just for me. I usually scout two weeks ahead of the troops. I wanted to explore the valley here and the spring. Expedition scientists are digging around an ancient Wupatki ruin we discovered northeast of here.”

“What do you say, Hanna,” said an enthusiastic Lorenzo, “We could take Antoine up the mountain to the start of the spring and picnic there.”

"That might be a little too much for me," said a pregnant Hanna. "You go ahead, Lorenzo. Leave the sheep on the upper pasture with Bandit in charge."

"Alright, what say we bed down for tonight and start early in the morning," offered Lorenzo.

"Sounds fine to me," said Leroux, "Mind if I bed on the porch."

"Not at all," said Lorenzo, recalling the winter night he slept on the porch before meeting Hanna.

"Wait a minute," said Leroux, slapping his forehead. "I have a letter for you, Hanna. Mr. Rosenstein at the dry goods store heard about the expedition and made the trip to Taos to pass on this letter. Sorry, it is so late arriving to you. Goodnight. Thank you for the excellent stew."

Lorenzo kissed Hanna goodnight and pulled over the cover, anticipating an early rise on the morrow. Hanna carried her letter and candle back to the table, sat down, and opened the envelope addressed to her in the care of Rosenstein's Dry Goods store. She pulled out a folded note and a second sealed envelope, setting both on the table. Hanna unfolded the letter.

Hanna,

I regret to inform you that your father, Chris Sandler, passed away last Tuesday, December 4th, '49. He asked if I could mail the letter he wrote to you six weeks back, if or when a post office became available, thus the long delay.

The winter fever swept through the camp before we could leave for Mokelumne Hill to try a new field. Your letter reached Auburn the last week in December. I took it upon myself to open it and could sense the love and support you showed for Chris. I read the letter aloud over Chris's grave. I hope he heard the words and is resting at the success you have had on the ranch and the loving husband you have found.

Chris was a good friend and partner. He stood by me on at least seven occasions.

Sincerely and with the deepest sympathy,
James Scott Knodel

Hanna opened the second envelope:

Dearest Hanna,

I hope this letter finds its way to you. I think about you and the ranch often, but not too often, or I would go crazy. Four of the boys here in the camp did go crazy. I can't say I'm gold-rich at this point. I have been working the pan and the long tom here in Auburn for a year. I build up a pouch of dust and a few pea nuggets, think I'm ahead, then prices for meals and supplies at the camp stores jump up again and wipe out my dust.

When I get over my case of the sniffles, my partner, Jim Knodel, and I will move down to Mokelumne Hill. We hear that placers in that camp clear the amount of gold dust I have in my sack in a single day. On our claim here in Auburn, we sift for a month to achieve the same amount of gold.

Now I'm just trying to eke out enough gold to compensate for the time and work I have put into this venture. My stubbornness has about had it. Either way, in one month down in Mokelumne Hill, I will head home if I don't turn up a considerable amount of gold. Hauling and cleaning dirt from sunup to sundown six days a week in icy water is crippling my hands and back. I have seen more mud and grime, sin and depravity, and men of evil intent than I can ever get out of my head.

I long to scratch the soft shoulders of our sheep.

I continue to have faith that you are well. Despite the single-handed management of the ranch, I trust that you are smiling over your efforts at the end of the day. You are capable, that is sure. I will see the San Francisco Mountain peaks again soon.

Your loving father,
Chris

Hanna read the letters a second time. Hearing her gentle sobs from their bed, Lorenzo came to the table and stood behind her, his hands holding her shoulders. Hanna turned in her chair, encircling Lorenzo's waist, burying her face in his nightshirt. "I am sorry you couldn't meet him," she said. "Jeremiah and the baby will never know him."

"I know," said Lorenzo, "but we have each other and the ranch he created, and you say Jeremiah looks a little like him."

Hanna nodded, stood, wiped her eyes with her apron, and dressed for bed. In bed, husband and wife hugged each other. Hanna extracted heavenly waves of love from Lorenzo. Lorenzo dreamt of California and the companionship of Antoine trekking further west. He dreamed of Hanna, how she had saved him from her father's fate, panning in dirty shanty towns on desperate mountains.

***

Lorenzo, Antoine, and Bandit shepherded the flock to the upper pasture as the sun broke through the treetops surrounding the meadow below the cabin. Leroux owned over four hundred sheep at his ranch in Taos, yet Bandit's skill and Lorenzo's gentle guidance impressed him. After settling the herd, Lorenzo and Antoine followed the creek through yellow-leafed Quaking Aspin. Corkbark Fir and Ponderosa Pine also lined the spring as well. Higher up, their boots swished through Alpine Avens, small yellow flowers spilling down among the boulders like a complimentary golden river.

Lorenzo's leg strengthened yearly; if Antoine saw Lorenzo's slight limp, he didn't mention it. The two reminisced about their adventures as only two war veterans could. They didn't need to brag; each story genuinely interested the other. Both men had traveled Cumberland Road. Both men had ridden the rails, hunted buffalo, and fought Mexicans and Indians. Both worked sheep ranches differentiated only by the size of the flock. Tales of shearing contests, fleece auctions, and slaughterhouses in Denver filled the time of the climb.

Dressed in fringed buckskin from head to toe, Antoine walked with a measured pace in the higher elevations of the Peaks. Lorenzo had no trouble matching the steps of the mountain man in the gentle climb. Antoine's rifle hugged his back, attached to his leather sling. Lorenzo carried his rifle by the muzzle, the stock extended across his shoulder behind him. Both men had bags slung from a shoulder resting along their left hip, but Antoine had tied his beaver hat to his belt with a string. Lorenzo didn't wear a hat. Compared to Antoine,

Lorenzo looked the part of a typical farmer in loose-fit trousers with a fall front, a solid blue wool shirt, and suspenders. Lorenzo maintained a clean-shaven chin, and his hair never curled more than an inch over his ears. Antoine's beard seemed at least twelve inches long to Lorenzo, with hair even longer flowing around his shoulders and back. Leroux looked like a woodsman who spent his life alone in the woods, a "bear," as Jeremiah had called him.

"Have you ever considered scouting again, Lorenzo?" asked Antoine.

"There are days, in the quiet of the upper pasture," Lorenzo said, "when I wonder about my life if I had continued during the gold rush that pushed me to the San Francisco Peaks.

"I would have ended up like Hanna's father, sick and broke. I would not be walking up this mountain if it had not been for Hanna's doctoring. No, she is the best thing that ever happened to me. She is my lucky charm."

"We owe a lot to the women we choose," Antoine said. "Juana has been the same for me. I can't get the whiff of rainfall in an untainted, untouched land out of my head.

"These days, I can't turn around without someone wanting me to show them the sunrises I have seen."

"Yes, you seem to be in demand," Lorenzo noted, "I'm not sure Hanna would understand what we're talking about. Her whole life has been on the ranch. She smiles at every sunrise as it is."

By one o'clock, the duo had reached the point where water poured down the ravine in streams out of the mountain, producing a fringe of green herbage. They sat down next to the gurgle and chewed jerky.

"I have been thinking about this, Lorenzo," said Antoine, gnawing loudly to finish a bite before proceeding. "I think you should come with me on this trip. I find I can talk to you. The soldiers are young recruits. The scientists are bothersome, and Captain Sitgreaves is disagreeable to the point where I sometimes feel like leaving the party to their own devices and heading back to Juana."

Lorenzo gathered gravel at the edge of the spring and scrubbed his hands, rinsing them in the cool water. Using his porcelain mug, he scooped a freshwater drink. Antoine followed suit.

"Let me think on it," Lorenzo said, starting the gradual descent back home.

The two descended in relative silence. The climbers reached the upper pasture, and Bandit met Lorenzo with a branch in his mouth. Master threw the stick several times and wrestled with the curly-haired dog for several minutes before ordering him back to work.

Bandit began to round up the three outlying sheep, running back and forth behind the herd until all the sheep, as one, began moving down the mountain toward the cabin.

"Lorenzo, I can tell you are capable," said Antoine. "You take care of your rifle, the ranch, and sheep. You've seen things and done things that indicate I could depend on you. I tried to tell Sitgreaves we needed two scout-hunters; careful not to disturb Indians we may contact."

Lorenzo still did not reply. He wanted to speak, *but Hanna would never agree,* he thought.

"It is a duty you can't ignore, Lorenzo," Antoine argued, "Hanna couldn't object to a Corps of Topographical Engineers Army order."

"No, Antoine, as much as I might wish for the experience, it wouldn't be under orders. Hanna would have to be completely OK with it. Me as well."

That night, with Antoine again asleep on the porch and Jeremiah quiet in the crib, Lorenzo broached the idea with Hanna.

"Never mind, Hanna," Lorenzo said minutes later. Hanna's glistening eyes and tears broke his resolution and burned in the pit of his stomach. *How could I think of such a thing?*

The couple went to bed, and Lorenzo leaned in for his goodnight kiss. He tried to dispel the tension in her shoulders. She responded, and the joint release of emotion they experienced while coupling provided a restful sleep for them both.

Lorenzo invited Antoine in the morning for breakfast, letting him know he would stay on the ranch.

Hanna, cheerful as always in the rising sun's light, provided the three of them and Jeremiah with pancakes and honey.

Antoine stepped off the porch, gathering his gear and shaking Lorenzo's hand. He bear-hugged Jeremiah and, at the last moment, picked up Hanna in a similar embrace. "You have a good man, Hanna," he said in her ear. After twelve feet, Antoine turned and waved at Jeremiah, who ran to the bear and hugged his leg.

Hanna looked over at Lorenzo, at ease with his decision. Then she turned to Antoine. The two men are honest, capable, and considerate. Good friends. She ran up to Antoine and gathered her son.

"How long will it take to get to California and back?" asked Hanna.

Antoine grabbed at the opening. "I would figure six months. Four months there, two months back."

"Lorenzo has to help with my baby. It should be easier this time, but I need him more than ever," Hanna said.

"I have thought on that, Hanna. I have a couple of porters, a Mexican husband, and his wife, that I could leave with you to help Jeremiah and the baby. Fernandez works on my sheep ranch and is a capable and agreeable fellow.

"I need a hunter and scout to back my play with the captain and any Indians we may meet.

"I'm almost certain Sitgreaves would pay two hundred dollars for Lorenzo's service under an independent contract."

Two hundred dollars! More money than Hanna had ever seen in one place. She turned to Lorenzo, eager but resigned. "If you stay for a week after the baby is born, could you catch up with the expedition?" she asked.

"Sure, I can," said Lorenzo, "but wait. Can Fernandez shoot? He may need to discourage the wolves."

Holding Jeremiah, Hanna walked back over to Lorenzo, pulling him aside.

"Husband, I can see how much this means to you," Hanna said. "I can see that you would stay. I can see that you will come back to the children and me. I ache for my father, but you are not a starry-eyed man like my father. I know you will return, my love."

Hanna emerged from the cabin, still holding Jeremiah, and addressed Antoine. "He is going with you, Antoine, but you must promise me this. He is not to gamble with this two-hundred-dollar fee you are promising. You saved him once. You better keep him safe again."

"Agreed," said Antoine Leroux

7 |Sitgreaves

Antoine and Lorenzo caught up with the expedition by traveling west from the valley, spotting the troop coming from the north midafternoon. Antoine, Lorenzo, and Captain Sitgreave parleyed until Lorenzo and the captain signed a simple contract for two hundred fifty dollars for Lorenzo's services.

The expedition had been without water for four days. Leroux led a small unit of soldiers and the pack mules carrying the rubber water tanks back to Antelope Spring to replenish the expedition's supply.

Having met Julia and Fernandez Murillo, Lorenzo accompanied the couple back to the cabin, getting to know the jovial pair and explaining the duties he expected of them. The Murillos, shorter than Hanna by an inch, spoke broken but understandable English. Fernandez's wrinkled and sunken cheeks, deep brown in complexion except for the cracks in his neck that didn't see the sun, seemed never to lose his smile. Julia, who had large hands and a waddling behind, gathered up Jeremiah, a newfound friend. Three days later, Julia and Lorenzo assisted Hanna at the birthing station to produce a baby boy after just three hours of labor. On September 18, '51, Hanna named her new boy Zachary Christopher Brennan.

On the second day, Lorenzo judged baby Zachary to be calmer than Jeremiah. Hanna and Lorenzo didn't feel the same nervousness over Zachary as when Jeremiah struggled to enter the world. Zachary, shorter than Jeremiah by an inch at this stage, moved arms and legs but not frantically, as Jeremiah had. Lorenzo held the baby after nursing, burping the little bug and handing him on to Julia. Three days later, Lorenzo saddled Shady and left for the expedition. He caught up to Antoine in the scientists' camp at the base of Williams Mountain.

Lorenzo wandered the camp looking over the shoulders of the artists finishing sketches of the mountain. Another explorer pressed wildflowers in a three-inch-thick book. The soldiers smoked and chewed tobacco around their fire, separated from the scientists by twenty yards. Lorenzo carried his bedroll over to Antoine, stretched out on his furs, his beaver hat covering his eyes.

"I ain't a sleepin," he murmured, not moving, "Is that you, Lorenzo?"

"I made it, Antoine," Lorenzo replied. "I have a new son named Zachary. Mother and baby are fine. Julia and Fernandez have things well in hand. Hanna is very appreciative."

"Happy it is working out. You and I will push ahead at daybreak. I like staying at least two hours before the Sitgreaves party."

Excited to explore unfamiliar territory and be helpful, Lorenzo woke up first, rolled his bed, and restoked the fire. Then he made coffee. The brew roused Antoine, and the two left the expedition on foot in fifteen minutes, leaving their mounts with the porters.

Antoine struck out about a hundred feet ahead of Lorenzo, indicating with hand gestures which trees to mark, clearing small brush to form a trail for the troop to follow. Lorenzo, lagging, blazed trees and continued clearing. They worked, stopping for a chew now and again and searching for streams to replenish their canteens. The scouts broke off around four o'clock to locate a suitable campsite for the night. The Ponderosa Pines were becoming sparse, replaced in numbers by

Pinyon Pine and Fir. Luckily, their elevation still afforded a small creek for water. The body of the expedition arrived within the hour, and the porters and soldiers set up camp.

Antoine and Lorenzo reported to Captain Sitgreaves and Major Kendrick. Leroux sat down in a folding chair in the captain's tent.

"Captain," Antoine said, "We are moving into lower and hotter valleys until we run into the Colorado River.

"That means we must fill every container we can carry with water out of the creek we found today."

"Right, Antoine," Sitgreaves said, "We'll issue a rationing order tomorrow. The guarded reservoir will be off limits to anyone whose canteen goes dry during the day, and a refill from the tank won't occur until the next morning."

Next, Sitgreaves asked about Indian sightings.

"We're both watching for natives," said Lorenzo. "Nothing to report yet. So far, we have tree cover that is keeping us inconspicuous. Of course, that situation will also change as we move into the desert. I suggest we route through any Yucca gardens, cholla, and scrub whenever possible."

Antoine concurred, and Sitgreaves appeared pleased. "What's your estimate on getting to the Colorado River, Antoine?" asked Kendrick.

Leroux scratched the back of his neck, "We have at least another day in the high forest," he said. "Another seven days to the Colorado River. We'll try to find water here and there, more of a concern than the natives."

The pines entirely disappeared from the landscape, replaced by tall Yucca as the expedition paced into chaparral country. The temperature stayed in the high seventies. The first day of water rationing proceeded uneventfully. Over the next four days, two privates attacked the sergeants guarding the mules carrying the company's water supply. The sergeants prevailed, arresting and restraining the privates.

The expedition spent twelve hours crossing a dry, flat valley on the sixth day. In their nightly report to Captain Sitgreaves and Major Kendrick, Antoine suggested that Lorenzo and he scout to the north in hopes of finding an easy path through the jagged highlands. Lorenzo pointed north to a high mountain covered with Ponderosa Pine. By climbing high up that mountain and using the spyglass, the scouts would see the Colorado River or determine the next week of travel. The captain agreed.

The scouts traveled all the next day without finding a worthwhile gap in the rocky foothills to explore or water to fill their dwindling canteen supply. That night, Lorenzo went to bed with a mouth dry as toast and no spit to swallow. "If we don't find water or passage tomorrow, what say we turn back?"

"We must be close," Antoine argued. "As a last resort, we can reach the great canyon by heading north. That mountain ahead will provide water. Look, snow on the peak. If nothing else, there is water."

After a night's sleep, the two started trekking early. Lorenzo allowed himself a sip of water, swirled, savored, and swallowed. His resolve returned. *If Antoine, seventeen years my senior, can make it up that mountain, I'll be next to him.*

Late morning the ground turned into gravel - all sizes, flat and walkable for at least twenty yards. The Black Mountains parted, and climbing up the side of the ancient riverbed, Antoine could see a green horizon through the dry ravine in the distance. The scouts had found a gap in the rocky upland to the Colorado River. In four hours, they were filling their canteens at the river bank.

***

The expedition camped at the base of the foothills about four miles east of the river because Antoine advised against camping at the riverbank until he and Lorenzo could scout the area. An abundant water supply like the Colorado River is a magnet for natives and explorers alike. The water team cautiously led the mules carrying the rubber water tanks back from the river to the expedition camp. Within a day of silent scouting to the north, Lorenzo spotted a camp of Mohave Indians on the bank of a fertile field along the river. Major Kendrick moved the expedition south along the river for safety reasons after one day's layover.

The evening before breaking camp, a contingency of the Mohave approached the expedition site. Judged by Kendrick and Leroux as a peaceful approach, the major ordered the soldiers to stand down, a circle of peace was established, and gifts were exchanged. The Indians provided fruits and vegetables in exchange for iron and steel tools the soldiers could spare. Antoine offered a pouch of flavored tobacco, and Lorenzo provided one of Hanna's blankets. The illustrators among the scientists offered desert yucca sketches and a mountain painting.

The meeting lasted until midnight. Antoine functioned as an interpreter. Although he did not know the Mohave language, he knew words from the Ute and Apache people, and with the help of sign language, he kept up a quiet conversation.

In the morning, the Mohave group returned. More women came, wandering through the tents, curious about the cooking techniques, standing over the artists and scientists as they worked. Major Kendrick put the camp breakdown on hold, not wanting to give notice of his intentions to the Indians.

The Indians stayed all day. More Indians came in the evening bearing more fruit and vegetables, looking for gifts.

The women wore bark strip skirts from waist to knee with nothing covering their breasts. The men wore simple breechcloths.

Captain Sitgreaves worried about the effect the women had on the camp men. The soldiers approached the Mohave women with trinkets to get a closer look. Antoine cautioned against allowing any affront to the Mohave women. The officers kept the enlisted soldiers in check but decided to move out the next day. Major Kendrick and Captain Sitgreaves, with Antoine's help, shooed the Mohave women out of the camp and ordered preparations for breaking camp at dawn. The women appreciated the soldiers' attention and appeared unhappy about leaving the expedition camp.

As the company broke camp at sunrise, ten to twelve arrows flew over the tents, landing harmlessly near the cook's station. The startled soldiers glanced around, finding no injury among their numbers. A second volley and a third arrow grouping came down on the camp. A cry of pain echoed in the rock cliffs behind the tents. An arrow had scored a human target. The expedition doctor, Samuel Woodhouse, holding his right leg below his knee, hobbled into a clearing by one of the campfires. An arrow protruded two inches out of the back of his calf. The feathered shaft sticking out of the front of his leg rocked with each step.

Lorenzo Brennan, the nearest thing to a doctor, helped the man to a folding chair, calming him. The cries of pain subsided as Samuel's breathing normalized, "Thanks, Lorenzo, this fucking thing hurts like hell," said Samuel.

"I'll get Antoine," said Lorenzo, "he'll know what to do."

Major Kendrick and Antoine had gathered a small force to pursue the warriors back into the scrub to the north.

"I know what to do," Samuel said, "just give me another minute."

Blood seeped out of both sides of the wound. Lorenzo worried the doctor might pass out. Samuel took a few deep breaths, the soldiers and Lorenzo standing over him. Having made their power known to the expedition, the Mohave warriors retreated, and no more arrows fell from the sky.

A soldier retrieved a second chair for Samuel to prop up his leg. The doctor's satchel contained his surgical saw. Samuel asked Lorenzo to saw off the shaft's feathered end while another soldier held Woodhouse's leg and the rest of the rod immovable. Lorenzo's first few rakes to get the teeth started jerked the pierced leg. Samuel grimaced through clenched jaws, sucking air as the saw caught and cut through the shaft. Turning as white as the patient, Lorenzo looked to Samuel for further directions.

Antoine appeared at Lorenzo's side, "The Indians have dispersed back to their camp. We've got to get that arrow out, right doctor?" said, Leroux.

"Right," said the doctor, "make a clean, fast pull, Antoine, be ready with soap, water, and the bandage from my bag, Lorenzo. Wrap the wound tight."

The two scouts made ready and, on the count, pulled the shaft, bathed the wounds, and wrapped the punctures with a length of cloth. Samuel tied the wrap off himself.

The expedition set off south along the river. Lorenzo and Antoine stayed within shouting distance of the rest of the group, the path ahead obvious along the well-traveled Mohave trail. The doctor rode one of the mules while other soldiers led the rest of the mounts along the way.

Lorenzo walked as quietly as possible through the scrub thirty feet away from Antoine on the other side of the path. He hoped to realize any threat from in front of the company before an arrow might find him. Seventy-five feet behind the scouts, a unit of soldiers led their mules along the path. Then the scientists and artists plodded behind the soldiers. The porters and supply mules came after the enthusiasts and, finally, the rest of the soldiers, protecting the rear of the expedition from attack.

The captain posted sentries that night, but with no Indian sightings, the civilians' fears eased.

Lorenzo, on his bedroll, could not unwind. Having dealt with Woodhouse's arrow wound, he imagined Mohave arrows from the sky striking him in the back. Antoine, smoking his pipe, relaxed on his bedroll next to Lorenzo.

"Want a chew, Lorenzo?" said Leroux. "You're fidgeting like a mink mother watching for a fox."

Lorenzo crossed his arms and breathed deeply, attempting to lie still. "I'm worried about Hanna having to deal with wolves around the corral," he said.

"Fernandez will manage that," said Antoine after a strong draw, "tell me about the new boy. What is his name again?"

"Zachary," Lorenzo said.

"Just like Jeremiah, is he?"

"I reckon not much, maybe," said Lorenzo, warming with thoughts of the calmness of his new son. "Jeremiah has reddish brown hair. The little wisps on Zachary were a black match to Hanna's. He's calmer than Jeremiah; he didn't cry much at all. I hope he grows. Smaller than Jeremiah at birth.

"Jeremiah likes the thought of a brother but is impatient when he plays with Zachary. He'll need patience before Zachary is ready for roughhousing."

"Do you think you'll have more children?" asked Antoine.

"Bound to, I guess," said Lorenzo. "I know Hanna wants a girl. It'll happen."

"Juana had three miscarriages after our daughter, Catarina, was born. Catarina's a grown woman with her own family now. I would have liked to have had a son, to be honest. You have boys to look forward to. With Jeremiah and Zachary."

"That is true, Antoine," said Lorenzo, "Got to make it home first."

Lorenzo still couldn't sleep. He left Antoine and wandered the camp for over an hour, checking with the sentries. The nervous scout laid down and planned the steps to take him back to Hanna. Finally, he slept.

Leroux and Brennan scouted ahead of the expedition along the Mohave trail for five more days. On the afternoon of the sixth day, the two spied another Mohave camp a half mile distant and a short distance from the river. The two retreated and reported to Captain Sitgreaves. Lorenzo suggested preempting the inevitable meeting with the Mohave by setting gifts for them just outside the perimeter of their camp. Within an hour, the Indians found the donations and reciprocated with their own favors for the expedition. Two elders from the Mohave camp and a young warrior stood next to the presents of fruits and vegetables.

Lorenzo, Antoine, and Major Kendrick approached the presents and elders with hands out in a peaceful gesture of goodwill.

"Hola, la paz esté con ustedes," said the young warrior in excellent Spanish.

Antoine stepped forward. He could speak fluent Spanish in addition to French and a bit of German. "Buenos días," he said.

Leroux explained in Spanish the expedition's intent to pass by the Mohave village in peace. Sitgreaves' group aimed to find the Gila River junction with the Colorado River and then travel west to California. The Spanish-speaking warrior told Antoine an eight-day walk would bring the expedition to Camp Yuma at the intersection of both rivers. The company bypassed the Mohave camp and bedded down for a five-day layover. Sentries spotted Mohave warriors lurking in the scrub, but Major Kendrick forbade any contact between the expedition and the base. The directive was to no avail. An officer overheard a Private bragging to another soldier of his success in bedding a native with substantial bosoms behind the chuck wagon. The soldier was arrested and suffered ten lashes administered by Captain Sitgreaves.

On November 22nd, '51, the expedition packed up and moved off using the same sequence of scouts, soldiers, scientists, porters and mules, and soldiers in the rear.

In charge of the rear guard with a contingent of soldiers, Sergeant Denton kept a watchful eye on the path behind them.

Private James Jenison yelled up the line to his commanding officer. "Sergeant Denton, Sir. Request permission to go back. I left my knife on a rock next to my bedroll. Five minutes run to the camp and back."

"Permission granted," said Denton. "Make it three minutes."

The expedition came upon an acre size field. The open space made Antoine nervous and feel unprotected. He and Lorenzo hurried across and urged the rest of the men to move forward. Private Jenison broke out of the scrub, yelling and running as the rear guard made it halfway across the meadow.

Fifty Mohave warriors, horizontally striped in white paint up and down their arms, legs, torso, and face, took five steps forward, firing six arrows into Jenison. The arrow wound in his neck spurted blood as he died. It appeared that the warriors of the two Mohave villages the expedition had encountered had joined to satisfy the perceived affront to the Mohave women.

The soldiers acted instinctively, dismounting and giving over their mounts to the porters. The porters corralled all the mules, hobbling them as fast as possible.

Major Kendrick ordered the rear soldiers to form up in two lines, one prone with the second line of soldiers kneeling behind them. Antoine and Lorenzo moved to the right side while the soldiers protecting the scientists formed up for an attack from the south.

Lorenzo, crazy with fear, took a prone position, his rifle ready. Antoine kneeled next to him.

Get down, stay down, Lorenzo thought, heeding the advice of his friend Daniel during the Battle of El Brazito.

The warriors advanced on the soldiers. Unwilling to start a bloodbath, Kendrick sought Antoine's help in a parlay. In answer to the captain, Antoine stood and rushed to a grove of small fir trees to his right. From there, perhaps he could signal for a parley. Arrows flew, and Lorenzo saw one strike Antoine in his upper right arm. Another shaft creased Antoine's left wrist. Antoine went down, and the warriors, sensing success, moved forward again.

Kendrick gave the order to fire.

The Mohave warriors were confused when four of their numbers went down.

Lorenzo saw his chance. Tossing his rifle to the soldier to his left, he rose and ran to Antoine, who bled profusely from an arrow wound at his temple. Blood covered his face. Lorenzo pulled Bear to his feet and leaned him against a tree. Kneeling, he leaned into Antoine's stomach, hoisting the man over his shoulder. Lorenzo turned and ran toward the protection of the soldiers. As he fled, an arrow whistled by his ear, the feather cutting his cheek.

Uninjured Mohave gathered up their wounded warriors and melted away in the chaparral.

Samuel Woodhouse rushed to where Lorenzo laid out Antoine to staunch the blood from above his temple. He wrapped a cloth bandage around his head while Lorenzo held a cloth on Antoine's wrist to slow the bleeding. Woodhouse finished the head wrap and switched positions with Lorenzo, who began cleaning the blood from Leroux's face. After wrapping the wrist, Samuel focused on the arrow in Antoine's upper arm, extracting the shaft similarly.

Leroux screamed while Samuel removed the stubborn arrow, "Jesus! Fuck! Brennan," he said, "Woodhouse is trying to kill me." Lorenzo ignored his friend, demanding that he drink some of the expedition's precious whiskey offered by one of the soldiers.

Kendrick ordered the company to move out. Soldiers helped Antoine and Samuel onto their mounts, and Lorenzo, picking up his rifle, moved out to his scouting position.

8 |Look to the Mules

Four days passed along the Colorado River without further Indian ambush or encounter. Captain Sitgreaves suspended the scientific investigation to reach Camp Yuma's safety. On the morning of the fifth day, Antoine, Lorenzo, Major Kendrick, and the company cook met with Captain Sitgreaves in his tent.

"That's it, Captain," said Moses Gibson, the negro chef. "We've got the mixins for flapjacks that will feed half the camp. Salted meat is gone, beans almost gone."

"Antoine, you and Lorenzo go on a hunt ahead of us and shoot us some meat," said Sitgreaves.

"I don't know about that, Captain," said Leroux. "Lorenzo here is our best shooter, better than me, but neither of us has seen much in the way of animals along the river here. The Mohave has a lock on food in the territory, and you saw how hungry those folks were at both the camps we crossed."

"We have to have food," said the captain.

"Not if it ain't there to be had," said Antoine.

"So, what do you suggest?" asked Sergeant Denton.

Lorenzo, his stomach rumbling from the reduced meal portions of the last two days, just wanted to get home. "Push on," he said. "Get to Camp Yuma, stock up on provisions, and make haste on the last leg to San Diego."

"I can't tell these folks and soldiers just to swallow spit and march, Captain," Gibson said.

Captain Sitgreaves rose from sitting behind his folding field desk. "Alright, Moses," he said, "work with Samuel

Woodhouse (head scientist) and Major Kendrick here and agree on the equipment we can bury and come back for when our bellies are full. Shoot three mules, cook 'em up for the company, rationed, of course."

Dying of thirst seemed a distant memory to Lorenzo, replaced by the fear of starvation. Visions of his bones picked clean by coyotes and vultures now haunted his sleep. *Got to get home to Hanna and the children. Bandit, my friend, I'm on my way.*

The mules, as scrawny from lack of grass as the soldiers from rationed mule meat, were dying routinely now. Sometimes, sentries spotted Yuma Indians, curious about the expedition's intent. Warning shots sent the Indians away. On the ninth day of starvation rations, Antoine and Lorenzo spotted the tents and jacals of Yuma Camp on a hill well above the river.

The two scouts, preceding the expedition by an hour, found empty tents, no forage for the mules, and an abandoned quarter master's tent. They found nothing but wind-swept sand and dust. Lorenzo, having been hopeful that Camp Yuma would fill the emptiness in his belly and his spirits, sat on a rock, kneading his temple while Antoine continued to look for any small cache of provisions.

The rest of the expedition straggled into the camp, greeted by Lorenzo and the news of the camp's abandonment. Kendrick appeared shocked. Captain Sitgreaves shook his head in disbelief and sat beside Lorenzo on the rock. Major Kendrick ordered two soldiers to scour the camp and report back as if Antoine and Lorenzo must have missed something so obvious as the provisions store.

Antoine walked up to Major Kendrick, accompanied by the two soldiers, "There ain't shit here, major," he said.

The soldiers had scattered about, sitting on the ground, preserving energy. The artists and naturalists surrounded

Samuel Woodhouse with the same look of consternation as the soldiers.

Captain Sitgreaves stood and addressed the officer, "Order assembly, Major," he said, straightening and speaking firmly, "We have two hours before we make camp. We'll push on downriver. This evening we'll decide between continuing on the river or cutting across the desert to San Diego. Agreed?"

Major Kendrick so ordered, and the expedition set off.

The soldiers, the scientists, the porters, and the forty emaciated mules continued down the trail along the river. Lorenzo kept going, concentrating on putting one foot before the other, with Antoine walking at his side.

"Sorry, I roped you in, Lorenzo," said Antoine.

Concentrating on a picture in his head of Hanna, brushing back a wisp of hair while setting the table for the family dinner, Lorenzo turned to Antoine. "Nothing for it, Antoine," he said, smiling, "I have reason to keep going and stories to tell Jeremiah when I get home. No regrets."

In two hours, as the two scouts began to look for a suitable campsite, they spotted tents, a corral, and sentries guarding what must be the garrison they had expected to find at Camp Yuma.

A spontaneous cheer by the expedition soldiers brought the sentries to attention. The commanding officer of the camp emerged from a tent. He stood in front of the sentry to greet the newcomers.

Major Kendrick and Captain Sitgreaves threaded through the soldiers. The scouts stepped aside.

"First Lieutenant Thomas Sweeney, Second Infantry, at your service, gentleman," said the lieutenant, coming to attention.

Captain Sitgreaves returned the address, "Captain Lorenzo Sitgreaves, here, Directing the Corps of Topographical Engineers survey of a path to San Diego from Santa Fe.

"This is Major Kendrick, in charge of security. Where would you prefer that we set up camp?"

While the expedition soldiers and scientists bivouacked, Lieutenant Sweeney met with the expedition officials. Officers Sitgreaves and Kendrick, scouts Leroux and Brennan, and the naturalist/physician Woodhouse attended. A soldier set up folding stools for those in attendance. Sweeney introduced Lieutenant Edward Murray, who arrived mid-month from San Diego to relieve Lieutenant Sweeney.

"I am certain you expected a bigger reception," said Sweeney, "I've been in charge of Camp Yuma since June. I moved my ten-man unit to this location to use the backdrop of the river to protect the camp. We have defended the camp against two skirmishes with Yuma warriors."

Major Kendrick nodded, "We have also had our share of Indian encounters with the Mohave to the north," said Kendrick.

"Lieutenant Murray arrived here with fifteen recruits," Sweeney said. "He brought five months of supplies to relieve me, but with hostilities imminent with the Indians, we decided we couldn't afford to send the wagons back to San Diego without an escort: too dangerous. Twenty-five soldiers are here now, and Lieutenant Murray brought only enough combined provisions for two months. Those provisions are running low."

"That is unfortunate," said Captain Sitgreaves, "We were counting on restocking our provisions for the final push to San Diego."

"We need provisions," said Samuel Woodhouse, "We have at least two men in desperate need of sustenance to survive the week. The rest of our party is not much better off."

"That is unfortunate, Mr. Woodhouse," Sweeney said, "We are on extreme rations ourselves. I would say we are at the end of our rope all around. Suggestions?"

Having survived severe conditions in the past, Antoine Leroux spoke up, “Join forces, strength in numbers, but we can’t stay here and starve. As Lorenzo Brennan here says, make haste for San Diego. I bet we can do it in fifteen days.”

“It took us twenty-one days to get here, Leroux,” said Lieutenant Murray.

“You carried too much,” said Antoine. “All we have to do is get there. Our incentive is a two-inch steak.”

Captain Sitgreaves agreed. “We need to save the records and as many samples as possible,” he said. “Major Kendrick and I will support your decision to join us and abandon this place until the army can provision it adequately and offer protection against attack. We’ll need to bury more equipment for future retrieval. We should be ready to move out in three days.”

“Mule meat,” Lorenzo said, “more mule meat, but I’m always happy to see something on my plate. San Diego, here I come.”

On December 3rd, ’51, sixteen soldiers entered the camp under the command of Lieutenant Davidson on orders from Captain and Brevet Major Heintzelman, Second Infantry, to reinforce the force at the base. He brought no additional provisions and agreed with the consensus to abandon Camp Yuma and Camp Independence on the river despite orders.

All the soldiers and expedition personnel left the Colorado River heading west to San Diego on December 6th.

***

The expedition's physically exhausted, mentally foggy, and ravenous members entered San Diego on December 18th, twelve days after leaving the river. Haggard soldiers carried various artifacts from the expedition, tools and tents, essential water, and food they had slaughtered the day before. The journey had begun from the Zuni Pueblo at the end of September with more than one hundred and forty mules. Only thirty-one mules survived the trip. Indian ambushes had left three men dead and eight wounded during the eight-hundred-mile journey.

Despite the hazards, loss of equipment, and endured deprivations crossing the Mohave and Colorado Deserts, Californians recognized Captain Sitgreaves, calling the expedition successful. The journey received a glowing report in the San Diego Herald newspaper.

Having no further obligations with the expedition, the two scouts pursued their own agendas. Antoine stayed in the hospital for three days while his wounds were routinely redressed. After visiting a barber for a shave and a haircut, Lorenzo reserved the bath trough in the barber's backroom for an additional two bits. Then he rented a hotel room and slept intermittently for two days. He waited for Antoine's release. Lorenzo wandered down to the new wharf. Supplies from the east are offloaded and stored in the depot for distribution to the forts of the west. He wandered through the construction near the pier for two hours and then returned to bed.

Leroux and Lorenzo Brennan sat down in the morning to a steak and eggs breakfast.

"Captain Sitgreaves has requested we sail with him and the scientists up to San Francisco," said Antoine. "From there, he is sailing back to Washington to report on the expedition. Sitgreaves and Woodhouse will write up formal accounts, and we would meet with congressional members to add color."

"Sorry, but no thanks," said Lorenzo, "you can provide more than enough colorful tales on your own. I will go home to Hanna and the boys as soon as I'm paid."

"Let's hunt down Captain Sitgreaves about our pay. How will you return to the territory?" asked Antoine.

"I have been planning that trip in my head every hungry day since we left the Colorado River," Lorenzo said.

"You're going it alone then," said Antoine.

"Got to. Got to get home," said Lorenzo. "I'm planning on twenty days. Taking thirty days' worth of provisions."

"Well, I've said it before, Lorenzo, you're capable."

Finding Captain Sitgreaves in his hotel parlor, the two scouts inquired about their fee.

"All taken care of," Sitgreaves told them. "Go see the Quartermaster at the new San Diego Depot. I gave him letters confirming your contracts and services rendered yesterday.

"I'm sorry you won't join us in Washington, Lorenzo. If I don't see you again, have an uneventful trip home," said Sitgreaves. Then, as if getting another idea, the captain said, "Just give me a minute."

The captain busily took pen to paper before looking at his two scouts.

"Here's another letter for the stable handler," Sitgreaves said. "If you think it may be helpful, Lorenzo, pick one of those mangy mules. "Thank you again. Your contribution to the expedition was immeasurable." The three shook hands as friends, and Antoine and Lorenzo headed to the Presidio.

The Quartermaster at the barracks handed Antoine bank notes and coins totaling one thousand dollars. He gave Lorenzo twelve Liberty Head twenty-dollar gold coins, nine silver dollars, and one dollar in change: $250 total.

Once outside, Lorenzo turned to Antoine, "I'll be buying supplies and packing for the trip, Antoine. I'll be taking off this afternoon," Lorenzo said.

"We ship out tomorrow," Antoine said while bear-hugging his friend. "Lorenzo, glad for your company and help.

"Saved my life back there on the Colorado River. Those striped Injuns appeared intent on sticking me to death. Au revoir mon ami."

The two scouts walked away in different directions. Lorenzo headed for the stables in the Presidio. The handler mucking one of the stalls couldn't read the letter, but he had seen the seal at the bottom before and asked Lorenzo what he wanted.

"I'll need to see the mules brought in by the expedition four days ago," Lorenzo said. "This letter says I can take one off your hands."

The handler led Lorenzo to a grazing field on the south side of the stables. The scout found one mule that made the trip in decent shape and attitude. The mule he sought munched on the grass near a fence. This mule, skinny on the last day to the point of skeletal, had kept his head up moving forward. The light brown mule had recovered much of his weight.

Lorenzo spent half an hour leading the mule, brushing his neck and scratching behind his oversized ears. The mule enjoyed the attention, not stubborn at all on the lead. He led the mule to the handler and signed the letter from Sitgreaves as a receipt.

After retrieving his saddle and horse, Shady, from another stall, Lorenzo led both animals to the only general store in the newly incorporated city. He purchased a second canteen and two canvas-covered rubber bladders for water, each able to carry two gallons of water. With rationing, the water should last eight to nine days and get him across the Sonora desert to the Colorado River. Lorenzo figured another eight days following the river north to the pass through the upland. Then ten more days to the San Francisco Mountain Peaks and home.

Lorenzo purchased provisions for a thirty-day trip, including salt pork, bacon, and twenty meat biscuits for making soup. He also bought beef jerky, flour, salt, oil, and maple syrup, his sweet weakness. He acquired hard candy to suck on during the day as well. Lorenzo selected an eight-foot square canvas tarp to cover his goods on the mule and to use to form a tent. He included a breakdown spade, plenty of flint and tender for his possible bag, and assorted sundries.

He bought grain, oats his mounts would have to carry, and a separate water bag. He purchased a knapsack with attached leather shoulder straps in case Sunny and the mule gave out, and he had to hoof it the rest of the way home.

Lorenzo purchased a Sharps breech-loader rifle and made sure he had three boxes of cartridges. He also bought a Paterson Colt repeater, a revolver Lorenzo had used in the Mexican/American War. He kept his old rifle as well. His experiences with the Mohave and Yuma Indians on the expedition gave him cause to worry. He imagined a time when trading blankets and bracelets might not be sufficient to keep the peace. Alone on the trail, Lorenzo wanted to account for himself if backed into a corner. Lastly, he purchased a backup compass. The scout had copied Samuel Woodhouse's crude maps of the expedition's travels. He would not lose his way in the desert.

Lorenzo wished Antoine could double-check the supplies or make suggestions, but Leroux had boarded the ship with Captain Sitgreaves for the trip to San Francisco. Lorenzo slung full saddle bags over Sunny's hips just behind the saddle. He loaded the remaining provisions and equipment on the mule pack saddle, covered the stack with the tarp, and roped it tightly and securely.

Returning to the store, Lorenzo took time to peruse the women's clothing. The proprietor approached Lorenzo. "If I may suggest," he said, "the fashion this year dictates full skirts like this one in bright red. A matching bodice for day wear and a complimentary evening bodice for special occasions. These "engageantes" attach to the sleeves of the bodice and add that frill so favored by women."

Lorenzo, frowning, shoved the red dress aside on the rack. "My wife is beautiful, and I don't believe she needs this frill. I'm not sure we'll attend an evening affair soon."

"Certainly, sir," said the clerk, "sometimes it is hard to know what women believe is pretty; that's why I suggest the fashion of the day."

"Hmmm," Lorenzo muttered. "I went hungry thinking about buying a present for my wife. I favor this dark purple skirt and day bodice. Yes, this is the one."

"Excellent choice, sir. The bright green vertical pinstripes on the bodice make this combination perfect for every day and evening. How about petticoats? Two petticoats to complete the look?"

"I have no room to pack a petticoat. Just wrap up the dress and bodice as tightly and neatly as possible. Hanna can come up with the petticoats," Lorenzo said.

On the toy shelf in the corner of the store, Lorenzo picked out a peg top and a small bag of glass marbles for the boys. He realized they would have to grow into the toys, but the thought of them playing together in the future heartened the man.

Shady and the man's mule stamped impatiently on the street outside the store. Lorenzo glanced up to the sun: two o'clock. No more excuses. He mounted Shady and led the mule out of town.

9 |Lonesome Trek

I'm the world's worst horseman, Lorenzo kept repeating to himself. *Don't think about it, you idiot; you've got a long way to go.*

In Portland, Maine, where Lorenzo grew up, families would rent a horse and buggy if necessary. Otherwise, destinations in the city were within walking distance. When he joined the Maine Militia, he volunteered for horse handler duties. Better than walking to New Mexico, he had figured, naively. He had been unfamiliar with saddle sores, stubborn dangerous horses, or their upkeep.

Now, eight days out from San Diego, Lorenzo hoped to be crossing the Colorado River by now. Lorenzo dismounted, leading horse and mule along the trail. The stiffness in his back was so painful he couldn't stand riding any further. His butt felt so sore the traveler could hardly bear returning to the saddle. He had pushed himself into a twelve-hour riding day, eating lunch while standing beside Shady.

From daybreak until noon, the traveler rode Shady and tethered the mule to the back of his saddle. After lunch, Lorenzo pulled his saddle bags and saddle off Shady, untied the ropes covering the tarp over the supplies, unpacking the mule. He moved the mule pack saddle over to Shady and loaded his horse with the supplies and tarp, tying it off securely. Saddling the mule and mounting him reluctantly, Lorenzo continued on the trail. Six hours later, he made camp, made a fire, and ate supper in the dark. After cleanup, he crawled into his makeshift tent and slept, his mind churning over the next day's travel. Home a day closer. He mounted and moved down the trail by dawn.

The wind picked up, and the sand hit Lorenzo's face like tiny icepicks. He kept moving forward but much slower. Lorenzo's bandana covered his nose and mouth, tied to his neck like a road bandit. He tried to muzzle both his mounts so they could easily breathe, but both horse and mule shrugged off the extra shirt Lorenzo used for the purpose. After three hours of fighting the windstorm, the sun lowering and invisible in the blowing dust, the sand obscuring the trail like a six-inch snow shower, Lorenzo forced himself to stop. He couldn't risk wandering off course in the storm or getting turned around. He put up his tent, skipped dinner, and bedded down.

The wind subsided, and the shifting sands settled into new habitats by ten p.m. Lorenzo moved on toward the Colorado River late morning, now a day and a half behind his self-imposed schedule.

The extra sleep eased Lorenzo's sore butt and renewed his spirit. He broke up the monotony of the landscape by thinking up names for the mule. So far, the mule had endeared himself to Lorenzo. It walked steadily, oblivious of the time or length of the day's travel. His light brown coat stood out against the monotones of the parched landscape. Lorenzo spoke each name aloud. Repeating it over and over with different inflections. The mule could care less and just kept walking. 'Brazito' came to mind after the battle in the war. 'Santana,' sounding Spanish and rolling off the tongue nicely. 'Geronimo,' after the famous Apache warrior.

Lorenzo toyed with each name for an hour. The process passed the time. Lorenzo thought of the term 'Chance,' hoping his luck would hold until he got home. Then Lorenzo thought of 'Spirit,' the mule who always kept his head up. 'Buttercup,' soft and gentler, so far, than Shady. 'Quicksand,' after the storm. When more names began to make Lorenzo lose track of the ones he liked, he decided on his first choice: 'Sunny.'

Shady, Lorenzo's horse, dark to the point of blending into the shadow of a tree, had the disposition of an outlaw, a shady character. Sunny, bright in color like the dawn of a new day, dependable as the sunrise, and steady, as if he would walk around the world if given the order, didn't bat an eye at his new name. Sunny paired with Shady; it made sense.

Near the end of the day, Lorenzo sighted the river. He camped well back and lit no fire, respectful of the Yuma Indian encampments in the area. In the morning, he would scout his path across the Colorado River.

In the morning, the experienced scout sat on a slight rise surrounded by scrub. He spent the first hours of daylight watching the Yuma Crossing at the Colorado River for Indian travel. The shallows had long been established as the best place to cross the river on the trail. Granite outcroppings on both river banks forced the water through a one-hundred-foot bank to bank opening, the narrowest point south of the grand canyon far to the north. The Colorado River, filled with silt, offered dangerous quicksand patches, muddy, fast-moving waters, and depths from inches to sometimes ten to fourteen feet. Nevertheless, crossing the river at this point, although very swift and deep, could be accomplished.

Until five months ago, the Glanton gang had operated an exclusive ferry a mile upriver. A Yuman war party had attacked the Glantons (notorious for robbing and killing traveling immigrants and Indians.) The Indians killed nine of the Glantons and burned the ferry. The tension between the Americans, the Yuma, and the Mohave tribes culminated in the siege and eventual abandonment of Camp Yuma.

While scouting for the Sitgreaves expedition, Lorenzo checked out the trail ahead toward San Diego with Antoine. The porters and handlers corralled the mules and horses that still lived, including Shady, and sent them across the river from east to west. The mules carried the tents and equipment. The porters floated all the perishables across with little loss.

Lorenzo planned his crossing. He wouldn't dally, but he would be cautious. He did not want to lose time or provisions. The clouds in the afternoon lingered into the night. The moon, heading for full, would be rising around 9:00 pm. At 8:00 pm, Lorenzo detected no one else in the area, and Lorenzo put his plan into action. Shady would be the first to cross. Lorenzo stripped naked and led Shady into the muddy rush of water. Twenty-five feet into the river, the water became too deep for the man to keep his footing. Shady began to swim. The horse jerked on the lead, but Lorenzo held fast, aiming downstream to allow the river force to aid in the crossing. He struggled with the water rush for fifty more feet. Lorenzo's feet touched the river bottom. He led Shady out of the water and tied him to a bush thirty feet from shore. In the dark, Shady became invisible.

Lorenzo swam back to the west bank, scrambled up the rocks, and dragged his duster to the water's edge, loaded with his provisions. Once there, he tied half-empty water bags to the tarp's corners. The scout dragged the floatable affair over two branches tied together for stiffness. Swimming across with his makeshift raft and pulling the sticks and duster along in the water, he moved the provisions off the canvas duster and hid them in the brush near Shady. His food and clothes remained dry. He swam back across the river as the moon peeked over the horizon.

Next, Lorenzo side stroked the crossing holding the Sharps rifle out of the water. Two more trips brought his army rifle and the new revolver across dry. Nervous in the brightening moonlight, he swam back for the mule.

"Come on, Sunny," Lorenzo whispered to the mule. "Your turn." He fed Sunny oats he had reserved at the bank for enticement. True to his nature, Sunny carried the rest of the equipment and made short work of the Yuma Crossing.

Lorenzo air dried, dressed, packed the mule, saddled Shady, and took off northeast, away from the river, under a full moon. Two hours later, he set up his cold camp in an open space amongst the scrub.

On January 11^{th,} '52, the traveler sat on a boulder observing the landscape of the river. He could see twelve miles across the valley from the mouth of the pass through the Black Mountains. The expedition had used the access to get to the Colorado River via the wash from the east.

Lorenzo continued his twelve-hour riding day marathon for ten days after the river crossing near Yuma. Saddle sores toughened. Exhausted, his eyes smarting, Lorenzo's painful back kept telling him to stop and rest. Sunny nudged his neck from behind, nearly pushing Lorenzo off the boulder. The stubborn mule wanted to get going.

"Give me half a minute, Sunny," said Lorenzo. "When I can move, I will." He had picked his way along the base of the Black Mountain uplands for eleven days where no trail existed. He traveled by the light of the full moon between nine at night and six in the morning to avoid any chance of meeting with Mohave warriors.

Lorenzo decided exhaustion shouldn't stop him from continuing on the well-traveled path through the pass, yet he didn't get up. "Five more minutes, Sunny."

Ten minutes later, Lorenzo scratched Sunny behind his jaw. "Here I go," he told Sunny, but he still didn't move. With eyes closed, his rock-hard seat passed for an imagined feather bed.

"Now, Sunny," Lorenzo said, "Help me up." He reached and grabbed Sunny's reins, standing. Lorenzo mounted and turned

Sunny toward the trail, picking up Shady's reigns in his other hand and moving off. As always, Hanna's face entered his lonely consciousness when he journeyed toward home.

Hours later, glancing up from the path through the pass, he thought he saw movement far ahead. Lorenzo started weaving up the rise off the trail. Up, up, the steep scree until he couldn't ride further. Dismounting, Lorenzo continued leading his mounts. He found a huge round hole in the mountain up ahead. The tall man led the horse and mule right through the opening, which provided a hidden view of the path and the pass below. A band of Mohave walked in the direction of the river. Warriors, women with papooses, three horses pulling travois piled with tents and supplies, and children running around. Lorenzo counted forty-five Indians all told. *Friendly?* As they came closer, Lorenzo believed they struggled. They looked emaciated! A starving group can be dangerous, and Lorenzo prayed they would not sniff his presence. With all three of his weapons, Lorenzo readied for a chance attack.

Lorenzo thought of war and the battles he had survived. The terror of anticipation is even worse than the battle itself. At the end of his time at war, he, like his friend Daniel Martensen, had concluded that killing Mexicans had been a waste for them and himself. He had nothing against them. They were simple farmers, ill-equipped against the Americans. In some ways, lambs to the slaughter.

The Indians far below him reminded Lorenzo of the Mexican farmers. He had no reason to hate them or want them dead. They tried to scratch out a living. He just wanted to get home. His rifle ready, Lorenzo hoped they would pass uneventfully.

Shady stamped his feet, loosening a rock that tumbled down the scree, picking up additional gravel and stones and making too much noise. Three Mohave looked up, and two children, intrigued by the hole in the rock, began climbing the rock debris to explore the formation.

Lorenzo's gut tightened as the two boys scrambled. The loose rubble challenged the youths. After climbing to within twenty-five feet of where Lorenzo willed Shady to keep quiet, the boys turned back down toward the pass, skipping in the gravel until they regained the path, running after their families and moving off toward the river. Crisis averted. Lorenzo waited an hour for stragglers. Then he led Shady and Sunny down to the trail. He rode through the pass, continuing for six hours; camping outside assumed Mohave territory. Lorenzo lit a fire for a hot meal, the first in almost two weeks.

***

The light from the moon no longer allowed practical travel at night. If Lorenzo kept pushing, he would be home in eight days, no more than ten. One of his water bags contained enough water to get to Antelope Springs. Luckily, he hadn't taken a chance at the Colorado River to refill his water supply. He would have run smack into the returning Mohave band.

Lorenzo's food supply should hold out for twenty days. Stretching the journey to twenty-eight or thirty days would cause problems.

For the next five days, Shady and Sunny carried the man higher and higher in the uplands leading to the San Francisco Peaks.

The trail narrowed as the great Ponderosa Pine Forest surrounded the rider. In the meadows, leafless Aspen swayed in unison with the January wind. Lorenzo began to hear a clanking noise ahead of him on the trail. He distinguished the sound as metal pots jangling together. He heard cowbells as well. At one turn on the path, Lorenzo came upon the behind of a loaded burrow methodically plodding east. Animal traps, pots, pans, and saddle bags hung off the burro's sides. At the next small meadow, Lorenzo moved up even with the donkey while staying fifteen feet away from the old man coaxing two belled goats forward along the trail.

"Hello there," Lorenzo called out. The hunched-over old-timer halted his trek. Startled, he turned toward Lorenzo, sizing him up.

"We seem to be fellow travelers," said Lorenzo, "I'm heading home. I have a cabin in the San Francisco Peaks." Lorenzo couldn't help staring. The old man wore a plaid wool cap on a painfully sunburned forehead. The wild white frizzy hair sticking out from underneath the hat made the man look like a dandelion about to lose its seed head in the wind.

The man's grease-ladened beard and mustache hid the rest of his face. With one eye closed, and head tilted, Lorenzo realized the old man's right eye wept with opaque goo. The untucked plaid shirt functioned as his clean-up cloth. Likewise, the thighs and butt of the stranger's pants looked glossy with grease. His right boot sole flapped when he turned, separated from the leather upper.

"What are you after, mister," said the man, sounding angry.

Lorenzo ignored the tone. "My name is Lorenzo Brennan. I mean no harm. I want to pass by. I have been away from my family for a long time. Just want to get home."

The man relaxed and stuck out a hand to shake. "They call me 'Sifter,' 'Sifter Cawdell.'"

Lorenzo didn't want to but decided not to offend the man, accepting the handshake. "I'll just go around and move on down the trail." He tried to get away from the mess of a man. He almost asked the man if he was 'OK' but decided not to open any worms. Lorenzo moved off. Turning back, Cawdell appeared lost, confused, and very wary. *I am a sociable man, but not with that one.*

Three hurried hours later, Lorenzo set up a temporary camp, lighting a fire, frying up salt pork, and soaking a meat biscuit in the juice. He imagined Hanna's flapjacks steaming on a plate in front of him covered in maple syrup. Lorenzo had refused to dwell on his boys. Now he missed them with an almost unbearable ache. Reluctant to head into his tent, Lorenzo stared at a million stars. So far away. Home, closer, reachable. He soaked in memories provided by the expedition and his friend Antoine Leroux. Peace, a moment of peace.

The clang of pots broke his prayer. Lorenzo had set up his tarp twenty feet off the trail. The sudden appearance of Cawdell and his entourage in Lorenzo's camp meant, like or not, a time to be social.

"Got space for a weary soul?" asked Sifter, not waiting for Lorenzo to agree or object. "You found a nice soft spot here in the ferns. I'll just spread my blanket over here.

"Sifter's the name. Sifter Cawdell."

"Lorenzo Brennan, of Antelope Springs up the San Francisco Peaks valley," said Lorenzo. Sifter had forgotten their earlier meeting on the trail. Or he just wanted a fresh start. Sifter smiled from the moment he stepped into the clearing and never stopped.

"I have one last cup of coffee," Lorenzo said, reaching for the pot. Cawdell untied his mug from the cord wrapped around a ring on his makeshift burro pack saddle. Lorenzo poured the last of his coffee into the cup. Sifter sat down with significant effort, Indian style, close to the fire and far too close for comfort near Lorenzo, sloshing half the coffee to the ground.

"Looking for gold, are you?" Sifter asked.

"Just traveling home," Lorenzo said, "I should be there in three more days…" he broke off. Cawdell, a stranger, need not know about his family.

Sifter ignored the tall man. "Struck it rich myself, twenty years ago up near Sutter's place. Been living my dream ever since. Just a born wanderer, I am. Living off the land with my friends here is the way of it. Fancy hotels or ranches aren't my nature. Hell, I could buy twenty ranches if I had a mind to."

Lorenzo didn't argue the lie. Miners had discovered gold around Sutter's mill only four years ago, not twenty.

Cawdell continued his tale. "Yep," he said, "Had two big claims jumped over the years. I panned my last one until I had enough dust for ten men. Then I left the scrubbers and prostitutes behind.

"Buried my gold where only I can get to it occasionally if I need a bit of it."

Sifter stopped smiling. "So, you can stop following me."

That did it. Lorenzo had suspected the man of being crazy from their first meeting. Sifter's strange tale confirmed the assessment.

"I don't want your gold, Mister," Lorenzo said, "I'm just on my way home. Now, I'm heading to bed. I start at dawn, so I won't see you in the morning."

"Then why are you following me?" Cawdell reiterated.

"Not following you. Don't want your gold. Good night," said Lorenzo, with finality. He crawled under his tarp, pulled the blanket to his chin, and felt for the cold steel of his repeater by his hip. Tonight, Lorenzo cocked the hammer and tried to sleep. He planned to be down the trail before daybreak, leaving the mad geezer behind. Looking out the opening, Lorenzo saw Sifter shrug, untie his blanket from the burrow, and spread it out twenty feet away in the moss under a pin oak. Cawdell laid down and turned his back to the fire.

Lorenzo tried later to recall what he had been dreaming about, which awakened him. What saved him? When he awoke, Cawdell's face hovered inches from his own, his greasy beard tickling his chin. The grotesque expression froze on Sifter's face, and the dripping cloudy eye, the stink of the man's breath choked Lorenzo with terror. Cawdell knelt over him, a cocked bowie knife in his right hand high over his right shoulder. "You ain't gettin my gold," he screamed.

Lorenzo fired the repeater as the knife arced downward, setting the wild man back on his haunches. He toppled left, dead, blood muddying the dirt near the fire coals.

Crawling out of his tarp tent, Lorenzo grabbed the dead man under his armpits and dragged him over to the blanket on the other side of the clearing. Next, he built up the fire, lighting up the camp. He retrieved his spade from Sunny's pack. Using tentative pokes with the spade, Lorenzo found an appropriate site for a grave and spent the next two hours digging. The old man weighed next to nothing. Dragging him by the broken boot, Lorenzo pulled the body into the hole, bending the man's knees and bowing his head to his chest to fit the grave. Lorenzo shoveled dirt over the body and stomped the ground, packing the mound. He used a pine bow to sweep the campsite.

Satisfied, Lorenzo sat back down next to the fire. No apparent thought came to him except to be gone from the place. He packed his gear, roped the burro to his mule and the goats, put out the fire, and started in the pitch dark, not knowing the time.

Midmorning, Lorenzo, exhausted, began to shake. He found a clearing and built a fire. He laid down near the fire, covered himself with his blanket, and let the fire burn the shakes out of him.

In the afternoon, when Lorenzo woke up, the cold of Sifter Cawdell's icy skin still haunted him. He pulled his canteen off his saddle horn, wetness covering the outside, and discovered the knife slash; empty. *Sifter, you bastard.* All rubber water bladders were in the same state, slashed. He took the time to search through all the junk tied to Cawdell's burro. He found a canteen, but it contained no water. He found no documentation, claim deeds, or otherwise. He found no gold dust, not even a speck. The old galoot may have been delirious from lack of water.

To avoid the same fate, Lorenzo mounted and revised his three-day final leg home to two and a half days to the spring. In two hours, the thought of a drink of water replaced the haunting vision of Sifter Cawdell. He dismounted when he couldn't see the trail from the saddle and continued on foot, feeling his way along the path.

The happenings of the day eventually forced him to rest. He threw down his duster and covered himself with a blanket, unconscious within minutes. He wasn't in better shape when he woke up in the morning. Lorenzo discarded everything but the pack saddle from the burro. He retained the items on his rig, light from the remaining provisions. Sucking on a hunk of jerky, the traveler took off, struggling to swallow the salted meat.

Lorenzo, extremely parched and lightheaded by sunset, debated continuing in the dark. Twice he found himself leaning his head against Shady's neck as he walked, sleeping. Wandering off the trail in the night would be ironically ridiculous, dying so close to the cabin after the six-month effort to return to Hanna and the boys. He began slapping his face harder and harder when he felt himself drift. When he stumbled and fell to his knees, he wondered if he could stand again. He laid down, tied the rein around his wrist, and slept. No blanket, no comfort, didn't matter.

Lorenzo woke up with sunshine warming his cheek, foggy-headed but renewed enough to note familiar markings on the path. The branch in the trail heading up toward the spring seemed close. Or was he fantasizing?

The traveler found the trail to the spring in forty-five more agonizing uncertain minutes. Lorenzo sighed with relief. Shady quickened his pace up the trail, sensing water ahead. Lorenzo laid his head against Shady's mane and rested his eyes.

Hearing water tripping over river rocks and nearly falling from his horse, Lorenzo crawled to the water's edge and scooped water. Better than the best whiskey he could afford. He began to laugh, turning over on his back. *Sifter, you son of a bitch, I found your gold.*

***

The upper meadow full of Hanna's sheep bleated a welcome as a homecoming. Bandit sprung toward him, running full speed across the field. Lorenzo dismounted Sunny and kneeled, letting the dog lick his chin. Wrapping an arm over Bandit's shoulder, the master scratched and kneaded his friend's ears and neck.

"Buenos días," Lorenzo called out to Fernandez.

"Buenos días, amigo," said Fernandez, "We should bring the sheep down and surprise Hanna and Jeremiah."

Lorenzo smiled; a surprise was his intention all along. He had spent the day after making it to Antelope Spring recovering and cleaning up. A smooth chin was in order. Lorenzo hadn't shaved since San Diego, so he had sharpened his knife and spent an hour shaving. Stripping and washing all his clothes, the scout scrubbed them with sand and laid them out on the rocks to dry. Not all the splattered blood sprayed by Sifter's death rinsed out of his shirt, but it appeared clean and no longer smelled of sweat. Next, he had shed everything off the horse, mule, and burro and thoroughly brushed out the mats and burrs entangled in their manes and tails. He brushed their coats until no dust flew when he swatted them.

Before coming down to the upper meadow, Lorenzo bathed and scrubbed himself clean in a cold mountain pool. After air drying and packing everything on Sunny's pack saddle, he hurried down the trail until he saw Bandit.

He felt rested, excited, and ready to greet his wife. He prayed she would not be too angry. Lorenzo hoped the nine Liberty Head gold coins, five silver dollars, and change in his purse might soften her. Then he would present the dress.

The traveler let Fernandez and Bandit send the sheep into the corral, staying back until the shepherds completed their tasks. Then Lorenzo approached the cabin. Jeremiah looked up from playing with blocks on the porch.

"Daddy?" he asked. Jeremiah flew like Bandit into Lorenzo's arms, not waiting for an answer, burying his little face in the crook of Lorenzo's neck.

The commotion on the porch brought Hanna out of the cabin fluffing her hair back. She turned around when she saw her husband and returned to the house. Lorenzo, a bit quizzical, wondered if he should follow her inside. Within two minutes, she was back on the porch and in her husband's arms. She had brushed her hair and put on her best blouse tucked into her best skirt. *Ah, beautiful Hanna.*

"Lorenzo, I have been so worried," said Hanna, "You are home, thank Jehovah."

"Every day from the day I left, I thought of turning back, coming home," said Lorenzo, "but here, nine twenty-dollar Liberty Heads and five silver dollars. Clear. Nothing owed, nothing gambled. I fell more in love with you every day."

"You're home, darling. That's what counts," Hanna said, embracing Lorenzo and squeezing him. "I hear Zachary waking up. Time for you to get acquainted."

The family gathered at the dinner table, joined by Fernandez and Julia, who departed to their room in the barn after a bowl of berries offered by Hanna for dessert.

"I will give you a full report tomorrow morning, Señor," said Fernandez.

Julia asked, "Señora, when might we return to our home, do you think?"

"Let Hanna and I discuss things tonight," said Lorenzo, "we'll give you an answer tomorrow, Fernandez. The ranch is in excellent shape. You and Julia have been a godsend."

After the Mexican couple left the cabin, Lorenzo read Jeremiah's favorite book aloud. Jeremiah hugged and kissed Hanna good night, then hugged and kissed Lorenzo before crawling into bed. Jeremiah went to sleep within minutes.

Lorenzo pulled the good rocker out to the porch and set it next to Hanna's porch rocker. Lorenzo listened to the happenings of the ranch involving sheep, wolves, storms, and looming. Thankfully, most difficulties were manageable with Fernandez and Julia's assistance.

"I will take them as far as the new fort up in Navajo country seven days to the northeast," said Lorenzo. "I want to start tomorrow, get it over, and I can tell they want to get home.

"Julia can ride Sunny, and Fernandez is small enough to ride the burro. The army will loan them mounts to return to Taos, and I'll bring the burro and the mule back. Two weeks Hanna. I'll be back for good." The planning settled; Hanna began describing Zachary's growth.

Lorenzo was correct in the supposition that Zachary might be an easier baby than Jeremiah. The baby now slept through the night. Jeremiah had taken a shine to his baby brother, asking to rock him occasionally after dinner.

"Mostly, we just missed you," Hanna said, "Jeremiah will need some attention now that you're back."

"How about some attention for you, Hanna," Lorenzo said. Lorenzo went into the cabin, pulled out the skirt and bodice from his gear, straightened them as much as possible, and brought them back to the porch to display for Hanna.

"Here is the present I meant to buy you on that first trip to Albuquerque," Lorenzo said.

"You should not have wasted money, Lorenzo," Hanna said with a minor scold. "It is beautiful. I don't know where I could wear it."

"Wear it for me, Hanna," Lorenzo said. "That will be enough."

Hanna wanted to hear the details of the journey. Lorenzo tried to recount the expedition as honestly as possible but didn't wish to scare Hanna. Lorenzo told her about the white stripes the Mohave warriors painted on their bodies and the raining arrows that fell on the expedition camp. He told her about his squeamish sawing of the shaft stuck in the doctor's leg.

"Did one of those arrows catch your cheek, Lorenzo, Hanna asked. "You'll have a scar there," said Hanna.

"Antoine went out from camp to negotiate peace, and the Mohave warriors shot three arrows in him for his efforts," said Lorenzo, his voice quiet. "I retrieved him, carried him over my shoulder back to our line, and received this feather nick for my endeavor."

"God, almighty husband, what a chance you took," said Hanna.

"He is a good friend, Hanna; I had to," said Lorenzo.

Lorenzo sat and rocked for a time, silent. Hanna finally spoke, "I guess you had to."

The creak of the rockers slowed to still as each of them contemplated 'what if' scenarios from the past six months, Hanna and the wolves, Lorenzo and the Yuma and Mohave Indians.

Lorenzo reached for Hanna's hand, "I killed an old prospector on the far side of the mountain, Hanna. Shot him before he could kill me." Remembering the haunting face, Lorenzo held up his hands a foot apart. "He came this close, swinging a knife at my chest. I had to do it. Had to shoot."

Hanna shuddered, thinking of firearms, the deaths and destruction they cause, and the men who must carry them. Lorenzo decided he had confessed enough and offered no more details.

"Come to bed, my husband," said Hanna. "Hold me tonight. Warm my want. Swear to me you won't go on any more expeditions, fight any angry Indians, or kill any crazy miners."

Rising from the rocker, Lorenzo promised, "Hanna, neither wild horses nor an army could drag me away from you and the boys again."

10 |Return of the Bear

Temptation grabbed Lorenzo by the neck a year later. On December 22nd, 1853, Lorenzo finished his coffee, put on his coat, and gave Hanna a morning kiss. The sheep needed to graze in the valley today. An inch of snow covered the upper meadow, but the snow in the valley had melted.

Zachary waddled over to him, grabbed his leg, and sat on Lorenzo's boot to play the peg leg game. Lorenzo accommodated by swinging Zachary around the room as he walked, playfully trying to shake off his son.

Jeremiah, now four years old, made up his game with the top Lorenzo had brought back from San Diego. He couldn't master spinning the top independently, but he could twirl it around several times without using the string.

A knock on the front door startled the whole family. Hanna set the bowl of pancake batter on the counter while Lorenzo opened the door. Incredibly, Antoine Leroux stood on the front porch, a huge grin creasing his expansive beard.

"Bonjour," Antoine said, "Let a man warm up by the fire, perhaps?"

"Come in, come in, you rattlesnake," Lorenzo said.

Antoine entered, sat at the table, pulled off his beaver hat, and scratched his head where the cap had matted his curls.

Jeremiah ran over to Hanna, hiding behind her skirt. "Jeremiah, this is Mr. Antoine Leroux. Remember when I tell his stories, I call him 'Bear?"

"Bear," said Jeremiah. "You look like a bear. Can I see where the arrow got you?"

Leroux pushed his shirt up and showed Jeremiah his wrist scar.

"Does it hurt?" asked Jeremiah.

"No," said Leroux, "except when the weather changes, like yesterday. My wrist tells me when it will snow."

The boy looked at Bear quizzically, cocking his head at the crazy man. Since the stranger made no sense, Jeremiah broke away, went to the toy corner, and dumped his blocks on the floor, assembling them into a tower.

Hanna dried her hands with her apron, hiding her apprehension. Antoine appraised her, "Beautiful as ever, Hanna. How are you?" he said.

"Fine, fine, Antoine," Hanna said. "We're up to one hundred three sheep now. How about yourself."

"Too many to count," Antoine replied. "I'm hardly ever there. Too busy in Washington. I bet you'll be traveling to the ranch one of these days. You'd like Juana. She needs more friends."

Lorenzo went to Hanna, put his arm over her shoulder, and hugged her to him.

"Antoine, how have you happened upon our cabin again," Lorenzo said. He leaned over and kissed Hanna on her forehead to reassure her before returning to Leroux. "What story are you telling this winter day? You must stay and celebrate Christmas with us."

Antoine pulled out a flask from a pocket in his fringed buckskin coat. "I came to have a drink with you two," said Leroux, "Cups, please. I'll tell you all about it, but I'm parched."

He was happy to see his friend, but Lorenzo suspected another motive for the old scout's presence. He needed him as a scout and hunter again. Glancing over at Hanna, Lorenzo, excited and worried about Hanna's reaction, remained silent. If asked, would he go? *Probably, in a shot!*

Hanna gathered herself. "Forgive me, Antoine, but you are our first guest since Fernandez and Julia left over a year ago. How are they doing? They were so much help to me." She went over and picked up Zachary. "Meet our growing boy. He's the curious one. Zachary, this is Bear. Can you say Bear?"

Antoine reached out a hand to shake Zachary's. Zachary grabbed the hand and squirmed his way into Antoine's arms.

"Bear," said Zachary.

The tension eased. Hanna brought three coffee cups and the pot while Leroux bounced the giggling baby on his knee. Ignoring Antoine's flask, Hanna poured coffee into all three cups. Antoine added a bit from his flask to his coffee cup and gestured at Lorenzo, who covered his cup with one hand and shook his head to decline. Hanna turned to the stove and began making pancakes for Antoine.

"Lorenzo, I knew from Fernandez that you had made it back to the cabin with your scalp intact," said Antoine. "How did you get past the Mohave camp?"

"The timing was right, Antoine. I had a full moon. I traveled at night, stayed in the uplands, rather than take the river trail."

"Smart," Antoine said.

"Did you ever encounter an old prospector named 'Sifter Cawdell?" asked Lorenzo.

"No," answered Leroux, "of course that makes sense. Big country. Give you trouble?"

Hanna, bringing the last hotcakes to the table, put a hand on Lorenzo's shoulder and squeezed. Her grip conveyed caution to her husband.

Lorenzo glanced at his wife, then back at Leroux, shaking his head. "Just wondered. You're right. Big country.

"Well, as you know," began Leroux, speaking about his recent history, "I went to Washington. Damn, politicians loved the stories. Sitgreaves and Woodhouse submitted reports and journals, and I told the tall tales. Began to believe me after a while. Made two more trips there since.

"Big doings are cooking these days. The talk about the territory is heating up. The politicians can't wait to take a train to the Pacific Ocean. It ain't just a path and a way across the desert and the mountains anymore. The Sitgreaves expedition proved that possible.

"No, now even the river passages Sitgreaves promoted seem too slow. Roads, bridges, and railroads. That's what the people back east want. Where to build the railroad? That's the question. North, south, central? Slave or slaveless. Since the gold rush, the politicians know that tens of thousands of settlers and miners are making money and want a piece of it all. The Secretary of War, Jefferson Davis, created an engineering department and funded four major survey expeditions to find the best route to the Pacific.

Lieutenant Amiel Whipple approached me for advice on his proposed expedition west through your valley and on to Los Angeles, Alta California. He's young, just out of West Point, but he listens. I told him to double his proposed count of sheep and the rest of his provisions. I reviewed his map locating Leroux Spring."

"Leroux Spring," Hanna said. "Named after you! That is impressive, Antoine. Where is it?"

"Sorry," said Leroux, "that's what Sitgreaves named a branch of your Antelope Spring in his report. As you know, that water location is crucial to the success of any travel west from Albuquerque.

Antoine continued his tale, "The young man intrigued me. Whipple is in his early thirties, but business precluded my helping him out further at the time.

"Two months later, a captain named John Gunnison showed up at the Hacienda. He desperately wanted my help for his struggling expedition along the 39th parallel from Kansas to the Great Salt Lake. He buffaloed me into scouting for him. I only agreed because he approved my valet coming along. I'm old and known well enough to make such demands, along with a hefty salary and a substantial bonus if successful."

Antoine paused to pack and light his pipe. Hanna poured more coffee.

"I returned to his stalled expedition with him to help. Big mistake. One of my mistakes is going to get me dead someday."

While Leroux drew on his pipe, Lorenzo asked, "Why are you here? We're a fair distance from the Salt Lake." Lorenzo's anticipation and excitement grew. Would Leroux ask for his help? The tall man concentrated on presenting a calm demeanor, not risking another look in Hanna's direction.

"Because Gunnison is an asshole," continued Antoine. "He listened to me even less than Sitgreaves. He had no idea what to do or which way to go. The mountains we went over to get to the Green Valley pushed this old man's stamina to the limit and my patience.

"The party took four days to make the thirty miles to the top of Cochetopa Pass, bridging streams and hacking a wagon path through an aspen forest that extended to the crest. One geologist compared it to a crossing of the Alps. The crew dragged the wagons up the mountains, letting them down the steeper slopes with ropes. Rocky trails jarred our teeth, ravines had to be gone around, and we crossed the fastest mountain streams I've seen.

"I argued with Gunnison and lost increasingly. The expedition ended up at dry campsites for lack of an intelligent decision. Things came to a head when I told the captain to wait while I scanned the Wasatch mountains. The expedition went ahead. In my experience with peaks and passes, I can look at mountains from a distance and usually find a way. I scanned the Rockies ahead and estimated it would take me a month to find a way through. I told Gunnison to stay put, but he proceeded, like a man in a maze, trying this way and that.

"At that point, the whole venture hit me as stupid. Traveling from Albuquerque makes more sense than those mountains and the deep winter snow. I quit with Gunnison, backtracked with Fernandez, my valet, back down to Diablo Canyon, and found the Whipple expedition.

"The young man, elated to see me, signed me up, and I led him to your valley." Leroux sat back in his chair and puffed.

"Whipple's a young man, you say," Lorenzo interjected. "Hell, he is my age."

"Like you, he is capable. Yesterday we traveled through a storm that dropped at least twenty inches of snow on us," said Leroux. "It only lessened as we approached your valley ten miles from here. Whipple gathered his officers and called for a layover day. It is Christmas eve. There is going to be a celebration this afternoon and tonight."

Jeremiah heard the word Christmas and became interested in the attention Zachary received bouncing on the Bear's knee. The older boy kicked his stack of blocks and came to Lorenzo's elbow close to the shaggy man.

"And that is why I am here," said Antoine. "Come down with the kids. They can meet real soldiers and listen to Mexican songs. What do you say?"

"I don't know; what do you think, Hanna?" said Lorenzo. Jeremiah went over to Hanna, grabbed her skirt, and looked up at her, ready to plead.

"I'm not taking 'no' for an answer," said Antoine. "You both work hard and deserve a Christmas celebration."

"Hanna, you could wear your dress," said Lorenzo. "The one I brought back from San Diego."

"I can't walk down the mountain in this snow in my good dress," said Hanna.

Lorenzo countered, "Put the skirt on when we get to the camp. The boys can ride the toboggan down, and I'll pull them back up."

"Hanna," said Antoine, "I think you will find the naturalists interesting. I want to introduce you to John Bigelow. He is a physician who also studies plants and trees. I find him and his collection fascinating."

The matter settled; Antoine left for the valley, leaving a tortured Lorenzo thinking of questions unspoken and unanswered. The day had warmed, the wet snow bending boughs to the breaking point. Lorenzo went to the sheep sheds and offered them oats instead of a trip to the valley. Hanna packed her skirt into one of Sunny's saddle packs and saw that the boys had layers of clothes to stay warm, along with mittens and wool caps. When Lorenzo returned from the barn, he loaded the sled with the pack and the boys. He and Hanna strapped on snowshoes, and the family of four started down. Excited, Bandit circled the sled as it slid down in the snow. Lorenzo let the sled run its course in large openings, picking up speed for forty or fifty feet and throwing snow in the boys' faces as they screeched.

***

Hanna's sheep used the west end of the meadow for grazing, but now the field contained a diverse array of wagons and erected tents. The expedition had set up a corral that included dozens of mules. A second corral contained almost as many sheep as Hanna's herd. The soldiers and Mexicans had cleared dry ground in the center of the wagons and built a cozy bonfire. Ten men worked around a wagon and fire, preparing food and drink for the celebration.

Antoine led the Brennans to his own lavishly appointed tent. Fernandez Murillo had stretched a line inside the tent between two poles. Antoine's three trip outfits hung neatly on the line. Holding a stiff brush, Fernandez smoothed the suede of one of Antoine's overcoats.

"Fernandez," said the guide, "Look who I've brought from their high cabin."

Turning, Fernandez threw the coat across one of the cots and embraced Lorenzo and Hanna. "Mi amigos," he said. "It is so good to see you. Looking well, both of you. Is this Jeremiah? I didn't even recognize you: so big these days." Jeremiah suffered a pat on his head from the Mexican.

Hanna asked about Julia.

"Tending sheep and looming wool back home," Fernandez replied. "She keeps busy with the newest grandkids, Pepo, Juan, and Carlita."

Antoine, anxious to check in with Lieutenant Whipple, suggested the family accompany him to the command tent.

"Wait just a minute, Antoine," said Hanna. She left the tent and returned with the saddle bag containing her skirt and petticoats. Setting the bag down, Hanna returned to the sled, brought a wooden box of finely chopped straw, and handed it to Fernandez. While the valet held the box, Hanna fished around in the chaff and pulled out a chicken egg. "Take these eggs over to the cook's table. I brought two dozen. I'm sure they will be put to use."

Fernandez left the tent with the box, and Lorenzo stepped outside with the boys and Antoine to allow Hanna to dress.

When she emerged from the tent, Zachary ran up and tried to hug his mother but became ensconced in petticoats. Hanna swooped the boy up and handed him to Lorenzo. Picking up the hem of her purple skirt, she admonished Lorenzo. "You are in charge of Zachary, Lorenzo. I love my son, but I love my new dress as much and will not see it ruined."

While Lorenzo and Antoine laughed, the group set off for the command tent. Whipple bivouacked on the opposite side of the sixty-foot circle of tents. His residence looked identical to the tents on either side except for the thirty-one-star United States flag attached to a twelve-foot-tall pole next to the entry flap.

Antoine knocked on the tent pole, whereupon Lieutenant Whipple invited the scout and family in.

Lorenzo and Hanna shook hands with the lieutenant, noting he had a haircut similar to his own, just over the ears, and touching his collar in the back. Whipple combed his hair into a gentle wave on top and a slight curl in the back. He kept his mustache trimmed back from his upper lip, and his chin did not sport a beard. Whipple's eyes suggested intelligence and enthusiasm with quiet confidence. The lieutenant welcomed the Brennans to the Christmas Eve celebration, gesturing them to sit on stools before his desk. Lorenzo grabbed Jeremiah by the waist to stand at his side. Zachary sat on Hanna's lap while Antoine remained standing.

"I need to thank you, Mr. Brennan," said Amiel. "As I understand it, you are responsible for the current health of our scout Antoine here. He continues to be of great service to the expedition and the country, for that matter."

To Lorenzo, there seemed to be an easy admiration between the two men, one young, one old.

Another knock on the tent pole brought a man dressed in dark pants and a buckskin hunting frock to the corner of the desk.

The man addressed the lieutenant, “The weather is clearing, Amiel. What are your intentions for moving on? The lower elevations will have less snow, and Möllhausen and I can get back to collecting samples.”

Amiel stood again, “John, let me introduce you to Lorenzo and Hanna Brennan. This is John Bigelow, our surgeon and chief botanist on the expedition.”

“Hanna,” said Antoine, “this is the man I wanted you to meet.”

“Glad to meet you, Mr. Bigelow,” said Hanna, “I would indeed enjoy seeing your collection. I am an amateur herbalist; I wonder if you have collected a San Francisco Peaks Groundsel sample. I’ve only seen it on our mountain. Covered with snow today, but with the melt, you could collect a sample tomorrow.”

“Interesting indeed, Mrs. Brennan, “John Bigelow said. “If you wish to accompany me to my laboratory tent, I can show you my entire expedition collection. If you spot your species of groundsel, I’ll add the colloquial name to the register.”

“Right,” said Hanna, standing. “Lorenzo, we should see Mr. Bigelow’s collection. We have time before dinner, don’t you think, Mr. Bigelow?”

“Yes,” said Bigelow.

“You go ahead, Hanna,” said Lorenzo. “I want to see the map Lieutenant Whipple is working from with Antoine.”

Lorenzo masked his intent from Hanna with his natural vacant look. Her heart sank; *Her husband would ask if they needed his services as hunter and scout. Lorenzo, you can’t go. I’ll tell you why later.*

Hanna left the tent with John Bigelow in a bit of a huff, but not before depositing Zachary in Lorenzo's arms. "This one's in your charge until dinner," said Hanna.

Amiel pulled out the map of his expected path west of Bill Williams Mountain. The intended route would see the expedition turning north at the Colorado River and crossing somewhere nearby instead of following the Colorado south to Fort Yuma like the Sitgreaves expedition. Once through the hole-in-the-wall pass that Lorenzo had traveled two years ago, the company would offer gifts and incentives to the Mohave camp. Whipple wished for peaceful trade relations and a different result from the Sitgreaves fiasco.

At that point in the conversation, Amiel suggested he had to take care of something to fulfill his promise to Bigelow for departure from the valley on the morrow. Lorenzo did not pursue his desire to join this railroad survey to the Pacific Ocean.

Carting Zachary on his hip, Lorenzo returned with Antoine to the old scout's tent so that Fernandez might assist Antoine in dressing for dinner. Fernandez had laid out an appropriate outfit. As Antoine dressed, Zachary played with Antoine's boots, stuffing any loose item he could find into the Hessians. Lorenzo rolled a smoke, lit up, and breathed tobacco with a deep inhale. He attempted subtly to ask Antoine's intentions in his regard. As usual, his attempt failed, "So Antoine," Lorenzo said, "you want me to come along again? Am I right?"

"Lorenzo," said Antoine, "accompanying Fernandez and me from here on out has been my intent since leaving that windbag Gunnison high in the Wasatch mountains."

"After talking with Fernandez and seeing the color drain from Hanna's face when you did not accompany Bigelow and her to see the expedition plant collection, I have decided not to take you away from your beautiful wife again."

"Oh," said Lorenzo, "I guess with Fernandez, you figure you won't need me."

"I could use you, Lorenzo," said the scout. "There is another reason I quit with Gunnison. I have developed Asthma these past two years. It kicks up once or twice a month around the ranch and more often when I visit Washington. Any higher up the mountain from your cabin becomes pretty sticky for me. The worst feeling in the world is being unable to breathe, trying to fill your lungs with real air. I'm fifty-three in five months. This may be my last trip."

'That sounds like you need me more than ever," Lorenzo said.

"Fernandez will see to me," said Leroux, "I'll be fine. However, I will not ask you to come along, my friend. I don't think you realize it, but Hanna is pregnant."

"What?" said Lorenzo, closing his gape, "That's ridiculous. She would have said something."

"Fernandez figured it," said Antoine. "He has five grown daughters with families, thirteen granddaughters, and three grandsons. He is sure of it. She is with child, third or fourth month."

"Si, Señor Lorenzo," piped in Fernandez. 'I'd bet my Sunday sombrero on it. We, men, don't catch on so quickly sometimes."

Zachary, done playing with the boots, tugged on Lorenzo's pant leg, "Papa, let's get Mommy," he said, "Hungry."

Lorenzo hoisted Zachary as he stood and swiveled the boy up to his back. Zachary reached around his father's neck to hang on. One little hand stroked Lorenzo's Adams apple, investigating the lump, seeming to question and learn. Lorenzo said as he parted the tent flap, "I better find my wife, Antoine. Fernandez, I'll see you at dinner."

The tall man and boy walked across the campground. Lorenzo remembered the agony he felt watching the Mohave boys climb up the scree toward where he hid behind the hole in the rock near the Colorado River. At the time, he sweated wet, worried he would never return to his two boys to watch them grow.

Hanna, Jeremiah, and Zachary. They were his adventure, his future, his responsibility. Now, another little critter would add to the fold. I can be a foolish man.

With renewed resolve, Lorenzo searched for the rest of his family and found Jeremiah and Hanna meandering between the soldier's tents toward the bonfire. He kissed Hanna's cheek, thought better of it, and embraced her for a long hug. The family continued together to the bonfire circle.

The soldiers had used block-and-tackle harnessed to mules to drag fallen trees over to the campfire, supplementing the limited number of stools for seating. The Christmas Eve dinner included antelope steaks or mutton chops, roasted potatoes, onions, pickles, and a cookie for dessert. The Brennans, guests of honor, sat at the lone folding table with Lieutenant Whipple, two of his fellow officers, and two of the naturalists, including John Bigelow.

Lieutenant John Jones sat next to Lorenzo. "Thank you for the eggs,' he said. "I would call them a Christmas miracle," He leaned in close to Lorenzo. "I mixed up a delightful eggnog with the rum we stashed and my assortment of spices." The man stood and lifted his tin cup. "The cooks are pouring eggnog for all. A toast to our distinguished leader, Amiel Whipple, our intrepid scout, Antoine Leroux, and his friends, the Brennans, who brought this eggnog gift to our Christmas Eve table."

Everyone raised their glass and drank. The expedition slurped eggnog, consisting more of rum than egg or creme, tasting as good as the finest champagne at a Parisian society gala.

Lieutenant Whipple, seated next to Hanna, thanked her for the eggs. "You have added a special touch to our party tonight. Men are more civil in the presence of a woman. Especially one so attractive. These men will remember this night, Hanna, and your beautiful dress, as will I. Lorenzo, you are indeed the luckiest of us all this Christmas."

"And thankful I am," said Lorenzo.

For the next few hours, the Company gathered around the campfire. The soldiers smoked and polished off the eggnog, making continuous toasts to whomever they could tease. The Naturalists told lighthearted jokes. Lorenzo and Hanna joined in a songfest that echoed eerily through the ravines of the San Francisco Peaks. Lorenzo kept looking over at Hanna, staring. "What," Hanna would say, or "What are you looking at."

The Mexicans in the expedition interjected their native songs, whooping and howling and dancing in circles around one of their sombreros thrown on the ground. They then left the ring, keeping to themselves near the edge of the meadow.

The Americans in the circle sang Christmas carols. The night turned colder, and the sky cleared, delivering a million pinpricks of starlight.

The Brennans were about to leave when the Mexicans began firing their guns and rifles into the forest, laughing at the snow falling off the overladen pine branches. Jeremiah began to run toward the spectacle to catch a better view.

"Jeremiah, you come back here," said Hanna. "You stay right here next to me."

In the distance, ten Mexicans standing shoulder to shoulder pointed their rifles at the sky above the forest. Another of their company walked along the line making sure all the rifles pointed in parallel unison. Then he yelled, "Uno, dos, tres," On the fourth count, ten rifles exploded in a salvo that avalanched the snow off the three closest trees.

The sound cracked the night like a crack of lightning hitting yards away. Jeremiah covered his ears and shook his head, trying to understand such a loud noise. Zachary just giggled.

This was great fun for the Mexican herders as they moved around the meadow's edge, firing, laughing, and watching the snow tumble off the trees from the shock waves. After ten salvos, the riflemen exhausted the surplus ammunition Lieutenant Whipple had issued for the celebration.

Five minutes of silence followed. Jeremiah pointed to a man holding a torch to the bottom of a standing dead seven-foot jack pine through the space between two tents. The needles caught fire, exploding into flames, and sparks reached high toward the stars. Soon, every lone pine in the area looked like a roman candle.

The Brennans returned to Antoine's tent, allowing Hanna to change out of her best dress for the trudge up the mountain to their cabin. Lorenzo packed the sled, propping Zachary, asleep, in front of Jeremiah.

Lorenzo shook hands with Antoine, giving him an extra hug. "Good fortune and safe travels, Bear," he said. "Don't worry about us. We'll take care."

"Like I've said, Lorenzo, my friend," said the scout, "You're capable."

Husband and wife grabbed the sled rope together and left the expedition camp, traipsing up in the snow toward home.

A week later, as Lorenzo relaxed with a book at the table, reading by candlelight, Hanna sat down and asked for his attention. "I'm pregnant again, Lorenzo. It is a girl."

Lorenzo leaned over the table and kissed his wife.

"I know," he said, returning to his book.

11 |Black Spider

Hanna spent an April morning inventorying the sheered sheep fleeces rolled up on a shelf in the barn. She had to count all the dried and carded fleeces from this year's shearing. Hanna had worked like a crazy woman to finish all the carding before the baby came. The size of her flock meant she needed to start spinning soon. She would sit during the process, a perfect activity for the last eight weeks of her pregnancy.

Her husband had repeatedly asked her to slow down. Pointless, given her nature and pride in keeping up the ranch. Since the departure of Leroux and the Whipple Expedition, the Brennan family stayed put for the rest of the winter. The weather Gods were promoting spring. Snow had been absent from all but the summits of the San Francisco Peaks since the first of April.

Practice pains had been occurring for a couple of weeks. Hanna chalked up the early pains to the accelerating speed of delivery for subsequent babies since Jeremiah's prolonged labor. Zachary's birth had been more bearable and for a much shorter period. Her little girl may continue the trend.

While carrying a bucket of water to the chicken coop, Hanna stopped and set the pail down. She cupped her stomach with both hands and concluded that the practice pain was not. When the pain stopped, Hanna set off for the barn again. The pain began again before she made it to the barn. *Not ten minutes apart.*

On the third such pain, Hanna tried to remember when the baby had kicked up her last storm. She had been busy that morning with breakfast and hoeing. Was it a week ago that Lorenzo had laid his hand on her while the baby kicked him?

Now that the pain had ended, Hanna felt all the areas of her huge tummy. Nothing seemed wrong. No movement. Then another pain, more intense, more prolonged; five minutes since the last.

It's happening. How could I have miscalculated? She hobbled back to the cabin as the pain intensified. Hanna grabbed linens and blankets. *Thank God Zachary is napping.* She headed toward the barn. She knew she would never have time to find Lorenzo and Jeremiah. They were tending the sheep in the low meadow. Sweat poured from Hanna's every pore. She spread the clean linen over the dirt floor in the barn. Hanna dragged the birthing chair from the corner of the barn to the center of the sheet, bunched her skirts, and sat in the birthing chair. In seconds, another stomach pain began. Minutes later, another, then another, and another. She lost count.

Close to exhaustion, Hanna pushed involuntarily, screaming through pain; intense stars flashed behind her eyelids, and pain traveled from her jaw to the back of her neck, tight with tension.

The baby came out, falling into the pile of linen beneath the chair. Minutes later, liquid, blood, afterbirth, and sac gushed through the hole in the chair seat, flooding the linen below. Immediate relief. Hanna leaned her head back to rest and recovered her senses.

What about the baby? Silence filled the darkened barn.

Hanna looked down and saw the mass lying beneath the chair pooled in blood, the chord encircling her baby's neck and winding under her tiny arm. She knew her Miriam was stillborn. Hanna leaned over the side of the chair and threw up. That didn't help. She shifted her focus. The crack of sunlight through the barn wall boards made millions of dust particles dance up, down, and swirl. The roughhewn beam above housed a trail of ants madly chewing tiny holes. She still thought of dying. *Hell, this is Christ's hell. My poor baby girl. God, what have I done?*

After Lorenzo corralled the sheep an hour later, he and Jeremiah approached the cabin. Entering, they found Zachary standing in the crib, rattling the sides, his shirt wet from crying and repeating, "Mommy."

"Where is your mother, Zachary," said Lorenzo, hoping a cup of coffee awaited him. "Is she still picking berries for supper?" Carrying Zachary in the crook of his arm and leaving Jeremiah to play with his toy farm wagon on the porch, Lorenzo walked up to the garden. No Hanna. The barn and the fleece inventory were his next guess. In the dim light, he opened the barn door and found his wife slumped in the birthing chair, skirt bunched at her knees. Then he saw the mess.

Lorenzo threw Zachary on the hay bales and rushed to Hanna's side, taking her hand. It felt ice cold, despite the day's heat and the barn.

"Hanna, Hanna," Lorenzo said. When she opened her eyes and swiveled her head to meet his gaze, he sighed, "It's OK, Hanna, I'm here."

"Tired," said Hanna, pointing. "Perfect spiderweb near the beam." Lorenzo looked up to see a black spider scurry along its web to the rafter.

"I'll get it," he said.

"No," Hanna said, "I focused on it until you came. Didn't look down."

Lorenzo nearly cried at her plight but thought better, "I'll get a kettle on for warm water. You stay here and rest, then we'll get you cleaned up and into bed." He grabbed Zachary, returned him to his cabin crib, and threw in Jeremiah's blocks for the boy to play with.

Lorenzo returned to Hanna with the kettle, a pail of fresh water, and rags. While she slept, Lorenzo cut the cord with the shearing scissors, spread a small baby blanket on the milking table, picked up the baby girl, and wrapped it in the small coverlet, wiping her skin clean of blood. He guessed Miriam measured about twelve inches head-to-toe and weighed only a few pounds.

Lorenzo gathered the linens and blood, cutting around the chair legs to not wake Hanna.

Hanna stirred.

"Let's get you cleaned up and into bed," said Lorenzo. Hanna did not resist. Lorenzo soaked a washcloth and cleaned Hanna's bottom, thighs, legs, and feet. Carrying her to the cabin and their bed (skirts and all), he undressed Hanna, covered her in blankets and quilts, and built up the fire.

"Lorenzo," called Hanna, "What about the baby."

"Miriam is stillborn," said Lorenzo. "I have cleaned her up and wrapped her in a blanket."

"I'm ready for her now," said Hanna.

"Are you sure, Hanna?" he asked.

Hanna began to wail, "Lorenzo, I'm so sorry. It's my fault, I know, but what did I do wrong?"

"Nothing," said Lorenzo, trying to think of words to comfort his wife.

"But she died," said Hanna. "She's gone. I don't know what to do. What could I have done?"

Neither parent had answers. Lorenzo sat by the bed, holding Hanna's hand. Hanna sobbed for minutes, then fell asleep again. Lorenzo didn't move.

Hanna woke suddenly, frantic, "Where's the baby? Where is Miriam?"

"Are you sure, Hanna," said Lorenzo.

Hanna calmed herself awake, “Yes, I need to say goodbye. Bring her.”

He fetched the baby wrapped in the blanket from the barn and laid her next to Hanna. He left his wife and baby girl to make tea at the stove as Hanna whispered, “Hello, Miriam, my baby girl. I’ll never forget you.”

12 |Beasts of Burden

Sitting at the cabin table, his slate before him, Jeremiah seemed stuck. He had written the first six rows of his three's factors:

3 x 1 = 3
3 x 2 = 6
3 x 3 = 9
3 x 4 = 12
3 x 5 = 15
3 x 6 = 18
3 x 7 =

"Stop fidgeting, Jeremiah," cautioned Hanna. She continued peeling potatoes on the porch while watching her eldest as he studied. "When you get up to ten, you will be done with your lessons for today."

Jeremiah, nearly crying, said, "My eyes are tired, Mommy."

Hanna used a stern voice, "No excuses," she said, "and you are to address me as 'Teacher' during school time. Keep going."

Zachary sat opposite his brother. Tomorrow would be his sixth birthday. He felt big and old and wanted Jeremiah to play cowboys and Indians in the low meadow where Daddy tended the sheep, and Bandit could join in their game. Zachary could not go down the mountain unless accompanied by Jeremiah or one of his parents.

"Hurry up, Jeremiah," he said, "so we can play."

Jeremiah performed a right-handed scratch of his long brown hair above his ear.

"Mommy," said Jeremiah, "Zachary won't let me think. Go away, Zachary, go away now."

"Teacher," said Hanna, "You are to address me as 'Teacher."

Hanna started on another potato. Noticing his mother's concentration on the potato, Zachary snuck from his chair, circled the table, and whispered, "twenty-one" in Jeremiah's ear. The younger boy returned to his seat.

Jeremiah wrote 21. His thinking thus jogged, he finished the table:

3 x 7 = 21

3 x 8 = 24

3 x 9 = 27

3 x 10 = 30

"I'm done, Teacher," declared Jeremiah gleefully.

"Alright, Jeremiah," said Hanna," leave your slate on the table for me to check. You and Zachary can see what your Papa is up to."

Like a lightning bolt, Jeremiah shot out of the cabin, picked up his toy rifle, and ran down the trail toward the valley. Zachary stopped to pick up his toy bow, arrow, and feather headband and ran after his older brother.

After finishing the last potato, Hanna set the pot of potatoes on the stove, ready to boil for supper. She glanced at the slate on the table. Zachary hadn't fooled her. She had seen him answer Jeremiah out of the corner of her eye.

Although Zachary did not previously attend her school, Hanna mused that her youngest son absorbed the knowledge that rubbed off his older brother during lesson time. She decided to pull out the slate reserved for Zachary the following Monday and start him writing his ABCs.

Hanna believed in the importance of education, as did her mother, Rachel Sandler. Hanna had read every book on her high shelf in the cabin twice. Every time the family traveled to

Albuquerque, she would order a new book from Rosenstein's Dry Goods and pick up her selection from the previous year.

Zachary could pick out words in the children's books she read to her sons at bedtime. The differences between her brown-haired son and her raven-haired youngest reflected the parents they resembled.

Jeremiah learned in return for free time to play and spend with his father. Zachary, the curious one, asked a hundred questions daily and wouldn't leave Hanna alone until he received an answer. Hanna sensed that Zachary couldn't wait to read the books on her shelf. She let him leaf through the ones with illustrations.

Jeremiah may become a hunter or rancher, whereas Zachary might be better suited for business or academics. That is not to say that Zachary shied away from his chores. Zachary constantly attacked tasks with a sense of wonder, whereas Jeremiah had to be coaxed along.

Zachary gained a reputation with his brother for accepting any dare Jeremiah dreamed up, sometimes to their detriment or even danger. Zachary admired his older, bigger brother so much that he hung on every word Jeremiah uttered. Every second Jeremiah allocated to spending time with Zachary thrilled the younger child. Luckily the two boys got along.

Hanna opened the trap door to the root cellar and went down to get the sack of root potatoes for planting, her afternoon chore. She checked the sprouts on the potatoes before putting them in her carry burlap, counting out twenty. Hefting the gunnysack, Hanna took two out and put them back in the storage sack. *Be careful, don't overdo it.* She climbed the ladder out of the cool cellar and headed up to the garden.

In a clearing near the garden, Hanna stopped at the marker for Miriam's resting place, as she did on most trips to the meadow. She set down the gunny sack, clasped her hands together, resting them on her expanding stomach, and stood for a moment over the grave. *This time you will have a sister, sweet Miriam.*

Three years passed; the stillbirth took a tremendous toll on the Brennan family. Hanna's melancholy mystified Lorenzo. To him, a baby is a means to an end. A person to help with chores, hunt with, or spin and loom with her mother. To him, Miriam had not existed.

Lorenzo sympathized with the bond that held Miriam to Hanna, but he couldn't feel it. He just couldn't. To Hanna, her San Francisco Peaks had exploded in a volcano of second guesses and guilt. Months passed before Lorenzo spotted a genuine smile from his wife. He also began to see the stillbirth as somehow his fault. This tore up the clueless man. He kept trying to figure it out to help his beloved wife.

And there had been three miscarriages since.

And now, Hanna was pregnant once again. Hope and trepidation surrounded the cabin as if both Lorenzo and Hanna went about ranch business with their fingers crossed. Hanna had passed well beyond the weeks that marked her miscarriages. She also had surpassed the marker for Miriam's stillbirth.

She retrieved the hoe and spade from the garden shed and knelt beside a prepared row. Hanna spaded a hole large enough for her first starter root and pressed a healthy potato into the earth, covering it. "Grow, please grow," she whispered.

Emerging from the cabin trail, the boys hid in the tall grass at the meadow's edge. "Zachary," Jeremiah whispered, "See if you can sneak up on Papa like a ghost and scare him."

Zachary crawled on his hands and knees fifty feet to reach his father. Lorenzo awoke as Zachary made it halfway. Peeking from beneath his lowered hat, he remained still. When Zachary rose, ready with both hands to scare his father, Lorenzo surprised him first by jabbing Zachary and shouting, "Boo."

Zachary jumped back, effectively scared and startled. His father jumped up, swooping Zachary into his arms and tickling him. “Think to scare me, eh? We’ll see about that. Where is your brother hiding?”

Jeremiah ran over, attempting to tackle Lorenzo, who played along, falling to the ground and tickling his boys. Bandit came over to protect the boys, nipping at Lorenzo, circling his family, barking, and rousing the sheep.

The boys, escaping from their father's clutches, ran off to retrieve their toy armaments and discuss the boundaries of their cowboys and Indians game.

Lorenzo let them go. *Two fine boys*. He pondered Jeremiah, at eight years old, only a couple of years away from learning to shoot a rifle, becoming a hunting companion. He couldn’t figure Zachary out. Too young. Took after his mother. Kept Lorenzo on his toes.

The leaves of Aspen trees sprinkled along the edge of the meadow between the Ponderosa Pines had begun to go yellow. Lorenzo sometimes lost track of days and dates. He thought today to be either September 11th or 12th. Zachary would be six on the 18th. Lorenzo had spent the last four nights after the boys were asleep building a tree fort hidden in the forest close to the cabin. The tree fort would be quite a surprise for Zachary’s birthday, and both boys would be thrilled.

1857 had been a pretty easy year, and pleasant weather helped speed the shearing. The trip to Fort Defiance saved four days off his past trips to Albuquerque. All the supplies the Brennans needed for the year had been on hand at the fort. Lorenzo arranged with the station master to order some of Hanna’s frillies and precious books from her friend Mr. Rosenstein in Albuquerque. With the shorter travel distance, Lorenzo made the trip to Fort Defiance twice a year.

Bandit came running up and barked at Lorenzo. Turning back toward the trail to Albuquerque, Bandit ran twenty yards and barked in that direction, then turned back and scampered up to his master and barked again. *Something's up.* Lorenzo reached for his rifle.

"Boys," yelled Lorenzo, "Come back over here. Jeremiah, Zachary, come here, now. Bandit, go!"

The dog took off, racing toward whatever lurked down the trail, the line of first defense. A wolf? A bear or just a herd of antelope?

As the boys gathered at their father's side, out of the pines, a lumbering beast they had never seen before came into the meadow. As tall at the shoulder as a Clydesdale but uglier. The man atop the animal had a dark complexion. Indian? He had a blue cloth wrapped around his head. The man wore a white robe with long, billowy sleeves. He had on sandals.

The stranger, lost in the flowing robe, resembled a white-stemmed, blue topped mushroom. He raised an arm and fist to signal whoever followed him to stop. Then he urged his mount forward and leaned down to speak to Lorenzo. "Is this the trail to Leroux Springs," the man asked.

"The pool beyond the meadow is filled with water from the spring," said Lorenzo. "Is that… Is that a camel?"

"Yes," the mushroom man said with a distinctly British accent. "My name is Hadji Ali; I'm the handler for the Beale Expedition." As he spoke, men on mules leading camels packed with supplies and equipment emerged from the Albuquerque trail and fanned out behind Mr. Hadji Ali.

Then, another man riding a camel emerged from the forest, flicking a riding crop to urge his mount forward, reigning up next to Hadji. A distinguished gentleman with hair neatly trimmed at the ear and a bushy mustache; the rapt attention of the other riders told Lorenzo that this man would be the leader, Beale?

The man failed to acknowledge the Brennan family and spoke to the mushroom man. “Are we there, Hi Jolly?” the man asked.

“Just at the end of the meadow, another mile or two,” said Hi Jolly. “According to this man… I’m sorry, sir, I haven’t asked your name.”

“My name is Lorenzo Brennan,” said the tall man. “These are my two boys, Jeremiah and Zachary.”

The leader had eyes only for the end of the meadow and the trail ahead. Nodding acknowledgment of Hadji’s comment, he urged his camel forward, then turned the gigantic head back toward Hadji. “Brennan, you say, Lorenzo? The name comes to mind from a talk Antoine Leroux told all over Washington. Sir, are you familiar with Antoine Leroux?”

“Antoine is a dear friend,” said Lorenzo.

“Well then, sir,” the man said, holding a hand out for a shake, “We will need to talk. My name is Ned Beale. President Buchanan appointed me to survey the trail from Arkansas to California. Gonna build a road to accommodate immigrants settling in the territory.”

Lorenzo couldn’t wait to tell Hanna about the possibility of a road to Albuquerque. With a wagon road, they could load sheep for sale to butchers in Denver, just like the Leroux Hacienda. Of course, Amiel Whipple had been on a similar quest for a railroad, so Lorenzo would not hold his breath.

“A wagon road would be most welcome, Mr. Beale,” Lorenzo said. “The Whipple group spent Christmas Eve at that end of the meadow in ’53.’

“Hi Jolly, we’ll make camp there,” said Beale. “There’s space and good grazing for the stock. Mr. Brennan, we’ll be in the area for the next seven to ten days, surveying back to the east and beyond in the west before we move camp."

"I'll let you settle and stop in the day after tomorrow. OK?" asked Lorenzo.

"Make it sooner, if you can," said Beale. "Plans are essential. The more facts I can glean about our course ahead, the better."

"Tomorrow then," said Lorenzo. "Come on, kids, let's get our herd to the cabin. Nice meeting you, Mr. Hadji. Mr. Beale, nice meeting you. Bandit! Home! Now!"

Zachary bravely spoke, "Daddy, can we ride the ugly horse?

Lorenzo looked up at Hi Jolly, who gave a slight nod. "Another day perhaps, Zachary," Lorenzo said. "Let's go tell your mother about the camels."

***

Lorenzo sauntered into the surveyor's camp the next day, passing the corrals. He counted more than twenty camels. They lounged with their legs folded underneath or stood around chewing. He saw one camel fling his head, shaking white gobs of chew from his mouth. Occasionally, a camel would bray, sounding more like a lion than a horse. Lorenzo kept his distance.

Another corral housed too many horses and mules to count. Many of the soldiers were in the field with their mounts. Dogs ran through the camp. The twenty, two-man tents lined up in military precision reflected the strictness of Beale's command. The number of tents would account for forty soldiers and surveyors. Lorenzo headed to the tent with the flagpole and American flag waving out front. In the distance, the tall man spotted yet another corral filled with sheep. The Beale Expedition seemed well stocked. Ned Beale had taken to heart the stories of the Sitgreaves and Whipple expeditions brushes with hunger and thirst.

In the command tent, Beale sat alone, hunched over his desk. One corner of the desk held maps neatly stacked and fanned on one side for easy reference. The documents stacked on the desk's upper right corner comprised the communications necessary to run the camp. Centered in front of Beale, the proposed trek map from Albuquerque to the Alta California border held his attention.

Beale looked up upon Lorenzo's entrance, stood, and shook Lorenzo's hand, inviting him around the desk to collaborate over the map.

Getting down to business, Beale said, "These three points map the locations of water between here and the Colorado River. First question, Lorenzo, how accurate?"

"Two out of three are dead on, Mr. Beale. I'd say the middle point is off," said Lorenzo.

"Ned, the name's Ned," said Beale. "Where should we count on acquiring water in that area."

Lorenzo picked out a scrap of paper from the wastebasket, ripped off a small piece, and positioned the corner on the map where he believed Beale would find water. "The desert changes with the seasons and nature's whim, Ned, but you should find water close to that mark," he said.

"Thank you," said Ned. "That means my plan is pretty good."

"Those are pretty fair distances between water sources. Make sure you have enough water barrels to make it. One gets awful thirsty in a September/October sun," said Lorenzo.

"That's the thing about camels, Lorenzo," Ned said. "They can carry a load of seven hundred pounds daily with a fraction of the water and grain requirements of the mules and men. I've learned a great deal of respect for the creatures. I suppose camels can't swim, so we'll have to raft across the Colorado River. That's the only downside to 'em."

The two men discussed the nature of the Mohave Indians Beale would need to deal with. Ned seemed to Lorenzo to be less conciliatory than Whipple or Sitgreaves. The man might get into trouble underestimating the desert Indians.

After answering dozens of questions from Ned, Lorenzo asked about Antoine. "I'm a bit surprised Antoine isn't with you," he said.

"Antoine?" said Beale, "Yes, surprised me as well. I greatly admire the man, even if only half of his stories are true. He returned my invitation with a letter expressing his regrets. Said he would not accompany me on the wagon road exploration. He mentioned his age, which at fifty-six doesn't seem old. He just said he decided to retire from scouting."

"It may be due to his health, Ned," said Lorenzo. "He has Asthma. The mountains affect his breathing these days.

"Now, when will we see this wagon road?"

Ned poured them both a short whiskey, sipped, and smiled. "Congress has funded a road. First, we survey, then come back through and build the road. Complete the road's Albuquerque to California border leg by the end of '58. The leg of the road from Albuquerque east to Fort Smith, Arkansas by the end of '59."

Lorenzo's eyes widened. Never one that could conceal, his smile just kept widening. "A road would mean a great deal to our sheep ranch, as you can imagine," he said.

"We're on schedule so far," said Ned. "Indians, mountains, or weather could hold us up, but from the reports I have scrutinized, I believe the plan will hold.

"Ned, I must return to my chores," said Lorenzo. "Thank you for the discussion, and trust you'll stay the course. Might you find time for a home-cooked meal at our cabin tomorrow evening? Antelope steaks are on the menu."

"Lorenzo, I thank you for the information you provided. I will call on your household at six o'clock," said Beale. "How would that be?"

13 |Proposition

The next evening the Brennan family, Ned Beale and his 1st lieutenant, Jack Simmons, crowded around the table in the cabin. Hanna served carrot soup, pickled beets, baked potatoes, and antelope loin steaks. Jeremiah, fidgety as ever, asked to get down, but Hanna suggested that he stay still at the table if he wished to have berry pie. Zachary listened intently to the table discussion, understanding little of it.

"Mrs. Brennan, that meal alone would keep a man close to your stove," said Ned. "What a fine dinner."

"Why, Mr. Beale," said Hanna, gesturing at Lorenzo. "Did this man indicate he would be going with you to California? Because if so, he knows he can keep going, and you can have him."

"On the contrary, Hanna," said Beale. "Lorenzo pointed out yesterday his need to stay close to home for the birth of his baby.

"However, there is another matter I've been pondering since meeting you, Lorenzo. The meadow below is the ideal place for a supplies station for the building of the wagon road, a little over halfway to the Colorado River from Albuquerque. I would use the camels to pack supplies to store at the station. My men will build a log warehouse, but I need an honest station master. Someone to dole out supplies to the work crews and track requisitions for reimbursements from Washington or Philadelphia.

"You fit the bill for the job. You know these parts, you have good relations with the Indians, and you will stay close to the station for the next few years.

"I'd pay $120.00 monthly for your services, Lorenzo."

Lorenzo looked at Hanna. No help there. He plastered his best poker face on his demeanor, saying, "Something to think about, Ned," Lorenzo said. "I'll stop by again tomorrow with my answer. I appreciate the offer."

After the guests left down the trail to their camp and Hanna put the boys to bed, Lorenzo turned to Hanna. "What do you think, Hanna? The extra money would provide a good cushion for a few years."

Hanna sat down at the table, inviting Lorenzo to do the same. "Your hours are filled with shepherding and taking care of the stock and the barns," Hanna said. "I don't see where you could find the time to run a supply station. Are you thinking of getting out of the business of the ranch?"

"No," said Lorenzo, "But I guess you're right. Hard to do both."

Lorenzo had been salivating at just such a prospect. Station Master, a new adventure, something different than counting sheep.

"The money is intriguing," Hanna said. "Let me think."

The tall man sat on his hands so as not to show his nervous excitement. *Let her work it out. She always does.*

Hanna rose from the table and put a kettle of water on the stove for dishwashing. Lorenzo gathered dishes and took them to the porch to rinse, scraping each plate into the slop bucket for the animals. Back at the stove, he set the stack of dishes and forks next to Hanna for washing and found a towel to help dry them. Hanna laughed aloud. *He wants this.* Lorenzo usually smoked his pipe on the front porch while she washed the dishes.

Hanna finished the dishes, tidied the stove, and wiped the counters and table. She dried her hands and sat on the porch in her rocker. Hanna massaged her stomach with her hands as if to ask the baby for advice.

"What about a part-time station master," said Hanna. "You might work four to five hours a day at the station. The warehouse in the valley should be no more than fifteen minutes from the ranch. When you are not there, a sign on the door could direct the driver or customer to our cabin, and you could go down and unlock the stores and help load."

"That might work," said Lorenzo. "A heavy work week, but the money we could save in a couple of years would protect us from a bad year or two, diseases the sheep might catch, any number of disasters."

"We should be realistic, Lorenzo," said Hanna. "I don't want you to work yourself to death. The boys need your time. I need you."

"But short term, it would mean so much for the family," Lorenzo responded.

"There are positives about it, I know. You wouldn't be galivanting around with Ned Beale, for one. The money, of course, and the more we help with the wagon road project, the sooner we'll have neighbors and a road to market the sheep."

"So, I will tell him this tomorrow," Lorenzo said.

Hanna looked to the sky, still thinking, planning, calculating. She said, "Lorenzo, how much would we have to pay a ranch hand to help with the sheep."

"Around twenty-five dollars a month."

"Say thirty dollars a month," said Hanna. "Room and board included. That would leave us ninety dollars a month out of the hundred twenty dollars Mr. Beale offered."

"That's a great idea," Lorenzo said. "Then Jeremiah can take over the herd in four years."

"Alright," said Hanna. "Let's write this down." She walked back into the house, found a quill, ink, and paper, and began writing, discussing more points as she wrote.

Lorenzo Brennan agrees to:

1. Work four hours daily as Station Master manning the supply station to be built near Lorenzo springs and within fifteen minutes walk of the Brennan's cabin.
2. When not personally at the station, Lorenzo will be on call. Directions on the warehouse door will lead drivers and customers to the cabin to gain assistance from the Station Master.
3. At the government's expense, the Station Master will hire a driver to transport from Albuquerque or Los Angeles by wagon materials and tools to complete and enhance the wagon road.
4. The Station Master's fee shall be $130.00 per month.

"One hundred thirty dollars a month?" Lorenzo asked Hanna, panicking that the deal might fall apart at that demand. "Ned said one hundred twenty dollars a month."

"I know," said Hanna. "But you're the best man, the only man for the job.

"Poker, Lorenzo, play the game well this time."

The next day Ned Beale agreed to the conditions as Hanna had written. Lorenzo had an easy time with it. Instead of bluffing, he told Ned that his wife had agreed to the terms and would not let Lorenzo take part unless Ned acknowledged all the provisions. Lorenzo walked over to the camel corral while Ned composed a formal contract. He called Hadji Ali over to the fence, "My youngest son has a birthday in three days. I want to bring the family down to see the camels. Might it be possible for my birthday boy to ride the camel? With your assistance, of course."

"Certainly, Mr. Brennan," said Hi Jolly. "Bessie loves the children. Your boy will receive a much-spirited ride."

Lorenzo walked back to the command tent and signed the prepared contract. As Ned and Lorenzo shook hands, Ned said, "I will divert a crew tomorrow to cut the trees necessary for building the station. The logs can season until our return trip from Los Angeles. I want to evaluate the wagon road route next winter, so count on us in January or February. My crew will help you build the station before moving to Albuquerque."

***

Zachary woke up to his mother opening the stove door to stoke the fire and add a layer of firewood. Birthday. The boy climbed out of bed over his still-sleeping brother, dressed, and climbed down from the loft. He stood expectantly next to his mother at the stove. Hanna gave the boy a basket. That meant eggs for breakfast. Without a word, Zachary went out to the porch. The morning glow of dawn began brightening the valley. After his eyes adjusted to the grey fog swirling halfway down the trail, the boy ran to the chicken coop attached to the barn. He opened the gate and shooed the chickens to get to the nests in the hen house.

Returning to the cabin, Zachary presented the basket of eggs to Hanna, "When can I open the presents, Mommy?"

"After morning chores," Hanna said.

Dejected, Zachary asked if he could play until his mother had breakfast ready. Hanna asked him to set the table first, which he did, before running back outside. Bandit brought the boy a stick to throw. The two spent ten minutes on a throw-and-fetch game and headed to the barn.

Shady, Sunny, and Stumpy (the mule Lorenzo inherited from his encounter with Sifter Cawdell) received a chin and ear scratch from the boy, who had to scale the pen to reach the animals. He shinnied along the top rail until he could grab the bag of oats hung on a hook. The horse and mules followed him and slurped the grain out of his hand.

Presents! After morning chores! Zachary scooped chicken feed from the barrel near the coop and scattered the grain in the yard for the chickens to peck. Next, he grabbed a bucket and hiked up to the spring, dipping and gathering a quarter bucket of water (all he could carry) and took it back to the coop, pouring the water from the bucket into the poultry drinker. Zachary decided to make one more trip to the spring to top off the water trough. He and Bandit walked back to the cabin side by side. Bandit stayed on the porch while Zachary entered, now hungry and excited for his birthday celebration to begin.

Hanna hadn't cracked any of the eggs yet. Stirring sounds from the loft meant Jeremiah would be descending soon.

Shaving over the wash basin in front of the mirror, Lorenzo, suspenders flapping against his knees, called out, "Coffee."

"On the table," said Hanna as she set a mug down. The aroma of coffee filled the cabin, giving Zachary hope that the family day had begun.

After breakfast, the morning chores progressed. Lorenzo and Bandit cut out fifty sheep and shepherded them to the upper meadow to graze. Jeremiah groomed and fed the horse and mules, and Zachary picked corn and the last of the tomatoes from the garden. Hanna cleaned the cabin and rested, not taking any chances with her kicking baby.

Lorenzo had completed the morning farm chores by noon, and Hanna had baked the birthday cake. Lorenzo brought the sheep down to the second corral. He would take the sheep left behind during the morning's grazing to the upper meadow later in the afternoon. Lorenzo, as excited as Zachary, gathered the family to unveil the birthday surprises for the boys.

Lorenzo led the family down the trail toward the valley, continually checking on Hanna, appealing to the boys to slow down and give Hanna the time she needed.

The family walked to the camel corral, and Lorenzo sought out Hadji Ali. Hanna wanted to see the camels as much as Zachary pleaded to ride one. Hanna had moved to the San Francisco Peaks at the age of twelve. Her books provided her with an extensive worldview. Today she would experience the sight, stink, and touch of a real-world creature few in America ever could.

Hanna hugged Lorenzo's arm, awed. Lorenzo looked down at Zachary, jumping up and down. "Zachary, stand still and politely ask your question of Hi Jolly."

The younger boy stopped fidgeting, clasping his hands together in front of his chest. "May I please ride the camel? It's my birthday."

Hadji Ali told Lorenzo to pick up Zachary and approach his camel from the side. Lorenzo handed the boy to Hadji, who positioned him in front of him in the camel saddle. Without another word, Hadji turned Bessie and switched him in the rear, and Bessie took off in a dash. The lumbering giant trotted through the open gate on the far side of the corral, held open by a second handler. The camel broke into a run back across the meadow.

Hanna gasped, "Lorenzo, too fast, he'll fall off."

"Be that as it may, Hanna," said Lorenzo. "The boy will learn, one way or another."

Zachary did not fall off. Ten minutes later, Hadji handed the boy back to Lorenzo. The boy wobbled when Lorenzo set him down, rebalancing. Then he resumed his pre-ride excitement, repeating, "I rode a camel, I rode a camel."

"Thank the gentleman," said Hanna, putting a hand on Zachary's shoulder to help him stand still.

"Thank you, sir."

Lorenzo turned to his eldest son. Jeremiah wanted no part of riding the camel. He ran fifteen feet away and kept shaking his head from side to side. Lorenzo cajoled the boy for a minute and then shrugged, disappointed. But Hanna felt the experience highlighted the difference in the boys. Zachary took on the dares his older brother laid on him, looking forward to new adventures and learning new things. Jeremiah remained comfortable in the world he knew, Bandit, the ranch, and his family.

After thanking Hadji Ali, Hanna decided the family should walk to the command tent and thank Mr. Beale if available. When they arrived at Beale's tent, Lorenzo detoured to the medical tent next to Beale's and peered in. A bearded man inside sat at a small desk writing in a journal. Another man, his right wrist bandaged, brushed by Lorenzo, walking out toward the body of tents.

"Hello," said Lorenzo, turning his attention to the man at the desk. "Sir, might you be the company surgeon?"

The surgeon introduced himself as Jonathan Stewart and asked how he could assist.

When Hanna entered, Mr. Stewart understood. He ordered the boys and Lorenzo out of the tent and examined Hanna's stomach, asking her all the pertinent questions. The doctor requested Lorenzo to join them and offered his diagnosis. "Hanna, I'm sure you realize you are close.

"I have assisted in only three other births, but I would say, based on those experiences, that you must not worry. The misfortunate pregnancies of the past may be behind you.

"Still, if the expedition has not moved on by the time you go into labor, I would be honored to gain further experience in childbirth by assisting."

Trepidation versus excitement. The words of the surgeon moved Hanna multiple notches toward excitement.

After an even more careful hike back to the cabin, Lorenzo led the boys and Hanna through a thicket west of their home to a giant oak tree. Lorenzo had assembled ladder stairs and a platform ten feet off the ground surrounding the tree.

"Boys, what do you think?" Lorenzo asked. "We can add a built-in table or a cupboard for each of you."

"Zachary, Jeremiah, what do you say?" said Hanna. "Quite a surprise. Lorenzo, sometimes you amaze me."

Both boys rushed to their father, hugging his legs and thanking him. Then they broke away and climbed up on the platform.

"Maybe a railing around the edge," said Hanna to Lorenzo, then she shouted to the boys, "be careful until your father adds on a fence, so you won't fall off."

Late that evening, after the other half of the sheep had grazed, the family sat down to dinner, roast haunch of mutton with red-currant jelly and gravy over potatoes. After dinner, Zachary opened his two presents: a neatly pressed and folded hand-me-down nightshirt and a winter knit hat and mittens. Hanna brought the cake to the table and lit yet another candle for Zachary to wish upon. He blew it out, and the family enjoyed the cake.

Hanna allowed the boys two pieces.

***

The Beale expedition construction crew spent two weeks in March '58 completing Lorenzo's punch list for the new warehouse/cabin. The team built a counter near the front door where Lorenzo would conduct business, with drawers for office supplies and documents. The foreman constructed a table, sanded and planed the top, oiled the surface, and positioned it behind the counter. Lorenzo reserved space near the table for a stove, which was ordered, and on the way from Albuquerque. Hungry travelers and road construction crews would appreciate a roofed meal on occasion. Lorenzo had nailed down the last of the wood for the boardwalk. The porch ran along the entire front of the building. He had checked off twelve other small tasks. The ground slope on the west side of the building would allow wagons to back up to the barn door. Men could load or unload supplies, lumber, and grains from a wagon bed directly on the warehouse floor. Wagons would soon roll along a completed wagon road from the east and the west.

The Beale expedition had made it to the coast of Alta California and traveled back to the meadow, again using the Camel Corp, arriving on February 14, '58. Ned and Lorenzo met that day, reviewing procedures and timelines before Ned drove the expedition toward Albuquerque, proving the ease of use of his surveyed route for winter travel.

Two-thirds of Beale's group had moved on, but a crew stayed behind to build Lorenzo's supply station from the logs felled the previous September. As soon as the wagon road crew completed the road from the Colorado River to Lorenzo Springs, supply wagons would begin to arrive. Lorenzo would inventory and fill requisitions of the road crews continuing the road construction to the east. When Beale returned to Arkansas, he intended to hire another crew to build and improve the wagon road west to Albuquerque, meeting the wagon road crew from the Colorado River.

Lorenzo and Hanna planned a meal to celebrate the accomplishments of the construction crew. They brought fixings for a stew and a cake for dessert down from the cabin. Jeremiah waited for the meal, getting to know the crew's stock of mules and horses. Zachary wandered into every corner of the new building, opened every drawer in the counter desk, checked underneath the boardwalk for critters, and tagged along after the carpenters, asking about each tool they picked up.

Hanna carried baby Sarah in a papoose as she prepared the cooking fire and stew. She had given birth to Sarah six days after the Beale expedition moved away from the meadow. Dr. Stewart had missed his opportunity to assist with the delivery. Because of the stillbirth, Lorenzo, accustomed to the process, helped his wife tie, cut the cord, and clean his wife and baby girl. The birth turned out to be much like Zachary's. The baby girl cried within a minute of birth, as did Hanna. The stress from years of miscarriages and the stillbirth poured forth from Hanna like a flood. She shook with relief and held the baby beside her the entire first night. Hours after the delivery, successful breastfeeding caused another fountain of tears from Hanna. She kept assuring Lorenzo of her happiness, despite the tears.

The day after Sarah's birth, Zachary sat in a chair while Lorenzo placed the baby in his lap. Zachary examined the baby as Lorenzo had, checking fingers and toes and squeezing her little legs through the blanket. Her eyes were dark. She had a wisp of blond hair.

Jeremiah stood next to Zachary while his brother held the baby. Close enough for his liking. He let Sarah try to grab hold of his finger.

Lorenzo feared a baby girl. A girl would present unknowns to an inexperienced man, but Hanna continued to beam, and he felt overwhelming love and support for the strength of his wife.

The supply station was completed, and Lorenzo chatted with each crew member over a stew dinner, thanking them for their work and the quality of the structure. The crew began to pack up and planned to leave at noon or 1:00 pm the next day.

After the crew left, Lorenzo sat in a chair on the supply station porch for an hour, ready for business. He locked the station and mounted the sign on the door describing his on-call status.

Lorenzo encircled his wife from behind in bed, clutching her tightly that night. Sarah slept five hours a night, and the boys weren't stirring.

He had a new, important job, and Lorenzo figured brighter, prosperous days would be ahead. Lorenzo would be turning forty. He lived with a beautiful wife and three healthy children. His savings from the Sitgreaves expedition now sat in a Denver bank. The revenue from the sheep ranch would increase after the completion of Beale's wagon road. Lorenzo had a steady income as a station master. *I have to admit, I'm a lucky man.*

***

During the first week in June, the east/west wagon road crew showed up in the meadow and set up camp. The horses and mules danced in the corral. Working dogs herded sheep into a pen. Steve Pembroke entered the warehouse office, finding Lorenzo behind the desk totaling figures in a ledger for expenditures and revenues for May. Steve worked as the supply wagon driver for the construction crew. He had made several trips to the supply station, bringing or acquiring material for the road crews. "I got something you might be interested in this trip," said Steve.

Lorenzo met the driver at the wagon of supplies parked at the dock. Behind the buckboard, a box held two puppies squirming over each other. "What have we here?" asked Lorenzo.

"A couple of Australians," said Steve. "Both of their parents are great working dogs. I've noticed that Bandit is slowing down, and I thought…."

"If these puppies turn out to be half as good as Bandit, I'm going to be obliged to you," Lorenzo said.

Lorenzo tied ropes around the dogs' necks that afternoon and looped them under their front legs, forming a simple harness. The excited puppies, a sire, and a bitch, ran ahead, tugging on the leads, trying to drag Lorenzo forward. Lorenzo had no way to surprise the boys with the dogs. Jeremiah heard the squawking, and he and Zachary climbed down from their tree house and ran to greet their father. Both boys sat down on the rocks near the cabin, and the puppies swarmed over them, licking and nipping to the boys' delight.

"I want this one, father," Jeremiah smothered the puppy. The dog sported a fluffy black coat with two white splotches on his chest and looked about eight weeks old. "He's the biggest of the two, and I'm the oldest. Can I have this one?"

Lorenzo looked at Zachary, scratching the other puppy behind the ears and petting its back. "What say you, Zachary?" he said.

"Sure, Daddy," said Zachary. "This one likes me. Jeremiah should get the big one." The tinier puppy, born in the same litter, had a white chest and forelegs with a merle pattern in blue and white from the back of her neck to her tail. On both sides of her neck were tan tufts. She had blue eyes.

"Alright, it's settled," said their father. "The girl puppy goes to Zachary, the boy to Jeremiah. You two will have to live and breathe these dogs. Train them for the next couple of years to sit, stay, and come when you call them. After that, we'll set up a round pen and teach them how to work."

All the puppy yapping brought Hanna out of the cabin. She considered the consequences. "We'll have to create a barricade in the corner of the cabin by the table until they are potty trained," she said. "How is Bandit doing with them?"

"I'm afraid Bandit just can't get that excited about anything these days, Hanna," said Lorenzo. "Trained, these two dogs are just what we need with the herd getting so big."

"When do you think they will be ready to work the sheep, Daddy?" asked Zachary.

"Not for three or four years, depending on how well you two train them. They will be your responsibility. Your dogs," said Lorenzo. "Let's take them to the upper pasture and introduce them to Bandit and Abelardo."

Hanna returned to her stove. The puppies wrestled with each other, anxious to be active. Each boy took the lead and followed or dragged their puppy up the mountain. Lorenzo herded them in the general direction. Bandit sighted the puppies entering her domain and sat down and growled. Abelardo Sanchez, hired by the Brennans to help with the sheep while Lorenzo spent time at the supply station, stooped down and gathered Jeremiah's puppy. "What a surprise, Señor, no?" he said.

"Yes, I hope a pleasant surprise," Lorenzo said. "Bandit is over thirteen years old. We need to bring along new dogs. The boys will train them.

"Boys, you listen to Abelardo. He has trained sheepdogs. The puppies are you boys' responsibility, but we will teach them discipline."

Abelardo put down Jeremiah's puppy and picked up Zachary's. "Ah, chica bonita, Zachary," he said.

"What does that mean, Abelardo?" said Zachary.

"Pretty girl," answered Abelardo, holding the puppy to the sky and examining her ocean-blue eyes. "Chica means girl in my language," answered Abelardo.

Abelardo had a craggy face, burnt by the sun for over sixty years. His wife had died, and his children had families in Albuquerque. Like the dogs, he was a match made in heaven when Hanna found him looking for work. Able to work still and willing, he indicated the worst thing for him would be to sit around in his son's home living off his boy's charity. The spry old Mexican came to live at the Brennan ranch. Lorenzo helped construct a room in the barn hay loft for him, and Abelardo became a family member, eating dinner at the Brennan table daily.

Back at the cabin, Zachary held up his puppy so that Hanna could see the color of its eyes. "Chica Bonita," announced Zachary. "This is 'Chica Bonita.'"

"Chica," said Hanna. "That's a good name for a dog. What are you naming your puppy, Jeremiah?"

"I don't know, Mother," said Jeremiah. "He's bigger and stronger than Zachary's dog. Blacky.

"He is a hunter, the way he pounces on Zachary's puppy. Like that black wolf father scared off last week." Both boys had seen the wolf advance, snarling, crouched in its advance on the corral. Bandit alerted Lorenzo, who fired at it from the porch, scaring it back into the woods. Jeremiah, in particular, had been impressed with the speed and strength of the dark-as-night animal.

Abelardo, who had come along with the boys, ran with the thought. "Lobo, Jeremiah. Lobo Negro, you're right; your dog will look like a wolf rounding up the sheep."

"What do you think of 'Lobo,' Jeremiah?" asked Hanna.

"Lobo and Chica," said Lorenzo. "A good start, cabin training next. I'm hungry; let's eat."

14 |Rose-Baley

At the end of July, to Lorenzo's surprise, a party of travelers out of Albuquerque entered the meadow. Their scouts inquired about a water source in the area. The station master directed the scouts to Leroux Spring and the valley beyond to the west. One scout explained that the group of immigrants consisted of two separate wagon trains headed by Mr. L.J. Rose and Mr. Gillum Baley. The two expeditions had combined for the journey to California in Albuquerque. The scouts reported back to their respective leaders. Soon, drovers on horseback directed a herd of close to two hundred red Durham cattle, as well as fifteen spare horses, past the warehouse,

Five minutes after the stock left the meadow, four ox-drawn prairie schooners plodded by Lorenzo, observing from the porch of the supply station. Alpha Brown, the head of a family moving along with the fourth wagon, came over and introduced himself and his wife, Mary, who waved from the wagon as it went by.

Mr. Rose had hired Mr. Brown to manage his train. He pointed out the members of his family as they walked by. Julia (age 7), Orrin (age 5), and his daughter Relief (age 13, from a previous marriage). His wife Mary also had two daughters from an earlier marriage: Sophia Fox (age 15) and Sarah Fox (age 13). Supplies packed high in three covered wagons suggested to Lorenzo that the party had provisioned well for their trip to California. Six oxen attached to each wagon strained to pull the three ladened prairie schooners.

The Rose family passed next in a small wagon pulled by two mules. The conveyance reminded Lorenzo of a Portland, Maine, city ambulance. Mr. Rose ventured over to Lorenzo and Alpha Brown and introduced himself.

The three men moved to chairs on the station porch. L.J. lit a cigar, Alpha rolled a cigarette, and Lorenzo relit his pipe. Lorenzo mentioned his history with the Sitgreaves expedition, and the other two men pelted him with questions about the Indians along the Colorado River.

Twenty minutes after the Rose wagon left the meadow, half-a-dozen grubstake drovers and another herd of cattle appeared. Alpha told Lorenzo that the seventy-five cattle and riding horses belonged to the Baley-Hedgpeth outfit.

After the stock passed, eight loaded Murphy wagons, pulled by eight oxen each, rolled by the three men on the station porch. The tall-sided freight wagons measured sixteen feet in length, and Lorenzo knew they could haul four to eight tons each. The diameter of the rear wheels on the giant wagons dwarfed the men walking along.

Lorenzo mused as the wagon train passed. These were well-provisioned immigrants that would not require his mercantile goods. No sale. Alpha Brown said the parties traveled with forty men and fifty to sixty women and children.

Alpha introduced Gillum Baley and Joel Hedgpeth, who stepped up to the three seated men on the porch and leaned against a post. Baley had brought his wife and six children along on the journey west.

Hedgpeth and his brother Thomas left Nodaway County, Missouri, with the Baley clan for the rumored lushness of California.

"This past week has been stifling hot," said Joel. Lorenzo, your pine forest this side of the San Francisco Peaks sure feels fresher."

"After we're settled in the valley," interjected L.J. Rose, "we'll stop back at the station for help with water supply locations between here and the Colorado river."

"Glad to help," said Lorenzo. "Why don't I bring my family to your camp? My boys can meet the children in your group, and my wife, Hanna, and our baby girl need the diversion."

The wagon trains camped in the valley near Leroux Spring. The going had been rough out of Albuquerque, and the valley offered a welcomed respite from the intense heat and aridity of the high plains desert. Beale's road construction crew had completed their work only halfway to Albuquerque. The scouts from the Rose-Baley trains followed tree blazes, cairn stacks, and survey markers to get to the developed portion of the wagon road.

After the party rested, a half-dozen adventurous souls hiked up Humphreys Peak, the highest point in the territory, where they found snow and ice, unusual in July.

The Brennan family visited the camps every other afternoon. They temporarily shifted chores to Abelardo to allow the boys to meet and become acquainted with the children. Mary Brown, in particular, was interested in Hanna and the two boys. Her oldest daughter from her first marriage, Sophia Fox, an invalid (age 15,) stayed near her wagon knitting.

Sallie Fox (age 13,) Mary's second child from her first marriage, and Julia Brown (age 7) latched on to Jeremiah (almost ten, and Zachary, nearly eight.)

While Hanna and Mary discussed the upcoming bottling and preserving tasks, Sallie, Julia, Jeremiah, and Zachary led Chica and Lobo to Leroux Spring. The children coaxed the puppies into the freezing water, but soon the dogs splashed in the ankle-deep stream, yipping and biting the water sprayed at them by Jeremiah. The boys had removed their boots, so only a couple of inches of their knee pants got drenched. The girls in long skirts looked a little bedraggled.

"Julia and I got to dry out before we go back," said Sallie. "We better sit in the sun and ring out our dresses."

"Sure," said Jeremiah. "Our pants are drying out. Zachary and I can play jackstones on that flat rock next to the stream. You two can watch while we dry out."

"We'll play too, Jeremiah," said Sallie. "I'm the best in my Sunday school class back home. I'll beat both of you."

This challenge could not go unanswered by Jeremiah. "I bet I can beat you," he said.

"OK," Sallie wiped her mouth with her hand. "If I win, you must let me kiss you," she said.

Jeremiah's eyes widened. He worried she might beat him at Jacks. A girl better not kiss him. Jeremiah glanced over at Zachary running around, attempting to tag Julia. "Ok," he said to Sallie after Zachary ran past, out of earshot, "but you can kiss Zachary, not me. If I win, Zachary will kiss Julia."

Jeremiah untied his sack of stones from his belt and dropped them haphazardly on the game boulder. The contest between Sallie and Jeremiah remained tied through the threesies round. At foursies, Jeremiah won the game. They were his stones; after all, he had that advantage.

Sallie wanted to play again, "Two out of three," she said. Kissing a boy, any boy, seemed to her a grownup activity. A pursuit that she had as yet not experienced.

Jeremiah declined. "I won the game. Zachary kisses Julia." He advanced on his younger brother as Sallie discussed the matter with Julia. "Zachary, you get to kiss Julia," said Jeremiah.

"I don't want to kiss Julia. I don't want to kiss anybody," said Zachary.

Jeremiah tried a different approach. "I dare you." He let that sink in a bit. "Why are you scared? Are you a scaredy cat? I double dare you," he said.

Zachary pondered the dare and the respect he might gain from his older brother. Jeremiah climbed trees like a tree frog and beat him at Jackstones every time. His older brother could chase and catch any boy or girl playing tag. "I'll kiss her, but I won't like it," he said.

With a committed step, Zachary approached Julia, keeping her hands clasped behind her back. She was examining the scuffs on her shoes. Zachary frowned. Kiss her cheek? Her mouth? Inches away from Julia's nose, Zachary made his decision. He put his arms around her so she couldn't turn and run away, bent his head down to look at her, and kissed her on the mouth. Julia stared at him during the kiss. Zachary backed off after three or four seconds. He turned to Jeremiah, dare accomplished.

Jeremiah and Sallie stared at each other in amazement. Jeremiah put his arm around Zachary's shoulder, and the two brothers began walking back to the Brown wagon, each coaxing their respective puppy.

***

On August 1st, the Rose contingent split with the Baley group and left the valley. Following Lorenzo's directions, a small party searched for the spring's location west of the valley. They returned after locating a meager spring fifteen miles west of the supply station.

By dividing the parties, the leaders felt the limited water supply ahead would serve two smaller groups spaced a day or two apart. The Brennans walked down the valley to wave to the Brown family moving out. Sallie ran back to the Brennan family, grabbed Jeremiah by the shoulders, and kissed him on the mouth. She spun around and rushed to join her family without saying a word. Jeremiah, stunned, turned to his mother and shrugged.

The Brennan family settled back into ranch life. The boys now had added dog chores. They spent half an hour with their puppies and Abelardo each morning, working on the dog training commands: sit, stay, hush, and come. A separate lesson in the afternoon between one of the boys, his puppy, and Abelardo reinforced the morning lesson.

Chica immediately bonded with Zachary, so Hanna had to tell him to put his puppy down to eat, work his other chores, or climb the ladder to the loft and bed. Within weeks the puppy looked around to find Zachary. Trotting over and looking up for attention, which the boy always provided.

Jeremiah, being older, stayed a little more aloof. The male Australian reacted in kind, reticent unless required to pay attention during lesson time.

The Rose wagon train made it as far as the Colorado river by following Beale's wagon road through Sitgreaves Pass and down to the valley. Over the next few days, L.J. Rose moved their camp south, looking for an ideal crossing site. He settled on the bank of the river amongst a copse of cottonwood trees he planned to fell to build rafts. The Mohave Indians the immigrants met along the river ranged from friendly trading partners to covetous cattle rustlers curious about the white women.

Ten men worked on rafts while others, including Alpha Brown, herded the cattle closer to camp.

Sallie Fox struggled toward her mother's wagon carrying a heavy bucket of water from the river. She set the bucket down to rest for a minute. With hands at her waist, Sallie scanned the prairie horizon and noticed movement amongst the scrub a hundred yards distant. Now she could see action and Indians surreptitiously approaching the camp in an arc in front of her.

Terrified, Sallie screamed, "Indians! The Indians are coming. Indians! The Indians are coming. They're going to kill us!"

Alpha Brown heard his stepdaughter over the braying of the cattle. He took off at a gallop along with the other cowhands and reached camp just as the hundreds of Mohave warriors charged.

Sallie ran to her wagon. Mary hauled her up into the wagon. "Get under the mattress with the other children," she yelled over the gunshots. Mother had crawled under the mattress in seconds, joining her children, pulling blankets over the family.

Arrows falling from the sky began sticking into the mattress and the wagon's side. Sallie looked out the knothole next to her head. She was horrified when her father staggered into view, trying to reach their wagon, arrows sticking out of his thighs and back. Alpha Brown fell to one knee ten feet in front of Sallie, and she started to scream. Mary clapped a hand over her mouth. "No noise; we must be quiet."

When Sallie looked through the knothole again, more arrows protruded from Alpha's back and neck. Alpha went down. Dead.

Bile rose in Sallie's throat as she attempted to remain noiseless. Then another arrow found the clapboard crack near Sallie's side, piercing her. She cried out. Again, Mary clapped a hand over Sallie's mouth, but when she saw the arrow that had struck her daughter, she took her hand away, gathered a corner of a blanket, and stuffed it into Sallie's mouth. "Bite down on this as hard as you can," Mary whispered. "Don't think of anything else but biting that blanket and staying quiet."

Sallie bit the blanket and used it to wipe tears away from her eyes. She saw warriors through the knothole shot dead, falling backward, and exploding in blood. The pain shot through her side when Julie bumped her knee. Excruciating pain. She bit the blanket and concentrated on watching the battle through the knothole. She cheered inwardly as one after another of the Indian warriors fell. Finally, the Indians vanished from her narrow perspective. The camp became silent. No movement.

The immigrants emerged from their hiding places to assess the state of the camp. L.J. Rose addressed the group, "We can't stay here," he said. "They will surely be back. Our only chance is to hope Mohave warriors have not attacked the other group. Our combined strength should be able to hold them off. We need army assistance to get any farther on this trail. Leave everything and be ready to move out in a half hour."

Once the mattress had been removed from the Brown family, one of the men broke the arrow close to Sallie's side and wrapped her in bandages until she could gain further assistance from the surgeon traveling with the Baley party. Four men bound the eight dead men in chains and committed their bodies to the river. Mary prayed while men carried her husband's body to waste deep water, letting him sink. Her second husband, as good a husband as her first (who had died of yellow fever,) became a familiar ache in her chest.

***

Immigrants began to trickle down Beale's Road after the Rose-Baley wagon trains departed. They arrived from Albuquerque, Santa Fe, and Fort Defiance when the construction crew completed the wagon road to the supply station.

On a cold late October afternoon, a haggard-looking man hailed Lorenzo and Abelardo, walking toward them from the cabin. The working duo, replacing a post in the sheep corral, stopped to meet the stranger. The shaking man, a member of the Rose-Baley party, needed supplies to make it back to Albuquerque after failing to cross the Colorado river. Lorenzo accompanied the man back down the mountain to the supply station. He found the remnants of the wagon trains and settlers that had looked so stately on their exuberant east-to-west travels in July.

While the families set up camp for the night, Lorenzo walked back to the ranch and, with Bandit's help, herded a dozen sheep down to the hungry party.

Lorenzo inventoried all the supplies the desperate families requested. As he handed out blankets, food staples, and cooking utensils, he recognized Mary Brown standing in line. Standing beside her stood Sallie Fox, her daughter, sickly, jaundiced, eyes lowered. With others needing Lorenzo's help, he had no time to inquire about his friend Alpha Brown.

L.J. Rose and the other wagon train leaders did not approach the supply station. Someone would need to sign the supplies requisition. Lorenzo did not charge the desperate camp members as they received his handouts. Instead, he believed he could submit his expenses to the government agent at Fort Defiance for reimbursement.

After a couple of inquiries, Lorenzo found L.J.'s tent. He knocked on the tent pole, and L.J. stepped outside. "Family's getting dressed for bed, Lorenzo," he said, "been a long day, a long couple of months getting back here."

Lorenzo showed L.J. the requisition, requesting a signature, explaining that he would submit the bill to the territorial government. Rose signed.

"What happened?" Lorenzo asked.

"Too many encounters," said L.J. Rose. "Friendly Indians, looking for presents in trade for vegetables. Other Indians were not so friendly."

"That matches my own experience," Lorenzo said. "We know so little of their story. You can't be sure of their intent."

"True. Well, the last day of August," L.J. continued, "the men were constructing rafts on the east side of the Colorado River. The next time I looked up, hundreds of Mohave Indians appeared out of the bush and attacked. Arrows dropped from the sky like hail. Our firepower held them off while the women ran to the covered wagons with their children. One of their chiefs leading the attack stepped out before his warriors, taunting us. Gillum Baley, a Black Hawk War veteran, took him down with a single rifle shot. The Mohave warriors retrieved the chief's body and retreated from the battle. The whole ordeal lasted less than two hours. Eight of our party died, including Alpha; another thirteen were wounded.

"Being low on ammunition and manpower, I decided that our party should leave the area hurriedly. We headed back to the protection of the Baley party, still camped in the mountains. We could only round up ten horses and seventeen cattle of the train's livestock. It has been a strenuous walk back here to the supply station." The wagon train captain shook uncontrollably in the recall. Lorenzo encircled the man's shoulders with his right arm, rubbing Rose's arm until L.J. settled, drying his tears. L.J. Rose returned to his tent and family.

That evening, Lorenzo recounted the fate of the immigrants to his own family over dinner without mentioning names, not leaving out any details. He admonished the boys to leave well enough alone but to realize the dangerous nature of the frontier where they lived.

15 |Last Chance

Lorenzo worked the supply station the rest of the year and a half of '59 while the Beale wagon road construction crews finished their work to Fort Smith, Arkansas. The Brennans modified their plans for the station, gradually stocking items that immigrants would need to cross the desert.

News of the Rose-Baley wagon train's failure to cross the Colorado River, and the party's subsequent return to Albuquerque, discouraged all but a trickle of immigrants attempting the trip to California.

Lorenzo heard from travelers of the ensuing Mohave war along the Colorado River. The United States War Department sent an expedition to the site of the Rose-Baley attack. Upon arrival, the soldiers established Camp Colorado at the location to protect immigrants traveling west, and soon the camp received a new name, Fort Mohave.

In late August, Steve Pembroke, Beale's supply muleskinner, brought news of a battle between a squad of fifty soldiers led by Captain Armstead and two hundred Mohave warriors. The soldiers routed the natives in a pitched battle fought twelve miles south of the fort along the Colorado River. The encounter left twenty-three warriors on the field, while only three Americans received wounds.

"That clinched it," said Steve, "Mohave Chief Espaniole sued for peace, and the war is now over."

"Good news for a change," Lorenzo said. "Hanna and I expected to see more wagons coming through by now. The San

Francisco Peaks have been peaceful this whole time. We've been lucky, but our savings are invested in the station."

"The word is spreading," said Pembroke. "I spoke to a wagonmaster organizing supplies in Santa Fe and another in Fort Defiance. You'll see results soon, I reckon."

"We better," said the station master. "I've staked out a small addition to the station. I think a saloon would do fair business. Hanna figures a thirsty traveler would pay fifty cents for a drink by the time they reach the spring."

"You'll be needing wood from Denver, right?" asked Steve. "If you have a list, I can have what you need in four weeks. An exclusive run."

"I just happen to have a materials takeoff ready for you," Lorenzo said. "I'll travel with you as far as Albuquerque. When you get to Denver, I'll wire money from my bank to the lumber yard's bank to pay for the supplies.

"I'll be back here working on the foundation while you return from Denver."

The two men hiked to the cabin to review their plan with Hanna. She thought of a couple of changes and additions. "Lorenzo, pick out ten sheep for Steve to take to Denver and enough grain to feed them. That will give Steve profit from a full wagon load to Denver, and the sheep can help buffer the cost of the lumber for us."

"That's my gal, Steve," said Lorenzo, "Always thinking."

Steve returned with the wagon load of lumber and hardware at the end of September. By that time, Lorenzo and Abelardo had dug the foundation trench with help from the boys. The builders had stacked and cemented rocks around the perimeter of the sixteen-by-sixteen-foot addition. Lorenzo also continued a porch foundation across the front of the proposed building.

The men completed the framing of the building in three weeks. Steve volunteered to stay for ten days to speed up the process. Lorenzo applied clapboards to the structure at the end of October. Then he began shingling the roof. The advantage of a small building project is that each task finishes quickly, shortening the overall time to complete the entire construction.

On November 15th, Lorenzo installed the door and a wide window in the front of the saloon. He then mounted a 2"x10" board atop the center of the porch. He did his best with the lettering on the sign. In red paint, the name read: **Brennan's Last Chance Saloon.**

Brennan's Station became busy at the end of August '59 when word reached Santa Fe and Fort Smith, Arkansas, of the peace treaty with the Mohave Indian tribe. At least one wagon or wagon train passed by the station every week. Lorenzo had never worked so hard. Besides inventorying, ordering, and receiving supplies, Lorenzo waited on an ever-increasing number of customers. Lorenzo also continued with half of the chores at the ranch. He also worked on building and finishing the saloon.

Three men stopped in for drinks the day Lorenzo put up the sign. At four bits per pour, Hanna figured a three hundred percent profit. She had suggested setting up the bar on the honor system with no bartender. Hanna had agreed to Lorenzo's saloon scheme stipulating that the premises would not harbor gamblers. She mounted a sign next to the entry door and lettered it with the words: **No Gambling, No Gaming**.

The bar business took off at the end of December after Steve Pembroke delivered the stove to heat the saloon. Lorenzo filled authentic Henry McKenna bottles from a barrel of Mckenna Whiskey. He ordered one barrel at a time, and Steve Pembroke delivered it from Albuquerque and Denver after originating in Kentucky. The bottle has twelve lines neatly painted on the side, each marking a chargeable drink. A customer requests a bottle of the only brand Lorenzo carries, McKenna. The consumer then takes the bottle to the saloon and pours drinks. The customer sits at a comfortable table or on a stool before the bar. When done with his drinks, the bottle is returned to the station. Lorenzo counts the marks consumed and charges the customer accordingly. The bar provides an adequate supply of clean glasses.

The immigrants following the Beale wagon road typically had wives and families. They were more interested in journeying to California than getting drunk and causing trouble. The men usually moved on after two expensive drinks. Lorenzo limited the drovers and wagon train hired hands by the number of pours in the bottle. Suspicious troublemakers were handed a half-full bottle of McKenna to limit their intake.

***

In 1860 Brennan's Station and Saloon prospered from the resurgent immigrant drive west to California. The increasing stream of clients consumed the supplies as fast as Lorenzo could order and stock his shelves. The business in the lower meadow made more profit than the sheep ranch. Yet, the sheep ranch profit also doubled. Lorenzo contracted Pembroke regularly to take sheep to the slaughter. The herd had begun to grow exponentially. A bulletin board on the wall in the station advertised sheep for sale. Settlers who miscalculated the length of the journey to the Colorado River bought sheep to provide food on the hoof for their family.

As additional advertising for the sheep, Lorenzo constructed a twenty-four-foot diameter pen to keep a few ewes, rams, and lambs ready for purchase. The enclosure doubled as a training ring for Chica and Lobo.

Chica moved to the head of the puppy class. Zachary worked with Chica every spare moment because his father emphasized the importance of immediate and unconditional obeyance to simple commands. Obedience class became another chore that kept him from the tree fort and his make-believe Indian war. Zachary, although two years younger, concentrated on puppy lessons passionately. He loved his dog and wished her to grow in excellence.

The puppies cried when put into their pen at night. Jeremiah buried his head deep in his pillow to get to sleep. Zachary stayed awake until Chica dropped off. After a week, Zachary snuck down the ladder while the rest of the family slept. He carried Chica up to the loft, which was dangerous and awkward. He went back down to grab some clean puppy potty straws. The boy grabbed the extra blanket from the foot of the bed and slept on the floor. This way, he did not disturb his older brother. Chica cuddled to his chest. If Chica awoke at night, Zachary plopped him on the straw to go. When Hanna went out to work in the garden, Zachary worked with Chica to climb the loft stair ladder. Chica became brave enough in six weeks to ascend to the upper floor alone. Hanna and Lorenzo never said a word about this routine. The dog quieted in Zachary's arms at night, and the parents slept better. With one dog quiet, the other calmed on its own.

The dogs were two-year-olds. Jeremiah would be eleven in November and Zachary nine in September. Lobo, more obtuse than Chica, followed directions from Lorenzo, Abelardo, and to some degree Jeremiah. When not in obedience training, Lobo wandered. Trainers needed to cajole Lobo into paying attention and learning the basic commands. The dog, like Jeremiah, focused on living free. The boy had more important priorities than dealing with Lobo. Learning his lessons in Hanna's school or sticking to his ranch chores were equally onerous.

Lorenzo saw himself in his eldest son and loved the boy's ambition for independence. He kept a stern hold over Jeremiah to appease Hanna. He was secretly proud of his son's ability to figure out ingenious ways of circumventing his chores.

On Jeremiah's tenth birthday, Lorenzo laid a canvas-encased rifle on the table. When Jeremiah unwrapped the covering, he found what looked to be a brand new M1841 "Mississippi Rifle," the stock gleaming with fresh wax. Lorenzo had rubbed the barrel raw with the finest sand at a pool next to the spring. After the sanding, Lorenzo had oiled the barrel and all the delicate parts of the firing mechanism. Lorenzo had spent two weeks late at night in the barn reconditioning and refinishing his rifle as a present for Jeremiah.

Lorenzo's friend in the Mexican/American war, Daniel Martensen, had brought an M1841 from Portland, Maine where he and Lorenzo had joined the Maine militia. Fellow soldiers envied Daniel's percussion lock rifle, far superior to the standard issue muskets most soldiers shouldered. Assigned to burial duty after the Battle of Brazito, Lorenzo spotted another M1841 rifle beneath a dead Mexican officer. Without a second thought, he traded his musket for the percussion lock gun; surviving the war was paramount.

The tall soldier had held onto the rifle since the war. During the Sitgreaves expedition, he had been issued a breech-loader, leaving his M1841 rifle at the ranch. Hanna had used it to drive off wolves. After buying the Sharps breech-loader in San Diego, the M1841 had been relegated to a rack above Lorenzo's and Hanna's bed in the cabin. Jeremiah hadn't noticed its absence during Lorenzo's reconditioning activities.

The boy made two fists and shook with excitement when he saw the rifle, hardly able to touch his dream.

Zachary, amused with Jeremiah's excitement over the rifle, did not understand the allure. His big brother's happiness made Zachary happy. That's what mattered. Chica, Lobo, and Bandit all became excited over Jeremiah's enthusiasm for his birthday present.

"Hush, Chica," said Zachary, "Sit, Chica." Chica looked up at Zachary and followed both commands.

Whereas Jeremiah now had the long gun he had been dreaming about, Zachary lived and breathed his dog, Chica. From the first, Zachary and Chica developed a rare bond. When Sarah was born, Zachary became "the middle child." Lorenzo favored his firstborn. That was OK with Zachary; he worshipped his older brother as well.

Sarah drew Hanna's attention, which Zachary also understood. Who wouldn't love Sarah, his baby sister? So delicate, smelling so fresh after a bath in lilac-laced water.

Zachary may have become lost as the middle child in the Brennan family if not for Chica. The loveable puppy and Zachary became joined at the hip. By six months, Chica heeled next to Zachary's left side on a leash or off, looking up every few seconds for assurance from Zachary. The boy always noticed, ruffling Chica's ears, scratching the dog under his chin, or running his hand down the puppy's back. The well-behaved dog and child trainer were a source of pride to Lorenzo, Hanna, and Abelardo.

Hanna thought Chica was the most beautiful dog she had ever seen. Like her favorite wool blanket pattern colors, Chica's coat from a fluff ball puppy had grown more mottled in blue, grey, and white. The fur patches of burnt sienna bursting from her flews gave the dog distinction. She looked like smudges of color streaking across the field when she ran.

Zachary, so young when he began hugging his puppy, worked diligently at training her, first to sit, then come, then heel. Day in, and day out, Zachary worked on the commands, hugging and petting the dog whenever she correctly interpreted the boy's order.

Chica could speak and hush as Zachary desired. The dog also understood and obeyed the rest of the family's commands. Lobo, in contrast, obeyed his commands after three repetitions. Lobo, the stubborn; Chica, the lover.

Hanna began giving Zachary the shorter books on her shelf to read on his own. The boy could still understand the content if he skipped the big words. He sponged ideas and knowledge, looking up at Hanna, smiling in satisfaction. Zachary began dreaming of a world beyond the cabin. The wagon trains that passed through intrigued him. Where were the people from? Where were they going? California? Why, how?

Jeremiah's long gun became the incentive for completing school studies and chores daily, including training Lobo. When Jeremiah struggled to concentrate in cabin school, Hanna would point to the gun rack and shake a finger. If her eldest son made too many errors on his chalk tablet, Hanna made him repeat the lesson. If Jeremiah became frustrated or belligerent, Hanna took the rifle from the rack and laid it on the table's edge.

The incentive of the rifle helped Jeremiah achieve higher marks in school. The same holds for the ranch chores Lorenzo or Abelardo assigned to the boy. Lorenzo controlled the supply of ammunition Jeremiah needed to practice with his rifle. After completing his list of tasks satisfactorily for the day, Lorenzo or Abelardo distributed ten rounds of paper cartridges and Minié balls to Jeremiah for shooting practice.

Lorenzo could not influence Jeremiah's training of Lobo either by access to the rifle or lack thereof. Lobo mirrored his master's attitude toward learning. The dog learned what he could get away with. The dog was as intelligent as Chica. He knew the exact limit of misbehavior that would bring on the ire of Lorenzo or Abelardo. Jeremiah wanted a hunting partner, and Lobo happily filled the bill.

As the puppies grew, so did the boys. By the end of the summer, Zachary had caught up to Jeremiah in height. His knee pants no longer stretched to his knees. Hanna teased the boy about his long neck and big feet. She predicted he would be as tall and lanky as her husband. Jeremiah, like Lobo, had a solid chest and shoulders, but he reflected Lorenzo in his face and hair. Zachary had a softness around his mouth, thin lips, and ebony hair like Hanna.

If a convoy consisted of four or more Conestoga wagons, the tired immigrants invariably camped for at least a day or two in the meadow near Brennan's Station and Last Chance Saloon. The California-bound children, thankful for the layover, would spot the Brennan boys working their dogs at the sheep training ring. Lorenzo told the children they could watch from the station porch if they remained silent.

Lobo's session always came first. The dog's wanderlust could only be suppressed for a spell. For the first week of a new task, Abelardo or Lorenzo would issue a command, over and over, while Lobo, on a twenty-foot lead, responded. If Lobo executed the order thrice, the adult trainer would praise the dog, scratching his favorite spot behind the ears. If the dog did not follow a command, Abelardo would yell, "Stay, Lobo! Stay, Lobo!" Often repeating the 'stay' command three times until Lobo obeyed. The trainer would restart the sequence of three 'come bye' orders in combination with the 'stay' command. The 'come by' command meant Lobo would need to circle the pen to the right. The sheep inside the enclosure also moved into a herd to the right side of the ring.

Satisfied that Lobo understood, the lead passed to Jeremiah, who continued with the same sequence. Abelardo offered a critique of the young trainer's technique. After fifteen minutes, Jeremiah disconnected the lead and tried the same command sequence independent of the leash. Jeremiah kept his fingers crossed as he issued that all-important first sequence off-leash. If Lobo did not respond or thought to run off, the trainer reconnected the leash and tried the drill again. If Lobo interpreted Jeremiah's command, the session ended. The boy and his dog would run off to practice with the M1841.

Jeremiah would return to the cabin with his allocated ammunition, grab the rifle and hurry up to the shooting range he had helped Lorenzo construct. Targets of various silhouettes, squirrels, deer, wolves, or concentric circles painted on wood stood like gravestones at distances of thirty feet, fifty feet, and seventy feet down range. A live squirrel venturing across the range offered a moving target. Lorenzo allowed Jeremiah to shoot at a bird alighting on top of one of the stationary targets. After two weeks of Lorenzo's supervision, Jeremiah practiced alone.

During shooting practice, Jeremiah hit a squirrel four weeks later, blowing its hips and tail into a bloody mess. The squirrel crawled, screaming, blood trailing, for three feet. After more twitches, the animal stilled. Jeremiah hid from the sight of the squirrel with his back against a tree. Then he walked back to the cabin, not looking back, stomach pain in his pit and a catch in his throat. Two days later, he returned to the dead squirrel site, but a fox had scavenged away all traces.

Zachary waited during Lobo's class. Chica, lying in the grass at his master's side, looked up at the boy, anxious to begin the day's lesson.

As Lobo and Jeremiah raced off, Abelardo called to Chica. With a wave of his hand, Zachary sent the dog off. Attaching the long lead, Abelardo reviewed the 'come by' command with the dog. After five minutes, the drill changed to the 'away' command, which meant Chica should turn the herd to the left. All the practice occurred outside the pen containing the sheep.

Abelardo beckoned Zachary to join him and take over the lead. After Chica received attention from his companion, the dog and boy enjoyed the next ten minutes of the drill. After a series of practice commands, Abelardo suggested disconnecting the lead. The dog responded to all the 'come by' orders. Chica followed the 'away' command, but with difficulty, looking mournful when Zachary yelled, 'stay' if the dog seemed confused. The duo had only worked on the 'away' signal for two weeks. Zachary showed such patience, for a young lad with his dog, that he amazed Abelardo and Lorenzo. The boy gave a firm 'stay' command, but never with a harsh voice.

Chica's training astonished and delighted the children watching from the station porch. After his session, Chica gleefully played fetch with the children. Zachary did not care to go up to the shooting range, content to glean stories from the children of their hometowns and travels.

Gold leaves began to fall. Those still attached to the aspens glittered in the low afternoon sun. Lorenzo brought the rocker from the cabin and joined Hanna while she knitted and rocked on the front porch. He sighed and bent to kiss her on the forehead before sitting. Lorenzo could hear the boys in the distance, the tree house still providing hours of daily fun. Bandit slept at Hanna's feet. Lobo wandered by, sniffing, moving off toward the barns. Lorenzo closed his eyes.

Jeremiah and Zachary came around the corner of the house, waking their father from his snooze. Hanna came out of the cabin carrying Sarah, who played with the worn, dirty wooden blocks Jeremiah had first used when he was younger.

Looking up, Sarah smiled, "Miah, will you help me?" she said.

"Naw, I'm going to go shooting," Jeremiah replied.

"I'll help you, Sarah," Zachary said.

"Goody," said Sarah. She gathered most of the blocks before her outstretched legs, shoving four blocks toward Zachary. "Those are for you, "Sack," she said.

Zachary laughed. "I only get four blocks… Well, ok."

Zachary sat on the front porch and stacked his designated four blocks. Sarah took pity on him and kicked two more blocks toward him.

Lorenzo leaned toward Hanna. "Zack and Sarah get along, don't they," he said.

"They do," said Hanna. "Rightly so."

"I've been thinking of taking Jeremiah hunting," said Lorenzo.

That tidbit did not escape Jeremiah's notice. "When, Dad? When do you think we can go? I'm ready!" he said.

"I guess tomorrow morning," Lorenzo said.

"What about Zack?" asked Hanna.

"A couple more years, if he's interested."

***

Lorenzo called softly up to the loft to wake Jeremiah. Jeremiah climbed down the ladder dressed in layers for the morning chill in two minutes. He retrieved his possible bag, ammunition bag, and rifle. Lorenzo slung a coil of rope over his head and shoulder, along with the canteen and rifle. The dogs would stay in the cabin, at least for this trip. The man and his son began to hike up the mountain. They reached one of the high ridges that led to the even higher San Francisco Peaks by ten o'clock. They stepped down on the far side of the crest to an outcropping, sitting down for jerky and a slug of water from their wooden wagon canteen.

Lorenzo began scanning the valleys on the far side slope, three miles from the cabin. He pointed down and right, “do you see that buck munching flowers in that meadow?”

“I see it, dad,” said Jeremiah. “The wind is blowing up the hill. Doesn’t that mean he won’t see or scent us?”

“He might not,” Lorenzo said, “or he may bolt at any moment. We need to approach and still be blind to him,” asked Lorenzo?

“How about that boulder on our far left. I don’t know if it’s close enough for a killing shot, but we’d be closer,” said Jeremiah. At the words ‘killing shot,’ Jeremiah’s stomach tightened. As father and son descended toward the boulder, Jeremiah recalled the squirrel he had killed weeks before. He had not shot at a live target since that day. His foot slipped on rubble, sending a small amount rolling noisily down the hill. The boy and Lorenzo stopped still, but the buck in the meadow hadn’t heard the disturbance.

“Concentrate, boy,” whispered Lorenzo. “Another mistake like that, and we may go home empty-handed. Watch each of your steps. Concentrate.”

Jeremiah nodded. Thoughts of blood and guts from that crawling, near-dead squirrel kept his stomach churning.

The hunters made it down to the boulder. The buck had moved down along the wildflowers a bit, but the situation couldn't be more ideal except for being too far away for a shot. From their vantage point, Lorenzo spotted a second, smaller boulder fifty feet further to the left among a copse of trees. Lorenzo also realized he could kill the deer from their current position with his breech-loader. However, this would be Jeremiah’s day if they could get to that next boulder.

Jeremiah crept with his dad down the slope further. He shunned all thought except getting to that boulder in silence, moving like a snail to avoid disturbing the animal in the clearing.

Once they were in position, Jeremiah peeked around the boulder; his stomach began to crash again.

Lorenzo whispered in the boy's ear. "Wait for the buck to turn toward us," he said, "you want to hit him in the chest, just like the silhouette in the shooting range. Don't hurry your shot. If we miss this one, there will be another chance again."

Jeremiah's shooting practice paid off. He calmed, knowing he could shoot and hit his target. He cocked his M1841 and waited for the buck to turn. The horned beast began sniffing, suspicious, lifting its head, scanning the meadow and beyond. Jeremiah released his breath, just as Lorenzo had taught, and squeezed the trigger. The clap of gunpowder exploding echoed back from the opposing mountain, and the big seven-point buck fell.

"Don't move, Jeremiah," Lorenzo said. "You got him good, but if he gets up and runs off, tracking will be rough in this terrain."

Lorenzo raised his gun and fired a shot for good measure. The buck didn't twitch, reinforcing that Jeremiah had killed the deer with his first shot.

Jeremiah, relieved and proud, approached the deer. It did not crawl away like the squirrel. A sure shot, an immediate kill; that, Jeremiah decided, was the only way to hunt. The only way he would ever kill from now on.

Lorenzo and Jeremiah constructed a travois for the next two hours to transport the carcass to the cabin, then proceeded with the gutting. After turning the buck on its back and slicing it open, Lorenzo pulled out the entrails (stomach, intestines) and cut the organs away from the body. At every step, the father began the cutting, then handed the knife or saw to his son to complete the task. They gutted the deer down to the essential tenderloins that would keep the Brennan's in meat for a time.

They attached a rope to the travois and encircled one end around their chests. Together, Jeremiah and Lorenzo pulled the travois up to the outcropping where they had spotted the deer. By dinner time, cold with wet sweat, they made it back to the cabin. Zach and Hanna congratulated Jeremiah. Hanna sent them both up to the spring for a bath. Refreshed, the two voracious hunters ate dinner, beaming at the family sitting around the table. Jeremiah and Zachary went off to the tree house. They sat at the platform's edge, and Jeremiah told a rapt younger brother about his adventure.

Hanna put up with the same story from Lorenzo while they rocked together on the porch.

"That boy did us proud today, Hanna," Lorenzo said. "He is an excellent shooter. Takes after me, I'd have to say."

Lorenzo, I don't know when I've seen you smile more," said Hanna. "you're just bursting, aren't you?"

"They are great kids… Jeremiah, Zack, Sarah." Mused Lorenzo, "I could not be happier, darling. And you are the best of it all. I love you dearly."

16 |Whispers of War

On an unusually muggy day in late June, a man walked through the open station door and approached Lorenzo standing behind the counter. He wore a black frock coat over a wrinkled linen shirt wet with sweat. His boots must have been his pride because he had tucked in his pant legs, and the toe boxes looked spit-shined.

The stranger leaned on the counter. In his right hand, the man carried a rag of a bible; the pages so fanned Lorenzo wondered about the legibility of any passage.

"Sign says 'saloon,' but I don't see no one in there," the man said. "I'm thirsty."

"We're open, sir," said Lorenzo, thinking a half bottle, not a whole. "We operate on a serve-yourself basis. Is that your wagon?"

"It is," said the man. "Name's Levi Keller. My wife, daughter, and I are going to San Francisco. I understand that sinners are abundant in the gambling town. Figure to set up my 'Church of the Original Sin' in the town."

"Never heard of the 'Church of Original Sin.' Are you Mormonite?" asked Lorenzo.

"No," said Keller, "I collect the souls of prostitutes. Turned over fifty ladies of the night back to the 'way' since leaving Kansas City."

Lorenzo made up his mind. He pulled a bottle of McKenna's from the cupboard beneath it and set it on the counter. Whiskey covered three lines on the near-empty bottle. Levi grabbed the bottle by the neck.

"Will you join me, sir," Keller offered.

"Pour your drink in the saloon, Mr. Keller," said Lorenzo. "Glasses are on the far side of the bar."

"Just looking to be neighborly, friend," said Levi. "The family's asleep in the wagon."

"That's ok, Mr. Keller; I'm figuring out my May accounts. Busy time for me at the moment. You can pay or bring the bottle back, and I'll figure out your bill then. Four bits a line."

"Not a problem, sir," Levi offered. "My donation box is flush. Good citizens along my path encourage my work."

"I suppose your work is important," said the station master.

"Indeed," said Levi. "Come on over to the saloon with me. Kansas City's all astir with the news of the candidate for President the Republicans chose in Chicago."

Torn between his tasks and wanting to hear news of import, Lorenzo asked the man. "What was the outcome?"

"Abraham Lincoln for President, Hannibal Hamlin Vice President," said Keller.

"We know of Lincoln, even out here in the territory. I hear he is taller than me," said Lorenzo.

Levi Keller looked up at Lorenzo, stretching to his full height. "I sincerely doubt that sir," he said, "but he is tall, I hear."

"He stands for territories free of slavery, doesn't he?

"That he does. Says so right in the party platform," Levi said. "I got a stack of flyers in the wagon if you're interested."

"Now you're talkin, Mr. Keller," said Lorenzo, "I can't join you for a drink, but you earned yourself a drink on the house if I can post that flyer on my message board."

Levi left the station, returning from his wagon with three copies of the Republican platform and three posters depicting

Lincoln and Hamlin. The banner in the picture espoused 'Free Speech, Free Home, Free Territory.' Lorenzo used brads to nail the poster to his message board and then excused himself.

Lorenzo mused the man may be God-fearing, but Levi's religious leanings were the strangest of all the peculiar persuasions he had heard about among the immigrants. Brennan, originally from Maine, had listened to Daniel Martensen, his friend from Portland, rant on the evils of negro slavery. Hanna, he knew, would be interested in this political development. Living where they did, in the New Mexico Territory, Lorenzo could not vote in the upcoming November election.

When Levi Keller returned the empty bottle, Lorenzo collected payment for the three McKennas, minus the free drink he had offered, and the wagon, pulled by two mules, rolled on down the road.

A group of immigrants passed through on November 3rd, crowding into the station for warmth. They bought seven of Hanna's wool blankets, flour, sugar, and two sheep for mutton down the trail. Lorenzo said goodbye and thanked the group as they passed through the station's front door. That is when he noticed that the Lincoln poster had been torn to shreds, littering the floor below his message board.

"Say, Mister," he called after the last of them. "No cause to vandalize my board."

A bearded scruff of a man pushed through the others and leaned over the counter, a snarl turning his mouth ugly. "We are sons of the great state of Mississippi. That man, Lincoln, is a skunk that needs slapping down," the man said. "If you say you support that abolitionist lover, we may just rip the whole place apart."

Lorenzo pulled his Paterson Colt repeater out from beneath the counter. His hand held the gun rock steady. "Time for you folks to move off," he said. "I'll post what I want on my property. Now, shove off."

One of the taller men strong-armed the mean one out the door. Soon, the three wagons in their train passed out of sight at the end of the meadow. Lorenzo nailed up his second copy of the poster.

The poster had caused a stir among travelers since the day he had nailed it up. Fifty percent of the people felt the way the snarling man felt. Other immigrants praised Lincoln, appreciating his stance on slavery in the territories.

On the 10th of November, Lorenzo heard from Steve Pembroke that Abe Lincoln had won the presidential election back on the sixth. Hanna, when she heard, danced a jig around Lorenzo. Lorenzo picked up little Sarah and waltzed around in the cabin. Hanna joined hands with Jeremiah and Zachary and two-step shuffled behind her husband.

The Beale Wagon Road, Brennan's Station, and Last Chance Saloon became the information pipeline's midpoint between northern sympathizers from Kansas and California. The Butterfield Overland Mail stagecoaches served the southern sympathizers in the far southern portion of the territory. The unique Pony Express operated further north through the Utah territory to Sacramento, California.

Rumors abounded of a pending joining of the Overland Telegraph Company of California and the Pacific Telegraph Company, allowing wired communication between the coasts. Most immigrants stopping by the station could not comprehend a wire connecting America's east and west coasts, unable to believe the idea was possible.

Hanna Brennan prided herself on her knowledge of current territorial, national, and international events. She read every flyer and newspaper Lorenzo could collect at the station. She listened intently to the women's gossip from the wagon trains that passed through the valley if they planned to spend more than two nights there on the way to San Francisco.

News of national events accelerated after Lincoln became president. Two weeks after the inauguration, the southern states seceded from the Union, establishing the Confederate States of America.

Hanna began to worry. The arguments at the station had increased in intensity since Lincoln rose in prominence. The men on both sides of these arguments bragged about forcing a resolution in their favor. Hanna had heard horror stories from Lorenzo of the Mexican/American war. She no longer danced jigs in the cabin.

Word reached Hanna in late April '61 of the attack by the Confederacy on Fort Sumter in South Carolina. The news seemed remote and surreal, far, far away. She could no longer remember the travel from the east to her dear mountain as a small child.

She knew that Antelope Springs and the supply station resided in the territory west of Texas (a slave state of the Confederacy.)

Hanna did not bottle her fears. She concentrated on the vital work on the ranch. Hanna never dwelled on what might happen to the farm, Lorenzo, and the children. She had lived in peace with the Navajo Indians surrounding the mountain and hoped that would continue. Hanna had native friends. Others respected the ranch, blankets, and sheep she provided for their clans. Most were not aware of the Brennan ranch at all.

"What are we to do, Lorenzo," Hanna sighed one night, the children quiet in their beds.

"Least of our worries, Hanna," said Lorenzo. "We've got the shearing to do. Things will settle down, or they won't. The territory isn't a state. What's the gain? We're safe. I don't know what this will do to immigrant travel. Wait and see, I guess."

"I hope you're right," said Hanna. "There are days I wish we hadn't started the station and never come down the mountain.

"I like what we've done, Hanna," said Lorenzo. "Someday, I would like a neighbor, maybe a town as well."

As the wagon traffic increased that spring, the Brennan boys skirted around the rim of trouble. Jeremiah began to look at the girls with curiosity. He thought the dares he extracted from Zachary promoted his image as controlling their destinies.

The girls, likewise, continued to find the boys fascinating. Jeremiah was a force, someone to pay attention to. Zachary was cute and fearless. The Davenport sisters, Emily (age 12) and Laura (age 11,) thought so, traveling with their parents in a lone Conestoga wagon drawn by two oxen. According to Emily, the family had relatives in Santa Clara, California.

Jeremiah tried to cajole the girls into hiking up to Leroux Spring. The girls declined; their mother did not allow them to leave the immediate area around their campsite. Laura suggested they play jump rope a short distance behind the wagon, out of adult earshot. The boys agreed, and all four children took a turn jumping while two others twirled the rope. After analyzing the girls' skill levels, Jeremiah increased the stakes. Emily, the cutest girl he had ever seen at the station, intrigued Jeremiah. She had long, bright red hair, braided and pinned up in a circle on the top of her head beneath her bonnet. Jeremiah decided he could kiss this girl.

"Whoever goes the most jumps without missing gets to dare one of us," Jeremiah said, winking at his brother.

All four contestants were sweat laden by the time they miss-jumped. Jeremiah went last and would have won, but his bootlace loosened, and he fell short of Zachary's count by eight jumps. Zachary had noticed his brother's interest in the redhead, so he looked at Laura. "Alright, Laura, give me your best kiss," he said.

Jeremiah, frustrated, took Emily aside, hoping for a conciliatory kiss, while Laura ran over to Zachary. Zachary put an arm around 'his girl' and leaned down for the kiss. Laura's brother, James, appeared from around the wagon. He took in the scene, crossed to Zachary, and spun him around, away from his little sister. Zachary, confused at the magical appearance of the boy, gaped, mouth open.

'Stay away from my sister," the thirteen-year-old James yelled, swinging at Zachary. Zachary flinched at the last moment, turning his head. James's haymaker glanced off his cheek and left eye. Zachary fell to the ground. He lay there shaking spangles from his eyes as James jumped on him, pummeling him in the stomach.

Somehow Jeremiah managed to pull James away from Zachary, punching and rassling in the dust. The sound of the crying girls brought yet another brother running to their aid from the station porch. The two brothers ganged up on Jeremiah. Zachary's head cleared, and despite the pain in his cheek, he jumped on the pile of three boys, twisted the newcomer's arm behind him, and held on; the boy's face turned into the dirt.

Contending only with James, Jeremiah fought with the fury of an Apache. Crawling away, James received a kick in the butt from Jeremiah. The girls had run off. Zachary shoved his captive, who bee-lined after his sisters and brother.

Jeremiah turned to Zachary. "Let's get home," he said. The brothers ran from the meadow and halfway up to the cabin. Exhausted, they collapsed beneath a Ponderosa, looking down the valley to see if anyone followed them. Jeremiah, looking over at Zachary, sweat, wetting Zach's shirt and back, disheveled, one hand patting his swelling left eye. "Showed them, I'd say," he said.

"I guess we did," said Zachary. "Thanks for the help."

"Little brother," Jeremiah acknowledged, "you helped me just as much. We better get up to the spring, bathe, and let our clothes dry." He rose and pulled Zachary up. He put an arm around Zachary's shoulder. Arms around each other's shoulders, the two set off. Even though his eye throbbed with pain, Zachary felt warmth in his chest. His brother respected him. That mattered.

Lorenzo waited for the boys in the rocking chair on the porch as they approached the cabin, looking as straightened up as they could manage, Jeremiah attempting to conceal a rip on the side of his shirt. Zachary's eye felt better, but he could barely see.

"Heard about some trouble at the station," said the father. "Joseph Olemyers was more upset for his girls than the boys,"

"Papa, we were just funnin…."

"Stop right there, Jeremiah. I don't want to hear it. I can tell by Zach's eye. Now, there is one thing I will tell you, and you better listen hard." Lorenzo paused, made sure he had the attention of both his sons, then continued. "If I hear of another case where either of you has disrespected a girl, I will switch the living daylights out of you."

"Alright, Papa," said Zachary.

"Good," said Lorenzo. "Now go and apologize to your mother for causing such a stir. That's quite a shiner, Zach. No more discussion. Understood?"

***

Lorenzo sat down on the rocker on the porch midafternoon on the fifth of July '61. Hanna heard the creak of the rocking chair and leaned out the doorway. "You're home early, Lorenzo," she said. "Anything wrong?"

"No," said Lorenzo, "nothing wrong. I just wanted to take it easy for a minute or two."

Hanna wrapped her hands in her apron. "Well, you're due," she said.

Sarah toddled past her mother and grabbed Lorenzo's leg. He picked her up and placed her on his knees, facing him, holding her hands. "Look at the way the horsey walks… walk, walk, walk," he recited to her, bouncing Sarah from one knee to the other. She giggled.

The father let out a boisterous laugh. "Look at the way the horsey trots… trot, trot, trot,"

As she rode Lorenzo's knees, Sarah, head flying right and left, never stopped laughing.

Lorenzo bounced the girl on both knees simultaneously, even more violently than when she trotted, saying, "Look at the way the horsey runs, Gallopy, Gallopy, Gallopy…." He parted his knees, and Sarah fell through, "Wheeeeeeeeeee." Then, standing, he threw the child in the air, catching her, swinging her down through his legs and up in the air once more.

"Again, Daddy, ride the horsey again.

"Ok, last time," Lorenzo said. After the second ride, Sarah ran to the end of the porch and played with her blocks.

The rocking chair creaked for another five minutes and then stopped, still. Five minutes later, Hanna leaned out the door again. She caught Lorenzo staring at the cloudless, blue opening in the trees over the trail to the valley. After all their years together, he had that vacant look that still mystified Hanna.

"You're sure nothing is wrong, Lorenzo," she asked. "Something about the war?"

"No, nothing," Lorenzo replied. "Heard from Steve Pembroke today that Antoine passed away."

"Oh no, Lorenzo, I'm sorry," said Hanna.

"Apparently," said Lorenzo, "his asthma and those injuries from the Sitgreaves expedition became too much for his heart."

"Is there anything I can do," Hanna asked?

"No," said Lorenzo. "I'll sit a while longer. I wrote a letter to Antoine's wife and sent it to Juana with Steve. That is all I can do." Lorenzo began to rock in the chair, tracking a lone cloud breezing by the opening in the trees. Hanna closed the cabin door.

***

At the end of July '61, the immigrants traveling the Beale Wagon Road dwindled to two or three families a month instead of the many wagon trains that had become routine after the road inspection in 1860.

Mr. Christopher Winstead stopped at the station on his way to the coast of California with his wife and three boys. He imbibed two drinks of McKenna's in the saloon and returned the bottle. Lorenzo charged him the usual four bits per line.

"Any news of events in the east," asked Lorenzo. "My wife is nervous. Thinks the war is heading this way."

"I guess, maybe," said Mr. Winstead. "I'm from Charleston, Virginia, or West Virginia, depending on how the wind blows. I'm sick of it. Looking for a fresh start. California seems more like the home of the free. Got three sons to think about, too."

"Keep your eyes open then, Mr. Winstead," said Lorenzo. "Mexicans, Indians, Chinese, Whites, you name it. They're trying to live together. Works sometimes."

"Can't be as bad as where I'm from. People on the west side of Virginia have been trying to break away from the east plantation elitists for decades. The war has set the two areas at odds. Even in western Virginia, families may fight with the union and against slavery. Next door, confederate sympathizers may be heading for Richmond to join relatives fighting with the south."

"That's a shame," said Lorenzo. "Neighbor against neighbor, friend against friend. In my day, you could tell your enemy by his color. Not that it made the war any better."

"Where did you fight," said Christopher.

"Chihuahua, among other places. Mexico. Got a family now. Hope to stay out of the current mess. From what you told me about this battle at Bull Run, a short war doesn't seem to be in the cards."

"I'm afraid that is true," said Mr. Winstead. "There's a fear sweeping Albuquerque on the news of the invasion of the territory by the Texas Cavalry Regiment led by Lieutenant Colonel John Baylor. They say he is a real bastard, the editor of a newspaper, *The White Man*, which advocates the expulsion of Indians from North Texas. His army won the day at Mesilla. Do you know where that is?"

"Down near the territory's southern border," said Lorenzo, "about ten days east of Tucson. Well beyond the border of Texas."

Christopher leaned over the counter, separating the two men, "He's heading north, they say. Declared himself the Governor of the Confederate Territory of Arizona."

"What the hell is that?" Lorenzo said, scratching his forehead.

"It's a section of the southern portion of the New Mexico Territory running from Texas to California."

"So that's it," said Lorenzo. "The rebels are trying to connect and maybe capture California."

Mr. Winstead began to collect his goods. He dug to the bottom of his pack and found a relatively recent copy of the *Philadelphia Inquirer,* placing it on the counter. Lorenzo thanked him and shook his hand. "Good luck to you, Mr. Winstead," he said.

The door opened behind Mr. Winstead, and another traveler entered.

"Hello, sir," said Lorenzo, "be right with you."

"I'm in a hurry, mister," said the man. He looked trail rough, his hat brim frayed, but he stood as tall as Lorenzo.

"Where are you headed in such a hurry," said Lorenzo.

"San Antonio," the man retorted, "then to Richmond to fight for the Confederate States of America. The war will be over before I get there if I don't get a move on."

"Alright," Lorenzo said with a shake of his head. He turned back to Mr. Winstead. "Nice meeting you."

Mr. Winstead waved goodbye and closed the door behind him. Lorenzo filled the scruffy man's saddlebags with the requested goods without conversation and saw him on his way.

When the man's horse left his sight, heading east, Lorenzo sat down in one of the chairs on the porch. He unfolded the *Philadelphia Inquirer* and read the reporter's extensive account of the Battle of Bull's Run near Manassas Junction, Virginia. The Confederate army had stopped the advance of the Union troops attempting to march on Richmond. Over four thousand men were killed in this one battle.

Skirmishes were occurring in other parts of the country.

Damn it, Hanna's right. The war is comin.'

More than two months passed with almost no road traffic before the wagon train came through on September 30th, 1861. After selling supplies, whiskey, and two ewes, Lorenzo helped load the wagons. He closed shop and climbed up toward the cabin, trying to formulate what he wanted to say to Hanna.

Increasingly these days, he contemplated soldiering again. Twelve years after his last war, Lorenzo fought with himself as much as he anticipated arguing with Hanna over enlisting. He decided to begin the conversation with Hanna by reviewing the latest news from Albuquerque. The leader of the three covered wagon caravan heading west had much to report. The wagon master passed along all the events he could remember to Lorenzo.

The Texas rebels had won at Alamosa, taken Fort Craig, and prevailed in a skirmish at Pinos Altos, driving north into the heart of the New Mexico Territory.

If the Confederate Army overran Albuquerque, it made sense to Lorenzo that they would head west along the Beale Wagon Road toward California. The battalion would join forces with troops crossing the newly formed Confederate Territory of Arizona on the defunct Overland Mail route, probably meeting at the Colorado River. The combined forces would attempt to occupy California and confiscate that state's abundant resources in gold and agricultural products to feed their armies.

Eventually, Lorenzo would have to pick a side or hide in the mountains. Since Daniel Martensen had hauled him down, straightened him out, and saved his life in that first battle so many years ago, Lorenzo had faced every oncoming fear of death head-on. He wouldn't rush off looking to be a hero, but he wouldn't run away.

The children rushed Lorenzo as he entered the cabin, and Sarah began tickling him under his chin. He responded with a belly laugh before picking her up, setting Sarah and her doll on his lap, and tingling his daughter's feet.

Zachary took center stage next, calling Chica to sit, facing the boy. On the command to sit up, Chica rose, braced by her two hind feet and tail, pawing the air with her front paws until released by the boy.

"Here's a new one, dad," the boy said. He told Chica to lie down, then, with a circular motion of his right hand and arm, said, "Roll over Chica, roll over Chica."

Chica looked confused for only three seconds, and then she obediently rolled over one whole turn. Zachary rewarded the dog with a full minute of generous hugs, scratches behind the dog's ears, and praise. "Good dog Chica."

Jeremiah typically showed off one of his targets from shooting practice. Today's achievement impressed Lorenzo. Jeremiah had shot away the bull's eye, replacing it with a one-inch ragged hole. "I started shooting from a kneeling position with no other support this week. Getting fairly good. Standing is next, Dad," said Jeremiah.

He could not match Jeremiah's shooting these days; Lorenzo told him so.

"Let's have a contest tomorrow, Papa," said Jeremiah.

"You're on," said Lorenzo, reasonably sure he would lose, even if he did his best.

Hanna, wiping her hands across the front of her apron, came over from the stove, a smile creasing her face, dimples deep next to her cheeks, beaming pride at her children and husband. Despite the demanding work of the ranch, meals, and wool production, Hanna always seemed cheerful. *Beautiful,* Lorenzo thought. In truth, whenever Lorenzo had time to spend with the children, Hanna was the happiest. *Nothing could make my life better*, she thought.

Watching Hanna approach, Lorenzo lost all resolve to proceed with the conversation hanging on his shoulders.

Later, when the dogs had quieted and the boys stopped squirming in the loft, Lorenzo related the news of the New Mexican invasion by the rebel army. He hoped Hanna might help him with an approach to the hard talk.

"I've been teaching the lessons of the Old Testament lately," said Hanna. "After I told the story of the Egyptian enslavement of my people and the Exodus, Zachary wanted to know about Abelardo."

"He is always thinking, isn't he, Hanna," said Lorenzo.

"Yes," she answered. "Always. Zachary wanted to know if Abelardo was our slave. I shut that notion down."

Sarah cried from her crib, and Hanna went over, picked her up, and walked the room with the curly blond-haired baby against her shoulder.

"You do an excellent job schooling those two, Hanna," said Lorenzo, deciding the time was still not right to bring up soldiering. "Slavery has played too large a part all over the States and territories for too long. No wonder, looking back, that it boiled up in war. I met all kinds during the last war. Made friends with the Missouri militia. Found them to be genuine, dependable, and capable.

"Could not say the same about the Texans I met. I swear if you weren't from the 'Lone Star State,' they looked down at you, even when I met them eye to eye."

"If you think about it, they put that 'Lone Star State' motto above the United States, even back in the day. The current invasion turns my stomach."

Yet, as he looked at Hanna, Lorenzo could not move the discussion further. Silence floated over the table, heavy, unbreakable.

Hanna put Sarah back in her crib and walked back to the kitchen. *He's decided. It is just a short matter of time.* Thinking of Moses and the Israelites, she knew she would support his departure and sacrifice.

Snow. Six inches of the powder coursed through the San Francisco Peaks on a windy Wednesday night, the second week in October '61. Beautiful and blinding in the morning sun's glare, the lower meadow and the trail down the mountain seemed to wash the war melancholy out of the Brennan family.

All bundled up, Sarah giggled while her brothers tore around in the snow. The boys then tiptoed to unspoiled snow patches, falling, flapping their arms, and making angels before the cabin.

Sarah laid down on the porch and attempted her angel. She rolled unhurt right off the porch, the snow on her face momentarily causing her to gasp and sputter. Zachary splashed snow on his face in sympathy with his young sister. Laughing, he brushed off his face, then hers, and hugged her. Sarah buried her head in the crook of Zach's shoulder to warm her face and dry off.

Lorenzo came out of the cabin, sat down on the lip of the porch, and strapped on his snowshoes. The unexpected snow would mean more work for the Brennans at the ranch and valley. Yet, after hugging each of the children goodbye, he tromped down the trail, smiling into the sun. *Look ahead, not behind*, he thought. A commotion in front of the cabin brought Bandit, Lobo, and Chica running from the barn to join in the snow romp. Abelardo trailed after the dogs, leaning against a porch post to watch the gathering of jumping dogs and excited children.

Fifteen minutes after Lorenzo left, Hanna opened the cabin door and called the children in for school. Flapping his arms across his chest for warmth, Abelardo headed back to the barn to shepherd half the flock to graze on the tall grass in the upper meadow; Bandit was assisting.

Snowfall in October comes and goes in a blink. By one o'clock, the snow had melted as the temperature reached sixty degrees. The boys completed their studies, and Hanna released them to their afternoon chores. Midafternoon, their duties complete in the barn, Jeremiah opened the door to the cabin, leaned in, and yelled, "Mom."

"Shhhh, Jeremiah," said Hanna in a forceful whisper. "Sarah is taking her nap."

"Zach and I are heading to the practice corral for dog training."

"Are all your chores done?" Hanna asked. "Including mucking the stalls?"

"Abelardo checked them over, Mom," said Zachary. "He said they looked good."

"Alright, you two. Bring your father home for dinner. Don't get into any trouble, you hear me?"

The boys were out of earshot. Jeremiah turned back and waved at Hanna on the porch. Halfway down, they noticed Conestoga wagons on the trail heading for the supply station. Chica barked a welcome from the mountain, and Lobo ran ahead to investigate.

17 |Double Dare

At Brennan’s station, a wagon master bought four sheep and two seventy-five-foot lengths of one-inch twisted jute rope from Lorenzo. Jeremiah and Zachary waited on the porch while their father finished with his customer. A rider on a red roan gelding entered the meadow at a fast canter, passed all the slow-moving wagons, and dismounted at the saloon. The stockman tied up his horse, read the posted signs, turned, and walked down the porch to the station's door. He flicked the rim of his Stetson to acknowledge the boys and entered.

The man swept his knee-length duster behind the handle of a Colt 1860 Army revolver. Jeremiah and Zachary trailed behind him. Lorenzo interrupted negotiations with the wagonmaster to set a five-finger bottle of McKenna’s on the counter. He handed it to the man with a short blond beard and gun. The man closed the door on his way to the saloon. Jeremiah tried to sneak out the door behind him to ask to see the gun and hold it, but his father guessed his intent. “Jeremiah,” said Lorenzo. “You stay where you are. Give me five minutes. Unless someone else shows up, I’ll be ready to go to the corral soon.” Lorenzo helped the wagonmaster load his purchases.

The six Conestoga wagons and five covered wagons in the train had circled a hundred yards away from the supply station and saloon. The hubbub in the wagon circle began to subside as the travelers completed camp routines. The children helped forage for kindling while the men sawed fallen trees for wood.

Women started cooking fires and trekked over to Leroux Spring for water.

Another man, much shorter than Lorenzo and a friend of the wagonmaster, entered and asked for whiskey.

The man appeared mild-mannered to Zachary, and Jeremiah didn't think twice about the gentleman. Clean-shaven and sporting a white shirt and string tie rather than a wool plaid, he conversed with Lorenzo and the wagonmaster before heading to the saloon. Even though he seemed relaxed, Zachary noticed the bulge of the man's holstered revolver beneath his coat.

"Zachary, you, and Chica are first. Let's go," Lorenzo said, "Jeremiah, after Chica finishes, I want to train with Lobo alone. He has to catch up. I'll take him to the other end of the meadow, so the wagons and stock won't distract him."

"Can I still practice shooting when you're done with Lobo?" asked Jeremiah.

"If there is still time before supper."

Lorenzo closed and locked the station door, hung his 'be back in thirty minutes' sign, and strode off with Zachary to the practice pen.

Chica began circling Zachary, trying to remain calm as they approached the fence forming a rough circle around the sheep. The dog sensed his favorite time of the day, herding sheep with his young master. Zachary could hardly wait as well. When the boy and dog reached the enclosure containing ten ewes and lambs, Chica sat, relaxed and ready, on Zach's left, waiting for his first command.

Staying fifty feet from the boy and his dog, Lorenzo said, "Zach, send her clockwise."

The boy bent over his dog, rubbing Chica's shoulders vigorously, looking eye to eye with his friend. Zachary extended his left arm and commanded, "Chica, circle right."

Chica exploded in a blur and circled the outside of the pen in a clockwise direction. The startled sheep moved around to avoid the dog. After circling the ring twice, Zachary said, "Lie down." Chica halted and squatted at Zachary's command, never taking eyes off the sheep in her charge.

"Good dog, Chica, stay."

"Send her away," suggested Lorenzo.

"Chica, Circle-left," said Zachary. The dog jumped into a run, circling the pen counterclockwise. The sheep also moved in the desired direction.

To evaluate the dog, Zach called, "Lie down." Chica did so. Zachary repeated a series of commands switching the dog's directional orders. Chica passed.

"Chica," said Zach, and when the dog heeled to his left leg, he bent down and hugged his pal. "Good dog, Chica."

Lorenzo decided Chica and Zach needed a new challenge. He went over to the pen and opened the gate wide. "Send Chica into the pen and give her the 'outrun' command."

Zach worked on this command for three weeks outside his lesson time with Abelardo or his father. Chica started sauntering into the pen, staying close to the fence. The dog circled the sheep in the animal pen far enough so that the sheep were between the dog and Zachary, who backed thirty feet away from the fence. Zach said, "Outrun them, Chica, outrun, Chica, outrun." Chica barked once and rushed forward. The sheep began exiting the pen. "Lie down, Chica," said Zach. He didn't want to disperse the sheep in panic.

"Chica, fetch now," Zachary commanded. Chica began moving back and forth behind the herd, steering them toward Zach. After giving the 'lie down' command, the sheep settled around Zach.

"Let's see if she can pen the flock, Zach. I'll stay near the pen in case she gets confused. See what you can do."

Zachary, sweating now from the tension of these first-time tests of his dog's abilities, praised his dog and then issued the 'penning' commands. Lorenzo had to assist in the end, but Chica began to get the right idea.

"That's enough for today, Zachary," Lorenzo said. "Chica is coming along now. You're doing an outstanding job with her. She is going to be a champion herder."

Zachary beamed as he walked back to the station. Seven or eight curious children were mulling around in front of the building or on the porch. A couple of women sat in chairs on the porch waiting for Lorenzo to return and reopen the supply store. Zachary spotted Lobo urging a boy about his size to throw something for the dog to retrieve. The boy obliged. Lobo's hind paws clawed grass as he gained speed chasing a stick. The dog returned with the branch, pressing it against the leg of the boy until he threw it again.

The snow had melted in the valley except for small patches among groups of trees still in the mountain's shadow. The sun had mostly dried the fields, but the water ran in rivulets toward the lowlands near Leroux Spring.

Zack found his brother on his knees, surrounded by three boys and a girl. Jeremiah tossed one of his jackstones in the air and gathered four stones scattered on the ground with his right hand. He caught the thrown stone before it hit the ground.

The game of Jackstones broke the ice between the Brennan boys and the immigrant children traveling west. Zachary interrupted the game, "Papa is ready for Lobo now," he said.

Jeremiah put the game on hold to avoid making his father wait. That would be a mistake that might cost the boy ammunition. Jeremiah looped his bag of smooth stones to a button on his knee pants. With some coaxing, Lobo pranced around Jeremiah as the boy walked in the general direction of the practice pen. Halfway there, Lorenzo called Lobo. The station master and dog took off on the quarter-mile trek to the meadow's far end. Jeremiah returned to his newly found friends, and Zachary was waiting on the porch.

Without the entertainment, Lobo provided chasing sticks or Jeremiah's attention-grabbing expertise in repeatedly winning at Jackstones, a lull developed in the children's activities. A couple of the girls suggested a game of Prisoner's Base. Jeremiah laid out the boundaries, and the girls chose a second captain. The young people from the circled wagons in the distance joined the new pastime.

Jeremiah, no longer the focus of the immigrant youngsters, shuffled off back to the porch, calling to Zachary, "Hey Zach," he said, "I've got to get a better look at the gun that trailhand holstered. Let's go ask him to show it to us."

"You can't do that," Zachary said. "We aren't supposed to go on that part of the porch by the saloon. We can't go inside; Momma would skin our hides."

"How would she know? Papa will be back soon. Now is my only chance." Jeremiah hopped up on the porch in front of the station. Since the station and the saloon shared a common wall, the walk along the porch to the tavern had only an invisible barrier separating the two establishments. Parents' admonishments not to go further in the saloon's direction usually held sway over the immigrant children and the Brennan boys.

"I'm going over there," said Jeremiah, "I dare you."

Zachary looked to the sky. He sighed and scanned the meadow, hoping to find Lobo loping back to the station with his father. No one was in sight as far as Zach could see. He had never refused a dare by his brother. Zachary shook his head from side to side. *This dare would have consequences.*

"Come on," said Jeremiah, "are you scared? I double dare you."

Zachary jumped up on the porch in front of Jeremiah and walked along the porch toward the saloon.

"You boys better come back over here now," said one of the women sitting in one of the porch chairs. She had grandmother-skin and a face set in a mean scowl. The other woman in the chair beside the grandma nodded and shook her finger at the boys.

"This is our place," said Jeremiah. "My father said we could," he lied.

Jeremiah shoved Zachary aside and strolled to the saloon, stopping just short of the doorway. Both boys could now clearly hear the ongoing conversation inside the tavern. Jeremiah peeked around the open door. His brother lay on the porch and looked around the bottom corner of the open door. He had a clear view of the interior from an ant's point of view.

"Windemere," said the blond bearded man leaning on one elbow at the bar. "Why don't you take your pasty face out of here and let a man drink peaceable." The casual, lazy-looking appearance of the man seemed in no way threatening to Zachary.

On the other hand, Jeremiah noted the man's duster folded back behind his holster and his right hand hanging loose only inches from his gun handle. Jeremiah was sure he had been right about the make and model of the revolver. Jeremiah would know for sure if only he would take it from his holster.

"You boys get over here," shouted the gramma from the front of the station. "I'll take a hand to you myself if you don't get away from that saloon."

Zachary looked sideways, catching sight of the second man's boots beneath the chair and table where the man in the white shirt sat. The gentleman held his gun at the ready in his lap. Zachary had no idea what kind it was, let alone the make or model. He would have to ask Jeremiah and now was not the time.

"I'm telling you, said the gentleman. "Stay away from my wife, you bastard."

"Or what," said Yellowbeard.

"Just stay away from my wife," the gentleman growled.

Jeremiah leaned down and whispered to Zachary. "I'm going to the window to see better," he said.

Scared at the sight of two guns and two men arguing across from each other, Zachary thought to tell Jeremiah. Before he could eke out a warning, he saw the gentleman grip his gun tight and raise it above the table.

The melted snow from the roofs of the supply station and the saloon had flowed together, spouting onto the porch where the two buildings met. The water had run along the porch wall to the right of the saloon door, where it puddled. Jeremiah backed up two steps and leaped over the little pond. Quick as a sprite, he climbed atop the bench at the window, peeking through a dust-encrusted pane.

"Your wife," said the man at the bar as he straightened to his full height. "Your wife. That woman hasn't been your wife since Albuquerque. You know it, I know it. Now get out of here. Git."

Zachary saw the gentleman's chair slide, then topple over backward. A gunshot echoed in the near-empty bar.

Lorenzo heard the shot on his way back to the station with Lobo, thinking nothing of it. Immigrants needed to hunt for food as much as he did. They went far away from their camp to be safe.

The two women on the porch scooped up their knitting needles and wool and ran to gather the children.

Zachary watched the bearded man draw his gun and grab his right shoulder with his left hand, blood seeping through his fingers. In obvious pain, the desperado raised his weapon and fired while still holding his shoulder.

The resulting explosion of glass caught the attention of the women and children huddled thirty feet away. A girl who knew Jeremiah screamed.

"Son of a bitch!" shouted Yellowbeard over breaking glass. Piercing his lips and steadying his bleeding arm, Zachary saw him straighten his arm and fire again.

The gentleman's gun thudded on the floor and spun out through the saloon doorway, coming to rest inches from Zachary. The smell of blackpowder emanated from the weapon. A wisp of smoke curled up for a moment from the barrel. Zachary had never been interested in Jeremiah's hobby; now, he began to shake with terror.

Chica leaped onto the porch to protect Zachary, whimpering and sniffing his face. The boy feared a bullet had pierced the thin wall of the saloon and hit his dog. He gathered Chica up to check her over.

Then Zachary noticed Jeremiah lying on his back, covered in thousands of multi-sized shards of broken glass, a jagged cross of blood creasing his face. Blood gurgled from his chest, sounding like a small rapid in a mountain creek. Then the flow lessened, the gurgle quieted, and Zachary saw the circular rim in Jeremiah's shirt caused by the ball fired from the gun.

Lorenzo heard the second shot, followed by a third. He knew now the gunshots came from the vicinity of the station. He started running.

Zachary wailed when he saw Jeremiah. He crawled on hands and knees across the puddle, sweeping away the glass to get to his brother. Reaching Jeremiah, Zach pressed his bleeding hands against the other's chest, willing blood to stay in Jeremiah's rib cage until his father arrived.

Yellowbeard staggered a bit as he pushed by the saloon door with his good shoulder. He bent down, picked up the gentleman's gun with his right hand, and hurried to the hitching rail, grabbing the reins of his roan. After stuffing the extra gun in a saddlebag, he gripped the pommel with his good left hand, put his left foot in the stirrup, and grunted as the horse took his weight during the awkward one-hand mount. He kicked his horse into a gallop and shot down the trail back toward Albuquerque.

Zachary, crying, paid no attention to the rider; he couldn't look at him. Neither did the other children. They came over to console Zachary, but the two women shooed them away from the gruesome scene on the porch.

Three men from the wagon train showed up on the run. One, the wagonmaster, ordered one of the women to forage for blankets. He stood for a long minute over Zachary, and his brother's dead, still body, then entered the saloon.

Lorenzo arrived with Lobo. He climbed the first step on the porch and stopped, spotting Jeremiah, still as all the dead men he had seen on battlefields. He grabbed the porch post and knocked his head against it, his stomach flopping and his headache tightening. Something was stabbing his heart. Zachary sat on the edge of the porch next to his brother, shaking uncontrollably. He could not move toward him. He couldn't move at all.

The woman sent to fetch blankets arrived as the wagonmaster exited the saloon, stepping back on the porch. She handed one of the coverings to the station master. He wrapped the blanket around Zachary, carried him to the station, and laid him on the cot behind the counter, instructing one of the women to keep him warm to avoid shock.

Lorenzo still hadn't moved. Neither had Jeremiah. Blood dripped ever so slowly off the edge of the porch, drip…

drip…drip. The wagonmaster returned and covered Jeremiah entirely with a blanket. *Good, he'll be warm now,* Lorenzo thought. The children were all sent away back to camp.

The three men entered the saloon, "Never saw Windemere fire a gun or a rifle," said the wagon master. "Left such thing to the scouts and hunters."

"Anyone see who committed this?" one of the immigrants said.

"The boy did, surely," said the other man helping with the body of Windemere.

"Long gone," said the wagon master. "Waste of time to follow him. None of us have the skill. Lorenzo could do it, but he's got other worries now."

"I guess we bury him at the far edge of the meadow toward California," the taller immigrant said. "I'm sure that was his dream. Like the rest of us."

"What about his wife… Lucy, right?"

"She's back in Albuquerque," said the wagon master. "I'll not be concerned with her comfort." The two men began the grave-digging task for the dead man.

Outside the saloon, Lorenzo sat down on the edge of the porch, his head in his hands. *Move, get up, get going*, he thought. Finally, the father did move. Retrieving a broom and shovel from the station, he swept up the glass, shoveling glass and sand containing the tiniest shards into a bucket.

The wagonmaster came over to Lorenzo. "I suppose you'll want to take your boy home," he said.

"Yes," said Lorenzo.

"I'll have a couple of men build a travois."

"Thanks," said Lorenzo. The wagonmaster went off to find more help. Lorenzo went around the outside corner of the saloon and retched what he could from his stomach. Mostly dry heaves. It didn't help. He needed Hanna, yet he couldn't think how to face her.

Two men carried Jeremiah's well-wrapped body to the travois, jutting back to the ground at an angle behind a borrowed mule an hour later. They rope-tied him in. Lorenzo found Zachary sitting on the side of the cot, head in hand but otherwise calm. At the sight of Zach's father, he stood and encircled Lorenzo with both arms.

"I think the worst of the shakes are over," the woman tending Zachary said. "He wants to go home."

Lorenzo pushed the boy back. He guided the boy outside without looking down and helped him into the mule saddle.

The wagonmaster waved the sympathizers away from the mule. "I'll come with you, Lorenzo," he said.

Lorenzo couldn't even thank him. Numb, he never looked anywhere but at the trail up the mountain. "No, I'll make it. We'll make it." Lorenzo walked along the mule's side, holding the bridle. Soon the mule, pulling the travois loaded with the boy's body, Zachary and Father walked through the overhanging aspens at the mouth of the cabin trail. The small crowd of immigrants turned to walk back toward the wagon circle, shaking their heads in sorrow.

When the travois broke into the clearing in front of the cabin, Zachary heard his father start to sob. Zachary's stomach churned again as it did on the station porch. He didn't want to be crying when he met his mother. The tears came just the same. He slid off the mule on the opposite side from Lorenzo and moved off toward the tree house. His father called after him, but Zachary ignored the station master and kept walking away. He snapped his fingers, and Chica caught up and heeled on the boy's left. The two climbed up to the platform. Zachary lay in the shadow of the three-sided enclosure he had helped Jeremiah and Lorenzo build. Chica lay down mainly on the boy, his muzzle underneath Zachary's ear.

Lobo, oblivious to the new order of things, tore off toward the barn. Lorenzo took the time to go after the dog and put him into one of the sheep's houses. Then he headed back to the cabin, each step becoming heavier, more leaden. Lorenzo stopped on the porch and knocked his head against the supporting post tightening his hands into fists. He opened the door. With a sixth sense of his arrival, Sarah sat on his boot, expecting a routine leg waltz. Then Hanna turned around from the stove. *Something is wrong, very wrong*, she thought.

Zachary heard the spine-chilling scream of his mother and began to shake again. He hugged his dog and tried to imagine what he and Jeremiah would do tomorrow after school:

- Check out the tree house
- Wave the wagon train kids goodbye
- Work the sheepdogs
- Head for Leroux Springs
- Try to beat Jeremiah at Jackstones.

Jeremiah would gather ten shots of ammunition from Abelardo or Father, grab his rifle, and head to the range to practice. Zachary would watch him go. At this thought, Zachary hugged himself, looking at an imagined revolver spinning near his left foot. Guns. *Why had Jeremiah been so fascinated with that man's gun?*

He imagined the snarling yellow bearded man straightening at the bar, aiming, and firing the Colt at his brother looking in through the window. In Zachary's story, the gentleman who fired his gun first became a ghost. Nothing made sense. *Would it have burnt my hand if I had picked up the smoking gun?*

Zachary returned in a dream to Leroux Spring, where he and Jeremiah hopped from rock to rock on one of Jeremiah's dares.

"Wake up, Zachary," whispered Hanna from the ladder at the edge of the tree house. "Time to wake up."

Zachary stirred, muscles sore from tension. *How long have I been sleeping*?

"I've your favorite stew simmering, Zack. Come down now."

"I… Jeremiah was… It's my fault, Momma."

"No such talk, son. Come down to supper."

Hanna vanished from sight down the ladder stair.

Zachary felt so weak climbing down from the tree house that he forgot about Chica watching him from the platform's edge. Chica barked twice, waiting for his command to come down. "Chica, it's you and me, I guess, from now on," he said.

Even as he whispered this maxim to his dog, he thought he heard Jeremiah sliding forward on the platform behind Chica to climb down.

***

In late November, the cold and snow decided to stay for the winter. The Brennan cabin, built on the mountain's southwest side, received a good share of sunny days, even though the temperature dropped sharply on clear nights. On the east side of the range, clouds and fog ruled the season.

Sunny days couldn't dispel the cloud inside the Brennan home. The family never talked of the gunfight that killed Jeremiah, but his brother's death hung on to Zachary like a lingering sore throat and never left. His father stared into the corners of the rafters, seeming to look for spiders. The boy could not interpret or penetrate his father's vacant gaze. Hanna tried to distract both Lorenzo and Zachary. She pulled one after another of her books from the shelf to share an interesting passage or read a difficult chapter to Zachary.

Hanna struggled to shake the sorrow out of Lorenzo. She tried not to display signs of her despair over her missing son. Subconsciously, blaming Lorenzo for her son's death, peeked through occasionally. Where had he been when Jeremiah went near the saloon? He shouldn't have overlooked the boy's misbehavior. *What's the use? Jeremiah's gone.*

Sarah became the sun and the moon in the cabin. As far as Sarah knew, Jeremiah had traveled west with the wagon train and would return next summer. Mother, father, and Zachary kept Sarah laughing in Jeremiah's absence to the limit of their buried emotions.

The boy left alive began to grasp his father's intense love over the years for Jeremiah. Lorenzo now tried but failed to hide the vacuum and ultimate despair he suffered over the death of his favored son.

Zachary should have grabbed his brother's shirt, holding him still when he began to jump across the puddle. Zach had seen the gun in the gentleman's lap. Frightened by the sight of the single-shot revolver, he hadn't spoken or moved.

Afraid. What if I had helped Jeremiah sooner, pushed him out of the way?

The bullet would have hit me... and Father would be OK.

18 |Burning the Bridge of Despair

The saloon, the station, and even the ranch shrouded Lorenzo in a constant nightmare of Jeremiah's last breath, which he had missed. He never entered the saloon again. He worked late hours at the station even though the travelers west had thinned to a trickle for the winter months. The stationmaster concentrated on exchanging supplies for money with minimal communication. The only exception to his feeling of emptiness came from immigrant news of Texan rebel confederates invading the territory. The talk started his blood boiling, temporarily rechanneling his constant memory of the blood covering his dead son.

Lorenzo talked Steve Pembroke into buying the station by making reasonable monthly payments to Hanna. Lorenzo offered Abelardo a raise, telling him his intentions to join the Union Army at Fort Defiance or Fort Craig. Abelardo promised to protect the generous Brennan family.

During the week before Christmas, Lorenzo crowbarred and sawed away a five-foot section of the connection between the station and the tavern. Then he set fire to the saloon, creating a massive bonfire on a snowy Tuesday. The flames from the frame building scorched the log station. Lorenzo closed and locked the station, hid the key for Steve, and started home.

Lorenzo turned around halfway up to the cabin and leaned against a tall Ponderosa. Smoke from the smoldering building blew east while snow settled on his shoulders. The bonfire and the onset of winter would erase all traces of the saloon and the stains of Windemere's and his son's dried blood. *I had a good run of luck,* he said into the wind. *Hanna... my love, a prosperous ranch, the trek to California, and the station...*

The children, how he loved the children, but above all Jeremiah...

He stopped and bowed his head. Looking up, Lorenzo spat snow and shook his head. *Should have figured my fortune would turn south someday. My luck always does. Thought I could beat my odds this time. Damn unlucky, that's me...*

Jeremiah, we got one good hunt in, my boy. This war will see us hunting together again. The cold had begun to work its way through Lorenzo's layers of clothing. He shivered and continued up the mountain.

Lorenzo sent Zachary and Chica to the barn for shepherd training, then sat down and fiddled with Hanna's bird figurine gracing the center of the table. Hanna sitting opposite Lorenzo took the statuette and set it next to her. Clasping her hands, she said, "So you're leaving."

"What?" said Lorenzo, startled. "Uh... Yes, Hanna, I have to go."

"I understand, Lorenzo," said Hanna. "Moses led the Israelites to freedom. I know we are in sync on this. Slavery in any form is morally unconscionable."

Lorenzo outlined all the arrangements he had made to provide for the family while absent. "Steve will make regular trips to the Denver slaughterhouse. By reducing the stock Abelardo and you will have an easier time. We can build back when I return.

"I burned the saloon down," he continued, waiting for her reaction.

"I saw the smoke," she replied and shrugged.

"That's it then," said Lorenzo, "I'll leave tomorrow before dawn so as not to disturb the children.

"I'll ride Shady. As old as he is, he should make it to Fort Defiance. They'll provide a younger mount if I'm conscripted into the calvary."

"That sounds like a plan, Lorenzo," said Hanna. "You've thought this through."

Hana paused. She kept her hands clasped but perfectly still on top of the table. She looked down for a moment, then up, straight at her husband. "Let me ask you something, and please answer me honestly. Are you leaving to fight for our cause, or are you leaving to get away from Zachary and me?"

Lorenzo put his hands flat on the table and bowed his head, unable to look at his wife. He thought of his answer for a full minute before speaking. Hanna waited, quiet.

"Hanna, I've got to get away. I can't face you now, knowing I caused the death of our son. It is eating me inside out.

"I love you more than life, yet my son is dead. I can't live with that, and I'm looking to the army to straighten me out under fire. I've got to get this ache out of my system."

Hanna believed she might explode if anyone touched her, sure the tenseness in her shoulders and neck must show. Yet, she also ached for Lorenzo to do just that, envelop her in his arms and never let go.

"But what of the rest of our family," said Hanna. "Sarah, Zachary, me. How are we to live without you?

"Do you realize Zachary wets his bed every other night? I hear him twisting in his nightmares. He needs a father. He needs you more than ever."

"I know he does, Hanna," Lorenzo croaked. "I know I'm a coward. This is a coward's way. I know that. Whenever I look at Zachary, I see Jeremiah's ghost standing an inch taller behind him. I can't look at Zach. Can't touch him. I've got to leave in the morning."

Hanna rose and returned to her dishwashing basin. Her back to her husband, keeping her emotions bottled, she bit her lip and said, "You can sleep in the barn to get an early start. I hope you make it back home after all this. We'll make the best of it."

Lorenzo rose and walked across to Hanna, stopping just short of her. *Reach out, take her shoulders, turn her around, and hug her. She loves me.* Tears formed but did not fall. He turned on his heel and went to the dresser, packed the travel satchel with his essentials, and left the cabin for the barn. He passed Zachary, heading toward the house. Neither said a word.

19 |New Mexico Volunteers

On January 24th, '62, three inches of new snow coated Taos. Midmorning, Lorenzo dismounted Shady in front of the church at the parish of Our Lady of Guadalupe. Snow slid off the roof on either side of the bell tower sitting atop the center of the front wall. The small, unassuming structure seemed to befit the explorer buried within. Entering through the arched central doors, Lorenzo removed his wool cap. Searching along the side walls of the nave, he found a fifteen-inch by six-inch copper plaque.

Set in the wall at waist height, a plaque read:

Antoine Leroux
1801 – 1861

"Finally made it over to pay my respects," whispered Lorenzo. "What's it been, seven years… More?

"At least you're missing the mess this country has come to. I'll see that the rebels don't overrun your hacienda. After all your work opening the territory, I won't allow them to set us back.

"Hanna would say 'Hi' if she were here. We sure could have used your counsel lately.

"Remember little Jeremiah? Took him hunting last year. First time. He's gone now. Hell, you can show him a thing or two. I'd appreciate it.

"So long, old friend."

Ruts in the snow at a fork in the trail near Fort Union convinced Lorenzo to continue east. No chimney smoke rose from the buildings a short distance to the north. Fort Union had been relocated.

A mile east, Lorenzo discovered an irregular-shaped stockade and substantial fortifications. The trenches in front of the walls looked to stymy enemy rushes. The traveler estimated over a hundred working soldiers and volunteers with shovels and pickaxes were reinforcing the mounds. Lorenzo could see three points jutting out of the angled walls in regular spacing. As he approached the front gate, he recalled the trappings of Fort Preble, a similar star-shaped fortress where he had enlisted in the Maine Militia in '46, fifteen years earlier. He was forty-four now, the Mexican/American war a distant satisfying nightmare that burned in his soul. *Too old to be here?*

The atmosphere within the walls reflected the same frenzy and urgency as the laborers outside the fort. A thousand men. There was a line of barracks to the right of the gate. The guard at the entrance directed Lorenzo to the offices.

The enlistment desk's corporal looked only a few years older than Jeremiah. "Looking to join the New Mexico Volunteers?" asked the corporal. "Any experience?"

"Veteran of the war with Mexico, from '46 to '48," said Lorenzo.

"How old are you, old timer?" the corporal asked.

"Forty-four. Old enough to take a switch to your behind, son."

"Alright, all right, no offense intended. How about skills?"

"Horse management, sheepherder, supply station master. Scouted for the Sitgreaves expedition with Antoine Leroux."

"Leroux, I've heard of him. He and Kit Carson chased Apaches during the White Massacre affair, right? Do you know Carson?"

"Never met him, heard about him through my friend Antoine."

"He's a colonel now, commanding the First Regiment of New Mexico Volunteer Infantry."

The corporal filled out the rest of the paperwork on Lorenzo but, in the end, still had no idea what to do with the forty-four-year-old white man. The New Mexico volunteers were 'Nuevo Mexicanos," young and inexperienced. Lorenzo had picked up a moderate amount of Spanish from working shoulder-to-shoulder with Abelardo on the ranch. The corporal shrugged and said, "Excuse me, wait here." He went through a door to an inner office and returned ten minutes later with another man closer to Lorenzo's age.

"Mr. Brennan, I'm Staff Sergeant James Tooley," said the soldier. "I'm thinking you might pass muster with an outfit of scouts down at Fort Craig under the leadership of James Graydon. Paddy Graydon, they call him."

"Scouting, I know," said Lorenzo.

"Most of Graydon's company, all but about twenty, will muster out this month," Tooley said. "He needs volunteers to replenish his unit, but he's particular. I'll give you a letter of introduction. Travel on down to Fort Craig. I believe he would appreciate your experience."

"What about a fresh horse?" asked the recruit. "Ole Shady out there needs to retire."

"If Graydon approves, you'll be equipped, horse included," said the sergeant. "What about Indians? What are your feelings."

"I've dealt most recently with Mohave, Utes, and Navajo," Lorenzo said. "My attitude depends on their attitude toward me. I've never lived among them, so I'll not pretend to understand their ways. My wife and I trade with the Navajo in our area."

"Alright," Tooley said, dismissing the corporal and finalizing Lorenzo's orders. "The quartermaster will replenish your provisions for the trip to Fort Craig. If you can't locate

Paddy's unit, report to Colonel Carson's First New Mexico Volunteers instead. Make haste. Push your nag. A ten-day trip; get there in eight. Reports indicate the Texas Rangers are heading north."

Lorenzo calculated he could make it to Fort Craig by the second week in February. The wagon road along the Rio Grande should be snow free and warm. His goal: avoid Indians and Texans, concentrate on the path ahead, and try to forget the mistakes that haunted him.

***

The sergeant at arms led Lorenzo into Kit Carson's office, handing Tooley's letter to the colonel. Carson read the letter and stood, appraising Lorenzo Brennan. The colonel kept a scruffy mustache, and he had tiny freckles that dotted his cheeks and forehead, framed by reddish brown hair. He appraised Lorenzo Brennan with soft blue eyes that belied his reputation for courage and daring. Lorenzo had heard of the colonel's sensitivity to his height from Antoine, towering over the colonel by more than eleven inches.

"Mr. Brennan," said the colonel. "Antoine Leroux and I go back years. A good man. Went to his funeral. His wife is a friend of my wife."

"I learned from the man," said Lorenzo. "Miss his advice."

"The letter from Tooley indicates you are assigned to James Graydon's outfit."

"I'm a fair scout, Colonel Carson, helped Antoine guide the Sitgreaves Expedition beyond the Colorado River."

"That being as it may," said Carson, "Graydon is a wild card. His unit is independent of my command. I find him reckless and demeaning toward his recruits, the 'New Mexicans.' How's your Spanish?"

"I've worked shoulder to shoulder with Abelardo Sanchez for nearly three years. He's been tutoring my boys. I know a fair amount," answered Lorenzo.

"Indians?" asked Carson.

"Live and let live. I've had good trading days and scary ones with Antoine."

Carson sat down, picked up two smooth stones from a dish at the corner of his desk, and massaged them with his right hand. Thinking stones, Lorenzo guessed. He looked up, "My first impression of you, Mr. Brennan, and based on my knowledge of Antoine's friends, I judge you to be a man of honor."

Lorenzo nodded, but Carson continued, "I offer this to you: If you determine Graydon ever moves beyond decency, I will entertain a transfer for you to my regiment."

"Thank you, sir," Lorenzo said. "I'm here to stop Texans. I hear we're about to."

"Yes, they are on the move. Dismissed," said the colonel as Lorenzo saluted. "Luck to us all."

February 10th, '62, Lorenzo secured more provisions and an order for a horse from the Fort Craig quartermaster. At the horse barn, Lorenzo led Shady up to the stable master. "My old friend here needs to retire," Lorenzo told the man. "His hind ankles start swollen in the morning and worsen by noon on a riding day."

The man took Shady by the bridle and looked him over. "Grey withers, quite a sway back," he said. "All the signs. I think you're right."

"I'll be scouting with Captain James Graydon."

Hearing that, the stable master scrutinized the tall man. "Good luck keeping up with that outfit, sir," he said, implying Lorenzo should be retiring with his horse.

"Get me a horse befitting Graydon's campaign. I'll be fine."

The horse handler brought a handsome, 14-hand strawberry roan gelding. "This three-year-old has trained for a year now," said the private. If you think you can manage this horse, he's got the spirit of a scouting horse. His name is Arrow; he's fast."

"He'll do, I'll do. Let's get acquainted, Arrow." Said the tall man. He spoke to the horse, brushing him, combing his red mane and the tangles in his tail. After twenty minutes, with no one else observing, Lorenzo strapped on his saddle and ten minutes later mounted Arrow. He walked the horse to the parade grounds and trained him for an hour to learn which commands gave the horse trouble and which he could count on. Arrow did a fair job with them, even backing up. Cutting left worked better than right, but not by much. Arrow had been well trained.

Lorenzo spoke to the gate guard, who allowed him a ten-minute ride outside the fort. Mentioning Paddy Graydon's name provided a measure of pull within the garrison.

Rider and mount broke into a gallop as the gate closed. Arrow flew straight and fast. Lorenzo bent over the horse's neck, Arrow's mane flicking at his face. The horse pulled up at a tug of the reins and stopped, unmoving. The tall rider turned the horse toward the fort and returned in another gallop. *Antoine would say, 'Arrow appears capable.'*

The guards opened the gates that afternoon while Lorenzo continued working with Arrow. A cloud of dust hovered on the horizon south of the fort. Leading the cloud, twenty riders on the run became distinguishable. The horses and riders burst through the gate in a few minutes, stopping at the commandant's offices. A young man, in his thirties, with a beard, dressed in ragged clothes, entered the office, dust flying from his shoulders. Four white men stood on the porch leaning against a couple of posts. The rest of the men, all Hispanic, remained mounted.

Lorenzo tied up Arrow and pushed through the men on the porch, entering the building. He stopped outside the open door of Colonel Canby. He had yet to meet Canby, but Captain Graydon, Kit Carson, and Canby strategized how to use the Fort's regiments to meet the Confederate Texas Volunteers. Lorenzo overheard the name 'Henry Sibley' commanding the Texans, referenced as if an old friend of Canby's. The meeting concluded, and as Carson and Graydon left the office, Kit saw Lorenzo and stopped Graydon.

"Paddy," said Carson, "This man has volunteered under high recommendation to join your spies. His name is Lorenzo Brennan. Scouted for the Sitgreaves Expedition, a Mexican/American war veteran."

Graydon didn't offer a hand or have time to evaluate the tall man. "I'm low on men; you'd be welcome. Are you ready to ride?" he asked.

"Give me five minutes; my horse is saddled; I just have to grab my bedroll," said Lorenzo.

"I'll leave you two," Carson said. "The New Mexico Volunteers will be on the march in twenty. We'll cover the right flank. The Coloradans will extend from the Rio westward. Canby's regiments will take a position in the middle and attempt to reach us to the right. Good hunting."

"Catch up to us," Paddy told Lorenzo, ignoring Carson. "We'll head southwest."

Lorenzo raced to his tent, rolled his bed, and grabbed his rifle, holster, Colt repeater, saber, and ammunition pouch. Strapping the bed bundle behind the saddle cantle, he swung up on his new mount. He and Arrow would have to finish their socializing under fire. They took off from the fort gate, trailing the distant puffs of dust.

It took Arrow and Lorenzo fifteen minutes to catch Paddy's hard-riding company. They had clumped together on a slight rise. Paddy and one of the vaqueros had dismounted and walked a few yards ahead of the group. Graydon held a spyglass on the horizon. The Rio Grande snaked west at this point, and the spy watched the Sibley Texan troops march north on the west side of the river toward the fort.

Lorenzo had stopped Arrow thirty yards short of the company and pulled out his glass, confirming the continued movement of the enemy.

Paddy walked back to his vaqueros and waved at Lorenzo to join him. "They're still moving," he said to the assemblage. Looking to the west and the sun dropping toward the mountains, Graydon continued, "Getting late in the day to start the fight. I reckon they'll get to within a half mile of the fort and dig in." Lorenzo nodded in agreement.

Paddy sent a unit to verify the Texan cannonry and a second unit to determine the shape of the enemy's stock.

Borrero's four-man unit galloped up within an hour and reported to Graydon, who sent them back to the Union front. A half-hour later, Clemente's unit rode up, and Paddy again sent him on to report to Canby's command station.

Dusk dropped across the desert as the Texas force began to dig in. A short distance away, the Union line looked impressive to Lorenzo in strength and position, backdropped by the garrison and huge mounds protecting the artillery. Paddy's spies broke through the line and headed for the fort. Paddy went off to report while the rest of his band headed for their group of tents. Some of the tents were empty due to Paddy's men mustering out. Men, in twos, dove into their tents. Lorenzo approached one of the men without a tentmate, holding the flap. "Mind if I bed in your tent?" he asked.

"Eres bienvenido, Leandro Garzon es mi nombre," said the man.

"Muchas gracias, my name is Lorenzo Brennan. I'm from west of Albuquerque."

"Hola, Lorenzo," said Leandro. "My Inglés, not so good."

"Same with my Spanish," said Lorenzo. "We'll get along."

The following morning, Paddy's raiders were out of the fort at dawn, patrolling the rear of the Union front on horseback, shouting encouragement to the New Mexico Volunteers and Union troops. Two thousand men dug in just beyond the fort's fortifications, ready to defend.

As Paddy had predicted, the force arriving from the south had spent hours before dusk the previous evening digging in, out of range of the Union artillery. Thousands of Texans faced the fort waiting for the command to engage.

At midmorning, word reached Captain Graydon to call on the command post for instructions. When he returned, his raiders, Lorenzo included, listened to their leader review his orders. "Colonel Canby thinks Fort Craig and our established defensive positions will win the day if the enemy attacks," he said. "We're to wait another hour."

Lorenzo, mounted on Arrow, closed his eyes; waiting was the worst part of the war. He looked out along the line. The nerves of the men were edging toward the breaking point. This would be their first brush with real danger.

There didn't seem to be much movement among the Texan line, although they were too far away for anyone without a spyglass to see detail. The Texas commander had evaluated the field and determined the fort was too strong to capture. A siege, perhaps? A withdrawal, possibly? Still a chance of an attack.

A rider galloped up to Captain Graydon and handed him a note. He spent only a moment reading it as if he knew its content. He looked up, smiled, and chuckled, "Canby's given us the go-ahead."

Paddy mounted his great gray and wheeled the horse to face his outfit. “I’ll see if I can roust them into a fight.” Turning the gray toward the Texan line, he spurred the horse into a gallop, leaping over two Union soldiers who, luckily, didn’t see him coming and stayed prone.

The Union line cheered the crazed man’s rush on the Confederate line, cutting his horse to the east at the last moment, firing at the soldiers along the line, and sneaking back into the mesquite scrub. He appeared again further down the line coming back west, firing his repeater and swearing, “gutless long-horn devils, fight, damn you, fight.” The soldiers began firing at Paddy. Graydon continued to weave in and out of cover, hiding for a time to reload. Then he sprung forward with blood-curdling Apache yells. Soldiers rose and began to pursue Graydon, but rebel officers called them back to their positions.

Upon his return to the Union line, volunteers and troops stood and hooted, amazed the Confederates hadn’t hit Graydon. They had heard the shooting and watched the gray horse travel along the Texan line.

But the confederate officers still would not order their soldiers forward.

Graydon led his volunteers around the west side of the Union force. He divided his unit into groups of four riders, spread apart by thirty yards. Each group, in turn, charged the end of the confederate line, firing their rifles at the backs of the Texans, inflicting minimal damage but attempting to unsettle the enemy.

Lorenzo had little time to learn the individual names of the men, other than Leandro, under his command. As ordered, his group lined up for the next charge behind Clemente’s unit.

A minute later, as his stomach flopped and his heart raced, Lorenzo, waving a saber in his left hand, Colt repeater in his right, led his screaming companions behind and along the

Confederate line, firing as he rode. A bullet ripped his shirt near his shoulder. Three bullets whizzed his ear.

His eyes fogged as the wind increased. Blowing sand bit his hands and face. *Stay on your horse… Hanna, Hanna, Hanna.*

Eyes clear now, and mad at his continuous stupidity, Lorenzo kept firing. He doubted his shots had reached a Texan. With his repeater empty, he turned Arrow and scampered out of range of the Texans.

A smattering of confederates turned away from the Union front. Most stayed focused. The raiders tried, mostly unsuccessfully, to jab a thorn in the side of the confederate flank.

Lorenzo reloaded safely away from the lines to prepare for the next charge. His heart pounding, he looked around at his battle-hardened group, readying for another rush forward. These Hispanics seemed nothing like the Mexican farmers he went up against in the war in '48. His resolute companions were fearless, ready for another charge. Lorenzo also noted the steadfastness and calmness demonstrated by the Texas forces.

The desert weather turned sour as Paddy led his men back toward the Union line. Thousands of men on both lines waited.

A bugle sounded from behind the Texas forces. Confederate soldiers began to back away. The practiced discipline they exhibited, even in retreat, impressed Lorenzo. The soldiers did not turn tail and run. They withdrew. This enemy would not panic like the Mexicans he had fought against in '46.

The Union troops stayed on the field for two hours after the Texans left the combat zone. Amid the sandstorm and darkening sky, the bluecoats and volunteers returned to the relative weather protection of the fort. Graydon's spies had more work to do. Lorenzo learned the names of the two other New Mexicans in his group.

Captain Graydon assigned Lorenzo and his three charges, Mateo, Cruz, and Leandro, to track the movement of the enemy force. Paddy picked Lorenzo, the low man on the roster, for the assignment. The temperature continued to drop. The sandstorm made visibly sighting the Texans impossible. As he and his companions followed the retreat, he thought he might be in earshot of the enemy, "Ride side by side, saddle to saddle, and ride quiet," he whispered into the wind.

The four spies walked during the night, leading their horses in the dark, stumbling in and around the scrub. The torches of the Texan force provided their only light. Impossible to know the direction of travel, staying close but not too close to the rebel conversations carried by the wind.

The wind never lessened during the night. If anything, the sandstorm strengthened as the haze of dawn tried to brighten the sky. Lorenzo led his unit away from the meandering Lone Star soldiers. The troop organization had broken down because of the storm. Groups of soldiers dotted the horizon behind and ahead of Lorenzo's position but not to his west, only toward what the spy perceived as the eastern horizon. Still unable to determine his position, Lorenzo called for his group to hunker down, rest, and watch the enemy congeal until they began to move as a body. The day continued to get colder. Sleeping without cover was as dangerous as enemy fire. Lorenzo's spyglass might help him suss out the Rio Grande to the east. If not, his group would dog the scattered army from Texas until the storm ended.

The Texas soldiers grouped up in the morning haze and began to march away from Lorenzo's spot. Light among the clouds indicated a turn of the troops to the east and the river. The billowing wind and clouds confused the sense of direction.

The mass of soldiers slowed, and Lorenzo heard distant splashing, cannon wheels creaking, and soldiers cursing the freezing-cold river they were crossing. In another hour, the Texas battalion was hunkering down. Lorenzo bade his fellows stay put while he ventured to the water's edge. The swirling sand, at times, settled enough to give Lorenzo a view of the activity across the Rio. The spy saw cooking fires, tents, and corrals for horses and oxen to the south between the fierce wind gusts. Lorenzo could not count the Texan heavy artillery located in the center of the camp as he lay prone on the flat of the prairie.

Behind the camp, a craggy prominence jutted up a couple hundred feet from the desert. It extended on either side of the base for hundreds of yards. Lorenzo crawled back to his unit and pulled out his map. In the dim light, he studied the winding river on the map, comparing the map to the sweep of the river in his view until he determined his position relative to the landmarks. "Visibility is still for shit," he told his crew. "The storm will give us cover. We'll travel south, cross the river, and get up on that high ground for a look-see."

The sandstorm ended after they crossed the Rio. The three New Mexicans concealed their ascent of the sharp granite outcrop by climbing up the opposite side of the camp. While Leandro counted the cannons, Mateo counted the stock, and Lorenzo wrote the dispatch to Captain Graydon at Fort Craig. His spyglass picked up listless soldiers in grub lines or walking between tents. The animals had scoured the corral of all vegetation. The horses seemed as haggard as the soldiers. Lorenzo described the state of the camp in his memo and sent Cruz to Fort Craig with the dispatch. Three hours after the messenger left for the fort, Lorenzo watched officers rouse the soldiers, preparing for departure. This surprised the scout, but he attributed the move to the lack of vegetation for the stock to graze.

Sibley's brigade headed north, staying a short distance from the river. Too soon to send another courier. Lorenzo had to determine the Texan force's intent. Would they set up across from the fort for an artillery barrage from across the river? Midafternoon the soldiers turned east just before they came upon the fort. The Texans marched away for an hour and a half before returning north. Lorenzo couldn't wait any longer. He sent Mateo back with an update.

He surmised in the dispatch that Sibley had decided not to engage Canby's force so effectively entrenched at Fort Craig. Instead, the confederates would bypass the fort entirely and continue north toward Fort Union, isolating Fort Craig by controlling the supply line between the two outposts. Lorenzo wrote that he would meet Paddy's crew on the west side of the Rio at the point of the original standoff.

Lorenzo and Leandro took off at a gallop to meet the captain when the Texas Rangers began camping for the night. They reached the assumed meeting place and built a fire, warming their three days' cold bones.

20 |Mules for the Enemy

Paddy and sixteen men of his company hailed Lorenzo before leading their horses and a couple of mules into the light of the fire. "Sir," said Lorenzo. "I thought the Texans would rest a day or two. The sandstorm took it out of them. But nope, they're on the move."

"Your dispatch stirred up action at the fort," claimed Graydon. "Canby's preparing a force to meet the bastards at Valverde ford four miles north of the fort. That's the only spot to cross the river near the wagon road north."

"Leandro and I can break camp here and follow you north," said Lorenzo.

"Not so fast, Brennan. I have a scheme that will cause the rebels to be hurt during their sleep tonight. You, Leandro, Cruz, Mahony, and I will raid the Texan's camp."

"Really," was all Lorenzo could sputter.

"Mahoney, bring the mules over. Not too close to the fire, mind you."

As Mahoney led the mules closer to the light of the fire, Lorenzo saw that the mules were both burdened. Boxes tied to the mules jostled as they walked.

"Yep, filled with 24-pounder howitzer shells. That'll wake the boys over there, put the fear of God in 'em and destroy half their stock."

Leandro gaped at Lorenzo, then turned to Graydon. "How do we get by the pickets, Captain."

"Very quietly. The Texans won't be suspecting our small force this far from the fort."

The tension in Lorenzo's shoulders traveled to his neck. He rotated his head till it cracked, hoping to relieve his despair. *The man is crazy.*

"The four men I called out mount up. The rest of you help the mules across the river and then be ready to give us cover when we return if any gray jackets come after us."

After warming his hands at the fire for one last minute, Lorenzo rolled his blanket, tied it to his saddle, gave Arrow a handful of oats, and crossed the river.

The five riders descended the scrub in the dark about seventy feet apart. Lorenzo, a bit out front, guided the group. Next, Mahoney led one of the mules. Then Paddy on his gray. Next to the captain, Leandro led the second old mule, so gray in the withers that the creature looked like it might fall over dead. The last in line, Cruz stayed almost one hundred feet away from Cruz, wanting no part of the mule bombs.

When Lorenzo could pick out enemy fires on the horizon, he dismounted and began leading Arrow on foot. Paddy swung his horse over to Lorenzo. "The mules will naturally go for the oats when they get near the stock over there," he said.

"No talking from here on in," said the captain. "When I signal, light the fuses, slap the mules, and send them toward the camp. Then get the hell out of there. They'll do the rest."

Lorenzo led his horse forward. With every ten yards, he felt more pressure in his stomach. The pacing pickets, sucking on lit smokes, became more defined in the light from the enemy fires. *Close enough, Captain, light 'em up.*

Fifty feet from the picket line, Paddy raised his fist high. Mahoney and Leandro lit the fuses. Lorenzo heard the "thwack." He mounted and turned Arrow into a trot to the west. He peered over his shoulder. The mules trotted ten yards, stopped, turned back toward Paddy's crew, and began to trot after the raiders.

Terrified by the lit fuses, Leandro and Mahoney broke into a gallop heading for the river. So did the mules, trying desperately to keep up. Lorenzo galloped away as well. In hot pursuit of Paddy's unit, the mission's fatal flaw, the mules' stupidity, threatened to blow Lorenzo and his companions to desert dust. One of the mules gained ground on Mahoney before slowing, exhausted.

The two explosions, seconds apart, set off additional explosions. The odor of gunpowder grew while the splat of bloody mule meat spewed across the desert. The confusion in the camp was indicated by the soldiers' yells and the agitated stock. Everything settled down when no destruction or injuries were discovered. The five spies reached the river, crossed, and gathered among their fellows.

Disappointed, Paddy's spy company headed for the fort. Paddy hoped the rebels would sleep with one eye open the rest of the night. The Texans didn't sleep at all. Officers ordered the rebels north to beat the Union army across the ford near Valverde.

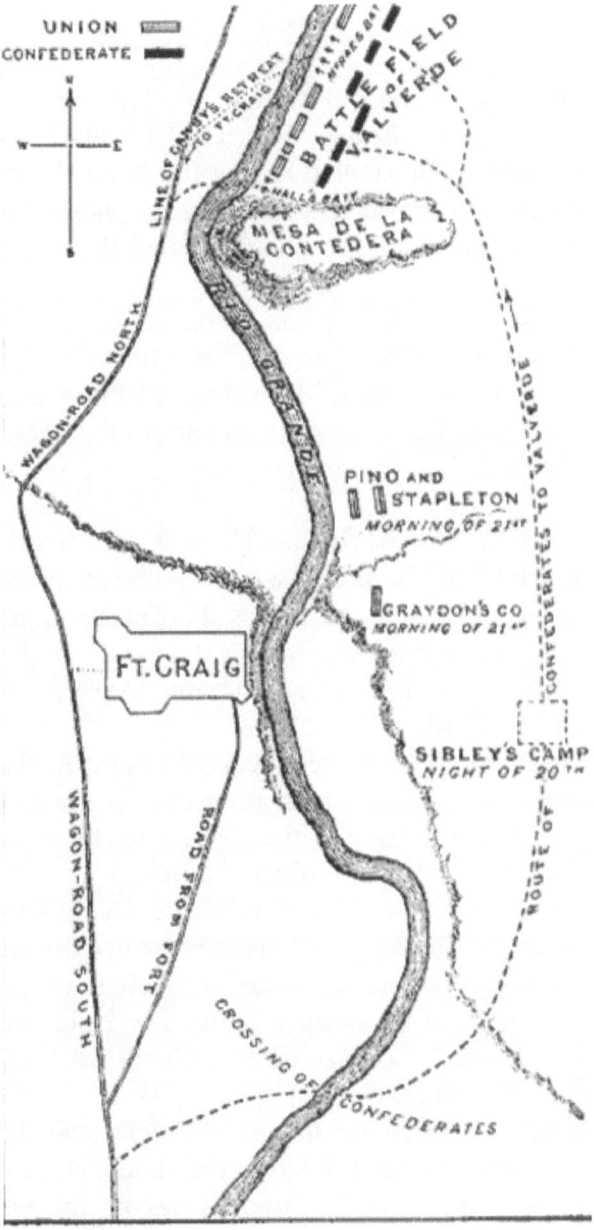

Valverde Battlefield

***

Lorenzo slept in the bed in his tent for four hours before Paddy rousted his spies. The date: February 21st, 1862. The sore forty-four-year-old scout saddled Arrow and threw the strap on a feed bag of oats over the horse's ears while he packed his gear. Then Lorenzo mounted his horse and joined the other spies moving north.

The Union forces, reaching the ford, moved through the shallows and set up artillery on the Rio Grande's east side. Paddy's spies crossed as well. They hugged the base of the Mesa del Contadero, heading southeast until they spotted the confederate brigade heading toward them on the way to the battlefield at Valverde. Paddy again broke his command into four groups of four New Mexicans. He sent back word to the officers at the ford of the progress of the enemy march. He ordered the free-flying spies to harass the Texans along their marching lines. Lorenzo's group streaked down from the mesa high lands, firing on the soldiers moving forward on their mounts toward Valverde.

During the second foray, Mateo received a bullet in his thigh. Lorenzo helped the wounded man return to the ford and the hospital tent on the west side of the river. With his remaining two New Mexicans, Lorenzo rejoined the fight.

Lorenzo could pick his sortie from his vantage point in the uplands of the mesa. The Gray Jackets scurried to a dry riverbed which provided cover and an excellent defensive position opposite the volunteers out of Fort Craig. The Union artillery began moving forward. Lorenzo spied Colonel Kit Carson on the west bank of the river.

Reinforcements arrived on the Confederate side, and the battle raged. Lorenzo pointed down in the valley, and Leandro and Cruz followed him toward a group of wagons rolling at the base of the Mesa from the south. As they approached, a company of lancers popped out of the Confederate force. Lorenzo's spyglass picked up the fringed buckskins of the defending Coloradan volunteers. They were rugged westerners, and they repulsed the lancers. When that skirmish appeared over, the lancer mounts were dead, and the confederate injuries looked extensive.

Graydon rode up, "We're to help out on the right flank," he said. The raiders galloped to the river, splashed through the ford behind the Union artillery, and emerged on the far right, joining Colonel Carson's New Mexico Volunteers crossing the river from the west.

Now in the thick of the battle, Lorenzo dismounted near Captain Alexander McRae's artillery battery. Terrorized by the whining shots landing amidst his fellow defenders, so far missing him, he fought on in a fog. Exhausted from over six tension-filled hours of inflicting damage on the territory invaders, Lorenzo continued to hoot and reload his fire-hot rifle. Picking out a gray coat in the distance, he would pull the trigger, reload the Sharp's rifle, and lift it to shoot with leaden arms. Half the time, he couldn't keep the rifle level, or it swayed away from his intended target.

Lorenzo became distracted by a ruckus at the opposite end of the Union line of defense. He couldn't tell exactly, but the soldiers on that side tangled in a pistol and saber fight. The Union soldiers were holding steadfast.

Yet another surge of the confederate forces began in the center of the field. Fresh Confederate reinforcements were gaining ground, leaving Union bodies strewn amongst the scrub. Lorenzo could see the fallen soldiers, either injured or dead. Every muscle in his body seemed to shake. He desperately wanted to mount Arrow and speed back across the Rio Grande.

Instead, Lorenzo somehow flushed fear from behind his eyes and began firing and reloading twice as fast, the horror in the field no longer diverting his focus from the approaching enemy soldiers.

A bugle's trill from the river's west bank broke through the battle's noise. Looking over his shoulder, Lorenzo saw a white flag waving high above a horse-mounted soldier. A truce was declared. A Union army retreat. Lorenzo didn't need a second invitation. He swung up on Arrow and dashed through the ford, joining the thousand-plus men heading back to Fort Craig.

The truce to deal with the dead and wounded held. Lorenzo found Paddy Graydon, one leg at the knee around the pommel of his horse, watching the listless procession heading south. The Graydon Raiders gathered behind him, trickling in by twos and threes until the outfit was complete. Graydon notified his men that one raider, Orlando Gorse, had died in battle. He called for a moment of silence in Gorse's honor. The men looked around at each other, blank in expression. They were still strangers in the brief time they had all known each other.

"What are our orders, Capitán?" asked Leandro.

"Same as always, scout out the bastards. Harass the shit out of 'em. Try to turn today's setback into victory for the territory."

Lorenzo couldn't think of anything to ask or say. He had not one ounce of energy left. The group rode west, departing from the contingent heading south. Lorenzo managed to struggle along near the back of the pack. His companions might label him too ancient to be a raider if he were last. *I am too old; that's a fact. Got to keep up.* Twenty minutes later, lulled by the gentle rhythm of the horse's cantor, head resting against Arrow's soft strawberry mane, Lorenzo slept.

21 |Over the Glorieta Pass

Slopes of the pass were covered in fresh snow powder. The snow absorbed the sounds of heavy breathing and occasional snorts from the horses. The gelding and the mare labored, high-stepping through the eighteen inches of white powder that filled the upper elevations of Glorieta Pass. The day before, the two scouts, Lorenzo and Leandro, had intersected the Santa Fe Trail heading east, following Paddy Graydon's orders. Lorenzo kept the pace reasonable. A lame horse: the last thing the messengers needed. Three more days travel to the Fort Union.

On the morrow, Lorenzo woke before dawn, nudging Leandro, who yawned, stood, and relit the fire, coffee on both their minds. The temperature had risen into the forties overnight, the wind blowing in a warm front. With a snow melt, the confederates might have a chance to gain ground on the two scouts. They ate a quick breakfast of hard tack and jerky while they packed gear. Twenty minutes later, Lorenzo and Leandro mounted and continued quickly along the trail. As soon as the snow disappeared in their path, Lorenzo alternated between a gallop and a walk to conserve Arrow's stamina. The scout kept a sharp eye out for Apaches, never quite overcoming the feeling that a Texan bullet or an Apache arrow may be whistling toward his back.

The two scouts dismounted around noon, and Lorenzo swept the mountains and trail to his rear with his spyglass. No sign of the confederates. He searched for Indian marauders; his spyglass instead picked up a body of blue coats in the distance to the east. He and Leandro mounted and galloped toward the Union camp. When they were close, Lorenzo waved the dispatch from Captain Graydon to secure passage, and an escort led the two scouts to the command post. Lorenzo recognized the hacienda of Martin Kozlowki. Martin had graciously offered Lorenzo a night's rest in his bunkhouse on Lorenzo's journey to Fort Craig in January.

Colonel Slough sat behind the desk in Kozlowski's study as Lorenzo entered on the run, stopped, and saluted. The colonel had rearranged the furniture to emphasize the desk and the commander's importance.

"Decorum, man," said the colonel, who glanced at another man sitting in a side chair to the colonel's right.

"Lorenzo Brennan, New Mexico volunteer, attached as a scout to Captain Graydon's company," said Lorenzo, laying the dispatch written by Paddy on the desk. Slough took it up, read it through, then handed it to the second officer.

"Mr. Brennan," said Slough. "Paddy wrote this dispatch two days ago. You have permission to speak freely; this is Major John Chivington."

The officer in the chair nodded. Both men had similar foreheads of receding hair, and their eyes showed the same intensity of purpose. The two struck Lorenzo as resolute, serious officers.

"We have been mobilizing our forces out of Fort Union," Slough continued. "Just today, regiments of the Colorado militia joined us after a rapid march from that territory.

"Our combined forces should be rested in two days. Then we'll meet Sibley's rebels and send him home.

"What would be your estimate of the confederate force's progress?"

"General, their vanguard force is no more than a day behind me. Now that the snow has melted, they will be here before you know it," reported Lorenzo.

"Mmmm," murmured Slough.

Lorenzo stood in front of the two men, both lost in thought. *For what are they waiting?*

Colonel Slough, head slightly bowed, began tapping his pencil on the desk, slowly at first and then increasing speed. Another two minutes passed. Suddenly, the man looked up and turned to Chivington.

"The Coloradans are exhausted…

"They'll have to march out. How many can be ready immediately?" said the colonel.

Chivington looked to the ceiling, calculating his response. "They are still trickling into camp," he said. "We have close to four hundred here presently. The Coloradans, exhausted from the march, are still itching to fight."

Lorenzo doubted this statement. No sane man itches to fight a war. Chivington stood and approached a blackboard swinging on a stand behind Slough.

"Brennan, can you sketch the trail back to where you think the enemy is riding toward us?" said the major.

Lorenzo stepped up to the board, drawing a rough arc representing a portion of the Santa Fe trail back the way he had traveled. Then he marked out three spots along the route.

"Working back from Kozlowski's ranch, here," Lorenzo began, pointing to each mark on his crude map as he spoke. "The next ranch is about here. Then you're in the mountains, and Glorieta Pass will be here. Further back down the trail is Apache Canyon, about here."

"The pass is strategic," said Slough. "If we can stop them there, we should control the field."

Chivington looked at the sketch. “Brennan,” he said. “Is there a chance we could make it to Apache Canyon before they do?”

“A slight chance. The horses would be worthless if you did make it there in time,” said Lorenzo.

“But we could ambush them from the high ground,” Chivington said. “The pass would be behind us as a fallback position.”

“Lorenzo,” said Colonel Slough. “You will be lead scout, attached to Chivington. Get his troops to that canyon.

“Chivington, hold off their vanguard while I gather the rest of our force and join you as soon as possible.

“Questions? No? Then dismissed”

***

Glorieta Pass:

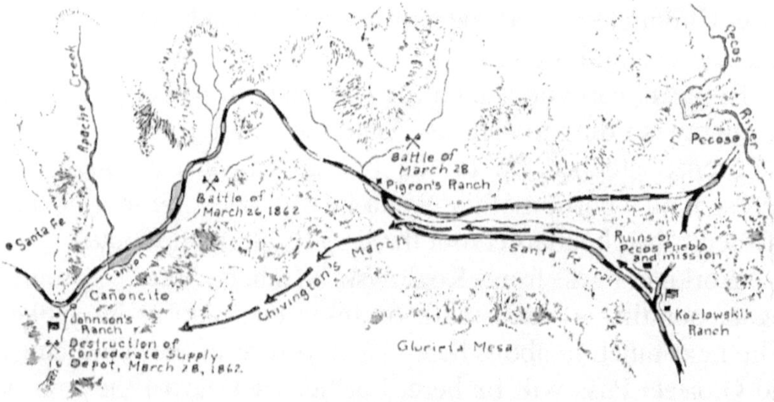

At one o’clock in the morning on March 26th, Lorenzo, crouching in the snow, looking through his spyglass, again caught a glimpse of a fire burning on the summit of Apache

Canyon. He turned and went down the slope fifty yards to where Arrow, Leandro, and thirteen New Mexican volunteers awaited his orders.

During the rush, chaos, and scurrying at Kozlowski's ranch to rouse and ready four hundred Colorado militia, Major Chivington introduced Lorenzo to Lt. Col. Manuel Chaves of the 2nd New Mexico Infantry. Chaves, familiar with the exploits of Paddy's raiders, picked out thirteen of his best men and placed them at Lorenzo's disposal, bestowing him the rank of unit captain. Lorenzo assigned Leandro, second in command to translate for half the team that spoke only broken English.

By traveling all night under a three-quarter moon, Captain Lorenzo's group entered the east end of Glorieta Pass. They dismounted, leading their horses through the pass, scouting for enemy advance spies or troops. The moon lowering in the west allowed the fifteen men and horses to walk the shadow in the valley: invisible to lookouts on either ridge. Lorenzo had spotted a fire up on the hill above their position. He led his men up the east side of Apache Canyon, gathering in a clearing hidden by golden aspens.

"It seems pretty quiet up there," said Lorenzo. "That could mean they are asleep or have less than ten men up there as lookouts." He waited while Leandro translated his words into Spanish. "At any rate, the risk is significant to try and go by them to see where the Texan force is camped.

"The fact that they have allowed a fire means they are dumb. Dumb enough that we might be able to surprise the sentries.

"We'll leave two men here with the horses. The rest of us will head up to the ridge, far enough away for them to see or hear us."

The newly appointed captain waited for Leandro's translation before continuing. "When we get up there, Leandro, you take six men and circle around their camp. I'll lead the others around to the left. We'll space out and close in on my signal if I believe we can surprise and overpower them. Otherwise, we'll melt away.

"Let's go," said Lorenzo.

When Lorenzo approached the campfire, he dripped sweat as he tromped through the snow along the top of the mesa. He worried he would collapse from the fear, tension, and exhaustion.

Sarah, his baby daughter, drifted through his conscience. *I can't wait to see how you've grown, Sarah Bee.*

Lorenzo could see three pickets standing guard and soldiers bedded around the fire, too grouped to count. More in number than his unit. He decided to withdraw, taking two steps back, about to give the 'melt away' signal. But the Texan picket before him peered in his direction, pointing his rifle. *Too late now.*

Lorenzo took three steps toward the picket, shouting, "You are surrounded." Lorenzo leveled his rifle at the Texan. "We have the drop on you. Throw down your weapons, or we'll shoot you like turkeys on a fence."

The others in his unit stepped forward at Lorenzo's voice. Due to the compactness of the bedded-down rebels, there could be no doubt about the outcome of a firefight. The pickets saw that their position was indeed hopeless and, twenty seconds later, threw down their weapons.

The New Mexico volunteers moved forward into the firelight. Leandro gave instructions in Spanish to disarm the enemy soldiers and tie their hands behind them. The sixteen prisoners, guarded, scrambled down the ravine. Five of the guards led the enemy mounts down the canyon as well. Arriving at the copse where they left their horses, Lorenzo pulled Leandro aside. "You'll have to take the prisoners," said Lorenzo. The sun peaked over the summit to the east.

“Where, Capitán?” Leandro said. “What should I do with them?”

“Chivington’s regiment should be at the pass by now. Find Lt. Col. Manuel Chaves, but you must return to the camp at Kozlowski’s ranch.”

“What’s your plan, Lorenzo?” Leandro asked.

“I’ll leave Arrow here. I bet I'll discover Texans a mile on the other side of the canyon. I’ll return here, pick up Arrow, and report to Chivington and Chaves.”

Because he had captured the Texan advance scouts, Lorenzo had no trouble finding and counting the four-hundred-twelve Texas Rangers about to advance into Glorieta Pass. Within another hour, he reported his scouting information to Major Chivington.

“Good work Captain Brennan,’ said the major. “We sent your unit back to the ranch with their prisoners.”

“Yes, sir, what are my orders,” said Lorenzo.

“Brennan, you look like six mules, and a stagecoach ran you over. When was the last time you slept? Four days, five?” Join your men at the ranch. I’ll send for you after we win the skirmish this afternoon.”

“Thank you, sir.” Lorenzo saluted and left the command tent. Back at Kozlowski’s ranch, Lorenzo headed to the bunk house, picked the bed in the furthest corner, fell upon it, and blessedly fell asleep.

***

Lorenzo woke up near noon the next day. He lay still for two minutes to determine where he had gone to bed, in this world or the next? Kozlowski’s ranch: that was the foggy answer. Instead of the solid, cold ground, his usual bed, the straw mattress had sent him to heaven for eleven hours. He remembered two trips to the latrine and two to the shitters but nothing of the coming and going of others in the bunkhouse.

Hunger bit him now. Lorenzo didn't have long to wait for the triangle clang announcing the lineup for lunch. He took his plate of beans and eggs to the corral to check on Arrow, leaning against the corral fence to finish his plate. The Union troops, New Mexico, and Colorado volunteers had returned to Kozlowski's ranch. Arrow looked fit and glad to see him, chomping at the hay Lorenzo offered. Lorenzo went to the end of the grub line, hoping for a second helping. That is where Leandro found him.

"Good morning Capitán," Leandro said. "You look a little better, I guess."

"A shave is next, and I'm going to wash out this shirt," said Lorenzo. "What happened yesterday? Did we win or lose?"

Leandro shrugged. "From what I hear, Chivington's four hundred met the confederate vanguard at about where we captured those pickets. Then our side pushed the Texans back over a mile until the Coloradans ran into their artillery. Chivington split his force in two, sending them up either side of the canyon and attacking from each side.

"Chivington had the advantage but decided to withdraw and wait for the reinforcements from Fort Union. There are over a thousand men here now. Word is tomorrow there will be cannon fire on both sides."

Lorenzo shaved. His hands were ice cold in anticipation of the day ahead. He didn't take time to wash his shirt, grabbing his spare shirt from his saddle bag instead. Then he hurried to the command tent, waiting in line with others petitioning the major or General Slough.

On his turn, he entered the tent and saluted, saying, "Captain Brennan, awaiting orders, sir." The three officers gathered around a blackboard full of chalk lines and 'X's.

"Hard time recognizing you, Captain Brennan," said Chivington. "We're thinking…."

General Slough interrupted, "I'll be taking over the command of the front line in the pass," he said.

"Chaves, here, will advance his scouts, that's you, Brennan, and lead Chivington's regiments up on the mesa to await the beginning of the skirmish. Like the Israelites at Jericho, Chivington's force will descend upon the Texans."

Outside the tent, Chaves pulled Lorenzo aside. "Start for the mesa now. We'll need the best route for getting up on the mesa and an easy ravine to navigate back down on the north side. Send a scout back every hour when you get up there with progress reports. My New Mexican and Chivington's Colorado volunteers will follow you up on the mesa at dawn tomorrow."

Lorenzo's unit took off for the mesa's base within twenty minutes. Lorenzo skirted the bottom to the south; Leandro took six men north. Not ideal due to the chance of spies observing their actions so close to Kozlowski's ranch.

But Lorenzo found a way up a mile south of the ranch, out of range of spyglass view by the enemy hiding near Glorieta Pass. He rendezvoused with Leandro's six men, and the entire unit worked up the Glorieta mesa. When they reached the plateau flat, Lorenzo sent one scout back to the Union camp to lead Chivington's force up to the top.

Meanwhile, Lorenzo rode Arrow in a circle, well back from the mesa edge, dropping off a scout every quarter mile with instructions to find a ravine down the valley. The group reformed two hours after sunset and compared possibilities for the descent. Lorenzo disallowed any fires, not wanting to make the same mistake as the Texan pickets two days prior.

Sam Gonzales, speaking in English and repeating his report in Spanish, had found the most ideal and direct ravine. He had traveled down to the prairie and back.

"Alright," said Lorenzo. "Sam, you head back to the ranch and locate Chaves. Lead them on to the mesa and your descending ravine and keep them at least a half mile back from the cliffs so the enemy in the valley doesn't discover our troops."

"What plans do you have for the rest of us, Capitán?" asked Leandro.

Lorenzo rubbed his chin, "I have been thinking here on the mesa how ideal this position is. In the morning, five of us will ride to the west edge. We'll be able to see the confederates moving forward, so we'll count them, judge their speed, and check their dig-in rifle positions.

"Jim, take the first watch. Get to sleep, the rest of you. Big day ahead."

Before dawn, Lorenzo saddled Arrow and selected three men and Leandro to scout to the west. The mesa stretched five miles, and canyons and ravines cutting the landscape made the journey to the west edge anything but straightforward.

Lorenzo pulled up, dismounted, and walked to a boulder on the mesa's edge. He located the Johnson ranch along the Santa Fe trail with his spyglass, guessing it to be at least three miles away. Too far to gather intelligence with the spyglass. Sweeping around to the north, Lorenzo picked up the glob of confederate troops heading into Glorieta Pass. Again, they were too far away to count.

Lorenzo decided he needed to get closer. Asking Leandro to accompany him, the two scouts picked their way down from the mesa. Tall scrub hid their advance on the ranch. Lorenzo dismounted, scoping the cattle farm, now a half mile distant.

The scout saw only a handful of pickets guarding supply wagons. All the troops had traveled to battle Slough's regiments, leaving the wagons unprotected.

Lorenzo stopped counting at fifty wagons. “That is a gold mine over there,” he told Leandro. “I hope we can convince Chaves to bring troops and capture those wagons.”

Lorenzo and Leandro pushed their horses to the mesa's base, then led them back up the ravine to the top. As they reached the plateau, Lorenzo began to worry that he had seen a mirage at Johnson’s ranch. He should have risked getting even closer.

The two scouts rode back east, again skirting the deepest canyons. At noon Lorenzo gathered his unit, telling them what he had seen. Chivington and Chaves appeared with their contingents fifteen minutes later.

Chivington and Lorenzo saw the battle at Glorieta Pass had begun through their spyglasses. According to orders, Chivington was due to attack the rear of the confederate force. He had over four hundred men prepared to descend the mesa.

Lorenzo and Lt. Col. Chaves approached Chivington with a different idea.

“Major,” said Chaves, “Captain Brennan has scouted west on the mesa and has spotted a group of the Texan’s supply wagons.”

Chivington turned his attention to Captain Brennan. “How many wagons did you find, Captain,” he said.

“I counted more than fifty, sir,” Lorenzo said.

Chaves said, “If we split our force on the mesa, we may be able to help defeat the confederates at the pass and cripple their supplies by capturing the wagons at Johnson’s ranch.”

Chivington shook his head. “Splitting the force would weaken our ability to defeat the Texans at Glorieta Pass. That would be a serious error in judgment. How long would it take to get to the wagons?” he asked.

“At least an hour to an hour and a half,” said Lorenzo.

“So, a three-hour round trip and then another forty-five minutes to get down to the pass and help out Slough’s force,” the major opined. “We’ll do both in that order. Slough will have to hold out four more hours.”

Lorenzo pushed ahead, and Chivington’s force made it to Johnson’s ranch in under an hour. Everything looked the same. A smattering of pickets and wagons; no soldiers in sight.

Chivington approached Lorenzo. “Captain, take your unit down the trail toward Glorieta and watch for the Texan force. The rest of us will push these wagons together. Every mule in the corral must be shot or run off, and every wagon burned. Now let’s get those pickets out of the way.”

Leandro and Lorenzo’s comrades rode north and found high enough ground that Lorenzo could see the tail end of the battle in his spyglass. Soon a colossal conflagration lit up the sky, the smoke blowing ash high in the air. The soldiers in action at Glorieta Pass and Pigeon’s Ranch up ahead, ducking cannon and rifle shots, took no notice of the smoke and fire.

Captain Brennan decided the time had come to rejoin Chaves and Chivington. On approach to the ranch, Lorenzo noted that only smoldering charcoal and iron wagon axles lay strewn across the ranch yard. The carcasses of more than fifty mules scattered about sickened Lorenzo, thankful he hadn’t drawn that murderous duty.

Lorenzo’s unit caught up with the Union forces as they ascended the mesa. On top, at the prescribed ravine chosen for the regiment’s descent into battle, Chivington again waffled.

Too late. The Confederates had pushed the union force back to Pigeon’s ranch, and ongoing skirmishes appeared chaotic and undisciplined. Chivington addressed his officers and included Chaves and Lorenzo.

“We’ll head back to our camp at Kozlowski’s with the prisoners,” said Major Chivington. “Join Slough’s regiments and defend the Santa Fe route north to Fort Union. Or we’ll pull back to the fort.

"By burning those eighty-three wagons, we have thwarted Sibley's intention to conquer the New Mexico territory for the Confederacy."

***

Lorenzo put down the pen, blotted his signature, then reread his letter to Hanna before sealing it in an envelope with wax:

April 12th, 1862

Dearest Hanna,

I think of you often.

I work hard, scouting and fighting. I am unhurt at this point. Undamaged, unlike so many others. Alive, unlike so many. They say 100 died at Valverde and more than 350 at Glorieta, but we turned the Texans back.

More than in the Mexican-American war, seeing so much death has tempered my anger and despair over Jeremiah's accident.

I now see Jeremiah's death as an early casualty of this great war. He is no different in death than the sons I have seen dead on the field before me. The brothers that have died. The friends, the fathers.

The trick to getting through war is to work so hard on the task at hand, be it scouting, spying, riding, or shooting, that dying, or living, for that matter, slips away out of mind and body.

I am trying to make sense of it all by helping to win this war for what I feel in my heart is right about the human spirit. You have taught me about freedom, equal opportunity, and brotherhood or a Union of like-minded souls; immigrants, Indians, negros, rich and poor.

I have decided to continue until this war is over. I am a Captain, reporting to Brigadier General Edward Canby. I am beyond enlistment age which is part of my disguise. I have an allowance for gambling, a pastime that encourages loose tongues. I will be gathering intelligence behind enemy lines. Do not expect regular correspondence.

Please know how sorry I am for leaving without expressing my great and eternal love for you. Wrong! Cowardly! I know! Give me another chance when I return to show my adoration for you.

Forever in love with you, Zachary, and little Sarah,
Lorenzo

P.S. Pray my returned luck holds.

Zachary Zig Zags

PART TWO

22 |Emancipation – Freedom

Hanna's war fears eased when word reached the supply station at Leroux Spring that the New Mexico Volunteers and Union Army had expelled the Texas Rangers from the New Mexico Territory. Visions of marauding rebels overrunning the ranch, taking the sheep and stock, and burning her cabin receded from her sleep. Still, she kept her family nearby just in case.

Occasionally, the three Brennans ventured down to the valley during uncertain times to order supplies or pick up a new book from Albuquerque by Simon Rosenstein. During one such trip in March of '63, Hanna learned of Abraham Lincoln's latest forthright message.

Steve Pembroke, or the clerk that staffed the store while Steve traveled to Albuquerque or Denver, kept the mountain family up to date on the war. Hanna and Zach, carrying Sarah on his shoulders, warmed themselves around the station stove while Steve filled the mule pack with Hanna's order. With toasted hands, she returned to the notice on the board, rereading one of the paragraphs aloud for Sarah's benefit.

"*And by virtue of the power and for the purpose aforesaid, I do order and declare that all persons held as slaves within said designated States and parts of States are, and henceforward shall be, free; and that the Executive Government of the United States, including the military and naval authorities thereof, will recognize and maintain the freedom of said persons.*"

The Emancipation Proclamation, Lincoln's executive order, foreshadowed the extinction of slavery in the entire United States. In the form of a very tall, bearded man wearing a stove pipe hat, Lincoln righted the off-kilter notions of slave owners about the spirit of America as established in the Preamble to the United States Constitution: *to form a more perfect Union.*

Steve returned from filling the mule pack on the back dock. "Almost forgot," he said. "We are now standing in the Arizona Territory. Congress passed the bill describing the boundaries, and Lincoln signed it on February 24th, two weeks ago."

"I don't understand," said Zachary. "I thought the Arizona Territory was some kind of illegal Confederacy description of the southern part of the New Mexico Territory."

"That's true, Zach," said Pembroke. "They had the gall to divide New Mexico along a horizontal line that favored their belief in the right to own slaves, pitting Northern New Mexicans against southern New Mexican residents. It didn't take. Thanks, in part, to your father and the New Mexico Volunteer militia."

"So, how are the boundaries defined now," asked Hanna.

"The line continues the divide of the new Colorado Territory and Utah Territory south to the border of Mexico. The boundary splits the New Mexico Territory into two equal parts, the Arizona Territory and New Mexico Territory. We're on our way to statehood, folks."

"But we're still at war," said Zach. "This is all meaningless if the Union army loses."

"Perhaps," said Hanna, "in combination with President Lincoln's proclamation, the will of the army and the resolve of free-thinking citizens will be renewed, and we will win the war."

"The fighting is intensifying in the east," said Steve.

Zachary turned back to the fire, suddenly cold, wishing for the end of the fighting, for the end of the war. *Father would come home; forgive me.*

Lorenzo had left the sheep ranch for Fort Union over a year ago. Zachary had withdrawn into a stupor of blame and shame, nearly destroying Hanna. She had recalled her mother leaving her when she was twelve. Her father had needed her, and Hanna had focused on the singular task of saving him. She had submerged herself in the work of the ranch.

She had done the same for Zachary and never let her guilt or Zachary's shame surface. She had put him to work, first adding Jeremiah's chores to Zach's. Soon, the exhausted boy slept through the night. Next, she made the boy shadow Abelardo and report his learning. Abelardo put the boy to work as well, speaking only in Spanish.

Hanna had hauled down the most essential books on her shelf for Zach to read and study. It was no concern to Hanna if he didn't understand the material. When he finished a second book, she made him go back and reread the first book, alternating between the two until he could explain the content of what he read each day to Hanna. Zach had always been a good student. Thoughts of Jeremiah and his father became buried beneath the pile of books and ranch chores.

Little Sarah transferred affection to Uncle Abelardo weeks after Lorenzo left. Now a precocious five-year-old. She extracted smiles from Hanna and Zachary, showing off somersaults and pantomiming wolves and mountain lions.

When Hanna received Lorenzo's letter in May, she had waited until Zach and Sarah were asleep before reading it by lamplight in bed. She wept, then laughed, then cried again. *The skinny fool. Who's feeding you*?

The morning after the letter arrived, Zach noticed Hanna's constant smile. She related the gist of the letter and described

Lorenzo's exploits as a scout with the Beale expedition, stories Zach had never heard. She didn't tell Zach Lorenzo would be home soon, only that he was fighting for the right of a slave-free New Mexico territory.

With the sheep stock reduced back to fifty, the upper meadow provided the needed grazing. The ranch on the mountain isolated the family from the war's violence, politics, and suffering.

Zachary took regular supply trips down to the station on Sunny, one of the Brennan mules. During one trip down to the valley on a sweltering day in September after his 12th birthday, he stopped just outside the open door on the porch to listen to the conversation at the counter between a young-sounding man and Josh, Steve Pembroke's clerk.

"No getting around it; you're a man on the run. That's sure," said Josh, judging the man as a northerner in dress and accent.

"And I ain't denying it neither," said the younger man. "I've had enough. Gonna start over in California if I'm not shot for desertion."

"No one to stop you here," said Josh.

"I ain't no coward, I'm telling ya," said the man. "I just had enough. Made it through Gettysburg. They're saying over three thousand of us died. 20,000 wounded. More on their side. I ran through fields of arms, legs, and bodies to return to camp and kept running."

"Was the battle decisive?" asked Josh. "Or will they be back at it again next month?"

"Oh, the Union forces won the battle. Lee and the Reb army retreated. Word is they're still running, just like me."

Zachary stepped into the station. Both men clammed up. The young man grabbed what little he could afford, shuffled, mounted, and rode west. Zachary, shaken, went about his business as well.

That night Zachary woke up lying on a sweat-soaked sheet. In the nightmare, he runs through a never-ending field of body parts piled high like haystacks, rifles, and revolvers abandoned and available every thirty feet. Zachary's carrying his shepherd's crook whittled under the direction of Abelardo. The weapons scattered around him fire, driving him back as he waves his stick at the bullets to fend them off. He runs again, soldiers firing at him from the cover of the woods in front and the tree line behind him, waking him as he senses a bullet painfully hitting him in the back.

***

The wind drifted the day's eight-inch snowfall in curves around each tree base in the forest. Powder on the up-mountain side of the trunks measured more than twelve inches, while grass, moss, or needles huddled on the down-mountain side of each Ponderosa Pine. The clouds had blown east an hour ago. The wind stilled, but the sun warming the other side of the mountain provided a bright glow in the sky for the boy. The forest floor on this side of the peak was dark.

On February 12th, '64, the youth hurried to search for the dog after haying the horse and mules. He did not bother to strap on snowshoes. In forty minutes, his freezing feet began screaming at him to turn back.

"Bandit," Zach called out. "Bandit come… Here Bandit…"

Zachary Brennan's efforts were useless.

Bandit had been missing for two days. Mother had cautioned him at breakfast that Bandit had reached the end of life and gone off.

"He's lost, cold, and scared, Mother, that's all," Zachary had argued.

"He's old," Hanna had replied. "So old. Think how gray he's gotten. He can't keep up with Chica and Lobo. Has no interest in the sheep? He's left us. That's the sorry truth, son."

Sarah had cried, running to hug Zachary.

Turning back toward the trail leading to the ranch, the boy had to admit the quiet surrounding him reinforced his mother's conclusion. He shrugged, hardened to loved ones gone and now his childhood dog disappearing from his life.

Late September, Hanna rang the triangle on the porch, signaling lunch. Zachary sauntered to the cabin for beans and soup. As he approached, Chica heeling to his left, Hanna tried to remember the last time she had measured his height. She would have to stand on a chair to assess it now. *Was he as tall as his father, at thirteen, taller?*

"Mother," said Zach, "I need to see Steve about a couple of salt blocks for the sheep."

"Alright, I have a list already started," said Hanna. "Take it down to the station after lunch."

Zach nodded, his thick black hair swishing his cheeks. Preferring his hair long and his boots shiny, he polished them every other day after work. His striped shirt with billowed sleeves showed sweat at the pits, and his pants had fresh dirt smudges on the knees. Zach's braces had little stretch left but still managed to hold up his pants. At 150 lbs. and with a six-foot frame, he rivaled Lincoln and Lorenzo for skinny.

Big enough now to sit in a regular chair, Sarah looked around, impatient. "Where's Uncle Abelardo, Mommy," said Sarah.

"Be here in a minute," said Hanna. "He's been late before."

Zach finished his soup and vegetables. "I'll go round him up," he said, and when Hanna nodded, Zach took off toward the upper pasture. Abelardo and Lobo had the morning shift with half the sheep. Abelardo should be herding the sheep to the shift corral for lunch.

Chica ran ahead when they approached the meadow. The sheep were milling around in two major groups. The flock munched on the plentiful grass. The contented sheep would stay and chomp the rest of the afternoon if left alone. Zach looked over to the pin oak at the higher end of the pasture. He did not see Abelardo, usually sitting on the makeshift log bench in the oak shade. A gnarled maple crook leaned against the tree. Abelardo never went anywhere without it, even into the woods to pee.

Chica circled something in the tall grass along the meadow's edge, twenty feet from the bench. Zach approached cautiously and found his mentor, teacher, and friend face down in the tall grass. Abelardo looked peaceful in death. Zach couldn't remember Abelardo's age, sixty-seven or sixty-eight. *Heart attack.*

Zach and Chica gathered the sheep and sent them to the shift corral. Then the boy told Hanna how he had found the old man. She clasped a fist to her mouth, shaking her head, tears forming. Hanna left the cabin to talk to Sarah, playing with her dolls on the porch. Hanna returned and sat at the table with Zach listening to Sarah cry.

"I'll go up with Sunny and use the small cart to bring him down," said Zach. "Will his family want to bury him in the Albuquerque cemetery, do you think?"

"Zach, in this heat? No," said Hanna. "We'll bury him next to Jeremiah up in the meadow. He's as much a part of our family as theirs. I'll help."

Hanna walked to the meadow while Zach collected half of the sheep and herded them to the pasture with Chica's help. Hanna had found a spot near Jeremiah's marked grave and handed the shovel to Zachary. Two hours later, Zach had dug a hole long enough to fit the old shepherd but narrow because the shovel had hit two granite boulders halfway along the length of the grave.

Hanna went back to the cabin twice to check on Sarah. After helping position the body in the burial place, Zach began filling the grave. Hanna completely covered the burial place before going down to the cabin and bringing back Sarah.

While Hanna was gone, Zach spoke to the grave in Spanish. “Hola, Abelardo. Como estás. Es un buen dia. Muchas gracias por toto. Descansa tranquilo, mi amigo.”

Sarah appeared and clung to Hanna’s skirt.

“This is where Abelardo will rest from now on, Sarah,” said Hanna. “If you like, you could gather some flowers and place them on the grave.”

Sarah took Zach by the hand and led him to the wildflowers growing on the south side of the meadow. Together they picked ragwort daisies and pink alumroot flowers, handing them to Hanna, who bundled them in her hair ribbon before giving them back to Sarah. She held Sarah’s hand and led her to the grave. Sarah got down on her knees and placed the bouquet on the center of the mound.

“Abelardo,” she whispered. “Can you hear me? I love you, Uncle Abelardo.” Then she rose and ran back to Hanna, burying her face in Hanna’s skirt.

Hanna moved the two of them back to the grave.

“Abelardo, you have been a lifesaver. Children, I don’t recall an unkind word he ever said. We will miss him dearly, won’t we, children?”

“I will,” said Sarah.

Zachary could barely croak out, “I’ll miss you too.”

The three Brennans shuffled over to Jeremiah’s monument. It read: Jeremiah Brennan, 1849 – 1861. Zachary shook his head, biting his lip, while Sarah looked up at both of them.

Sensing Zachary's sadness, Sarah sobbed until Hanna drew her away.

Two days later, Zach dismounted Sunny in front of the supply station. He told Chica to lie on the porch, which she did instantly. He glanced over at the grown-over space adjacent to the station. Zach spit, then walked into the station. He handed Hanna's list to Steve Pembroke, adding, "two salt blocks as well, Mr. Pembroke, and a new scoop shovel if you've got one back there."

"I do, Zach," said Steve. "How are things up the mountain."

"Abelardo died of a heart attack a couple of days ago. Mother wants to order a headstone for him." Zach handed over another paper with the inscription spelled out.

"Oh, what a shame. I am sorry to hear that, Zachary. A good man, Abelardo."

"He was. Sarah loved him like a father. He taught me how to train Chica. He taught me Spanish too. He'd been slowing down this past year."

"What will you do for help, Zach?" said the station owner.

"I'll manage."

"If you need a hand sometimes, get Josh or me. One of us can break away down here with a little notice."

"I'll keep that in mind, Mr. Pembroke; thanks."

"Steve! The name's Steve. Zach, you're head of the ranch until Lorenzo gets back."

"Alright," said Zach

"Wouldn't surprise me to see your father walk in and pound on the counter soon. It shouldn't be much longer. Business is picking up. More wagons are heading west again; refugees from the Confederate states lately. Burned out by Sherman's force, needing a fresh start."

"You think the war will be over soon?"

"The whole city of Atlanta is gone. One of the three biggest cities in the south. Cinders. Sherman didn't stop there either."

From what Zachary remembered of a picture in one of Hanna's books, Atlanta had been a stately southern city. Steve referred to the newspaper report that Sherman's forces destroyed over three thousand homes and businesses. Indeed a barbaric act; Armageddon?

The ranch will survive without Abelardo, but for how much longer?

Zachary helped Steve load Hanna's foodstuffs in the mule pack. He strapped the shovel on top and took off for the cabin, hopeful Lorenzo's return would soon dispel his battle nightmares. But then again, when it came to the conflict, he had lived through disappointment for years.

***

Until winter hit, Zachary viewed the additional workload due to Abelardo's passing as challenging. Before daybreak, he fed and mucked the horse and mule stalls, and after breakfast, he worked the morning grazing. His work schedule included the addition of Abelardo's afternoon shepherding shift. In deep snow, he pitched hay to keep the sheep healthy. He built a folding table and hauled it up to the upper meadow. While he kept one eye on the leisurely sheep chewing, he worked at the table on minor repairs.

Occasionally he directed Chica to gather a lamb or ewe. Lobo always came along as well. Chica's brother had little patience for the sheep, preferring to wander off and explore. Zachary didn't even try to keep him on command. However, the dog guarded Zach, Chica, and the sheep devotedly. Zach refused to take the rifle to the meadow, leaving it for Hanna. She was more than capable of protecting herself if threatened at the cabin. A wolf dwarfed Lobo, although Lobo was sturdy through the chest and bigger by two hands than Chica. Zach had once watched Lobo chase away a wolf.

Last year, at dusk one night, the dog stood against a young mountain lion while Zach banged his staff against a flimsy tin tobacco container and screamed at the cat.

The flock had increased to sixty-three, which meant more shearing work and fleece preparation, more spinning and weaving for Hanna. The thirteen-year-old shepherd worked from sun up to sun down and beyond, day in, day out. Growing now in his chest and shoulders from plowing the hay field, maintaining the vegetable garden, and carrying ewes and lambs.

Now big enough to manage a hoe, Sarah worked an hour each summer day on weeding the garden. She helped with the bottling of berry jam. The family worked and slept and worked.

Zachary took to studying by lamplight late at night. Hanna found him at the table two nights a week, head down on the cool pages of an open book. She urged him and Chica up to the loft and bed.

That winter, the work grind stirred in Zach an inherited wanderlust. He imagined his father in the east spying for the Union, visiting cities like St. Louis and Philadelphia. He pulled down books from the shelf that described foreign countries and vast seas. He wanted those experiences. He began dreaming of leaving the ranch.

The boy had no idea if his father was dead or alive, but he hoped Lorenzo would return daily to free him from the ranch. Hanna encouraged his daydreams, speculating with Zach about careers he might consider in the future. She settled on him becoming a lawyer like her hero Abraham Lincoln. She pointed out Abe's modest background, the intelligence of his speeches, and his strength of character.

The harsh December of '64 brought more snow than Zachary could recall, colder too, according to Hanna, adding to Zach's despair. The workload never varied in the deep snow; it just demanded twice the effort. Constantly exhausted, Zach's sleep shifted back and forth between dreams of Chicago's sprawl and the U.S. Capitol in Washington, the Eiffel tower in Paris, and the nightmare war battle he always lost with just a shepherd's crook for a shield.

The first three weeks in January compounded the snow and cold of December. Snow so deep feeding the stock was the only chore Hanna and Zach agreed had to be accomplished. Otherwise, the Brennan family stoked the stove and stuffed wool remnants in the cracks that usually ventilated the cabin. Then a warm front settled over the mountain, bringing a bright cloudless week and sun that melted all but the mounds of snow in the worst drifts.

The knock on the cabin door late afternoon on April 17th, '65, startled Hanna, who was busy gathering potatoes from the root cellar.

"I'm coming, I'm coming," she said, climbing the ladder to the kitchen area. Again, a gentle knock.

Steve Pembroke greeted her when she opened the door. Not surprising. Besides Steve or Josh, Steve's clerk at the station, whoever visited?

"Did you come to help Zach in the hay loft with the broken pulley and crane?" she asked. "He's still up with the sheep. Shouldn't be too much longer, though."

"I can stay and help, but that's not why I came up."

"That's fine. Dinner will be ready in an hour. You'll remain, of course." Hanna yelled out the window. "Sarah, go up and hurry your brother along, please." Watching out the window, Hanna saw Sarah running to the barn and turning on the path toward the upper meadow. She shifted her gaze back to Steve.

"So, do you need Zach's help with something at the station?"

"No, Hanna, I'm all set, although you might be surprised at the traffic moving through on the wagon road. We may see a stagecoach soon."

From the corner of her eye, Hanna saw the flock emerge by the barn, Chica herding them into the corral. Sarah held her brother's hand until he had to close the gate. "Just a minute, here comes Zach," she said. Hanna made Steve wait while she cut a thick slice of bread from a loaf and smeared it with jam, placing it on a small plate at the table as Zach came in and sat down. He picked up the bread and took a big bite.

"Hungry, Steve?" he asked. "You've had mother's jam, haven't you?"

Steve could no longer contain himself, throwing his hands in the air. "I have news. Listen," he said. "Confederate General Lee surrendered to General Grant of the Union army on the 9th of April."

"What?" said Hanna. "If this is true…,"

"It's true, Lee dismissed his troops on their word of honor to stop fighting; nearly 30,000 confederate soldiers."

Pembroke extracted a newspaper from his inside breast coat pocket and smoothed *The Kansas City Daily Western Journal of Commerce* on the table. Steve read aloud, "*With cannons across the country falling silent, we have held on as a community.*"

Hanna prepared a beef stew dinner. Hanna brought half a berry pie to the table for dessert at the end of the meal. Sarah never let go of her fork until she finished her last pie bite. Zachary left the cabin for the barn and the evening chores. Steve helped Hanna with the dishes.

"You're quiet, Hanna," said Steve, throwing a towel over his shoulder. 'We should be celebrating."

"It will sink in, I'm sure," said Hanna, "But I immediately wonder about Lorenzo. Did he make it through, do you think?"

"I would bet on it, Hanna," Steve said. "Older soldiers may be slower, but they're wily. Lorenzo will come home, I'm sure."

Zachary returned from the barn. The three adults played cribbage accompanied by a bit of port wine to celebrate the momentous surrender at Appomattox. By the end of the game, Zach, exhausted, could barely lift the deck to deal, but he won. Steve left in the dark. Hanna lit a torch, handing it to him so he could see and follow the trail.

The day's chores had worn away Zach's stamina. The two cordial glasses of port helped him drift off. Regardless, he went to sleep the minute his head squashed the pillow. Tonight, the battle nightmare did not recur. It never would again.

23 |Jury of Peers

The unlocked back door provided the man easy access, but the screen door hinge screeched. The man of the house, still fully dressed, though it was after midnight, interrupted his reading of a book in the living room and entered the kitchen. He carried his shotgun pointed at the stranger's chest.

The trespasser backed slowly out the screen door. He held his hands up in the backyard, told a story about his horse going lame, and asked the homeowner to please lower the shotgun. The cowboy drew and fired twice as soon as the farmer pointed the scattergun at the ground.

The trailhand hadn't counted on a neighbor who cantered by on the way home from the saloon. The witness looked up precisely as the murderer pulled his gun. The Pima County Sheriff arrested the suspect within the hour, and the cowhand sat in the county jail for two months. A jury of twelve men in Tucson deliberated for thirty-three minutes and found the drifter not guilty based on his self-defense testimony, despite the neighbor's account that the homeowner's shotgun could not have been construed as threatening in any way.

The outlaw learned that day that he could carry out his quest with impunity among the sympathizers of southern Arizona. The trial scared the jailbird enough that he became highly cautious with subsequent murders. More surreptitious in his hunt, he became isolated, introverted, and angrier in his daily activities.

24 |Hanna Cries

The weather the last week in April turned summer-like. Temperatures climbed into the seventies on the San Francisco Peaks. The cabin became unbearable. Hanna packed a lunch basket and rang the triangle at two o'clock to alert Zachary.

When he approached with Chica by his side, Lobo, loping along twenty feet behind, he asked, "What's up, Mother?"

"We're all heading down to the supply station. I've got a basket of food for lunch. We'll spend the afternoon in the valley, in the cool shade of that big Ponderosa Pine next to the springs."

"Oh, Mommy," Sarah said. "Can I maybe get a licorice stick at the station?"

"We'll see, daughter."

"I won't argue with you, mother," said Zachary. "I'll leave Lobo in the cabin. The sheep will keep a while."

Down in the valley, the Brennans made their way toward the springs. Hanna stopped at the station and gave Josh her list of the necessary sundries. Steve Pembroke was away at least until late afternoon, according to Josh.

Hungry from the valley trek, the family devoured the sausage, bread, and cheese lunch.

The water running from the spring was ice cold and delicious to drink. After lunch, Sarah splashed her teasing brother as he ran up close to the stream. Hanna lay on a blanket, resting momentarily from a life of motherhood and ranch ownership.

Zach took Chica to the field and sailed her beat-up tin plate toy far afield for her to retrieve. On half the throws, Chica overtook the spinning disk, jumping and catching the saucer in her teeth as it spun through the air. Always, Chica returned to her master with the plate and dropped it at his feet, barking for him to throw it again.

Steve Pembroke ambled up to the Brennan family, "Hello Hanna, Zach, Sarah," he said. "Looks like you all found a way to beat this heat."

"Hi, Steve," said Hanna, sitting on a rock.

"Josh has your supplies ready," said Steve. "No hurry, of course."

"We better start back soon. Hopefully, everything will fit in my basket."

"If not, I have a knapsack back at the station if you need it."

Zachary approached. "Any more news from the East, Steve?" he asked.

For an answer, Steve turned his back to Zachary, walked over to the stream bank, plucked a green weed out of its stalk, and began chewing on the twenty-inch stem. Hanna sensed his reluctance. "What's wrong, Steve," she said. "Did the fighting start up again?"

"No, but I found out yesterday that on April $14^{th,}$ an assassin shot Lincoln. The President attended a play at Ford's Theater in Washington, D.C. He died, Hanna, Abraham Lincoln is dead."

"No, that can't be," Hanna began to rant. "After everything he has done, the dangers he has skirted in the last four years of war, how can this be." She sat down on the rock again. Shortly she began to cry, breaking into huge sobs; short of breath, she said, "How could someone kill that great man."

"I know Hanna," Steve said, "hard to believe."

"The $14^{th,}$ you say, Steve. That would mean while we celebrated, Abe Lincoln had already…."

"Yes!"

"When will this damn war truly end."

Late that night, Hanna couldn't sleep. Sitting on the edge of the bed, she reached underneath and picked up the book that lay out of sight. *Lorenzo's favorite, a Tale of Two Cities,* dogeared from multiple readings. The small table near the stove held one of his pipes. Hanna picked it up to smell the tobacco. On the wall near the dishpan hung a turquoise trinket Lorenzo had obtained for Hanna in a trade with a Mohave warrior near the Colorado River.

Still wide awake, Hanna set her candle on the table, grabbed a pen, ink, and paper, and wrote:

May 5th, 1865

Lorenzo,

News of Lee's Confederate Army surrender at Appomattox has reached our valley. It would seem safe to write to you now in the care of Fort Union. I hope this letter finds you.

Then, we heard of the assassination of our President, Abraham Lincoln, which thwarted our relief and joy at the probable end of the war.

As you know, I have been one of his most ardent supporters. I kept up with his policies regarding the war, especially the Proclamation of Emancipation that set slaves free in the southern states.

These past three years, I have believed that the two tall men in my life (you and Lincoln) have been righteous in your perseverance to win this war. I have focused on the farm, Zachary and Sarah. I have kept the emptiness in my heart due to your absence at bay.

As I thought of our great President tonight, I allowed myself to unravel a bit. Tonight, overwhelmed, I wept for a man I had never met. The hundreds of thousands of men who died in the conflict caused tears tonight. Tonight, I cried for you, my dearest, with a choking hope and plea that you are alive. I sobbed for Jeremiah.

I have such hope for Zachary. He'll be fourteen in five months, but he has displayed the strength and fortitude of a man full-grown. Since Abelardo died last September, Zach has accomplished the work of two men with never a complaint. When Bandit wandered off to die two winters ago, Zachary searched but never found him.

He still keeps up with his studies. With your help, I hope to fund all the books he will need to become a lawyer, like Abe Lincoln. That's how smart he is.

Sarah helps in the garden and with the canning. She is prettier than me but a more likable little girl than I have ever known.

I feel better for having written about my melancholy. I'll be able to sleep now.

Lorenzo, come home to me, my love. Come hold me. Renew my strength.

With love forever,

Hanna

***

The spring shearing dispelled all thoughts of a hoped-for homecoming of Lorenzo. Now, as fast at shearing as Hanna, Zachary helped her finish the sixty-eight sheep within a week. Zach then tended the fire beneath the boiling pot, swinging the beam that held the cast iron crock over to Sarah's station for scrubbing the fleece. The other end of the shaft held a second pot. Zach first dumped the dirty water and fetched clean water from the spring to heat over the fire. Sarah helped Hanna with the shearing scrub.

While the skins dried, Zachary left for the valley and worked on the summer hay planting. Hanna spent another week dying half the fleeces blue, her trademark wool color. While Zach worked the field, Hanna carded the wool. Sarah had her miniature carding station to work at. Mother and daughter carded wool halfway into June. Then Hanna commenced spinning the wool into yarn.

Zachary, meanwhile, had turned the garden ground in the small meadow behind the cabin next to the spring. Sarah helped plant seeds.

The shepherd sent the sheep to the upper meadow in shifts in the morning and afternoon. Chica took over once the sheep began grazing and ensured they did not wander. Zach could return to the garden work while the sheep grazed.

The glorious summer days on the mountain always filled Hanna with inner warmth. The mountain strived to please her; pastel wildflowers were abundant, and many green-hued leaves and red and purple berries were at her feet. The sky, light blue when the sun rose and dark blue in the afternoon as it descended behind the peaks, set off the exquisite colors in the forest surrounding Hanna. Her world.

For Zachary, work seemed more rewarding in pleasant weather. He appreciated the warmth in his muscles, never minded the sweat in the hollow of his back, and drank the chilly water from the spring for refreshment. He often stopped to watch Chica running across the field, her mottled grey/blue coat flashing. The soft white and burnt sienna behind her flews whipped in the wind to the rhythm of her run. Each evening after supper and barn chores, he sat on the edge of the cabin porch and combed burrs from her coat. Chica licked his face, patiently enduring the occasional ouch from the comb. His world.

In late August, the days turned to swelter. Taking a break, Zach bathed in a two-foot-deep pool provided by the spring near the upper meadow. Naked, refreshed, and air-dried, he dressed and returned to work in the garden.

Hanna looked in the mirror over the wash basin on the dresser. She flipped her hair across her chest and brushed it to a soft natural wave. Then she pinned it up and threaded a green ribbon around the knot to match her skirt. Her blouse clung to the top of her breasts due to the summer heat. *Today?*

Around three o'clock, Lorenzo spotted the cabin in the distance. He waited as long as he could, "Hanna," he yelled, "Hanna are you there?"

In the cabin, Hanna turned her head. Had she heard his voice, or was she daydreaming again?

Then she heard Lorenzo plainly, "Hanna, Hanna!"

Hanna looked to the door, then thought a second and ran back to the mirror and her brush, picking it up and quickly setting it aside. *I'm OK!*

She rushed out the door. Only twenty feet from her husband now, she stopped on the lip of the top step, holding the porch post tight so as not to faint. With a breathless choke, she could not think where to start. “Lorenzo,” she said.

Lorenzo stopped on the second stair, his face even with hers. “My love,” he said.

Hanna dissolved into his embrace, every inch of her filling the spaces between them. Reacquainting her body with his. Broad shoulders, a tall frame, slim, but not as thin as she had imagined. He looked fit. More handsome than Hanna remembered. His face seemed just a bit wider.

The first thing Lorenzo zeroed in on when he saw Hanna was the wisps of gray setting off her raven black hair at her temples. He couldn’t have imagined how gray would make a woman more beautiful, but it did. He brushed it to the back of her ear. Her hair gleamed in the sun, silky and managed. He hugged her again, stepped back, and noticed the small lines at the corner of her eyes. He knew his forty-seven-year-old face looked older by five years after living in the rough for so many years. *How did she become more beautiful?*

Trim, with full, middle-aged breasts shoving her blouse, Lorenzo felt instant heat below his belt. He kissed his wife with a passion held back these past three years.

Sarah heard a man calling her mother’s name and climbed down from the tree house. She turned the corner of the cabin. Running to her mother, she stopped three yards away from the couple. *Who’s kissing Momma?*

“This is your father, Sarah,” said Hanna. “He’s come home to us.”

Sarah inched forward. Lorenzo kneeled and reached out a hand to his daughter. Hanna placed her hand on Sarah’s back and gently pushed her forward. Sarah reached out, and Lorenzo engulfed her outstretched hand with both hands and gave her a slow, firm handshake. He wanted to pick her up, crush her, and smell her skin and hair. He did not. She and Lorenzo would bond again in time. Hanna, in her letter, had been accurate. Sarah was beautiful.

Hanna fixed a pot of tea. "Sarah," she said. "Please fetch Zachary, will you? Tell him his father has come home." After Sarah left, Lorenzo stood and pulled his wife to him again. He couldn't get enough of her. Hanna finally shrugged him away to pour the tea. "Tonight, husband, tonight," she said.

A knock on the door interrupted Lorenzo's ardor. Hanna opened the door. A young man, inches shorter than either Lorenzo or Zachary, stood on the porch, hat in hand.

"Good afternoon, Mrs. Brennan," said the man.

***

Lorenzo had ridden up to the supply station with another rider on a sorrel. The two dismounted, and Lorenzo dug out his shaving kit from Arrow's saddlebag. He stepped into the supply station to visit for a brief time with his friend Steve Pembroke. The second man stayed on the porch, sitting in one of the rocking chairs.

While reacquainting with Steve, Lorenzo stood over the station wash basin and shaved for a second time that day. "We'll catch up later, Steve," said Lorenzo. "Right now, I'm itching to see Hanna."

"Certainly, Lorenzo, she will be relieved you are home."

"Steve, I have a friend on the porch, Kyle Cantor. Could you give him something to eat and send him to the cabin in an hour?"

***

"Hanna, Meet Kyle Cantor," said Lorenzo.

A bit startled, Hanna invited the stranger to sit for tea.

"Kyle served with me these last six months. I thought he could stay in Abelardo's room in the barn if you would allow."

"Certainly," said Hanna, "pleased to meet you, Kyle." Hanna sat down opposite the two men. She guessed Kyle might be about an inch taller than herself. He had reddish blond hair and acne running down the left side of his face from cheekbone to chin. The right side of his face appeared clear and smooth. Less than six hairs sprouted from his jaw. He had the makings of a handsome man once he made it through his awkward growth years.

Hanna couldn't help commenting, "You seem young, Kyle."

"Signed up last year when I turned seventeen, Ma'am," Kyle said. "Your husband saved me from an Apache arrow four months ago. I stood up to tamp my rifle, and Captain Lorenzo pulled me back just in time. The arrow thudded the tree next to my ear."

Lorenzo sensed Hanna's unease. "Kyle, I'll take you over to the barn. Show you where to bunk."

"Fine, Captain," said Kyle

"When you hear the triangle, supper will be ready," said Hanna.

Hanna stood, the two men rose to leave, the cabin door opened, and Zachary walked in, Sarah hiding behind her brother. Chica bounded in next, then Lobo.

Excited to see his father, Zachary didn't know what to make of the stranger beside him. *Short.*

"Hello, Father," said Zachary. "Been a long time. Will you stay long, or must you return to the fort?

Lorenzo, taken aback at his boy's height and question, grabbed the back of the chair, blood draining from his arms and legs, suddenly cold. *Where did that come from?*

Lorenzo said when he found his voice, "Hello Zachary, you look… You've grown."

"As I said, it's been a while, " Zachary said.

"Lorenzo," said Hanna, "What is your plan." She hadn't considered the possibility that Lorenzo would visit and not stay, but Zachary had been wise to ask.

"Why, I'm home, Hanna. The war is over; at least, it is for my unit. My men and I have mustered out."

Hanna hugged her husband in relief. "Then everything else will be fine," she said.

Zachary approached Lorenzo and shook his hand. "Great to have you home, Father," he said. Then he turned to the stranger. "My name is Zachary."

"This is Kyle," said Lorenzo. "Kyle Cantor. You could show him Abelardo's room in the barn."

"Sure," said Zachary, "follow me. Chica, come." Zachary led the way to the barn, gathering the reins of the taller horse, obviously his father's. "What's your name, I wonder," he said.

Kyle led his horse while Lobo scampered around, vying for Kyle's attention. "That's Arrow, a hell of a horse. This one I call 'Kicker,' and he will if you don't watch out."

"Good to know," said Zachary.

After bedding down the horses, Zachary led the way upstairs to Abelardo's room. Memories swept over the boy. He had often visited Abelardo in his room for Spanish lessons, advice, and conversation.

"Wow," said Kyle. "This is the nicest place I've stayed since I left home."

Zachary thought of many questions, "You and my father must have seen many soldiers die."

"Not really," said Kyle. "When I joined, The Union troops had driven the Texans out of the territory. Captain's unit spied under orders in Indian Territory and Arkansas. One skirmish with Indians might have cost me my scalp if it hadn't been for Captain Brennan."

"So, you shot Indians, mostly," Zachary said.

"I shot at Indians. Not sure I ever hit one. Your dad kept us out of sticky situations. He's someone you want around in a skirmish, that's sure. A crack shot too."

"Yes, I know."

"How about you, Zachary? What's your preference? I'd give anything to get a hold of a Henry Repeating rifle."

"No, sorry, I don't shoot. What will you do now that the war is over?"

Kyle blinked and turned away to open his satchel. He decided to drop that subject and asked, "How old are you, Zach? Can I call you Zach?"

"Sure, people do. I'll be fourteen in September."

"The Captain and I talked about me helping your family on the ranch here. He heard about your Mexican dying. I could give you a hand.'

"Help I could get used to," said Zachary.

Husband and wife tiptoed about the cabin after supper that night as if they had just met. After such a long absence, Lorenzo decided that sudden moves toward his wife would be inconsiderate. Hanna kept thinking about the strange young man her husband had brought home. She had dreamed about her family together in work and play on her beloved ranch, free of war worries.

Lorenzo picked up the pipe off the stove table and sat on the porch rocker smoking. It didn't help; he remained nervous as a cat watching a stranger approach. Hanna quickly dressed in her clean nightshirt, folding the top wool blanket back across the foot of the bed.

"Coming to bed, Lorenzo?" she asked.

"Ummm..." she heard from the porch. "Be there in a minute."

The night breeze had cooled the cabin, yet Lorenzo still sweated. He was torn between ultimate desire and respect for what he had put his wife through. He dressed for bed and lay next to her.

"Goodnight, Hanna," he said.

Hanna turned to him and crossed his chest with an arm, moving to a position of closeness. Lorenzo encircled Hanna with his right arm, and neither moved for minutes. Lorenzo thought her asleep. *Just as well.*

But Hanna stretched and kissed her husband lightly on his cheek. The coals smoldering in Lorenzo ignited. Soon, Hanna's ache and Lorenzo's burn crested, dissolving the torture of their separation, eventually turning into peace for both.

Sarah became a binding member of the family. She quickly became reaccustomed to her father's embrace, listening to him read *The King of the Golden River.* Sometimes he made up stories of leprechauns and fairies. During story time, Hanna worked at her loom, and Zach studied at the table. The connection between Sarah and his father looked so natural to Zachary that he couldn't help smiling. He could barely remember when he had been Sarah's age, imagining the little golden dwarf. These were sublime times for a family shrugging off the war years.

As September tipped into October, winter preparations predominated the work schedule at the ranch. With Kyle pitching in, Zachary appreciated the relief from the pressures of Abelardo's passing. Hanna had divided the chores equitably between Zach and Kyle. Lorenzo managed repairs and coordinated the work between the two hands. Hanna wove. Sarah continued with her schooling.

Kyle had to learn about sheep ranching. Zach could see that the young man learned quickly and worked hard. He sought to adopt the Brennan family as his own. Hanna discovered that

Kyle's father had taken to the bottle in the years leading up to the war. Kyle joined the territorial militia the day before his mother left to live with her sister in Kansas. He had never heard from her since.

Zachary surmised that Lorenzo had found a replacement for Jeremiah. Hanna realized it as well. As far as Hanna could tell, Lorenzo had reconciled with Zachary. Zach and Kyle got along as two hands would on a ranch. Yet, she could still appreciate the distance Zachary maintained from Lorenzo.

Over the war years, Zachary had pieced together the differences between Jeremiah and himself in his father's eyes. He wasn't Jeremiah and never would be.

A month after Lorenzo returned from the war, he and Kyle went on a three-day hunting trip and bagged a doe, bringing it home dressed. Lorenzo hadn't even asked Zach to come along.

Hanna could see that Lorenzo remained embarrassed about leaving the ranch work to Zach while he resolved his demons on the battlefield. A thaw would take time as each learned to respect the other beyond their father/son relationship.

In the meantime, Hanna kept Zach focused on his studies and dreams.

At fourteen, Zach had lived long enough without a father that he felt comfortable in his skin. He knew he could never be like Jeremiah or Kyle. When the time came, he would leave the ranch. Start a new life.

25 |Blacksmith

Patches of dirty snow littered the corners of the Santa Fe streets, heavy snowfall becoming less of a concern now that March had arrived. The blacksmith/foreman took charge. He rechecked both wagons parked in front of the Timmerman Storage Warehouse on Capital Avenue. The front gates of Fort Marcy on the west side of Santa Fe were within waving distance of the warehouse. The lumber and supplies for the new station seemed secure for the bumpy ride down Beale Wagon Road. Two carpenters the foreman hired to build the outpost climbed on the first wagon. The laborer and Eli climbed up to the buckboard on the second wagon. A man ran down Lincoln Ave. toward the blacksmith, waving a letter. Eli Blackstone stuffed the letter in a pocket and yelled, "Gid-yup, mules, Git."

February 21, 1866

Father,

Your new job as the manager and blacksmith for a swing station in the Arizona Territory sounds exciting. I hope the building project at the site the company chose goes well. Wells Fargo & Company seems pretty progressive. I'm sure a stagecoach route between Santa Fe and Prescott, the new capital of the Arizona Territory, will thrive.

I trust you will invite me to visit soon, although I cannot find Diablo Canyon in the Arizona Territory on maps here at the school. Regardless, what an opportunity for you.

This first semester of classes has been as exciting as it is challenging. Aunt Colleen has been a gracious host. Extremely strict, but I stay focused on my goal to be one of the first women accountants to graduate from Oberlin College. We both have the opportunities of a lifetime. Thank God the war is over. The freedom we dreamed of for our brothers and sisters in the south has been realized.

I look forward to my graduation and joining you on the frontier. I am confident I can put my skills to practical use in that newly developing land.

Oh, how I miss you,
Love,
Your daughter Eliza

***

By the summer of '66, Kyle could hold his own as a skilled shepherd. The shearing went well in the spring. The three men on the Brennan ranch turned and replanted the hay fields. They turned their attention to the garden, completing the seeding and starting the root vegetables.

The flock grew in count enough that Hanna and Lorenzo decided the stock should use the lower valley for grazing to allow the upper meadow time to regenerate. Hanna divided the sheep into two flocks. Kyle took half the sheep down in the morning, and Zachary guided the other half to the valley in the afternoon.

Lobo gravitated to the easy-going new hand. Neither took the other seriously. Through Kyle's coaxing and patience, Lobo quickened his response to orders.

It took seven months for Kyle to discover the headstones in the far corner of the upper meadow. Abelardo's, he understood, the timing obvious. The other monument for Jeremiah Brennan struck him as curious. He had noticed the Brennans trekking up to the meadow. Not as a group but individually. Now, if Kyle noticed Zachary or Hanna starting up the trail to the field when he could figure no requirement to do so, he followed. Sure enough, Hanna just stood by the headstone a while and then descended the trail back to the cabin. Zachary did the same.

Kyle noted that Lorenzo visited the site more often than either Hanna or Zach and spent more time there. The first time he followed Lorenzo, he discovered Captain on his knees, weeping at the marker. He never shadowed his boss again. Kyle even caught Sarah running up the trail, picking wildflowers and scattering them across the grave mounds.

It seemed strange to Kyle that no one in the family spoke of Jeremiah; they didn't go up to the meadow together.

Lorenzo talked Hanna into expanding the ranch by buying and raising more sheep. He proposed growing the additional sheep solely for slaughter. If the wool sheep stock increased, Hanna would need to hire a second spinner and weaver. She did not oppose Lorenzo's ideas. More business meant more profit and the ability to send Zachary and, eventually, Sarah to college: her dream.

The Pembroke Supply Station near Leroux Spring still provided the Brennan ranch with world news. The family joined occasional social activities when a wagon train camped in the valley for a day or two. A single Conestoga wagon often rolled by, ready to stake out a homestead on public land in California.

Kyle spent his half day off work at the ranch on Sunday afternoons, riding down to the valley and visiting with Josh at the supply station. Sometimes he volunteered to help Josh behind the counter or tidy up the warehouse. He also enjoyed showing new immigrants the best places to camp and accessing the water from the springs.

Gregarious in nature, Kyle met young people his age this way. He often participated in gatherings around campfires where stories and music livened his life.

One Sunday, a group of three wagons rolled past the supply station. Playing a game of canasta with Josh, Kyle set down his cards and hurried out the door. He noticed the four occupants of the second wagon, a man about his age, a boy younger than Zach (or at least shorter), and two young ladies. They all waved at Kyle. He smiled and waved back. Then the lead wagon stopped. The other two wagons stopped as well.

Kyle nonchalantly stepped down from the porch. He walked up to the middle wagon, where all the occupants were evacuating the wagon and stretching.

"Are you people thinking of stopping here for the night?" Kyle asked.

"Jason's in charge," said the man with curly hair. "He's in the first wagon."

"If you're stopping, I can show you the best camp spot near the springs."

"He's coming back this way," said the curly-haired redhead. "Ask him."

Kyle spent the evening with the Sorensen family from Alabama. The former militiaman made no mention of the war and his affiliation. He assumed the Sorensen family were confederate sympathizers, but the ladies were pretty, and the men seemed in good humor. Kyle helped all three wagons set up camp. The Sorensens asked him to stay for dinner.

Mr. Walcott, the wagonmaster, indicated they would need another day in camp to rest and fill all the water jugs for the dessert crossing. Kyle left the group for the ranch around ten o'clock, hoping he could talk Zach into coming down the mountain with him the next night to the Sorensen's sing-along.

Over the porridge and berry breakfast, Kyle broached the subject, "How about it, Zach, after you bring up the sheep, I'll help with the stalls, and we could ride down together. There are at least two in the group about your age. What do you say?"

Zachary only ventured away from the ranch on errands for Hanna to pick up and order supplies. He would take the opportunity to read any newsworthy items Steve Pembroke posted on the station bulletin board. Zach would look through Steve's pile of out-of-date newspapers as well. "All right," he said, "I'll go."

The two shepherds entered after tying up Arrow and Kicker (Kyle's horse) at the supply station. Kyle sauntered to the counter where Josh recorded inventory in Steve's catalog. Zach gravitated to the bulletin board. None of the new bulletins were of interest. Instead, he read an old yellowing notice in the upper right corner. The language in the text seemed lawyerly, which Zach thought would fascinate his mother. The small type and minute detail discouraged passing immigrants.

The notice presented another path to future independence for Zach, who was not yet fifteen. He asked Josh for a pen and paper and jotted down a summary of the information to show his parents.

The Homestead Act

Approved on May 20, 1862, and signed by President Abraham Lincoln.

THIRTY-SEVENTH CONGRESS
Sess. II Ch. 75 1862

An Act to secure Homestead to actual Settlers on Public Domain. ... That any person who is the head of a family, or who has arrived at the age of twenty-one years, and is a citizen of the United States, or who shall have filed his declaration intention to become such, as required by the naturalization laws of the United States, and who has never borne arms against the United States Government or given aid and comfort to its enemies, shall, from and after the first January, eighteen hundred and sixty-three, be entitled to enter one-quarter section... subject to preemption at one dollar and twenty-five cents, or less, per acre ...

SEC. 2. ... and upon filing the said affidavit with register or receiver, and on payment of ten dollars, he or she shall thereupon be permitted to enter the quantity of land specified: Provided, however, that no certificate shall be given or patent issued therefor until the expiration of five years from the date of such entry...

Kyle shouldered Zach away from the board, and the two left the station, heading for the wagon camp. He waved at John Sorensen and walked to the campfire, introducing Zach to everyone around the fire.

"We're from Alabama, Zach. How long have you been out here?" said John.

"Born here, up the mountain," Zach said.

"Big family?" asked the girl Kyle called 'Suze.'

"Father, mother, and younger sister, Sarah."

"And a brother that passed," said Kyle. "Right?"

"Yes, my older brother, Jeremiah. Five years ago."

"I'm sorry," said Suze. "You were close, I take it."

"We did most everything together," said Zach. Only the crackling fire broke the forest's quiet surrounding the wagons and gathered family.

John Sorensen dug into his pants, bringing out his harmonica. He trilled the length of it and began playing *Oh! Suzanna*. Voices scattered around the campfire joined in. Zach glanced over at the supply station. He mouthed the chorus politely, smiling through the vision in his head of the blood-stained porch and the wide-open dead eyes of his brother.

***

Hanna was very interested in Zach's report on the 1862 Homestead Act. One night after dinner, she urged Lorenzo to sit down with Zachary. She asked Zachary to show Lorenzo his notes.

"Lorenzo, I think we should pursue this," she said.

"Why? No one bothers us here. No one objects to our ranch or competes with our grazing fields," said Lorenzo.

Zachary remained quiet. He had already worked through the ramifications of the act to the ranch's future. He let his mother present the argument.

"Lorenzo, didn't the Whipple expedition survey the valley?"

"They did," said Lorenzo, "and the Beale expedition did too. The surveys covered fifty feet on either side of the road line. There are markers."

"So, the ranch is technically on land surveyed by the government."

"Yes, for a railroad. So far, I know of no immediate plan for a railroad."

"Don't you see? According to this homestead act, we could acquire a deed to this land."

"But why, Hanna? One dollar and twenty-five cents an acre is more money than we have. That's two hundred dollars. We could use the money to expand the herd. No one is going to bother us on the mountain. The valley is big enough for fifty settlers."

Zachary and Chica eventually trundled off to bed. Zach knew Hanna's plan would move forward before the last lantern was extinguished. Zach drifted to sleep, pondering the possibility of owning a ranch. *After I have seen Paris.*

26 |Swing

The man had been on the trail from the north for five days. Fourteen months had passed since the trial in Tucson, and he needed a drink. He had a five-day-old scruffy beard and happened to ride by a house just beyond the edge of town where a boy, judged to be about six years old, was sitting on an old swing. The ropes for the swing hung from the barn wench rail. That night the trail bum rode by the house four times in both directions.

He noted that three of them lived there, presumably husband and wife and the six-year-old.

Unable to control his excitement and under cover of the half-moon night, the stranger crept up to the house. He fired four times through an open bedroom window, moved to the next window, and shot the boy as he scrambled out of bed after hearing the other room's gunfire and screams. The man returned to the first window. Noticing a slight movement on the far side of the bed, he cocked the trigger and fired again. No movement. No sound. The stranger mounted his horse less than a minute after the first shot. He made it beyond the county line by daybreak.

27 |Help Wanted

Two men pushed through the door of the newly finished swing station, one of thirty stops on the run from Santa Fe, New Mexico, to Prescott, the Arizona territorial capital. The wranglers fed the horses and mucked the stalls. They stomped off the snow from their boots, hung up their overcoats, and Eli Blackstone stoked the stove.

Darcy Franklin flopped into the wing chair facing the fire. As the heat began to radiate, Eli took to the rocking chair, tapping tobacco on a rolling paper.

"I think you're in pretty good shape here, Eli," Darcy said.

"Yup," said Eli, "The miner's shack on the property helped the timeline. All we had to add was the bunkroom, the horse barn, and the stable. Of course, we don't have enough stock yet, but I'll wait until spring hits to worry. When did the boss say he hoped to start freight and passengers?"

"April," said Darcy. "Will you have hired someone by then, do you think? We're allowed two grooms, right?"

"Yeah," said Eli, "you'd think there would be men looking for work, but I've had trouble. How about you?"

"Haven't had any trouble at all. My station is close to Prescott, though; that might be the difference. Pretty isolated here."

"The Pembroke Supply Station is only forty miles west of here," said Eli. I'll put a posting there. The wagons roll through the San Francisco Peaks often, I hear."

Both men were from Ohio, blacksmiths both, and longtime friends. Eli's wife died the first year of the war, leaving Eli to care for their only daughter. Darcy, who still ran single, heard about the Wells Fargo station keeper positions in the New Mexico territory. With the war in full swing, both men spent the rest in Denver, training and planning for the Prescott-Santa Fe stage line.

The two fixed dinner; steak, beans, johnnycakes, and honey. After supper, they smoked cigars and sipped bourbon around the stove. They reminisced about bars they had closed back in Cincinnati.

As Darcy prepared to leave the following day for his station, #28, he snapped his fingers. "Almost forgot, the office has been holding a letter for you." Rooting in one saddle bag and then another, Darcy pulled out an envelope and handed it to Eli. "We'll communicate from now on by carrier letter, Eli," said Darcy. "Don't be a stranger."

Eli watched his friend ride off. On the rise, Darcy turned his horse back and waved. Eli waved back, the loneliness of the swing station already closing in. Two more months before the line opened up in April. The blacksmith/station keeper contemplated posting a job listing at trading posts along the Beale Wagon Road and the Pembroke Supply Station near Leroux Springs. He picked up the letter off the table, sat down to open it, and began reading.

January 8, 1867

Father,

Happy New Year.
I waited to write this letter until I knew what grades I received this past semester. I received A's in Algebra and

Accounting I. B's in the rest, including English Grammar, the first course I truly disliked.

I understand that you completed all your building projects in your last letter. The management team in Omaha must surely be impressed.

It troubles me that you are finding it challenging to hire the help you need to run the station. If worse comes to worst, I'll come out and help. I'm only half kidding.

Since my mother is gone, I must tell you that I have met a boy who has expressed interest in me. Aunt Colleen watches him closely in the parlor when he visits, so please do not worry.

I will stay focused on my studies and eventually travel west to join you. Peter is the exact opposite of you, father. A bit weak in the knees, if you know what I mean.

I'm looking forward to Accounting 2 this semester.

Your loving daughter,

Eliza

28 |Breaking Ties That Bind

The hunting trips shared by Lorenzo and Kyle became frequent. Lorenzo took venison steaks that the Brennan family couldn't eat down to Steve Pembroke before they spoiled. Sometimes an immigrant family would arrive when Lorenzo delivered the meat. Lorenzo generously divided the food between Steve and the travelers in those cases.

Whenever the hunters wandered away from the ranch on a two or three-day hunt, Zachary had to pick up all the work they left behind. He didn't resent Kyle for Lorenzo's attention, except for the extra work laid upon him due to their absence.

Lorenzo never pushed the hunting experience on Zachary. He realized his son's limitations in that regard. Zachary had strengths that Lorenzo did admire. He worked hard and studied hard. Smart. But he enjoyed Kyle's company. They spoke of the war, Indians, and living rough on the trail for months. Gambling. Asshole officers and likable fellow soldiers, alive and dead.

Hanna sensed the distance between her husband and Zachary. Whether she or Lorenzo could admit it, Zachary no longer wore knee pants. Despite his young age, he was a war child who had grown inside into a man. She believed time would soften the harder edges of their relationship, shortening the gap between them.

For now, Hanna kept Zach's focus on the future possibilities his intelligence afforded him. She spoke of college, suggesting the family could afford Kansas State Agricultural School. Or, with a scholarship, Zach might attend an eastern school, Columbia Law School in New York, for instance.

The snow melted off the mountain in the third week of March. Hanna made a list of staples, and Zachary hiked down to Pembroke's Supply Station to place the order.

Zachary walked up to the counter. Josh, shaking his head, gestured at the man standing by the bulletin board, affixing a notice in a space in the middle of the board.

"What do you need, Zach," said Josh.

"Got a list for an order on Steve's next run to Albuquerque," said Zach.

The man at the board turned to look at Zach, tipping his Stetson. Curly black hair evaded the hat around the man's ears. Not as tall as Zachary, but stocky. Barrel chested. Giant, strong hands. Smartly dressed, the man didn't smile, didn't scowl.

Something compelled Zach to walk over and offer his hand, to Josh's curious chagrin. "My name is Zachary Brennan, sir; I live up the mountain," said Zach. "Whenever I come down to order supplies, I check out the board."

"My name is Eli Blackstone, son," said the man, offering his own. A more powerful hand Zachary had never experienced. The man shook firmly without crushing Zach's hand, which Zach decided he could have done effortlessly.

"I'm looking for a horse handler. I guess you can read about it in the bulletin," said the man. Eli Blackstone stepped aside so that Zach, knitting his brow, could examine the notice.

The first bulletin Zach noticed described the murder of a family by an unidentified wanderer in the Prescott area. Then Zachary read the notice explaining the horse handler position at the Sunset Crossing swing station.

"Sunset Crossing, about forty miles east on Beale Wagon Road, isn't it?"

"That's right."

"Wells Fargo. I've heard of the company. I don't remember anything but desert at that point on the way to Albuquerque or Santa Fe."

"I guess you haven't been over that way in a while."

"True enough."

"I've built up a swing station there. The first stagecoach will be coming through after the first of April, on the way to Prescott."

"Will coaches be stopping here at Leroux Spring?"

"Not yet. Someday maybe, sooner than later, I expect."

Blackstone broke off and stepped over to the counter. "Got any jerky I could use for the trip back?" he asked.

Josh didn't look up, "Sorry, mister, not at present."

The statement startled Zachary. *Steve always had jerky on hand.*

"Josh," said Zachary, "Can I have four hardtack pieces, please? I'm famished."

"Just a minute," said Josh, walking into the back room and returning with the hardtack in a sack.

"Mr. Blackstone," said Zachary. "It's a sunny day. We could sit out on the porch. I'd like to hear more about the stagecoach run Wells Fargo is starting."

On the porch, Zachary gave two of the biscuits to Eli, saying, "I don't know what the deal is; I've never known them to be out of jerky before. Anyway, take a couple of these for your trip home." He split a third biscuit in two, handing half to Mr. Blackstone.

"How old are you, Zachary?" Eli asked.

"I'll be sixteen in September," Zachary said.

"Big for your age, I guess. You seem capable of handling yourself."

"I worked the sheep ranch for over three years while my father fought with the New Mexico Militia. I grew up fast during the war, like everyone else."

The burly man nodded, "How is your family now? Did your father make it home? Sorry, I apologize for asking."

"That's all right. Father did. A captain and scout for General Canby and others. He's home now."

"I don't suppose you could break away from the ranch to help me out. I posted a horse handler/groom listing, but you could apprentice with me. The blacksmith trade can provide opportunity, postwar."

"How much would you pay; I plan on attending college someday."

"I have been able to send my daughter to college with the wages I make smithing, and Wells Fargo pays very well. The poster says the job includes room and board, so your wages can go right in the First National Bank of Omaha."

Zachary stood and stepped off the porch. Chica jumped off simultaneously, assuming her master was ready to head home. Zach paced as Eli Blackstone watched and smiled. After three minutes, Zach came back to the porch.

"I need to speak to my parents, but I'm sold on the idea," said Zachary.

"Listen, I will continue to Aspen Spring and pin up one more flyer. I'll be back here in two days. We'll travel back to Sunset Crossing together if you take the job. Otherwise, you're a pleasant young man to have met."

"Thanks for the opportunity, Mr. Blackstone. I'll be waiting here."

On the long walk home, Zach thought about leaving. He had as yet never brought up the subject with Hanna or Lorenzo. Hanna would say he was too young. Lorenzo would say the ranch needed his help, especially with Lorenzo's plans for expansion.

Kyle didn't seem to be going anywhere. Hanna wanted Zachary to attend college, but that was a slim dream.

Blacksmith apprentice. Respectable, challenging work. Could Zach manage it? Once committed, there would be no recourse. He could save enough money to attend college in three or four years. That would be a good argument for Hanna. In Jeremiah's absence, Hanna might balk at her other son leaving. Could he stand firm and insist? Or would he fold?

What opportunities had Zachary ever seen posted on the board? The answer was one, Blackstone's horse handler position. Zach enjoyed horses and not just riding. He and Arrow had a connection similar to what Zachary felt with Chica.

Could he leave Chica, the one constant in his life besides his mother? That would be hard. He couldn't take her with him. That wouldn't be fair to the ranch. *Chica. I'll miss you.*

Halfway home, Zach had convinced himself the Wells Fargo job provided a path to independence and a future away from the ranch.

But what if Lorenzo or Hanna forbid it? Zach, all of a sudden, couldn't give up the notion. But fighting with Hanna was equally distasteful. He would stand up to his father. Lorenzo had left the ranch for years. But it would be exceedingly difficult, if not impossible, to stand firm with Hanna.

Zachary decided that his best bet would be to do it. He would leave before sunrise, meet Eli Blackstone, ride to Sunset Crossing, and overcome whatever challenging work might greet him at the swing station. Then in a couple of weeks, he would send a letter to Hanna via a Beale Wagon Road traveler.

Zach warmed his suddenly cold hands with his armpits. The gigantic step he contemplated might alienate his family. Of course, since Jeremiah's death, he lived in an ethereal state of alienation anyway.

Chica ran ahead and tussled with Lobo near the porch. Zach climbed to his room in the cabin and quickly packed his meager belongings in a valise. Hanna didn't notice.

Zach climbed down from the loft and impulsively went over and kissed his mother on the cheek. Small talk. "Do you need any help, Mother?" he said.

'Why, thank you, Zach," said Hanna. "Go ahead and set the table. We're having venison steaks provided by Kyle tonight."

After dinner, Zach and Kyle worked the barn chores. Kyle noticed Zach's enthusiasm. "What's put the fire in your pants tonight, Zachary?" he said.

"Nothing special," said Zachary, "Maybe a big day tomorrow, who knows."

"Something went on down at Pembroke's. A girl passing through?" Zach did not respond. He did not notice the hard look Kyle gave him.

After the barn chores, Zachary spent an hour playing fetch-the-saucer with Chica rather than studying. He stayed up as long as he could, reading in bed by lamplight. After that, he couldn't sleep, going over his plan, the position with Wells Fargo, and the strange buffalo of a man he would be working with.

The pros, the cons. Would Zach ever get a chance at college? Would he go on to travel to New York, to Paris?

Zachary crept down the ladder and out of the cabin when the sky brightened over the valley. He headed over to the stable and began to saddle Arrow. Zach would send Arrow back with the same traveler that carried his letter of explanation to his mother. He double-checked the cinches.

"The girl you met at Pembroke's must have been pretty amazing. Looks like you're going for good," said Kyle, startling Zachary from the doorway to the stable.

"I didn't mean to wake anyone," said Zachary.

"No hope for that; the barn walls don't keep out the wind, let alone the noise you've been making. Are you going to let me in on the big secret?"

"Go back to bed, Kyle. This has nothing to do with you."

"So, you're leaving."

"I am. I've taken a job over at Sunset Crossing."

"Whoa, boy, I can't see Hanna taking too kindly to that. We should go over and talk to the folks."

"This is something I have to do, Kyle. You can work the ranch now with my father. You will all be fine."

Zachary strapped the valise on the back of the saddle. He started to lead Arrow out of the barn. Kyle, standing in the barn door opening, didn't move, effectively barring the way.

"I'm a bit older than you, Zachary. Not smarter, for sure, but older. You can't go off like this."

"I've decided this way is best. Out of the way."

Kyle stepped forward and swung, catching Zach's left cheek as Zachary turned to avoid Kyle's fist rushing toward him. Dazed, pinpricks of light dancing in front of his face, he went down. "Can't let you do this, Zachary. I know what you mean to them." Zachary stayed on his knees, shaking his head to clear the stars, his anger mounting to fury. When he stood, Kyle faced the released frustration of a dangerous man.

Zachary circled the older boy to the left, fists up, thumbs tucked, like Lorenzo had instructed the boys. He stopped, measuring Kyle and the opening on his left side. He started to circle counterclockwise, then threw two jabs with his left and a full-force punch with his right.

Surprised, even expecting it, Kyle never saw it coming. He went to one knee.

He was a veteran of a gruesome war. A man who had survived Rebel gunfire and Apache arrows. Kyle stood again and waded back in.

But Kyle didn't have the reach of the tall boy nor the technique. He soon backed away exhausted, blood streaming from his nose and a cut above his eye.

It ended. Kyle and Zach both gulped air, bent over at the waist, Kyle spitting blood. They both noticed Lorenzo leaning against the opening, trying not to smile. *My boy can fight.*

"What's going on here," said Lorenzo.

Catching his breath, Zachary finally said, "I've taken a job with Wells Fargo Stagecoach, Father. I'm leaving. I thought it would be easier on everyone if I just left. Kyle had a different opinion."

"Let's go get you two cleaned up," said Lorenzo. "Your mother might have input. First, shake on peace. The war is over."

Zachary and Kyle shook hands, Kyle adding his off-hand on top. "Where did you learn to fight like that," he said.

Zachary turned away and started for the cabin leading Arrow. "Jeremiah," he said to no one in particular.

Hanna washed and dressed the wounds in the cabin as Zachary explained the circumstances again. Hanna seemed at a loss for words.

"Hanna, by the look of things," Lorenzo offered, "I think Zachary has made up his mind about this job at the swing station."

"I can't just say yes. I need to think," said Hanna.

"No time, Mother," said Zachary. "I'm meeting the station keeper this morning at Pembroke's."

The family and Kyle were quiet for a time. Hanna was holding back tears. Dressed and ready for breakfast, Sarah wandered from one adult to the next, trying to catch up on the discussion.

After a long silence, Lorenzo, strangely, provided what seemed to Zachary a rational solution. "Look, Hanna, Sunset Crossing is not at the end of the earth," he said. "Zachary, Hanna, and I will travel to the swing station in four weeks, and Hanna can see for herself. If she disapproves, then you'll come home with no argument. There will be other opportunities. You are welcome, of course, anytime you wish or need to come home."

Hanna absorbed Lorenzo's logic and accepted the approach. That would give her time to organize a rebuttal and write to colleges. Should she worry about her fifteen-year-old leaving home? No. She knew how Zachary conquered arduous work; he would undoubtedly learn life lessons if nothing else.

"Agreed," she said.

Zach smiled, but only for seconds. He was already running behind and didn't want to miss Eli Blackstone as he traveled through the valley from Aspen Spring. He spent five minutes hugging Sarah and telling her he would be back to visit soon. She wouldn't let go. Hanna finally transferred Sarah to her lap.

Outside, Zachary spent ten minutes saying goodbye to Chica, the hardest farewell. Kyle shook his hand again, wishing him luck.

Then he turned to his father. "Thank you, I just couldn't imagine your support, or Mother's either, for that matter."

"Oh, you have a long way to go to persuade her."

"I hope I can convince her."

"You will, son; I'm certain you will. Now, as to Arrow, let him be my present to you. Your bonus for taking my place during the war. He's an excellent cutting horse and needs to work like Chica. You are good with animals; I know you'll be a good horse handler."

Zachary, taken aback, couldn't speak.

"You should take the Colt repeater and my old holster. It would fit you."

Zachary answered instantly, "No! I'll be fine." *Don't spoil things.*

"Someday, you may need it, but only if ready."

"That is right, Father, when I'm ready. Goodbye, I'll miss you all."

"Work hard, son."

Arrow seemed anxious. The horse started with a jerk. Zachary patted Arrow's reddish mane, scratching behind his jaw. Looking ahead down the mountain, Zachary clicked his tongue twice but resisted kicking Arrow into a gallop.

29 |Blacksmith's Apprentice

After months of struggling to hire help, the tall lad had appeared before Eli as if in a dream. The boy carried himself as if fully grown, despite his age. He would write to Eliza, describing Zachary Brennan, easing one of his daughter's concerns.

The two riders moseyed during the three-day trip back to Sunset Crossing. After two months of living alone at the swing station, the station keeper never stopped talking to Zachary. They became acquainted as they traveled or prepared stew and beans around their campfire.

Eli described his father and grandfather, both blacksmiths, back in Ohio. Father Blackstone had died from a horse kick during an unguarded moment in front of the blacksmith shop. The grandfather trained Eli. The business couldn't have been better; the carriage industry in Cincinnati kept the shop constantly busy.

After ten years, Grandfather passed away, leaving the shop to Eli. On a day in July of record temperature, a young woman brought a carriage with a bent strut into the shop. Over chilled tea at the drugstore across from the blacksmith shop, Eli warmed to his future wife, Virginia, proposing three months later. Eliza, the daughter, born in 1848, grew up working the bellows and constantly sweeping and cleaning the shop.

The war turned Eli's world upside down. He closed his blacksmith's shop, traveled with the 84th Ohio Regiment to Maryland, and later back to Ohio. Less than twenty of the 84th

died of disease, and none died from wounds. Eli didn't speak of his wife much. Only that he wasn't with her when she died. His daughter, fourteen at the time, grieved her mother's death for a year. Eliza stayed with her aunt in Cincinnati, went to public school there, and eventually applied to Oberlin College.

"I'm telling you, she'll make a great bookkeeper," said Blackstone. "Gets As in her 'numbers' courses."

Eli had run down by the morning of their trip's second day. He never mentioned anything about his background or family again. Zachary would have liked to hear about his training as a station keeper.

Eli wanted to know about Zachary's background. The boy found it liberating to be away from the ranch. Reticent by nature in the shadow of his brother and father, the farm seemed distant in time and miles. He talked about his beloved dog Chica, training her, working with Abelardo, and learning Spanish."

"That will come in handy with the passengers and drivers that come through on the run," Eli said.

"I know enough to get by, that's all," said Zach.

"More than this Buckeye for certain."

Zachary related the procedures and tasks relating to raising sheep and wool production.

Eli said, "No doubt we'll see sheep herds and cattle herds coming in both directions along the Beale Wagon Road and the stagecoach trail."

Zach continued his story, "My father started the supply station at Leroux Springs. He scouted with Antoine Leroux on the Sitgreaves expedition."

As Zach spoke of the early expeditions and the creation of the Beale Wagon Road, Eli's eyes fogged over. To Eli, Zachary's heroes already seemed inconsequential and forgotten in the lexicon of a Midwesterner.

That is until Zachary mentioned that Lorenzo had served with Kit Carson. Eli kept a couple of the dime novels about Carson on the coffee table in the waiting area of his blacksmith shop.

"That man is probably the most famous man in this territory, that's for sure," said Eli. "What did your dad think of him."

"My father believed in him until Carson pushed the Navajo from their land north to the reservation."

"Wasn't he following orders?"

"I guess everyone did things they wouldn't stomach otherwise during the war, my father included."

"Well, Carson's still bigger than life, from what I've read."

"Shorter than you, actually, by three inches."

Zachary remembered his favorite story about riding the camel when he was six or seven. He felt extremely comfortable with his new boss. Looking at the bulk of the man riding next to him, it seemed to Zach that the work at the station would be challenging.

Still, it would be a new life. He had not mentioned Jeremiah. Whatever work lay ahead, Zachary would not invite the ghost of Jeremiah.

Zachary spotted the swing station on the horizon from miles out due to the increasing flatness of the desert. The woodland grasslands had given way to sparse prairie grass and scrub. The sun wasn't allowing even a wisp of a cloud in the blue.

Arrow quickened his pace as they approached, sensing the Little Colorado River, a drink of water, and the smell of fresh hay at the station. Now that he had arrived, Zach recalled the small adobe building blending into the landscape he had passed on previous trips to Albuquerque. A ten-foot breezeway connected the pueblo-style adobe building to a framed single-story structure.

"That's my home and the bunkhouse," said Eli. "Dining table, cook stove, and sofas and chairs. My room is off to the right, and the bunks are to the left. The barn will hold enough hay in the loft to keep the horses through the winter, stables below."

The barn looked highjacked from an Ohio crop farm, including red paint. The Little Colorado river flowed northward a thousand feet east of the ranch. Water at the bend in the river near the ranch flowed across a granite shelf stretched between the river banks. Wagons or stagecoaches crossed the river here without difficulty. The river never reached a vehicle's axles, even during the flash floods that frequented the Little Colorado River in the early spring.

"The corrals must be completed before the first horses arrive next week," Eli concluded.

Zach assessed the area marked off for the corral, "We'll need to fence an area for pasture about three times the size of the corrals." He said, "The vegetation is sparse out here, but you've got wheatgrass, Indian ricegrass, forbs, and in the spring, sagebrush, all of which the stock will eat."

"We'll put up the horses and see how many posts we can set before sundown," said Eli.

The ground was dusty, and the sandstone crust was an inch deep and as hard as iron. Pickax worthy. Sand further down gave easier to the post-hole digger. The two worked past dusk and completed twenty fence posts.

Eli showed Zachary the adobe blacksmith shop by lantern light. A ten-foot opening on the east side of the building had been cut away to allow for the height of a stagecoach undercarriage and sixty-inch rear wheels. Two steel posts on either side of the opening, connected overhead by a steel beam, held a hoist and pulley system for separating the coach body from the wagon base. Once detached, the blacksmith could wheel the underbody of the stagecoach into the shop close to the forge.

Inside the shop, the forge occupied half of the north wall of the fifteen-foot square space. The brick hearth extended from the wall five feet into the room. Eight rough rock courses brought the fireplace to waist height. A well on its surface held water for cooling and hardening hot worked pieces. The firebox behind the hearth contained a large pile of coal. The brick chimney rose to the opening in the roof to let smoke escape and light reach the blacksmith anvil sitting four feet in front of the hearth. A door in the east wall led to the breezeway. Next to the door, a workbench held tongs and clamps. Other tools adorned the wall above the workbench.

A hand-forged dog's head blacksmith hammer lay across the workbench as well. Zachary picked it up, hefted it, and quickly put it back so as not to embarrass himself. He figured it might take a while before he could swing it effectively. The south wall held the sheet metal, steel bars in various round sizes, and scrap left over from previous projects. The ceiling height in the converted adobe home allowed only three inches of clearance for Zachary's height.

Only the excitement of the day kept Zach awake during dinner preparation. Afterward, Eli promised to roust him to continue with the pasture fence at dawn. Zachary chose the bunkbed near the sole window in the room that housed four guest bunkbeds. He grabbed an extra mattress from one of the beds and piled it on his chosen bed. He turned down the lantern and rubbed his sore shoulders and neck, tight from post-hole digging. No images of chasing soldiers, no arrows sailing toward his back, nor the explosive noise of a Colt repeater squeezed into his subconscious. Sleep came quickly within the quiet of his new world.

The two men worked long days and completed the pasture fence in seven. They also finished adjustments to the corral based on Zach's recommendations. The day after finishing the corral, Eli shouted to Zach, pointing to the northeast. Zach propped up the saw he held on a post and walked over to Eli, keeping the station spyglass to his eye.

"They're coming," said Eli. "Right on schedule. Quite an organization, Wells Fargo, well organized."

"How many horses?" said Zachary

"Can't tell yet. We'll know in a couple of minutes. Might as well open the first corral."

"Yes, sir." Zachary strode over to the gate and swung it wide. By then, he saw three trailhands directing twelve horses across the river. In another minute, he closed the gate behind the herd."

"Name's Zachary Brennan," he said to the three hands watering their horses. One of the men looked Zach up and down.

"I'm Walter Farndon. Call me Walt. This is Milton Tabb and Irvin Teller."

"Good to know you," said Zach. "I can take over if you want. Feed and water and brush your mounts. Eli's making an early dinner. Will you be staying the night or starting back?"

"Boys, let's go see what Eli's cooking up," said Walt.

Twenty-five minutes later, Zach entered the dining area through the bunkhouse. Walt and Milton sat on the sofa smoking. Irvin looked nervous, pacing by the door.

"I'm telling you, let's get going," announced Irvin. "By tomorrow, we could be eating steaks at the Willow Saloon. Why waste time here."

"What's the yank, Irvin," said Walt. "We're already ahead of schedule. Relax."

Eli came around the stove and laid a pot of his tasty stew on the center of the table. "There it is, fellows, one scoop for each, please," Eli said. "Seconds if there is enough to go around."

Zach, starving, sat down at the table. He had already sampled Eli's stew four nights ago and recognized Eli as a great cook. Milton and Walt joined Zachary at the table. After bringing out the biscuits, Eli sat down. He had already served the coffee.

Instead of sitting at the table, Irvin moved to the door, opened it, and turned back. "I can't abide him," he said, jerking his head toward Eli. "I'll be off."

"Suit yourself," said Walt.

"I will. See you back in Omaha."

"Watch your scalp!" said Walt, but Irvin had closed the door.

The two wranglers stayed the night in the bunkhouse. In the morning, after a daybreak breakfast, Walt and Milton took Zach out to the corral. They identified the horses individually, offering hints of their personalities or potential problems with behavior. Zach wrote the horses' names, notes, and features in the station logbook. As they prepared to leave, Eli looked over Zach's notes and wished the handlers well on their return trip.

"This group will get you started," Walt said. "Your station was the last one to stock on our list. We'll bring a herd of cattle through next week and drop off six head here before moving on."

Eli nodded, "Steaks, on the way; they'll be much appreciated."

"And a wagon with hay and supplies," said Walt. "Any special requests?"

"Maple syrup," said Zach. "For the flapjacks."

"Got it. I know the management booked a run on April 5th."

After the trailhands crossed the river, Eli leaned cross-armed on the corral fence. "Tomorrow morning, I want to show you the workings of the forge," he said.

"Sure, Boss," said Zach. "I would like to get to know the horses this afternoon. Try a couple of combinations using the rig hooked to our hay wagon. See if I can pick out a couple of lead horses."

"Go ahead, Zach," said Eli. "Need help?"

"I'll call if I need help. Arrow and I should be able to manage them."

Lorenzo had been right. Arrow loved cutting out a horse and steering them to the holding pen. Zach haltered each trapped horse and strapped them into the rigging. It would be easier with two people, but it didn't look like Eli would find another wrangler by the time of the first run. Zach figured he needed to work out a method on his own.

Once six horses were in the rigging, Zach walked up to each horse, checked his notes, and spoke to each, offering encouragement and identifying the ones that seemed nervous. All the horses had trained to pull stagecoaches. Zach just needed to know them well enough to combine the team efficiently.

Within two hours of driving the six-horse team down the trail and back, he had identified Stinger as perhaps the most impatient, ready to go. Putting him in the lead with Bell, a steady mare, wasn't quite the ticket. The team tended to drift right; Zach had to correct the group with the left rein.

At the barn, Zach moved Bell to the second position behind Stinger and put Misty, another mare, up next to Stinger. That corrected the drift, but Zach wasn't entirely happy with Bell's new partner Ruby. The horse handler spent another two hours shifting the horses and learning each horse's strengths and quirks. The worst horse, Ranger, continually nipped at the horse to his right. Zach took him out of the team altogether. Instead, he brought Lightfoot into the mix. After another trip out and back, Zachary realized that Lightfoot might make a better lead than Stinger. On second thought, Zach created a second team of six with Lightfoot as a lead.

It was getting late, so Zach unfastened each horse and led it into one of the eight stalls in the barn. He spent another hour brushing the horses and treating them with grain. Eli called him to dinner.

The next morning before daybreak, Zachary met his boss at the stove as he made a pot of coffee. The two men carried their mugs over to the blacksmith shop. Eli instructed Zachary in properly building the forge fire, from kindling to coal chunks with an orange flame of fire. While the heat in the forge and shop continued to build, Zach and Eli returned to the station house for breakfast.

After hard tack and beans, Eli showed Zach how to work the bellows, keeping the fire hot enough to melt metal. While Zach squeezed the bellows and watched, Eli heated a length of iron in the fire. Using long-handled pincers, Eli extracted the red-hot iron from the forge, held it down on the anvil, picked up the dog's head hammer, and beat the rod into a square shape. Eli stuck the iron back in the fire when it cooled down and became unworkable.

Zach stopped working the bellows, grabbed the tongs, and got a good grip on the workpiece. As Eli had done, he pulled it from the fire and laid it upon the anvil. The apprentice, already tired from working the bellows for the last half hour, struggled with the hammer. He hammered the piece five times before it cooled.

"Again," said the boss. Zachary stuck the piece back in the fire and repeated the process. Whereas Eli had hit the part twelve blows before it cooled, Zachary could only whack it five times before he needed to rest his hand. He fired the iron again and worked the bellows until he thought he could manage the hammer again.

After the morning lesson at the forge, Zachary and Eli ate lunch. Zach then walked to the corral and hitched up his first six-horse team for the afternoon exercise routine.

After four days of getting comfortable with both horse teams, Zachary moved on to hitch up the units to the wagon as quickly as possible.

As far as Eli could determine, the stagecoaches would take a day and a half to reach the swing station from Santa Fe. The time depended on the weather; no coach mishaps or animal injuries. For the initial trip on April 5th, Eli had lunch ready with new steaks cut from the beef herd Walt and Milton had driven down from Santa Fe. After dropping off four cows and a bull at Eli's Swing Station, the cowboys continued moving the herd down the trail toward other swing stations and Prescott.

30 |First Run

At one o'clock on the fifth, Eli and Zachary heard the stagecoach conductor blow on his horn. Eli spotted the horses, traveling fast through the spyglass a half mile away. Eli responded by blowing three short notes on his own horn to signal all clear for the approach to the station.

When the stagecoach pulled up at the station, the driver addressed Eli and Zachary, standing together at the hitching post.

"Winchell Bandicoot's my name," said the conductor sitting to the driver's right. "This here is Charlie Bend."

"How's your schedule Winchell," said Eli. "We have steaks ready for the griddle if you and your passengers have the time."

The coach's door opened, and a man in a grey suit and bowler stepped down. The man politely took the hand of the woman behind him. Her hair was piled and pinned up high on her head, covered by a flat hat with a wide brim. A ribbon encircled the crown and passed through holes in the bonnet to tie beneath her chin. She had to duck her head to enter the door without knocking off her hat. When she reached the ground, she began to pound the dust away from the folds of her long skirt. The dress's color might have been dark blue beneath the dust, matching the ribbon on her hat.

A second man alighted from the coach. Dungarees and a striped shirt beneath a suede jacket made the man a rancher. He wore a wide-brimmed Stetson.

Winchell asked his customers, “What do you say, folks, steaks or hard tack as we travel?”

No one chose hard tack.

Zachary addressed the driver, “Mr. Bend, while you’re getting lunch, I’ll switch out the team and brush and feed yours.”

“You gotta deal, son,” said the driver. “Here’s the roster for the team. Watch out for Corky, the last horse on the right. Kicks too much for my liking.”

Eli first served up two steaks for Bend and Bandicoot while the passengers used the privy. The crew didn’t waste time with pleasantries. They ate and went back to the stagecoach.

The next three steaks for the passengers were ready in minutes.

Outside, Zachary had finished hooking up his best team of horses. He handed Charlie Bend a team diagram with names and a brief note about each horse's temperament.

“This is a pretty even group, Mr. Bend,” said Zach. “Ranger, up front on the right is a biter. The groom at the next station will appreciate him. I wouldn’t mind if he didn’t return. Any chance that the rest of them will see their way back here; they’re a good steady bunch?”

“No chance of that. Eventually, you’ll have the whole herd sorted, but let me take this team around the barn and down the road a mile before the passengers come out. We can adjust then if I think it necessary.”

“Yes, sir, Mr. Bend.”

After the test run, Winchell approached the coach and called up to the driver, “What’s your judgment, Charlie?”

“They’ll do,” said Charlie. “Go get ‘em out here, Winchell; let’s go. Excellent work, kid. See you on the way back. We’ll be making a quick switch, so be ready.”

Eli followed the passengers and stood beside Zachary to wave away the stagecoach. He turned to his horse handler and said, “Went well, I believe.”

“That Charlie Bend knows his stuff, all right, but I think he’s satisfied,” said Zach.

“Let’s go in. I’ll throw on two more steaks for an early dinner. The stagecoach from Prescott will pass through here six days from now on the eleventh.”

Throwing six new horses into the team mix meant that Zachary needed to evaluate, realign, and drill the groupings to his satisfaction. Daily, he worked on his iron rod to fashion it into a four-sided square surface. He could now carry the hammer for ten blows before the rod cooled.

On April 9th, Steve Pembroke stopped for lunch on his way back from Albuquerque to Leroux Springs.

“Got something behind the buckboard for you,” said Steve. “I’ll be right back.”

Returning to the table after trekking to his wagon and back, Steve tossed a wrapped, heavy package on the table. “It took a considerable amount of money to get that shipped from New York to Simon Rosenstein’s Dry Goods,” he said.

Zachary unwrapped the thick book entitled: *Les Misérables* by Victor Hugo.

“If you don’t mind waiting, Steve,” said Zachary. “I need to write a short letter to the family.

April 9th, 1867

Mother,

Thank you for the book. The work here at the swing station is challenging. Eli, my boss, is teaching me smithy skills. My strength in lifting the hammer and bringing it home accurately on the anvil has improved.

The Wells Fargo company continues to exceed my expectations as a well-managed organization. Do not worry about me. I am enjoying the animals in my care. Hug Sarah for me and say hi to Father and Kyle.

Your loving son,

Zachary

Zachary used Eli's sealing wax from the small desk beside Eli's bed. He gave the letter to Steve.

"I know she will want to come and fetch me when she reads this. I hope she waits a month or two. I do not want to return to the mountain yet. This is where I should be."

"I can see that," said Steve. "I'll speak to Lorenzo. Between the two of us, we can convince her. Eli, thanks for lunch. I'll see you next time, friends."

Two days later, Zach had his chosen team of horses rigged and standing by at 10:00 am. At 11:00 am, with no sign of the stagecoach, the horses began to stomp, restless. Zach pulled the hay wagon around and attached the horse team, eyeing the southern horizon so as not to be surprised when the stagecoach suddenly appeared. He took the team out for a brief run and quickly returned, stopping the horses inside the barn, out of the sun. He unhitched the wagon, offered each horse a two-hand grain snack, and began pacing again, too nervous to go into the station for lunch.

At 1:30 pm, he heard the bugle. He had misplaced the station horn. Spinning twice around, he noticed the horn on a chair in the shade of the barn. He grabbed it and blew the three-note signal for the stagecoach to approach.

Charlie, driving and yelling at the horses to keep their speed up, came into the yard at full speed.

Hauling back on the brake hard, "Whoa, you beasts, whoa," said Charlie. No conductor rode with him on this trip. He swung down and opened the stagecoach door.

"Potty break, folks. Five minutes. I'm releasing the brake in five minutes," Charlie said.

Zach gulped. His best time to change a team in practice was eleven minutes and thirty seconds.

Luckily, Eli came out from the blacksmith shop to help. Zachary unhooked the team from the stagecoach, asking Eli to direct the team into the corral, where he could unhitch the horses after the guests left.

Zachary ran to the barn, grabbed the temporary reins of the lead horse, and led the team over to the stagecoach. His hands were sweating, trying to manage the leather straps. Candy, the second swing horse on the left, kept trying to rear up, which agitated the other horses. Zachary decided to stop the team and regroup. "Whoa, there. Whoa," he said. Thankfully the six horses settled, including Candy. Zach relaxed a bit, and the horses sensed that as well. He completed the hookup and retrieved his roster, handing it to Charlie as he climbed back to the driver's box.

The four passengers were hurrying to climb into the stagecoach. None of the men on this trip dressed as fancy as the man and woman on the first stage from Santa Fe.

"Giddup," yelled Charlie. The horses and stage raised dust, crossed the river a minute later, and rambled northeast.

Zach shook his head. *That sure seemed fast.* He walked over to the corral and began to separate the team.

***

By June, Eli's swing station had assisted ten Santa Fe coaches, most of whom stopped for Eli's stew for lunch. The nine eastbound stages never stopped for more than ten minutes. Zachary could switch the teams in less than four minutes. When the Santa Fe stage stopped, Charlie offered advice on horse hitching strategy, explaining the traits of an ideal horse for the wheeler, swing, and lead.

Of the twenty horses Zachary could provide, he picked his steadiest horses to be nearest the coach. The 'wheelers,' Sue, Crusty, Samson, Diamond, or Jake, all stood close to sixteen hands. They were the heaviest horses in Zach's corral and the most dependable. The groom had learned that these horses responded quickly to Charlie's jerks on their reins to turn the team. Lightfoot, Stinger, Blue, Daisy, Corky, and Flash were interchangeable 'leaders,' the smallest and fastest in the herd. Zachary hitched the other horses, 'swing' horses, in the center. When Charlie Bend began each run, he gathered the leads from each horse to his left or 'near' side in his left hand. The three reins from the horses to his right, the offside he held in his right hand. The off leader, swing, and wheel reins were each held individually between the knuckles of his hand. He had the near leader, swing, and wheel reins between the knuckles of his other hand.

The whip stayed in its holder. The driver had his hands full of reins. Eli sold off horses in need of the lash to immigrants passing through.

Immigrants from Albuquerque or Santa Fe stopped for water or an occasional meal at Eli's table. The swing station junction saw more traffic from Conestoga wagons than stagecoaches. Iron wagon tires, axle skeins, or broken iron axle bands needed Eli's attention. Zachary's attempts at fashioning a horseshoe still did not meet Eli's expectations, but he could shoe a horse if the reserves hanging on the wall were the correct size. Otherwise, Eli took over the shaping, handing the shoeing to Zachary, who would shave the hoof and nail on the horseshoe.

Eli and Zach worked well together. A quick "yes sir, Boss" from Zachary and quick obeyance to Eli's request kept the never smiling, always sweating smithy in the leather apron pleased. Zach's hammer strokes became more robust, faster, and surer daily.

When Lorenzo and Hanna eventually did visit in June, both were amazed at Zach's size. Zachary had broad shoulders now. As he neared his sixteenth birthday, he still looked gangly, almost distorted between an unusually tall boy and a full-grown man. He felt embarrassed by his look: angular, almost sunken in cheek and jaw.

Hanna captured the attention of Eli, who fawned over her, fixing his best meals during the couple's two-day stay. By the morning of their departure, Hanna appeared convinced that Zachary's decision had been sound. Lorenzo asked Eli about Ohio. Lorenzo had never been that far north since leaving Maine during the Mexican/American war. He wondered if Cleveland and Cincinnati rivaled Philadelphia or New York in size and industry.

Eli wanted to hear about Mexico and the Colorado River to the west. The two men talked and smoked the first night while Hanna and Zach discussed the Victor Hugo book. Zachary compared the war between the states and slavery to the crippling effects of imprisonment described in the book. Zach's parents continued to Albuquerque on a supply run. The Brennans stopped briefly on the way back to give Zachary another book Hanna picked up at Rosenstein's Dry Goods. Another man by the name of Wilbur Dawson traveled with them. He looked not much older than Zachary. The box of his buckboard was covered with a canvas tarp. Hanna introduced Mr. Dawson to Zach and Eli.

"Mr. Dawson is an engineer, Zach," said Hanna. He attended Kansas State Agricultural School in the first graduating class. He's going to measure our property."

"That's right. I've got all my surveying equipment, and Lorenzo will be my assistant holding the leveling rod."

"Your mother talked me into this," Lorenzo said.

"My Dear," said Hanna, "I've been set on this since Zach first discussed the Homestead Act Lincoln signed in '62."

"As if anyone has ever bothered us," said Lorenzo, "or ever will on the ranch. Too much space out here for anyone to worry about crowding us. Now back in Maine, I agree, farms bumped up against the next farm everywhere."

"Well, just to be sure, I think it is time to have a legal document," said Hanna.

"I agree, Mrs. Brennan," said Dawson. "The travel on Beale Wagon Road is bound to increase, and if they ever build a railroad through here, you'll have stakes to point to."

31 |Lasso for Zachary

Wagons stopped at the station occasionally while traveling to or from Albuquerque, Santa Fe, Prescott, and Leroux Springs. Immigrants, mostly, headed west to escape conditions throughout the South. The Conestoga wagons that headed east held hungry visitors that had decided to cut their losses. Frontier life and self-sufficiency could defeat determined dreamers searching for riches in California. Zach could tell at a glance which of the wagons contained westbound immigrants and which held eastbound travelers by their demeanor. Westward wagons clipped along, parents and kids smiling and eager. Eastbound people never said much and moved slowly, conserving the little energy they had left, usually very hungry.

On the other hand, the stagecoach passengers contained professional businessmen, ranchers, government employees, and perhaps their wives. These people had business somewhere down the line. They just wanted to get to their destinations, finished with the dust and thirst of a desert trip across rocky roads. Sometimes relatives of established immigrants rode the stage to visit family members.

Miss Elizabeth Adair, the niece of William Adair, the first mayor of Prescott, traveled from Kansas to visit her favorite cousin for a month's stay. She and her chaperone, Cora Norton, were the only passengers on the stagecoach out of Santa Fe on Wednesday, October 14th, 1867. The rear axle cracked and disabled the carriage fifteen miles east of the station. Charlie Bend, the driver, wound baling wire around the two sections of the broken axle so the stagecoach could hobble into Eli's swing station.

Her reddish hair was straggly from the miles of dust and wind whistling through the coach; Miss Adair stepped down and nearly ran to the outhouse. Miss Norton headed for the bunkhouse, stopping to inquire about a meal.

"Charlie will have something for you," said Zach. "It's too late for lunch, but he always has beans and bacon handy." He shooed the women into the station.

Sweat from the late afternoon desert sun stained everyone's armpits and back. Zach could only imagine the heat Miss Adair concealed in her thick dark skirt. She looked close to fainting.

Charlie kept eyeing Miss Norton with sideways glances. She was attractive. A single man constantly traveling, Charlie picked up temporary relationships when an opportunity arose. Cora was a prospect.

Gathered at the table, Zach distributed plates and forks. He poured coffee and tea on request. Charlie told Eli of their predicament while Eli rounded the table, ladling beans from his pot.

"Lucky to have made it here," said Charlie. "Guess we're stuck. Another stage heading in this direction won't come by for another week."

"Mr. Bend," said Cora, "that is unacceptable. If a delay of Miss Adair's arrival extends to three days, you can rest assured the army will be thundering through here looking for savages."

Eli looked to Charlie, "Let's not get ahead of ourselves," said Eli. "Charlie, when the women get their fill, you and I can look at that axle."

The food seemed to perk up Elizabeth. As Zach began to collect the dishes, she stood. "I'll help, Mr. Brennan. If you wash, I'll dry."

Cora shook her head and put a hand on Elizabeth's wrist. Zach observed the silent exchange. He believed Miss Adair to be his age or at least close. Elizabeth regarded Zachary. Tall, lean; with a four o'clock shadow of light fur on his chin; she thought he might be nineteen or twenty.

"Thanks," said Zach. "I need to hurry and get to the forge to help."

Zach didn't say much during the cleanup. He felt self-conscious around girls, too tall, hands too big. The days in his past, when he and Jeremiah tricked girls into kisses, had been forgotten. Adair had a figure. Slim at the waist; not too top-heavy. She possessed a pert nose, and her red hair set off her brown eyes. Zach noticed.

As Zach approached, Eli bent down near the broken rear axle in the yard. "If we can get the stagecoach over to the hoist without breaking the axle in two," said Eli, "I think I can collar it in two, no, in three places."

Charlie nodded in agreement. Eli continued, "If so, I'm sure you could make it to Prescott and probably back to the big shop in Omaha for a new axle."

"How long," asked Charlie.

"I've got to fashion the collars and bolts. I'd say all day tomorrow. You could be on your way early the day after tomorrow. You could make up the time in two days and push into Prescott on time."

Cora, listening nearby, nodded approval. Elizabeth beamed at the chance to spend time with the strong wrangler close to her age.

Eli signaled Zachary to take care of the team. He unhitched all six horses and stabled them within a brief time. Elizabeth wanted to help, thinking she would be near Zach as they brushed down the horses and fed them hay. Zach handed her a brush and let her start on Bell, the gentlest of the bunch. Still, he warned her to mind Bell's hind legs.

"Zach," she said. "I have a quarter horse back home in Kansas."

"Oh, well, thanks again for the help," Zach said. "I have to get over to the hoist."

"We could go for a ride tomorrow sometime. You could show me around."

"Look around; this is it."

Miss Adair looked so disappointed; Zach relented. "I probably won't have time, but if I do, maybe we could ride to the Meteor Crater."

"I hope so, Zachary."

Zachary met Eli and Charlie at the hoist. They had cleared an area for the stagecoach under the hoist. The three men then muscled the stagecoach in between the two iron columns on either side of the wide opening in the blacksmith shop. Zach climbed a ladder and attached pulleys, blocks, and tackle to the two eye bolts six feet apart on the overhead beam.

Charlie attached the two block-and-tackle hooks to the structural support rail on the coach's roof. In the meantime, Eli had unbolted the coach's body from the wheeled frame. With Eli manning one of the blocks and tackle, Charlie and Zach hauling on the other, the three men lifted the coach off the chassis, tying each rope to stakes.

They rolled the frame into the shop. Eli blocked up the splintered rear axle, disconnected one of the wheels from the axle, and separated it from the opposite wheel.

Eli could now work directly on the axle. He indicated to Charlie that he saw nothing to change his plan of attack and set about forming the first six-inch wide by six-inch diameter collar. Zach manned the bellows and stoked the fire.

As the fire roared, Zachary excused himself and returned to help Miss Adair care for the horses. Zach complimented her on the sheen of the three horses she had brushed. Together they finished the other three horses quickly, working across from each other over the last horse, Lightfoot. The two had become comfortable with each other over the dishes and brushing. When it came to haying the horses, Zach tossed a pitchfork of hay for Lightfoot, that accidentally on purpose, showered Elizabeth.

"Why Zachary, totally uncalled for," Elizabeth said. She picked up a handful of hay, backed Zach into a corner, and washed his face.

"Enough," said Zach. "Truce." He laughed. She laughed. Zach admitted the girl seemed to lighten his hardened heart. *I might kiss this pretty girl as I used to on a dare.*

Cora Norton entered the barn and broke the mood.

"Come now, young lady," said Cora. "We must work out our sleeping arrangements in the bunkhouse."

"Yes," said Zach, "I better get back to the forge."

At dinner, Eli indicated his desire to return to work and finish the first collar, leaving the remaining two collars for the morrow. That left Zachary with dinner cleanup duties again. This time Cora raised no objections to her charge helping Zach. She and Charlie sat on the sofa, discussing the aftereffects of the war and the upcoming presidential race. It seemed certain to them both that the nomination for President would go to General Ulysses Grant.

Seeing Elizabeth putting away the last clean dishes, Charlie slapped his thighs and stood. "Enough, Miss Norton," he said. "How about a game of cribbage, anyone? Zachary, how about it?"

"Oh, I'd like to play," said Elizabeth. "I'm not very good, though."

"Alright," said Zach. "Break out your board and the cards. Miss Norton? Are you in?"

"Heavens, no, I have no idea how to play," Nora said. "I'll sit near Mr. Bend to learn."

At the start of the game, Charlie and Zach rattled off their scores as they played their hands. "Fifteen two, fifteen four, and a pair is six, and another pair is eight, and a run of three is eleven."

Elizabeth began slowly, but at the turn, she increased her confidence and speed in counting, and the first game went to Charlie, who took a big gulp from the small glass of bourbon he had poured to celebrate. Laughing during a game break, Charlie retrieved another mug, pouring a dram for Nora.

Surprisingly, Miss Norton slugged it down and inconspicuously held her mug out for a second pour.

Zach won the second game.

After three bourbon shots, Nora hung on Charlie's arm for the third game. Charlie made four apparent errors in judgment in his discards. Zach took every opportunity to inflate Elizabeth's crib, and she won the final match.

Nora excused herself to the privy. Charlie accompanied her to stand guard. Zach and Elizabeth took the opportunity to stop in at the forge to say goodnight to Eli. He had finished the first band, and the second collar looked half beaten to shape.

Instead of heading directly to the bunkhouse, Zach directed Elizabeth around the back of the ranch house. The night had cooled off into the sixties. The moon had risen three-quarters full. The low branch on the pin oak near the bunkhouse made for a tight squeeze to accommodate the boy and girl.

Zach resisted kissing Elizabeth (as much as he wanted to), opting to speak in a deep voice and hold her hand. For her part, Elizabeth felt excited, nervous, and adventurous in the shoulder-to-shoulder contact with the unassuming boy.

She asked Zach to write to her, promising to do the same. Zach said he might.

Zach took Elizabeth back to the bunk house where Nora had clothespinned a blanket partition to a rope tied across the room that isolated two of the beds for the women. Zach sympathized with Elizabeth when he heard Nora snoring twice as loud as Charlie. Still, as Zachary undressed, he listened to Elizabeth rustling out of her skirt and petticoats. The horse handler lay in bed and imagined what might one day be in store for him on the other side of the partition.

In the morning, Zachary woke to the same rustling of petticoats. He knew Elizabeth had arisen early, anticipating their ride to the meteor crater. Elizabeth and Zach met outside. "What would you like for breakfast?" Zach asked.

"A biscuit, maybe," said Elizabeth. "I don't want to wake up Nora. She is going to have a terrible headache when she does. I have never seen her imbibe, much less three shots of bourbon."

"Well, I can't take you to the meteor without a chaperon," said Zach

"Perhaps we could ride along the river and stay near the station."

"I guess that should work. Let's saddle up. I'll stuff cheese and bread in a sack for lunch. Water to drink at the river."

After saddling Arrow and Bell, the two mounted and trotted away. Zach noticed Eli stretching at the bunkhouse door and heading to his shop.

The winding Little Colorado River made for an exciting ride out. The only greenery in the desert hugged the shores of the shrunken creek. Arrow and Bell carried the couple out of sight of the ranch in five minutes.

Zach enjoyed Elizabeth's company. The riders dismounted at a tight bend in the river shaded by a desert juniper grove. Their hands kept brushing together while spreading the blanket.

Elizabeth, anticipating Western adventure, did not sit down on the cover.

They spoke of plans; college for Zach, finishing school for Elizabeth as she moved closer. Zach pulled her to him, embraced her, and kissed her gently. The girl nearly swooned in her excitement. Zach stepped back, "Let's eat lunch," he said. "I should think about getting back."

The tension eased a bit. The trip west now matched Elizabeth's dream of adventure and romance. Sitting on the blanket with Zach, eating the small snack he had hurriedly grabbed, Elizabeth felt as warm inside as she did from the sun on her skin. Her cheeks glowed red, and she never stopped smiling.

For his part, Zach already wished to move past Miss Adair. An older, more experienced woman might ride the stagecoach into his life.

"How old are you, Elizabeth?" Zach asked.

"Oh… I'm thirteen, Zach,' she said. "How old are you? Twenty? Close?"

The swirl of dust zigzagging along the Little Colorado River to the south solidified into a rider heading their way. Zach began gathering the blanket and leftover snack, stuffing the items in his saddlebag. Soon, Charlie Bend pulled up but did not dismount. "Need you back," he said. "Eli finished the axle. We're leaving, pronto."

Relieved, Zach lifted Elizabeth into her saddle without the help of a mounting block. Then, in one sweeping motion, he swung up onto Arrow and led the threesome back to the station.

Cora Barton stood rigid in the barn with her hands at her waist while the three horses approached. Elizabeth slipped off her saddle without assistance and started for the bunkhouse. Miss Barton followed her. Cora said, "Have you no shame, young lady. Unchaperoned, alone, with a…, with this ranch hand," her voice low but angry, wagging her finger at Elizabeth.

Elizabeth turned back. "Zachary showed me the greenery along the river. A perfect gentleman, I might add."

"When your uncle hears about this, you'll be sitting in your room for a week," said Cora.

"I just thought to give you consideration for your hangover from the night of bourbon sipping with Mr. Bend," Elizabeth said, turning again toward the station.

"Oh, well," said Cora, "we'll say no more of the matter. Next time wait for my permission and company."

"Of course."

Zach nodded at Charlie, and the two met Eli at the shop. They hoisted the stagecoach cabin, wheeled the chassis from the shop underneath the hoist, lowered the cab, and bolted the connections. Collared and straight, the repaired axle turned in the newly greased mounts, slippery as butter.

Zach hurried to the stable and hitched Charlie's team. In twenty minutes, Charlie climbed up to the driver's box, stood, and yelled, "Stage pulls out in five minutes, with or without passengers. Your choice, ladies."

Elizabeth ran out of the bunkhouse with her overnight satchel and handed it to Zach, who secured it to the top rail. Taking Zach's elbow when he climbed down, she made to drag him behind the coach.

Zach guessed her intent and shrugged her away, walking over to Miss Norton and grabbing her satchel. He tied the bag on top of the coach next to Elizabeth's, "I guess this is goodbye," Zach said.

"I'll write letters and send them with the returning stage, Zachary," said Elizabeth. "You'll write too."

"Eli keeps me pretty busy, Elizabeth. I'll see."

Elizabeth stretched on her toes, kissed Zach's cheek, and whispered in his ear, “I love you.”

Zachary went white with shock, then led Elizabeth quickly up the folding step into the stagecoach.

“Hi-yah,” said Charlie. The team strained and pulled away from the station. Zachary, too stunned to speak, returned Elizabeth’s pleading wave. He looked at Eli and shrugged, “I surely do not know what that was all about,” he said.

Eli laughed, “You’re lucky you’re a hundred fifty miles away from Prescott. How about lunch?”

32 |Winter Break

During the winter, the scheduled stops by the Wells Fargo Stagecoaches dropped to once every other week. The westbound Santa Fe coach came through on Wednesday, barring severe weather. The Prescott run heading east stopped by the following Thursday.

The three letters Elizabeth Adair sent Zachary over the winter months amused him. Zach couldn't help comparing them to a young child's letter to Santa Claus as he read them. They were flowery, practically dripping with perfume, with little hearts drawn in the corners of the pages. He didn't write back.

Zach arranged with Charlie Bend to give him a unique signal on his arrival horn when Miss Adair rode his stagecoach back to Kansas. Eli managed the horse team switch that day while Zachary saddled Arrow and rode west to the Navajo trading post.

He needn't have bothered. Elizabeth had found the new love of her life two weeks before leaving Prescott and only exited the stage to use the privy.

Zach spent time out of the winter air forging horseshoes under Eli's supervision. Horseshoes and nails. Zach was an expert nail maker with a quarter barrel two-thirds full to prove it.

***

In the spring of '68, Wells Fargo notified Eli that beginning the first week in May, there would be two runs per week between Prescott and Santa Fe. Zach asked Eli for two weeks off to visit his family. The weather cooperated, and he accomplished the trip home on Arrow in two and one-half days.

As he emerged from the mountain trail canopy into the cabin yard, Chica caught sight of him, leaped onto the porch, and barked. When Zachary dismounted, Chica recognized him, jumped from the porch like a bullet, and nearly tackled his old friend. The commotion brought Hanna out on the deck, as well as Sarah. Zach brushed Chica away after intense reacquainting ear scratches just as Sarah leaped into his arms.

"Zachary," Sarah cried, "You've come home. Mother, look how big he is."

Hanna joined in on the hug. "What a surprise, Zachary," she said, wiping tears away with the hem of her apron.

"I'm here to visit, Mother," said Zach, "Before the busy season at the station."

"For how long?' asked Sarah.

"Six days, I guess. We start double weekly runs the first week in May."

"Get settled in the loft, and we'll all go up and surprise Lorenzo and Kyle in the upper pasture."

Zachary, Hanna, and Sarah stopped by the barn where Kyle worked on the shearing gate.

"Hello, Kyle," Zach said, passing through the shadow of the barn loft. "Getting ready for the shearing, I see."

"Hi Zach," said Kyle, "Planning on starting tomorrow if I get the pen and gate in shape."

"I can help for four days," said Zachary. "Trading my hammer for shears will be nice for a change."

Hanna gave the two to catch up with the past year's events at Eli's Stagecoach Station and Pembroke's Supply Store. Then she hurried Zach along, anxious to show him something up the mountain. The three Brennans left Kyle to his work on the gate.

When Lorenzo saw Zachary coming into the meadow, he leaned his staff against the old oak tree and embraced his son. This startled Zach to the point of incomprehension. A hug from his father was unheard of. Recovering, Zach squeezed his father firmly.

Chest to chest, the two men, equal in bulk and height, found the event unfathomable, incredible. Zach hung on for as long as he could until Lorenzo stepped back. *My father is glad to see me.*

"Lorenzo," said Hanna, "I'm going to show Zachary the markers."

Hanna's husband stayed with the sheep while Hanna led Zach and Sarah along the creek until they met a cleared three-foot path, arrow straight, heading due north. Five minutes later, they came upon a concrete boundary marker. According to Hanna, the three-foot obelisk sat on the northwest corner of the Brennan homestead. Looking down the mountain to the south, Zach eyed the surveyor's cleared path until it vanished over a rise. Looking east, crossing the hill on a gentle slope, Hanna pointed and led the way.

In twenty minutes, the Brennans found the northeast monument. Turning south and heading down to the valley, they approached the southeast marker. The open field in the valley made finding the final post a little trickier, but a half hour later, Sarah shouted about her discovery.

"I had no idea, Mother," said Zach. "All the land within the corners we just walked is your property?"

"It will be after all the requirements of the homestead act are met," said Hanna. "Our ranch property encompasses the northeast side of the pasture. The Whipple and Beale survey markers mark the promise of a railroad just south of our property. West of the marker where we're standing, the pasture continues past the supply station for another mile. One day we will have neighbors. The land in the valley here will be valuable."

Zach insisted the three of them stop to say 'Hello' to Steve Pembroke at the supply station. Steve, happy to chat with Zach about the stagecoach line, offered Sarah a licorice stick. Hanna needed to get back to start supper, and the three took off up the cabin trail.

"I've got another surprise for you, Zach," said Hanna, "back at the cabin, but I think I'll wait. Shearing starts tomorrow."

"Alright, Mother," said Zach. "Now I'm curious."

Zach visited the tree house at the cabin, reminiscing on the platform until Lorenzo and Chica brought the flock down to the corral. Chica chased the old tin plate thrown by Zach (peppered with so many teeth marks and holes Zach could hardly make it fly.) The boy and his dog gloried in each other's company, the blur of Chica proving her stamina hadn't waned. The game lasted until dinner.

Lorenzo called Zach awake before dawn the next day. Kyle entered the cabin and sat expectantly at the table. Zach climbed down from the loft and sat next to Kyle, ready for the stack of flapjacks Sarah brought to the table. Lorenzo and Hanna also sat down, and everyone ate in anticipation of the challenging days' work ahead.

Zach settled into the rhythm of the shearing alongside Kyle, equally as accomplished with the razor-sharp tool. The three days of shearing and two days of pelt washing passed quickly. Zach enjoyed his time with the family and felt ready for another long stretch working at Eli's forge.

He still had much to learn from Eli. Eli had begun teaching Zach the skills of a farrier, essential to operating a swing station in the desert. Making or shaping a horseshoe to fit a particular horse's hoof would soon be one of Zach's main tasks. As it was, Zach trimmed the horses' hoofs and replaced their shoes every ten weeks. More often if needed.

Increasingly, patrons came from Santa Fe, Albuquerque, and even the long way from Prescott to commission decorative ironworks by the Master blacksmith. Farmers brought their plows for repair.

In the morning, Zachary prepared to leave for the swing station at Sunset Crossing. Hanna asked Zachary to sit at the table. She brought out a series of pamphlets, a half-inch thick catalog, and a series of letters, fanning them on the table.

"I wrote to the Kansas State Agricultural school," said Hanna. "That is where Wilbur Dawson, our surveyor, attended college. He knew the names of the admissions advisor and helped me ask the right questions."

Zachary rifled through the catalog, stopping at one interesting course description after another. He didn't want to leave. *So much to absorb.*

"I'm not sure I've saved enough money, Mother," said Zachary.

"The prices are in these letters. I think you will be surprised," Hanna said, beaming. "I know you could do it, get in, I mean. Wilbur agreed and would give you a recommendation. They have something called work/study to defray the expense.

"Take all the information with you. Study it, write to me."

"I will, Mother," said Zach, "Thanks."

33 |End of an Era

The news reached Eli and Zachary by way of Charlie's stagecoach on the 25th of August. The letter from the Wells Fargo Omaha office thanked the station keepers for their service, but the run between Prescott and Santa Fe would be closing in the middle of September. A crew from the Omaha office would be arriving to herd the stock north and close up the buildings in the third week of September.

"Zachary, call Charlie in, will you please?" said Eli.

When Charlie entered the bunkhouse, he shrugged, "Hell of a note, Eli; I'm affected as well. I'll have to split runs from Omaha to North Platte with Regis Knox. The split means less salary, less bonus."

"The letter doesn't give a reason," said Eli.

"Money, of course," said Charlie, "They still aren't getting the traffic they expected on this run. The stagecoach lines have become second fiddle to the railroad buildout in Kansas and Nebraska."

Eli sat in silence for a minute. Only a minute. "Well," he said, "I'll move the shop to Albuquerque, Santa Fe, or Prescott. Tucson, maybe. The desert air agrees with me. Not going back to snowy Ohio. Towns can always use another blacksmith."

"That's the truth of it, Eli," said Charlie. "What will you do, Zachary? You could be a top hand somewhere. You are great with horses."

"I have been saving to attend university," Zach said. "This is the push I've needed. I'll be fine, except I'll miss… this place.

“I thought smithing might provide a livelihood,” Zach continued, “but the last time I took the keg of nails I made to Santa Fe, they gave me only $15.00 for the lot. I understand a machine can create them now for half of what I hoped to get for mine. Jenkins at the hardware store said not to bother him with nails anymore.

“A master blacksmith will always be in demand. But that is not me.”

“The letter says we’re to start selling off the assets and inventory,” announced Eli.

***

The stranger rode up to Eli’s shop three days after the letter arrived. A rare overcast September sky suggested a possible rainstorm that morning. Zach watched the man dismount and slap his bay on the shoulder. The horse snorted and moved sideways out of the path of the tobacco gob that the man spat at the horse’s front hoofs. Zach frowned. *Spiteful.*

Seeing Zachary, the man beckoned him over from the barn. The dust-covered cowboy swept his slicker behind the holstered gun on his left hip. “Are you the only one here?” the man said. “Heard a blacksmith worked here, but you ain’t the one I heard about, that’s sure.”

“You’re looking for Eli Blackstone. He runs this place,” said Zach.

“Git him, kid; I’m on the move. Are you the only crew?”

“Yes, sir, I’m the horse groomer. I’ll see what’s keeping Eli.”

Zachary took off for the bunkhouse, looking over his shoulder at the outsider. The man now stood in the doorway to the shop, his eyes adjusting to the smoking forge.

Eli stood at the stove, chopping a carrot into a stew pot. The Wells Fargo stagecoach would be pulling in around two o'clock. Eli tried not to disappoint Charlie Bend and his passengers with a lack of hot food for a late lunch.

"Fellow out there seems to know about you," said Zach. "Likes his gun."

"Oh," said Eli, setting down his butcher knife. "Anything else about him?"

"He's not exactly kind to his horse. Seems to be in a hurry. He looks to be checking out the shop."

"Best I get over there," Eli said, pulling off his apron, grabbing his hat from the hook near the door, and heading for the shop. Zachary followed.

The man waited at the anvil. Proud of his workplace, Eli did not appreciate uninvited guests or customers in his shop.

"I'm Eli," he said, offering a handshake, "and who might you be?"

The man picked up a pair of tongs, avoiding returning Eli's handshake. Innocent enough.

"Turk Corbin," the man said, spitting another gob into the smoldering coals.

"How can I help you, Mr. Corbin."

Corbin looked at Eli, glanced at Zach, and then back to Eli. He smiled, relaxed, and said, "I'm the new trail boss for an outfit out of Albuquerque. I'll be heading up a drive from the Albertson ranch of 450 head of cattle to the railroad at Abilene, Kansas."

Zachary couldn't reconcile this man as a trail boss. Corbin's three-day beard growth didn't help his appearance. He had black hair, like Zach's, which stuck out from his wide-brimmed Stetson in wolf-like fur chunks. The man didn't look like the professional ranchers that came through on the stage. Zach could tell he wouldn't want to work for the man. A trail boss had to be hard, Zach guessed.

"I'm still unsure what you're looking for, Mr. Corbin," said Eli.

"Oh, I'm just scouting around these parts a bit. I want a decent iron grate for the drive. Heard you could make me up a large grate three feet by two feet. It should fit steaks for the crew all at once. Hands don't like waiting while a shift eats. Best to get it all done in one shot."

Eli scratched his chin. "Couldn't get to it until a week from Friday. I must send Zachary to Fort Defiance to sell off our scrap steel. Where are you camping? He could deliver the grate when I finish it," he said.

"South, three miles, on the river. Best I pick it up on my way to Albuquerque on Saturday, September 12th. I've got a couple of errands in Prescott and Tucson to take care of, so that schedule works for me. You say the kid here won't be around?"

"That's what I said. Wells Fargo won't be through until next Tuesday, so I can send him off. Four dollars for the grate, half now."

"Sure," said Turk, digging into his money belt and tossing two dollars on the anvil. "That should cover it. I'll be back Saturday the 19th, early afternoon."

Turk Corbin turned and walked out of the shop without saying goodbye. He shoved the bay out of his way again, mounted the horse, swung around, and galloped off.

"That man is not pleasant," said Zach.

"No, he is not. That's why I charged him four instead of two dollars for the grate," said Eli.

It rained for ten minutes during lunch to cap off the strange morning.

After lunch, the two men stacked the dishes. Eli put a hand on Zachary's shoulder, spinning him face to face.

“I’ve changed my mind,” Eli began. “After Charlie takes off this afternoon, I want you to make the trip right away to the Indian Agency at Fort Defiance instead of waiting until next Tuesday. I’ll manage the team switch for the days you are on the road.”

“Alright, Eli, why the shift?” Zachary said.

“Something about that fellow, I guess, all swagger, but I’ve learned to be cautious when I get jumpy about someone. Between the two of us, we should be able to manage any trouble he might present.”

***

Zachary snicked the reins, saying, “Keep it up, you two.” Bell and Candy both picked up the pace. Zach worried. He had set off for the swing station two days later than Eli had figured, compensating for the lost time by constantly encouraging the two-horse team to pull the buckboard faster. He had dallied at Fort Defiance while waiting for a shipment of sugar to arrive from St. Louis. His top box contained enough perishables and staples to last until the end of September and the station's closing. The weight of the supplies didn’t overburden the horses at the fast pace set by the young driver.

Passing the time on the six-day journey back to Sunset Crossing, Zachary had worked out his entire plan for attending Kansas State Agricultural School classes. He read the material his mother had collected from the school to the point of memorization. She had been right. His savings in the First National Bank of Omaha would cover the school's tuition and projected supplies for at least one year. Zach felt confident the wages made in a work/study program would provide funds for room and board.

Holding the reins in one hand, he turned the page of the catalog of courses with his right hand and tucked the open document back under his thigh. Still holding the reins with his left, he grabbed the folded book with his right and held it up to read the following course description.

Structural Systems I

Credits: 3

Introduction to design of steel structures. Theoretical and practical bases for proportioning members, their connections, and layout specifically for applications of buildings.

Note

3 hours of recitation per week.

Engineering is definitely in the running.

No longer a daydream, Zachary felt sure he could achieve his plan for college by next year. Engineering, Law, Agriculture, Animal Husbandry. He would try a course from each discipline that interested him, settle on one, and pursue a degree. He looked up from his dog-eared catalog in time to steer his horses into a rare desert curve in the trail. He snicked the reins again. "Git up, Bell, Git up, Candy," he said, looking up at the late afternoon sun. "Hay and oats in another hour if you keep pace."

Arriving at the station, Zach drove the buckboard straight into the barn. He unhitched the horses and put them in two separate stalls. He gave each a feed bag of oats, picked up a brush, and began rubbing Candy down.

Voices filtered across the yard, drawing his attention. When he looked out the barn door, he saw Turk Corbin's bay horse at the hitching rail, but no Turk. He could hear the growl of a voice only as a murmur, but it made Zack shiver. Turk Corbin had shown up a day early.

Remembering Eli's trepidation about the stranger, Zach started toward Eli's shop, picking up the hay hook hanging by the barn door as he went by.

Dusk had settled on the swing station.

Quietly, the wrangler made his way into the shop through the framed hoist and pulleys, passing into the dark space, the canvas flap across the door pulled back and tied down. Barely silhouetted by the impending outdoor darkness, Zach stayed silent, still, out of sight of Eli and Corbin. They both glowed in the reflection of the forge fire, confronting each other across the anvil.

The flames' steady low roar and snap radiated heat even against Zachary's chest and cheeks twelve feet away from the anvil. The smell of coal and oiled steel permeated the shop, but the sweat stink of the two men dominated. Eli was bare-chested except for his leather apron. The stranger, less significant looking without his duster, was wearing an unbuttoned vest with volumes of curly hair pushing through the spaces between the buttons on his pin-striped shirt, ripped at the elbow. Corbin still wore his Stetson even in the stifling air of the shop; a rat had chewed along the brim above the man's right ear. His unkempt appearance haunted Zach, reinforcing his impression from their first meeting. In the devilish flame of the forge, Corbin exuded tense emotion. *Danger*.

This close, the stranger's murmurs were clear.

"You're telling me, boy," said Turk Corbin, "after two weeks, you still haven't bothered to make the simple grate I ordered and paid for."

"Corbin, as I promised when we met," said Eli, "I will have your grate ready tomorrow. It is my business how I run my shop, but I have never missed a promised deadline. If I have to work all night, your grate will be ready tomorrow."

"**Mr. Corbin** to you, boy. Don't forget it."

Eli shoved his long poker back in the fire and turned to Corbin, "That's it, I've had enough of you," he said. "Get out of my shop. I'm done with you."

Zach watched, choking on bile, as Turk Corbin drew his gun left-handed, straightened his aim, cocking the hammer of the walnut-handled 1860 Colt army revolver. Eli swept his right hand back, grabbed the poker, and flashed the glowing point at Corbin, upsetting his aim as he fired, the poker smoking into the man's left wrist, the gun flying toward Zachary, landing and spinning at his feet.

Eli cried out in pain, dropping to one knee, the bullet passing through his upper left arm, blood spattering the wall behind him.

Zach froze. The spurting blood from Jeremiah spasming on the station porch filled his consciousness. In his head, the boy relived those moments; the screaming horror of that scene so long ago now reflected in danger playing out in Eli's blacksmith shop.

"You fucking nigger," said Turk while Zachary stared at the gun, twirling for the last time at his feet. Corbin began sucking the back of his left hand burnt from the hot iron. With his right hand, he pulled out a hideout from an inner waistcoat pocket, aiming again with a straightened arm at a downward angle at Eli, who clutched his blood-soaked left arm with his right hand, looking to faint.

"There ain't many of you burrheads in the territory," Corbin laughed maniacally, "I smoked three of you black devils down Prescott way. You'll be the next notch."

Zachary shook his head. Neither man closer to the light of the fire noticed him. He leaned over to take up the gun. His hand shook so badly that he stopped and made two fists to steady his hands.

Pick it up. Pick it up.

Too late, Turk Corbin fired the derringer. Eli fell back. Turk stepped in, cocking the ridiculous little gun, sticking it against Eli's chest where he lay, and pulling the trigger again.

Zach, backing soundlessly out of the shop, turned and ran for the barn, hoping to make the barn cover before Turk Corbin emerged from Eli's blacksmith shop. He imagined a gunshot and a bullet piercing his back the whole way. He made it behind the barn door as Corbin emerged from the shop, the ripped-off sleeve of his shirt wrapped tightly around his left hand.

Even in his hurt, the assassin meanly smacked the bay before awkwardly mounting his horse. He wheeled around twice in the yard, eyes searching the buildings and grounds for any watchful eyes. Zach ducked back into the barn shadow.

Turk flew off at a gallop waving his hat high in the air and shouting "Hallelujah," repeatedly.

Zach collapsed to the ground, leaning against the barn door.

***

The swing station wrangler stood over the blood-covered body of his boss. Biting his lip and clutching and unclutching his fists, Zachary, awash in shame, with flashing lights at the back of his eyes from a migraine, his knees shaking as he looked down, fell to his knees.

I'm sorry, Eli. I couldn't pick up the damn thing.

Another half hour passed. The first of Zachary's waking nightmares began. *What if he comes back? What if he finds me? He'll want to locate me, eliminate the only possible witness. He knows me.*

Still shaking, Zachary walked to the corral and whistled for Arrow, leading him into the stable. In ten minutes, his horse saddled, and his belongings cleared out of the bunkhouse; Zach was ready to travel. Where? He had no idea which way to go.

The half-moon night could light the way for a while. He mounted Arrow and turned to the stagecoach trail toward Santa Fe. *No, he might come across Turk Corbin.* Manhattan, the town housing the Kansas State Agricultural School only a two-day hard ride from Abilene, where Turk Corbin would be driving the cattle from Albuquerque. Zachary didn't figure on going anywhere near where Turk Corbin might be. He wheeled Arrow around to the trail heading southwest to Prescott. *No, too close to Corbin territory. Corbin may come there as well.* Zach turned Arrow again, *due west to home.*

Zachary nudged Arrow forward. A hundred yards from the ranch, he stopped and held his right hand at eye level. His shaking had subsided. He looked back at Eli's shop. *Time to do the right thing.*

Zachary turned Arrow back and hitched him to the rail. He retrieved the spade and shovel from the barn and walked behind the bunkhouse. He stopped at the pin oak growing on the slight rise that blocked the winter wind from the building. Zachary began to dig.

The image in his head of the blacksmith's helper bedeviled Turk for two days. On the morning of the third day, as he knifed another notch on the butt of the walnut handle of his gun, Corbin decided to double back to the Wells Fargo swing station. The tall ranch hand that hung around the barn when Turk commissioned the cooking grate might cause trouble. Best to find out where he stood. He could always argue self-defense like that first time in Tucson. The jury of sympathizers had clapped him on the back after announcing the not-guilty verdict. No one paid heed as Corbin rode in and hitched his horse in front of the blacksmith shop. Two men worked at loading an oversized buckboard box with furniture from the bunkhouse. Three others were examining the horses in the grazing corral. Turk noted that the best horses were gathered in the barn corral.

Two other men were hauling everything out of the blacksmith shop, loading another wagon.

The crew on site proceeded with stripping the station clean in preparation for abandonment. Turk hailed one of the furniture movers, "Looking for the blacksmith," he said, "I got business with him."

"See Jim Grier over at the shop," said the mover. "He might be able to help you."

Turk sauntered over to the pile of bricks, the remnants of the forge ready to load into the wagon. Fire bricks are valuable.

"Looking for the blacksmith," said Turk to the man in charge.

"Never knew the man, but it's ironic how he died just before my crew came in to dismantle the place," said Mr. Grier.

"That's too bad," said Corbin, "I heard he would be good at making a wrought iron piece for my front entry. Rode from Albuquerque to see him."

"You can see him back of the bunkhouse," said Grier.

And that was that, decided Turk, as he rounded the corner behind the building and saw the grave. The flat mound pointed due east as far as Turk could determine, on the side of the rise beneath the tree. The burial place had been carefully dug by the wrangler he sought. No one working to clear the station had an answer as to the whereabouts of the horse handler. No one knew of the circumstances surrounding the death of the station master. If the kid had dug the grave, he hadn't told the tale and had not connected Turk to the killing.

Turk Corbin skulked about the swing station the day Zachary rode up to the barn at Hanna's sheep ranch. As he brushed down Arrow, Lorenzo, Chica, and half the flock ambled down the trail from the upper pasture.

"Zachary," said his father, "Good to see you. Unexpected, but welcome, of course. Have you seen your mother yet? I think she is in school with Sarah in the cabin."

Zachary sighed and let the comfort of his family and childhood home wash away the tension in his chest. He enveloped his father in his arms, a gesture that seemed second nature now.

Over dinner, Sarah related the incident involving the chickens and the wolf, and Kyle detailed Lobo's run-in with a bear. Hanna looked inquiringly at her son but decided that discussing college around the dinner table would be inappropriate. Instead, she brought forth the berry pie she had made that afternoon and the maple syrup the family liked to spoon over the dessert.

Zachary began to feel nervous again. He needed to talk to Lorenzo and Hanna. Should he tell them? Could Turk Corbin follow him here, endangering the whole family?

Before retiring to the loft, Zach asked to speak to them on the front porch. He pulled the rocker and another chair out of the cabin. Hanna and Lorenzo sat in the rockers, and Zach turned the chair around backward and straddled it, arms folded across the back of the chair.

Hanna could contain herself no longer. "Have you come home to prepare for college? Lorenzo and I have set aside funds to help out."

Zachary had expected her excitement, but he couldn't answer her, fumbling for words.

"Have you written to the college?" she asked. "Do you need help with the application?"

"No, Mother," said Zach, "let me explain. I have decided to put off college for a while longer. Circumstances at the swing station have altered my view at the moment."

"Why," said Hanna, "whatever happened?"

"Eli died."

"Oh, that's terrible," Hanna said. "Such a fine man."

"He was Mother, a stronger, kinder man I may never meet. Wells Fargo is shutting the station down. The business is slowing due to railroad building heading west."

"That's understandable," said Lorenzo. "There's talk of the railroad coming through here again."

"So, you could go to college now," said Hanna.

"Mother, I will go to college, but not now. I need to see a little more of the country first. I hope you will understand."

"You may not see another time for your education, Zachary."

"Perhaps, but this is something I have to do."

The mood had broken, and Hanna sat quietly while Lorenzo and Zachary spoke of the sheep, the increase in the flock, the market prices for mutton and wool, and plans for the next year on the ranch.

"I am heading to bed," said Hanna. "Zachary, I hope to change your mind about college. We'll talk again in the morning."

"Yes, Mother, we'll talk more in the morning."

Once Hanna entered the cabin, Zachary rose and stepped off the porch. "I thought I'd check on Arrow, father, come on, Chica girl."

"I'll mosey with you; good to see you getting along so well with Arrow," said Lorenzo.

"He's a great horse, Father."

At the stables, Zachary lets Lorenzo feed Arrow a handful of oats, old friends reacquainting.

"Leaning back against the stall, Zachary told Lorenzo of the murder of Eli Blackstone, leaving nothing out.

"I didn't want Mother to hear such words, Father, but it was horrible. The worst part is that the gun spun right before my feet. If I had only reacted. Eli would be alive today if I picked up that gun."

Lorenzo, leaning against the stall shoulder to shoulder with his son, looked straight ahead.

"That two-shot derringer could have plugged you and Eli, son," said Lorenzo. "Who knows what might have happened? It happened, that's all. You are right. This man Corbin must be crazy."

"But the gun was right there. I couldn't pick it up. I shook so, but a man would have picked it up, shaking or not. I couldn't. Guns. I can't get by it. First Jeremiah, and now Eli. Cowardice."

"No, son, stop thinking that."

"But Father, where did you come by it? The war in Mexico, the civil war? How come I didn't inherit something of that from you."

"Zachary, let me tell you this," Lorenzo said. He swung around, stood before his son, and looked into Zach's eyes. He grabbed Zachary's shoulders with both hands.

"No one is born brave, Zachary. No one. You can't learn bravery, either. You can't train for it or be ready for it.

"I was a coward when I was young, believe me. Anyone who tells you they don't start a coward reveals the worst lie to themselves and their fellow soldiers.

"I know you, Zachary, as a man of integrity. A diligent worker. A learner. A man who is kind to animals and friends.

"Don't belabor … this nonsense of bravery.

"I tell you, when your time comes, you will be the one to stand up. I can guarantee it."

Zachary, sobbing, wiped the tears from his face and hugged his father again.

"That means so much to me, Father," Zachary said softly.

Lorenzo broke their embrace and led Zachary back toward the cabin. "What will you do next, Zach?" he asked.

"I'm going to avoid Turk Corbin. He'll be up in Kansas near the university. Perhaps I'll try something new in California. San Francisco, maybe."

"That sounds like a plan, Zachary. I'll speak to your mother. When will you leave?"

"Tomorrow, I guess."

At first light in the cabin, Zachary found paper and ink and wrote the letter he had been thinking about for three days on the trail.

September 16, 1868
Miss Eliza Blackstone,

My name is Zachary Brennan. I worked for your father, Eli, as a horse groomer and apprentice in the blacksmith shop at the Wells Fargo swing station in the Arizona territory.

Straight off, I must tell you that your father died on September 11th, 1868.

I found him in his shop and buried him behind the bunkhouse near a tree. I drove a stake in the ground at the head of the grave and transplanted a wild grape plant near the stake to mark Eli's resting place. I hope the vine will grow, wind around the stake, and reach the tree nearby. I will check on it whenever I pass that way, but I am heading to San Francisco now.

I know that Eli wrote to you often and spoke of you daily. He was proud of your accomplishments at Oberlin

College. I am sending this letter in the hope of reaching you.

Your father was a good man. A capable man. An excellent blacksmith, a strong but kind teacher, and a great cook. He served all the passengers with dignity and respect. His stew usually won over any disgruntlement of the dusty trail.

My parents live in Antelope Springs, Arizona Territory, and they will forward any correspondence on your part to me. Their names are Lorenzo and Hanna Brennan.

I feel as though I know you. Eli and I talked our way through every cribbage game. I will keep the picture he showed me of you as a ten-year-old in remembrance of him. I would deem it an honor to meet you and get to know the daughter of such an influential man.

Yours truly,
Zachary Brennan

By ten o'clock, Zachary had said a solemn goodbye to Hanna, hugged Sarah, and shook Lorenzo's and Kyle's hands in farewell. Zach could tell by the look in Hanna's eyes that Lorenzo had not informed her of the events at the swing station. Hanna would gain nothing in the knowing. The same law that ruled in Jeremiah's shooting still prevailed.

The rule of law in the Arizona Territory existed only as far as a spinning gun. A gun Zachary couldn't pick up.

34 |Alta California Opportunities

Every muscle and bone in his body ached with a dull pain from the extended horse ride across Arizona and California. He took after his father in that regard. Something about their height or the angularity of their frames set awkwardly on a saddled horse. Long rides jolted them to the extreme.

A three-day horse ride from Pembroke's Supply Station to the swing station seemed like a lark compared to the twenty-day trip on horseback from the San Francisco Peaks to Los Angeles.

In Zack's estimation, the city of angels showed promise. Men worked on setting railroad tracks south of San Pedro. An old established church bordered a newly defined plaza. Although the telegraph had reached Los Angeles, a conventional bank had not as yet. Wiring money here: out of the question. Zach spent only one day wandering the city before heading north to San Francisco.

The Missions Trail between Los Angeles and San Francisco offered Zach's back and hips no favors. At least the saddle sores were beginning to heal. Zach traveled fast and light, fourteen and a half days between Los Angeles and San Francisco. The boy spent his seventeenth birthday alone on the trail. The stars that night over the Pacific Ocean calmed the boy. The night air still, a million pinpricks of blinking lights overhead. The wind whispered a song of the wild to him. His troubles seemed irrelevant within the vastness.

Days later, in San Francisco, Zachary paid the stable owner the stall fee and an additional quarter to sleep in a corner next to Arrow. His funds, borrowed from Lorenzo for the trip to San Francisco, were exhausted. Sleep had finally found him buried in the hay in the clammy stable, but he woke up at dawn on the 21st of October wondering about a bank that could transfer funds from his Omaha account. Then he planned to begin looking for a job.

From the livery at the corner of Montgomery and California streets, Zachary headed three blocks to Tadich Grill for breakfast. He glanced through the window of a hardware store as he passed by. The clock on the far wall read 7:45 am. The breakfast rush should be over by the time he sat down. Zachary began crossing the street to the diner when the soft rumble of an earthquake raised a brow: a new experience. The roar increased as the buildings on California Street began to sway.

His steps were now so unsteady Zach looked drunk and toppled to one knee. Others were running from the buildings into the street. Women screamed and clutched their babies or children, looking for shelter.

Trying to stand back up, Zachary felt dizzy. He saw an older man of about thirty-five running drunkenly along the street on his right. Bricks and cornices from a two-story brick building toppled on him, knocking him down and out.

Before a minute expired, Zachary's world stilled.

In Zachary's view, there wasn't much damage evident to the buildings. People poured out of the buildings into the street, fearful of aftershocks.

Zach trotted over to the man lying unconscious from the fallen brick. The gash on the man's temple bled steadily. Zach looked around, thinking of yelling out for help but decided the chaos would muffle his call among the hysteria in the street. Instead, Zach loosened the tie around the fallen businessman's shirt, pulled it away, and wrapped it around the man's head and across the wound, tying it tight. Blood soaked through the tie but slowed the flow to a trickle. The man's eyes opened, and he shook his head. He quickly shut them and moaned at the pain of the cut and bruise forming at his hairline.

"Lie still, Mister," said Zachary. "What's your name."

The man said nothing, then whispered, "Conrad, Conrad Mercer."

"Take it easy. I've never been in an earthquake. All these people think it isn't over. I should help you to the middle of the street at least. In another minute or two."

Two women approached. One of them asked, "Is he OK?"

"Pretty bad gash is all I've found. I don't think anything's broken," said Zach. "Is there a hospital?"

"Yes, the Marine Hospital at the Presidio, about three miles down California Street."

"I don't think he could make it that far," said Zach. "Maybe you could find a blanket to keep him warm until an ambulance arrives or at least someone with a carriage."

"Alright, I'll find something. I'll see what I can do."

A half-hour later, Zach gave up on the woman who went to find a blanket, but men on horseback started to appear, as well as carriages. Zach commandeered a ride to the hospital and helped admit the injured man. He left Mr. Mercer in the care of a nurse.

A relief station hastily set up at the church two blocks from the hospital offered Zach coffee. The smell of frying eggs drifting from the church kitchen drew Zach inside, overriding his fear that the building might shake down around his heels. He sat down at the table next to three other hungry volunteers. Eggs and toast appeared on a plate one of the church ladies set down.

"I spoke to an old timer over in the Mission District," said one of the men. "He said this was the biggest in the city's history. An exaggeration, but who knows."

"What do we do now?" asked Zachary.

"Watch out for aftershocks, stay on your toes, stay away from crooked buildings; they could still topple."

"I guess I better go see my horse," Zach said. He stood and carried his plate to the kitchen.

The days, weeks, and months following the 'Great San Francisco earthquake' became a California gold rush for Zachary. There was much to do. He ate at bread lines and charitable soup kitchens, staying in tent cities offered to people experiencing homelessness. He wandered through the cities and towns, volunteering to help dig out, salvage or rebuild quake-ravaged buildings. Zach soon heard that the leveled area of Hayward needed assistance. He rode over to the devastated town. Piles of debris lay everywhere. People wandered through the wrecked homes digging for family memorabilia, wailing in despair. The fear of an aftershock always hung over all that worked through the rubble.

Zachary foresaw months of work. He had no ownership of the place before or after the quake. But people everywhere needed his help. As long as he could scrounge food and a bed to sleep in, he decided to right the destruction of the great earthquake.

He was anonymous. At first, no one knew his name, where he was from, or why he was in the area. He became the man others sought for his strong back, arms, and hands. No one asked questions, and they all thanked him kindly.

Eventually, a man named Thomas Winslow noticed the tall stranger working independently and asked if Zachary would consider working for him. Winslow, who owned a construction company specializing in home building, had a band saw that connected to a portable steam engine via a belt.

Zachary worked with Winslow's crew for three weeks tearing apart collapsed wooden structures and bringing piles of uneven and jagged boards over to the band saw for the operator to clean cut. Then Zachary would sort the lengths salvaged in stacks of similar sizes for reuse.

After a while, Zachary determined that Thomas Winslow's company would hold the wood recovered hostage until the owners of the destroyed buildings paid a ransom for the work accomplished. The tall stranger quit the company, wandered to the next town, and returned to work with a hand saw, shovel, and claw hammer to help owners who offered him room and board.

***

Once a week, Zachary ventured to San Jose, and the soup kitchen tent was set up outside the San Jose City Hall on North Market Street. The First Unitarian Church of San Jose offered free food involving much more than soup and bread. The meal included grilled chicken and pie for dessert while it lasted. Zachary arrived an hour before the dinner line opened and waited patiently. The food tasted so good he came back repeatedly.

Zachary, always starving by the time the lineup began receiving food, looked down the line, counting the men before him. On this evening, the young woman doling out the small pie plates caught Zachary's eye.

Chocolate-brown hair pulled up and back, tied with a bow, dressed in an immaculate beige dress with yellow stitching and a modest bustle; the woman seemed out of place, cutting pieces across from mostly filthy men and families with sunken eyes.

There she served, the most beautiful girl Zachary could have imagined.

Taking the piece of pie the lady offered him, Zachary noticed a red smudge on her face. “Ma’am,” said Zachary, “You have a bit of cherry on your cheek.”

The brunette looked up and up again to glimpse the tall stranger, “Oh, thank you,” she said, taking up a napkin from the table and lifting it toward her right cheek.

“No, the other side, Miss…There! My name is Zachary, Miss…, Zachary Brennan. What is your name Miss…?” Zachary asked.

“Caroline, sir, Caroline Wainwright,” she said. “Was your home badly damaged?”

“No, Ma’am,” said Zachary, “I’m from Arizona. I arrived here the day before the quake. I’ve been helping with the rebuilding effort.”

A man two back in the line yelled, “Hey buddy, hurry along, get going.”

Zachary frantically stepped back out of the line to let the hungry people pass. He found a table close enough to observe the woman as she served. Zachary thought she was dedicated to the task, obviously caring about the fate of the people filing by. San Jose, her town.

After finishing his piece of pie, Zachary walked to the rear of the food preparation tent, lifted the flap, and walked over to a lady directing the activities of the chicken grillers and dishwashers.

“Ma’am,” he said. “It looks like your dishwasher could use a break. I’d be happy to assist.”

The heavily bosomed lady didn’t even look up. “George, this man will spell you for a while,” she said. “Stoke the coal fire under the washing vat, then take a break. Don’t go far; we’ll be done in an hour.”

"Yes, Mrs. Gains," the dishwasher said, handing the dishcloth to Zachary. "You're in for it now," he told Zachary, "you're hooked."

Twenty minutes later, Caroline Wainwright entered the tent and approached Mrs. Gains. "Any more pies, Betty?" she asked.

"Last three on the shelf behind the curtain."

"Great," said Caroline, grabbing two of the pies.

"I'll bring the third one out," said Zachary, wiping his hands and offering his best smile to the surprised pie lady. Outside the tent, he set the pie down in front of Caroline. "There you go, Miss Wainwright," said Zachary. "When we're done here, I would be pleased to offer my protection for your journey home."

"I tied up my buggy and horse on the side of city hall. I live just two miles away. I'll be fine," said Caroline.

"Well, Arrow and I will see you home safely, just the same." Without waiting for an answer, Zachary walked back into the tent and quickly finished the three stacks of dishes remaining. George had returned by then, and Zachary left George the task of loading the dishware in the buckboard for the short trip to the City Hall kitchen for storage until next week's soup line.

Zachary hurried over to Arrow, mounted, and turned him toward the side of the building. He found Caroline just climbing into her buggy and gathering the reins to the all-black horse hitched in front.

The polished-with-care buggy sported red pinstripes along the smooth curves of the cabin. The logo on the buggy's side contained a grapevine, and the word Wainwright curved into a smile below the crest. The black beauty that would pull the carriage looked like he could give Arrow a run for the money. Zachary had never seen such affluence. *And this is just her buggy.*

"Hello again, Miss Wainwright," he said. "Arrow, bow for the lady. Arrow, bow."

Arrow promptly folded his forelegs and knelt.

"Up Arrow, good boy."

"That is a fine horse. My ranch is just five miles down the road," said Caroline.

"No trouble at all, Miss Wainwright. I need to get the lay of the land hereabouts."

Caroline was correct; the ride to the ranch gate took only eight minutes. The massive stone columns stood on either side of a twelve-foot-wide wrought iron gate. A Wainwright grape vine crest hung on each of the stone pillars.

Zachary dismounted, opened the gate, and led Arrow and the black through. After closing the gate, he swung up on Arrow and accompanied the reticent Caroline for another three minutes up to the mansion.

Zachary tried to initiate a real conversation, telling the lady about his mother's sheep ranch back in Arizona and asking Caroline about the Wainwright crest. Anything to get her to warm to him.

Hopeless. Zachary had never brushed against high society. He didn't even know what that meant. Jean Valjean, the wealthy hero of *Les Misérables,* seemed the closest approximation to what he perceived might live in the vast house in front of him.

Caroline Wainwright was too beautiful not to try and break through her icy standoffishness. After these last months of manual lifting and sweat, Zach looked ragged in his work outfit. Maybe if he wore his suit?

Whatever the reason, Zachary could see himself losing the battle. He decided to retreat.

"Thanks for that delicious pie and grilled chicken dinner, Miss Wainwright," Zachary said. "I better shove off. I'll see you again sometime."

"Goodbye, Mr. Brennan," Caroline replied.

Caroline watched him ride to the gate, sitting tall and, she had to admit, handsome in the saddle. He was forward, bold even, but something about him fascinated her. Those ocean-blue eyes set against his black, sinister hair. Lips soft and thin. Those shoulders. Caroline shuddered. *Impossible.*

***

On Wednesdays, Zachary bought the *Daily Alta California* newspaper for fifteen cents. He read every article in the four-page paper, absorbing the news of San Francisco, the bay area, and California and exciting stories from the rest of the country. While reading, he envisioned Hanna's presence at his shoulder, urging him to add to his vocabulary.

On May 12th, 1869, at the top of the fifth column on page one in bold type, a heading summarized the ceremonies of May 10th in Utah. The article described the completion of the Transcontinental Railroad:

> **The Ceremony at Promontory Summit-Meeting of the East and West – Preparations for the Grand Ceremony – Description of the Spikes and Ties – Gifts of Various States and Territories – Address of Dr. Harkness, of Sacramento – Response by General Dodge – The Final Ceremony – Great Enthusiasm – Congratulations by Telegraph – Who Was There – The Final Banquet.**

The article generalized the celebration occurring in Promontory, Utah. The newspaper published the story two days after the driving of the golden spike but still beat the rival publications in town.

The news flabbergasted Zachary. He could now travel from San Francisco to New York in the comfort of a sleeping car on a passenger train instead of in a dust-filled Wells Fargo Stagecoach. The closing of the switch station in eastern Arizona and his subsequent travel to San Francisco now seemed almost fortuitous. The opportunities afforded by the railroad connection between the Atlantic and the Pacific and the telegraph lines connecting the coasts seemed immeasurable. Zachary's arrival in San Francisco, despite the setback of the great earthquake, put Zachary on the ground floor of a newly rebuilt and exploding city.

In the same issue, Zach found the following post in the last column near the fold on page three:

> **Notice: Increasing circulation of the Alta California publications necessitates hiring an additional compositor. Typesetting experience appreciated. A written application letter may be submitted to the Managing Editor, Harold Crenshaw, at 529 California Street.**

At a Chinese mercantile store, Zachary immediately purchased stamped stationery, envelopes, nibs, pens, and ink. Proceeding to Wagner's Beer Hall at 308 Dupont Street, Zachary spent two hours on a letter of application. After the third iteration, he copied the text as neatly and legibly as his roughened hands would allow. He addressed an envelope. Next, Zack visited the Roos Brothers Men's Clothing Store at Post & Kearny Streets. The salesman brought out a dark navy pen-striped wool suit. The tailor on duty lowered the hem of the pants appropriately for the tall man's height. Paid for with a draft from the Bank of California, Zachary, dressed in the new suit, set off in the early afternoon for the address noted in the paper.

As he walked, he became increasingly excited about the typesetting position, even though he had no idea what it might entail. Zachary had volunteered as a cleanup day laborer all over San Francisco and the bay area for seven months. Most of the final cleanup work would now be accomplished with heavy equipment, steam shovels, and dozers. The rebuilding would be the responsibility of the tradesmen.

The young wrangler knew his way around San Francisco, San Jose, Hayward, and the other communities he had helped after the quake. Zach transferred his funds from Omaha to the Bank of California. Depleted by half now with the additional cost of the suit, he had kept his expenses to a minimum by frequenting various charity soup lines and sleeping in homeless tents erected after the earthquake. His main cost entailed the stabling of his horse, Arrow. If at all possible, he would not sell Arrow. Zachary explored the region on horseback. He traveled into the foothills to escape the cities' closeness and the smell of the fishing wharves.

Making his way to the address on California street noted in the newspaper, Zachary stopped to admire the three-story brick structure. Large windows in the front. The building seemed solid and permanent like it had a history and a future.

"Zachary Brennan to see Mr. Crenshaw," said Zach to the middle-aged lady sitting at a desk tucked into a nook in the small lobby. The hallway leading away from the entry contained three offices on each side.

"Do you have an appointment?" said the receptionist.

"No," said Zachary, "I have an employment application I would like to deliver."

The receptionist said, "Just a minute; I'll see what I can do.

Zachary didn't sit down. He decided he had wasted his time and money. What made him think he could get a position at a newspaper when he had no experience and didn't even really understand the duties or skills required of a compositor? The placard on the desk clued Zachary of the receptionist's name, Amanda Costain. Minutes passed before she returned, followed by a man an inch taller than Amanda and four inches shorter than Zach.

The man wore rumpled pants, a wrinkled white shirt, no tie, and no suit coat. He chewed on a three-inch unlit stogey hanging from a corner of his lip. Zachary, looking down, noticed the man's friar haircut and bald spot.

"I'm Crenshaw," said the man. "You've got an application letter? Let me see it." Zachary almost felt the man's quick appraisal as he handed Crenshaw his letter.

"Don't know if you'll fit. Got to get your hands dirty around here, especially as low man on the totem."

"My name is Zachary Brennan," said Zach, offering a handshake. Crenshaw had broken into the envelope and read Zach's application, not looking up, ignoring a handshake.

"Horse handler eh," said Crenshaw. "Respectable occupation. Why typesetting?"

"I enjoyed wrangling; yes, sir, I did. But your paper had an article today about the transcontinental railroad's completion. I worked for Wells Fargo. I figure the trains could make my job obsolete.

"Besides, I have different goals. My sights are set on education and a profession."

"You may be right about the stagecoach. It may go the way of the Pony Express. Come back to my office so I can read this through again." Mr. Crenshaw turned and walked back to the first office on the left. He closed the door behind Zachary and waved him to the seat facing the desk. Mr. Crenshaw walked around to the other side of the desk. Standing in the light of the window facing California Street with clomping horses hurrying by and pedestrians chatting as they strolled, Harold Crenshaw reread Zach's application. Zachary heard the thrum of a printing press rhythmically chugging on the floor above. Finally, Crenshaw sat down, looking over at Zachary.

"Your application is beautifully written, Mr. Brennan. Says here your mother schooled you."

"That's right, she believed in the power of words. I learned a love of reading from her."

"Well, it shows, even in this brief letter. Let me get down to it. I need someone willing to work sometimes ten hours a day to meet our deadline and get the paper out. You'd start on the weekly issue, learning to typeset. If your speed hasn't met my requirements in four months, you're done, no frets.

"Besides the typesetting, you'd be responsible for the boiler and fueling the steam presses. We've got two of them now and a Gordon-type jobber press for pamphlets and business cards. If the fire dies or gets low, we miss our deadline; you're gone, no second chance. It's hot down there in the basement, sweltering. Think you can take it?"

Zachary smiled, "I bet it's not as hot as the forge I worked in Arizona. It reached 120 degrees in the desert outside. Hotter inside."

"Alright, cards on the table. As I said, four months to see if you can cut it as a typesetter. $10.00/week wages. That's half what you'll make if you get good at it. I expect you to stick with me for at least two years if I go to the bother of training you.

"There it is. If, after thinking it through, you still want the job, be here at 6:00 am Friday, and we'll put together the *Weekly Alta California* edition for printing and Saturday morning delivery."

"Oh, I'll take the job, Mr. Crenshaw," said Zach, "I'll be here Friday at 6:00. Count on it."

The northern two-thirds of the second floor of the Alta California building housed two large steam printing presses and two Gordon-type jobber presses. Lining the access aisle to the presses, material shelves, and layout tables held reams of paper of assorted sizes staged for the scheduled jobs for the week.

Four identical cabinets lined the west brick wall at the opposite end of the building. The windows on the north wall let in copious amounts of light without distracting the compositors. Each cabinet contained 10 - 36" by 24" by 3" tall composing cases.

Harold Crenshaw pulled the second composing case from the cabinet and set it on top of the cabinet. Sliding it down to the toe board. Then he extracted the top compartment, placed it above the first, and propped it at an angle for easy reach.

Crenshaw gestured at the first case he had set down, "This is your lowers case, closest because it's used the most." He pointed to the other case, "Upper case. Got it?"

Zachary leaned over Harold's arm, observing the many subsections of each case. Little lead pieces the size of an individually printed letter filled each section in the case. Upon closer examination, he noted that the letters were backward. The words formed from the backward letters would be legible with ink and paper applied.

Mr. Crenshaw removed the same two cases from the cabinet next to the first. He beckoned Zach to stand at his left elbow. "Take your copy sheet, clip it to your easel, and position it in an easy line of sight next to your cabinet.

"Pick up your stick and set the measuring point according to your layout sheet. That represents a column of the newspaper." Crenshaw picked up what looked like a six-inch ruler, except that it had a frame and hollow area. Harold referenced his copy and picked through the upper case for the letter 'T.' Using his left thumb to control the tension, he slipped the 'T' into the stick. "Place the slug so that the top of the letter is at the bottom of the stick; keep it tight and hold it with your left thumb while you look for the next letter."

The apprentice struggled a bit, his calloused hands still swollen from the shovel work of the week before.

“The nick in the slug always faces the same way,” said the editor. “Ok, watch me for a while.” With that, Crenshaw’s hands began to fly across the cases, loading his stick faster than a cowboy arms his empty six-shooter to ward off Apaches. His hands were a blur.

When the stick was complete, he took it to the steel frame on his layout table to the right of the cabinet and carefully transferred the group of letters.

“Next comes a spacer denoting the end of the column. Then we keep going,” Harold again let his hands fly over the cases, filling the stick repeatedly.

At noon three other employees entered the press room. Harold took a moment to introduce Zachary.

“This is Zachary Brennan, who hopes to be our new compositor,” said the managing editor. “This is David Beasley, press operator; Frank Eastham (we call him stumpy,) our other press operator; and Gunther Penrod, distribution stager.”

Frank had two missing fingers on his right hand. Zachary surmised he got too close to the powerful steam press.

“Let’s get going,” said Beasley. “I want to be home for supper for a change.”

“Well, grab cases and work on page four,” Crenshaw said. “I’ll be done with my page in twenty minutes, and then I’ll take page three.”

The crew left Zachary alone to struggle with his page of type. He began to sweat, trying to pick up speed and match the other two compositors flying across their trays. He dropped a half-full stick at one point, and letters flew underneath the press.

“Pick them up, Zach, before anyone steps on them,” said Harold. “After that, have Gunther take you down to the basement. He’ll show you how to fire the coal for the boilers. I’ll finish your page.”

"Yes, sir," said Zachary, still embarrassed for dropping his stick. None of the others deemed to notice his slow speed or clumsiness. Did they believe Harold wouldn't ask him back?

Lighting and tending the boilers in the basement gave Zachary no trouble. At three o'clock, the presses and the frames were ready to produce the printed newspaper. At 6:00 pm, Gunther pulled the last page away from the paper. It was his job to sort, stack, and tie off the piles of newspapers sent by wagon at dawn the next day to the post offices, the mercantile and grocery stores, and bookstores around the city and in San Jose and Bergs further north and south.

Zachary stayed and helped Gunther, only a few years older than Zach and a little daft, always laughing at everything Zach and the others said, funny or not.

Harold Crenshaw tipped his brim goodbye from the stairwell without further conversation involving Zachary. On the walk back to his hotel room, Zachary decided to show up on Monday and assume the spilled tray mess hadn't cost him his job. Even at $10.00/week, Zach would make more than at the swing station. He would work with words and stories and learn new and challenging skills. Soon, he would write to his mother, assuring her he had rebounded from the great earthquake and was intent on rebuilding his college fund.

35 |Daily Alta California

For six weeks, Zachary kept his head down, learning the nuances of typesetting, picking up speed, and concentrating on accuracy. He poured over the previous day's newspaper on his lunch break, searching for grammatical and spelling errors. He spotted letters out of order and mistaken substitutions, such as a lowercase 'b' for a lowercase 'd.' As with every chore the tall young man tackled, he completed his tasks with a critical eye.

He read all the articles in the *Daily Alta California* each day. The newspaper highlighted the arrivals and departures of vessels in the bay, and ship manifests from overseas for products heading to San Francisco and San Jose stores. Prominent citizens traveling from Seattle, Vancouver, South America, and sometimes New York and Europe received notable mention in the weekly edition.

Zachary came to work two hours early to get his type set by the deadline for the printing presses to roll. He steadily gained speed, but Tim and Roger, the other compositors, could finish their pages in half the time it took Zachary. The daily paper typically consisted of four pages, of which Tim contributed two pages, Roger: one page, and Zachary: one page. Roger also maintained the supplies in the warehouse on the third floor, delivering paper reams, ink, glue, etc., to the staging areas near the presses.

The boilers in the basement were Zachary's responsibility. He ordered the coal and received it, walking the coal wagon's ramp carrying bushel baskets of coal down to the bin in the basement.

When he arrived at work in the morning, Zach went first to the basement, stoked the coals in the furnace, and pitched more coal on the fire. He never minded tending the boilers. Duties with the boilers, furnace, and steam equipment kept him in shape and offered relief from the monotony of typesetting.

During the first weeks, the fear of failure kept piercing his thoughts, causing tension in his neck and shoulders, the pain triggering sleepless nights. Fighting through the pain reminded Zach of the saddle sores he wrestled with on his trek across the Arizona/California desert.

Strangely, thoughts of the pretty girl from San Jose, Caroline Wainwright, eased his late afternoon discomfort. The pain seemed to evaporate when he reconstructed her face in his mind. Zachary would shake his head to regain focus on his stick and continue. The pain would creep in again, and he would have to repeat his process.

His speed filling his stick matched the other compositors in eight more weeks. The tension headaches decreased in inverse proportion to his increased rate. He could relax, keep his accuracy higher than the experienced compositors, and nearly match their speed. However, thinking of Caroline Wainwright persisted, even after the headaches disappeared.

Next, Zachary turned his attention to the steam presses. Instead of arriving two hours early for work, he stayed late to observe the press operators, David Beasley and Frank (Stumpy) Eastman, for two hours at the end of his shift while they finished the daily run. He helped Gunther pile, count, bundle, and label each stack with the route address or newsboy's name who would deliver the paper. The intricate machinery and various moving parts intrigued Zach. By observing each sliding or rotating part individually, he learned the workings of the presses. If a press broke down, Zachary stayed to help tear it down, locate a spare part, and assist in the reassembling.

The stately Alta California building held an efficient, tuned collection of industrial machinery and resolute hard-working people. Harold Crenshaw's meticulous procedures impressed Zachary, as did the rest of the staff.

At the Alta California October '69 board of directors meeting, the chairman turned the floor over to the Managing Editor, Harold Crenshaw, for introductions to the board of new employees. Zachary, asked by Harold to attend, watched the proceedings with interest, assessing the upper management personalities and their interactions.

The Editor in Chief, Albert Evans, trusted Crenshaw to deliver quality, highly professional editions. They were different in stature and manner. Crenshaw seemed like a worker bee, constantly moving, conscious of every deadline, and encouraging his staff.

Albert Evans first impressed Zachary as a 'pompous snoot,' and the whole time Zachary knew the man, his opinion never changed. The man constantly sucked up to the other board members, twirling his waxed mustache points. While he fawned over the board members, he badgered and attempted to belittle Crenshaw and the rest of the staff to reinforce his superiority.

Zachary thanked his stars; he worked for Crenshaw and not directly under Evans. Zachary respected a worker like Crenshaw, but not the prima-donna in a long beard. The suit Evans wore reeked of high society, the lapels glossy in the extreme, his stance stiff as the collar choking his neck. Albert Evans shook hands with the new employee. His limp and wet grip caused Zach to wipe his hand on the seat of his pants before moving on to Mr. William Woodward. He also shook hands with Frederick MacCrellis. MacCrellis and Woodward owned the Alta building and published the Alta California publications.

The six other members of the board sitting at the table represented various businesses in the city, and they said nothing at the meeting. The short man at the end of the table fell asleep right after the introductions.

Harold Crenshaw announced a slight raise in Zachary's salary. Zach had passed the initiation and trial period of his typesetting apprenticeship.

San Franciscans know winter is approaching when the dampness in the air becomes constant, and the fog on the bay doesn't lift for days in a row. Thus, when Zach entered the Alta California building three weeks after the board meeting, Harold wore a printer's cap to warm his head. He reviewed edits with Amanda at her desk in the lobby.

Crenshaw looked up at Zachary, "Been waiting for you, Zachary," he said. "Come in a minute. Got a little errand for you." Harold led Zachary into his office and closed the door. The editor grabbed a portfolio from the corner of his desk and handed it to Zachary. He didn't let go of his end of the folder. "I need to rely on your discretion in this matter, Zachary," he said. "We've gotten to know each other in a business sense. This assignment is more personal.

"A couple of my friends have told me of their firsthand experience with your honesty. They commended your generosity in helping the recovery effort around the city after the quake. The construction company owner you briefly met, Thomas Winslow, cheated everyone in his reach during that tough time. Inexcusable. I would have exposed him in the newspaper, but Evans overrode me. Afraid to ruffle the wealthy patrons of the city."

Zachary had nearly forgotten the scoundrel. "I quit when I found out what a crook he was," said Zachary. "He should have been jailed, but reconstruction during that time of chaos mattered the most, I guess."

"Still, Zachary," Harold said, "I've heard of other instances. You got around, I guess, especially for being new in town."

"What is it you need, Mr. Crenshaw," said Zachary. Harold let go of the portfolio.

"I need you to deliver this in person to a friend in room 340 of the Occidental Hotel on the corner of Montgomery and Bush Streets.

"Does the name Samuel Clemens ring a bell?" said Crenshaw. "No? Perhaps Mark Twain, his nom de plume, have you heard that name."

"Yes," said Zachary. "I know he is an author and a lecturer, but I arrived too late in the city to attend one of his lectures. I understood he left San Francisco for New York in '66.

"True," said the editor, "but he returned after he voyaged on the steamship *Quaker* to the middle east and Europe to concentrate on authoring the book about his travels. He wrote the book that made the name Mark Twain famous in room 390 of the Occidental Hotel."

"So why the secrecy? If Clemens is your friend, why don't you deliver the portfolio? Is it valuable?"

"I believe the contents may well be valuable someday. You see, Alta California paid Sam's expenses for the trip and $20.00 a piece for every letter he sent back to the paper. The original letters are in the portfolio. Sam wants them back, and I don't blame him."

"I still don't get it, Mr. Crenshaw. Why the secrecy?"

"That's a long story. You might ask Sam if he's in a good mood."

"OK. When should I go?"

"I've handed off your pages to another compositor today. Zachary, I can tell you this much. My boss, Albert Evans, whom you met at the board meeting, has a history with Sam that makes my direct involvement problematic. Those two hate each other."

If asked, Zachary would have to agree with Sam Clemens. The straitlaced Evans did not impress him either.

Zachary couldn't imagine a situation that would intimidate his boss, the tough, dedicated Harold Crenshaw. Yet his curiosity silenced his questions, and he tucked the portfolio under his arm. "I'll be back."

***

The gentleman who opened room 340's door in the Occidental Hotel appeared to Zachary to be about five feet nine inches tall. The décor of the parlor consisted of a plush wool carpet, dark blue velvet chairs, and a settee. The heavy coverings kept the noise from the street and neighboring room movements minimal. Zach peeked through the door to the bedroom, which was just as lavish.

"Hello, Mr. Clemens; my name's Zachary Brennan. I brought the portfolio of the rest of your letters." Zach set the portfolio on the dresser.

Clemens wore black pants and a white shirt. The shirt looked recently ironed, but the tails of the untucked shirt were a study of wrinkles. The man's long black hair pushed against his ears, so curly Zachary could have laughed without Clemens saying a word. The bushy black mustache across his upper lip brought a measure of respectability to the author's handsome face. Despite an attractive countenance, the man's sloped shoulders and slight build suggested a man who used his brains over his brawn to Zachary.

"Well, sir, sit a spell," said Clemens. "You work at the publishing house. How do you like the work?"

Zachary sensed an urgency in Mr. Clemens's manner. As if the man hadn't had anyone to talk to, a sociable person cooped up in a small hotel room with no audience. Zach, known as a listener, found a seat at the polished chestnut table.

"How about a beer?" said Clemens. "A cigar? No? Don't mind if I do." Silence held the room as the author lit his cigar and puffed a couple of rings toward the ceiling. "You were saying?"

"I've been training as a compositor under Mr. Crenshaw since May. I hope to save up enough money to attend University in engineering. I'm learning. The mechanical steam presses intrigue me," said Zach.

"Now, that's a coincidence; I also started as a compositor. How is Harold? Great editor." Clemens laid a hand on the portfolio. "If it weren't for him and Col. McComb, who convinced the principals to finance my trip, this folder would be empty. I owe him. Say, ever think of reporting?"

"I don't know, Mr. Clemens," said Zachary, taking a big swig of the warm beer. "I read but haven't written much, except for school term papers for my mom and stories to amuse the family."

"You must be a pretty good writer, or Harold wouldn't have hired you."

"He did comment on my letter of application."

"You, see? If you had a chance, what would you write about?"

"I suppose the earthquake. I came to town the night before the great quake. We never had anything like that happen in the Arizona territory where I came from."

Samuel Clemens, living up to his reputation as an interviewer and reporter, spotted something in Zach's voice that indicated a story might be between Zach's words.

"A little young to come out to the coast alone, maybe," said Clemens. "Parents die? Indians? Cholera?"

"Nothing like that, Mr. Clemens. I worked as a wrangler at a Wells Fargo stagecoach swing station south of Santa Fe. The route didn't generate enough profit, so management in Omaha shut us down. My boss, Eli Blackstone, died then, and I needed to escape. A good man, Eli, not that old, and he taught me smithing."

Samuel rubbed his chin, silent for a minute, "Plenty there to write about, I can tell," he said.

Zachary had spent months pushing the images of Eli bleeding on the dirt floor of his shop out of his consciousness. He desperately wanted to change the subject.

"I better get going, Mr. Clemens. Just a question, though. Albert Evans, Mr. Crenshaw said you two don't get along. Is that the reason for the secrecy? It seemed to me that Harold wanted to come to say hello."

"I'll answer your question," said Clemens, "but you'll have to join me in another beer. I'll pop out and arrange with housekeeping to bring up a pitcher. Hold on."

Samuel left the room without bothering to tuck in his shirt or put on his shoes. Zachary picked up one of the books from a pile on the table. They were all new copies of the same book. He read the cover: *The Innocents Abroad or The New Pilgrim's Progress* by Mark Twain.

Cracking open the book slightly so as not to affect the crispness of the edition, Zachary read:

During that memorable month, I basked in the happiness of being for once in my life, drifting with the tide of a great popular movement. Everybody was going to Europe – I, too, was going to Europe. Everybody was going to the famous Paris Exposition – I, too, was going to the Paris Exposition. The steamship lines were carrying Americans out of the

various ports of the country at the rate of four or five thousand a week, in aggregate. If I met a dozen individuals during that month, who were,

Zachary replaced the book on the pile as the room door swung open. Samuel entered and sat opposite Zachary, relighting his cigar. "Won't be another moment or two. Ordered a charcuterie with bread and grapes as well. Getting hungry."

Zachary allowed his host a minute to enjoy his cigar, then prodded him again. "About Mr. Evans," he said.

"Disagreeably stiff," said Samuel. "Men of such importance to themselves should be housed in cages with mirrors all around for self-admiration.

"He's not your uncle, is he? Zachary, perhaps I spoke out of turn.

"He wrote lies about me in the *Gold Hill Evening News* in '66. I called him out for it and wrote about it when I worked as the local reporter for the San Francisco *Morning Call.* He has some hold over a few of the local policemen. Rumor was that he wished me arrested. That's why I left San Francisco. A city for which I have great affinity.

"Alas, I have a successful book, *Innocents Abroad,* and he has nothing. He no longer raises my dander. I don't want him to put the law upon me. When you start writing, Zachary, tackle the rampant police corruption here. There is a story in that as well."

"I guess the letters are pretty valuable," said Zachary.

"Maybe, but that is only one reason I'm here," said Clemens. "I finished my eastern lecture tour earlier this year, and now the beautiful Olivia Langdon has finally agreed to marry me, and the date is February 2nd, 1870. My sweet Lily absorbs my every thought.

"I decided this trip would be just the thing to distract me. Think of it. I am one of the first hundred people to travel by train on the transcontinental railroad from New York to California.

"I traveled from Buffalo, New York, to Council Bluffs, transferred to the Union Pacific Railroad, and ended up here. It took seven days to get here. Tomorrow, I will start back. The trip has been enlightening and exciting. When I return, I will concentrate on a home for Lily, the wedding, and our honeymoon in Buffalo.

"Is there a woman in your young life, Zachary? I saw a picture of Miss Langdon while steaming along on the *Quaker City* to Jerusalem. Love at first sight, from a picture, no less. She turned down my marriage proposal three times, but I finally won her. The fourth time I asked, she accepted."

"There is a girl I would like to get to know further," said Zachary. "She served grilled chicken in one of the soup lines when I worked on debris clean-up in San Jose."

"How is that going?" asked Samuel.

"She is the daughter of the owner of a large winery north of the city. Have you heard of the Wainwrights?"

"Yes, I have," said Clemens. "He married into a five-generation Mexican family in San Jose."

Zachary took another long slurp of beer.

"That sounds right. Anyway, I have only met Miss Wainwright once. I felt something there, but she had her family name in her mind. I didn't have enough prestige to warrant further pursuit. Something to work on."

"Don't give up," said the author. "I'm living proof. You seem poised for advancement. Think about reporting the news instead of typesetting it. Although summarizing church socials and cataloging steamer passenger lists to fill a column can get you down. The end game is worth the grind of getting the newspaper out.

"Sometimes the work is important. Sometimes the pen is mightier than the sword. Sometimes the words you write change the world's direction a little; the words mean something. That's a feeling unmatched, let me tell you."

The beer had relaxed them both. Samuel, the sociable, and Zachary, the listener, enjoyed their commonalities, and each intrigued the other with their life paths.

"But how can I tell if what I write is any good? What is skillful writing," asked Zachary.

"Ah," said Samuel. "Find the story."

The seasoned newspaperman leaned back in his chair, lit another cigar, and sucked and puffed until ash glowed in the low light of the hotel room.

"I can nutshell it," Clemens said. "Number one: Keep your eyes wide. Observe, don't miss the obvious, but also the not-so-obvious. Read in between the looks and expressions for the imperceptible but true.

"Number two: Follow your gut. If the story gets to you, it will get to others who appreciate your effort.

"Number three: Do the work, walk the streets, get the facts, all of 'em. Check your sources. Don't let your resource trip you up.

"Lastly: Discover the heart in the story. If you find it, the story is worth telling.

"Then it is a matter of being brave enough to pursue the story, draft the narrative, stand for and stand by it.

"That's it. Oh, and don't listen to a word I say. I got lucky with this book, right time, right place. I should thank Albert Evans for shooing me out of San Francisco. Funny how fate turns out to either benefit or destroys a man's life."

Zachary nodded, considering the fates controlling his life and the instances that may have changed his course. He decided not to return to work, a mistake at this point. He wouldn't be able to correctly spell two words on his stick. Zach poured more beer into Sam's mug and then filled his own.

Some brief time later, a knock on the door startled them both. Three men entered when Samuel opened the door, shaking Sam's hand. The first burly man clasped Samuel in a bear hug. "Samuel, or should I say, Mark, my man, ready to lose all that dough you made on the book?"

Samuel led the three men to the table, introducing the first man of the bear hug as Steve Gillis, his one-time lecture tour manager and longtime friend.

"Zachary here is new to the newspaper business. His background is horse wrangling and losing at cards, so I invited him to sit in."

"Zachary," said Gillis. "You've got nothing to worry about. No one in the country is a worse poker player than my good friend Sam, but he'll make you laugh until you loan his losses back to him."

The second man sitting at the table might have been brawnier than Gillis. "Sit and cut for deal. I got more pitchers of beer on the way. Names Tom, Tom Sawyer, good to know you, Zach."

Samuel slapped Sawyer on the shoulder, which never registered with Sawyer. "Tom's a fireman, but he's modest. After he's had six beers, I'll tell you of his heroics. Just don't steal the stories for your writing."

The third man appeared a bit more mild-mannered than the first two gentlemen.

"Last but not least, this is Bret Harte, another fellow typesetter and author," said Clemens.

"Wait," said Zach, "the *Overland Monthly* magazine, right? You wrote that remarkable story, *The Luck of Roaring Camp*."

"Hey Samuel," said Harte, "Someone with taste. All right, the beer has arrived; cut you all."

Zachary couldn't tell if anyone stacked the card deck, but Bret Harte pulled the king of diamonds and won the first deal. Harte picked up the deck and dealt the hands with the ante established and the pot built. "Five card draw," said Harte.

He waited a moment for everyone to look at their cards. On his left, Bret nodded to Tom Sawyer, "What do you say, Tom?"

The beer, the cigars, and new friends. They were older, yes, but they never professed superiority. They all had history along the Barbary Coast and fascinating stories to tell. Zachary worried he drank too much and wouldn't remember much from the memorable day and late night.

Zachary walked home in the wee hours through the thick San Francisco fog. Alone but for the click of his heels on the cobblestone, the sound instantly swallowed in the dew. He conjured snatches of Sam's squinting eye beneath a cocked eyebrow speaking of the foundations of decent writing. *Mightier than a sword, he'd said. What about a gun? Mightier than a gun?*

36 |Promotion

7:30 am, October 24th, 1872; only the second time Zachary had been late to work since he began typesetting in October 1869. Zachary hurried along California Street and entered the Alta California building as unobtrusively as possible, rushing directly to the stairs. On the fourth step, he heard Crenshaw yell, "Zachary, step into my office, please."

Zachary stopped and shut both eyes briefly, disgusted that he might be losing his job because he had forgotten to wind his mantel clock the night before. He turned back down the stairs and entered Harold's office.

"What's up? Boss," Zachary said.

"Sit down," said Crenshaw.

Zachary folded his six-foot-two-inch frame into the side chair before Crenshaw's desk. Harold pushed a stack of memos out of his way, folded his arms, and leaned on the desk.

"We've lost our Editor in Chief. Albert Evans was aboard the steamship *Missouri* that burned at sea two days ago." Harold said.

"No! That is horrible!" said Zachary

"Nevertheless, it is true," said Harold. "The company made me Editor in Chief at an emergency board of directors meeting. I'll also stay on as Managing Editor. Two big jobs, one man."

"If anyone can keep the paper rolling, it's you, Harold," said Zach. "The fact is Evans mired the paper in mediocrity. The newspaper is better off without the man."

"I can't say I disagree with you, Zach," Harold chuckled just a bit. "Here is the deal. I appreciate your initiative. In your three years, you've become an excellent compositor. You have learned the workings of even the smallest part of the steam presses and the Gordon Jobber.

"I'm not forgetting that night last December when you tore apart the number one press down to the base frame, found a machinist at 10:00 pm to make a replacement part, and put the press back together in time for the next day's deadline. All that occurred while David and Stumpy ran the number two press all night to finish the distribution bundles.

"I know your suggestions to Gunther on buying our paper stock have saved us a ton of money. You have a handle on the business side of things as well."

"During the war," said Zachary, "While my father fought the Texas confederates, I stayed in Arizona and managed our sheep ranch with my mother. We kept things going by watching what sums of money came in and being careful about what we spent. It rubbed off."

"With Albert out of the picture, the shackles are off. I want the *Daily Alta California* to become the most influential newspaper on the west coast. *The New York Times*, *The Washington Post, The Daily Alta California*. Has a nice ring to it!

"I need help from people with vision. I know you are young; I hear that all the time, but I believe we may accomplish much together.

"I want you to move up to reporting. You'll take the territory south of San Francisco for now. San Jose, Saratoga, Gilroy. Memorable stories, hard news, exposés. If the story is good, I'll include a byline. Expect another raise.

"Amanda spent most of a day tabulating; we carry over a thousand subscriptions south of San Francisco's city limits."

Zachary focused on the picture of Lincoln hanging on the wall beyond Crenshaw's head to maintain professionalism, yet his smile gave him away. "When do I start, Chief," he asked.

Harold went to his file cabinet and thumbed through manila folders from the second drawer until he found the folder he wanted, pulling it up a little to mark its place in the drawer. He extracted an application, turned to Zachary, and handed the paperwork to him.

"When you've trained your replacement," said Crenshaw. "Here is her application. I think Miss Angela Caswell might work out. Right out of high school, women are faster at this job than men… no offense, you are the fastest compositor here."

"None was taken," said Zachary.

The territory south of San Francisco placed Zachary near the Wainwright ranch and vineyards. He would see more of Caroline. The promotion might help convince her to become more than a riding partner.

More importantly, Harold Crenshaw, already an esteemed businessman in the community, would now be on the Board of Directors. As Harold's right-hand man, Zachary would have the opportunity to hone his writing.

37 |Boston Immigrants

Excerpt from the *Daily Alta California,* January 1, 1876, scissored and folded into a letter sent to Hanna Brennan, postmarked San Francisco. Zachary's first byline.

> SAN FRANCISCO USHERS IN THE CENTENNIAL YEAR
>
> Zachary Brennan
>
> A sea of umbrellas dripping rain protected thousands of San Franciscans as they counted down the last seconds of 1875, kicking off the celebration of our nation's one hundred years of independence.
>
> Spotlights illuminated the titles "1776" and "1876" in bold figures hanging on the Fire Alarm Telegraph office under the supervision of J. S. Urquhart.
>
> Shortly before midnight, the Fire Company ignited a large bonfire in Brenham Square. As the midnight bell began to toll, observers threw bombs into the fire, which exploded.
>
> Many enthusiasts surrounded the bell tower dispatching rockets and Roman candles upwards through the rain. A government employee struck the bell at the Plaza one hundred and ten times lasting over five minutes. The building shook as if in an earthquake from the rapid strokes of the bell. After the ringing,

> the crowd's "Happy New Year" roar echoed off the square buildings. Enthusiastic and patriotic, not to say bibulous, individuals filled the principal streets and discharged firecrackers, bombs, pistols, Roman candles, and all kinds of explosives.
>
> Shortly before the stroke of the midnight bell, the International Hotel burst out in a blaze of colored Bengal lights, which beautifully illuminated the streets. Showers of rockets and candle stars shot into the air.
>
> The first California Guard hailed the advent of the Centennial year in front of their new armory on Market Street near Eighth.
>
> The illumination of the Alta California office attracted a large crowd that showed its appreciation of the brilliant fireworks. At the moment of the death of the old and the birth of the New Year, The crowd cheered this journal vociferously and wished it a happy and prosperous New Year.
>
> There will be a general suspension of business throughout the city tomorrow. The banks, stock exchanges, courts, and public offices will close for the celebration. The national bunting will hang on the flagstaffs at all the military posts; in all probability, the forts will blend a harmonious note into the universal chorus of rejoicing.

***

Justin Ormond, wagon master, palmed water from the Leroux Spring pool on his face. A red handkerchief tied by his scouts high in the dead, stripped pine near the creek had been the agreed-upon signal for a place to camp. Turning back to the wagons stretching behind the supply station, he yelled to no one in particular, "Let's camp here for tonight, at least. I, for one, can't take another step." The date: May 27th, 1876, and the mountain air felt comfortably warm after the desert heat along the Little Colorado River.

The signal to make camp spread down the line and drivers turned the Conestoga wagons into a circle. Children poured forth, heading for the spring to swim. The campers prepared dinner and gathered fire materials as if they had been traveling all their lives.

The trip from Boston for this group of immigrants determined to forge new family histories had been desperately hard. Leaving the panic of 1873 and the resulting depression in the east behind, the group met with yet another disappointment upon reaching the Little Colorado River and the land promised by the American Arizona Colonization Company. The Mormons had already established plots and ranches in the river's fertile areas.

Most travelers had all but given their homes away in Boston to raise funds to purchase a wagon and supplies to reach the promised land. There would be nothing to return to in Boston, so Ormond kept the wagon train moving west.

That morning, Justin had met Steve Pembroke manning the supply station. After purchasing some items at the station to be sociable, Steve and Justin sat on the supply station porch for a smoke. Justin slowly approached the topic of settlement land in the area. He hoped Steve might have a suggestion.

"The best land I know of is right here in this valley. You could speak to Hanna and Lorenzo Brennan up on the mountain," said Steve, gesturing toward the trail up to the

Brennan ranch. "They have staked out their property. Seems like they may be willing to sell a parcel or two.

"As you can see, there is nothing here except for the supply station."

Justin rocked back in his chair until it hit the station wall and propped his boots against the porch post. He took another drag on his rolled-up and surveyed the view of the vast lush fields. Then he shook his head. "Starting from scratch here sounds great to me, but you know," said Justin, "these folks have already seen about as much hardship as they can take."

"I understand," said Pembroke, "based on what you've told me. …been happening out here since the days of the gold rush. Promises, empty as a rain bucket in the desert.

"How about Prescott? Southwest of here, maybe eighty, ninety miles. Somewhat established these days, but lots of opportunities. No promises from me, though; you make your own choice. California is five hundred miles due west through a couple of deserts."

Justin rocked forward and stood. "I guess we'll discuss things over the campfire tonight," he said. "Might be here a few days while we sort things out."

"Welcome as long as you'd like. If I see Lorenzo, I'll send him over to your camp. He scouted for the surveyors traveling to Los Angeles before the war. He knows the water locations and is a great resource and friend."

"I look forward to meeting him," said Ormond. "We'll circle our wagons for a stay when we spot the signpost our scouting party erects to guide us."

As it happened, Lorenzo Brennan did not come to the Pembroke Supply Station before the Boston wagon train moved out of the area. The immigrants experimented for a couple of weeks, laying out a village and dwellings before the members decided to move to Prescott as Justin Osborn had initially proposed. The stripped dead pine tree sporting the red handkerchief remained for future travelers, a significant sign of the abundant water supply in the area.

***

A knock on the Brennan cabin door caused Hanna's heart to skip. She hoped it might be Zachary. It had been eight years since her son had left. The letters they exchanged could never fill the hole in her heart from not seeing him daily. Her solace came from his achievements and advancements at the newspaper where he worked. The articles cut from the newspaper with his byline beneath the headline made her smile. He was doing well, although she still hoped for her son to attain a college degree.

The two men standing on the porch, hats in hand, seemed unthreatening. The man in a leather frock coat bowed slightly. "Am I speaking to Mrs. Hanna Brennan," he said. "I apologize for not sending ahead a note of introduction. My name is Thomas McMillan. If we may be permitted to explain our visit to you and your husband, I believe you may find interest in our purpose."

Hanna, her left hand gripping the barrel of the rifle kept next to the door, out of sight, smiled, "You are welcome to take seats on the porch and await my husband's return from the upper pasture."

"I thank you, ma'am," said the man, smiling. He had curly dirty blond hair, a small, neat mustache, and long sideburns. His tidy appearance contrasted with the rougher-looking man seated in the chair seven feet away. That man had unruly black hair, worn too long to fit his Stetson properly. His frayed wool-striped pant legs covered his boots. His gun and holster seemed to say about the man, “Watch out for me.” A ruffian, Hanna decided.

Hanna busied herself making tea, bringing cups and saucers to the porch, and offering tea to the strangers. Mr. McMillan accepted a cup of tea. The other man waved Hanna away without speaking.

After five minutes of talking about the weather in the early days of June ’76, Hanna noticed Lorenzo approaching the cabin. Having finished bedding down the sheep and the other barn animals, he had sighted the men on the porch and quickened his pace.

These days the limp from his war wounds received in the Mexican/American war had returned as a constant ache. Lorenzo relied increasingly on Kyle and his daughter Sarah, whom Kyle had married in the spring. They kept the ranch going and expanded Hanna’s holdings.

“Lorenzo,” said Hanna, “this gentleman’s name is Thomas McMillan, and we were just getting to the nature of his visit.”

“Thank you, Hanna,” said McMillan, rising to shake Lorenzo’s hand before returning to his seat.

“Pleased to meet you, Mr. McMillan,” said Lorenzo. “Just a minute, let me get comfortable.” Lorenzo brought out the rocking chair from the cabin to join the discussion.

“Now, how can we help you,” said Hanna.

“Not to beat around the bush, Mr. and Mrs. Brennan, I have decided to move my sheep enterprise to your beautiful valley. Three days from now, my entire flock will arrive from Australia through California. I wanted you not to be surprised. In early spring, my surveying team and I staked out the 320 acres abutting your land and began building a cabin for my family.”

“How many sheep are we talking about,” said Lorenzo.

"Five hundred to start, Mr. Brennan, but I'll expand my stock as the market will bear. There are more, smaller sheep ranchers coming along as well."

Lorenzo exchanged glances with Hanna, the expert in the family when it came to their sheep ranch.

"I have long dreamed of neighbors," said Hanna. "I suspect the area around Lorenzo Springs could support ten thousand sheep, wouldn't you, Mr. McMillan?"

"I would agree one hundred percent, Hanna," said McMillan.

"My only concern would be distinguishing whose sheep are whose," said Hanna.

"Of course," said Thomas. "That will be the responsibility of my foreman. If more ranchers arrive, we must establish brands to identify each ranch."

"I'd like to walk your property markers with you, Mr. McMillan. Give me an idea of your new spread and plans," said Lorenzo.

"No worries," said McMillan, "come to our camp in the valley, and I'll walk you up to the building site. Then we can walk the boundaries. While I'm here, could you give me a tour of your operation?"

"Hanna," said Lorenzo, "you want to come along?"

"Sure do!" Hanna said.

Mr. McMillan seemed impressed with Hanna's ranch. He praised the Brennans for the efficiency of the operation, smaller in scale than his own.

Lorenzo turned to the man wearing striped pants when they were about to leave. He offered a handshake, "Didn't catch your name, sir."

"I apologize, Lorenzo," said McMillan. "My foreman's name is Corbin. Turk Corbin."

Lorenzo put both hands casually in his pants pockets and nodded at the foreman, who neither scowled nor smiled. "See you around," Lorenzo said. The man did not respond. Both men mounted their horses and set off down the mountain.

Lorenzo kept his thoughts to himself. He recalled what Zachary had told only him and not Hanna about the man at the swing station that had murdered Eli Blackstone.

Hanna noticed Lorenzo's body language. "What gives with you and that foreman?" she asked.

"Nothing I can put my finger on," said Lorenzo. "His look, I guess. Did you notice he always kept a hand on his gun handle? I will watch him tomorrow, and if you come along, watch out for him as well."

"Oh, I'm coming, alright."

The next afternoon, McMillan displayed confident strength as he walked Hanna and Lorenzo around his property borders. Tents for the construction crew littered a quarter acre at the valley's edge, along with piles of lumber and various building finishing materials under tarps. The guests moseyed up to the house foundation on the rise above the construction camp. The wind carried the familiar smell of seasoning ponderosa pine framing the first-floor south wall of the house, braced in place. Thomas brought the Brennans into the fledgling structure to appreciate the view overlooking the valley where his sheep would graze. His home would be much closer to the valley than the Brennan cabin.

"Of course," said McMillan, "I hope to build a bigger place once the ranch is established."

Hanna nodded, thinking what she could see seemed twice the size of her cabin.

Thomas continued, "As I'm clearing, I'll set aside the big pines for hewing and squaring in my spare time. When the logs are fully seasoned, we'll build my wife's dream house."

Lorenzo watched for Corbin until Mr. McMillan informed the Brennans that he had left to meet his sheep herd heading over from the Colorado River.

Hanna found in Thomas McMillan, a fellow dreamer who might share her vision for establishing a town in the valley. He seemed willing to share the land with others wishing to build a community. Maps showed the railroad surveys connecting Los Angeles, Santa Fe, and Wichita or St Louis right through the valley where they stood.

After existing alone as a pioneer on the San Francisco Mountain for more than twenty-five years, Hanna envisioned neighbors and shops nearby. The gleam in McMillan's eye matched her own. She would be on the ground floor. Even though a woman, Hanna held powerful and valuable land assets along the route. The day would come. It seemed only a short time to Hanna, only three years away.

Without the presence of Turk Corbin, Lorenzo warmed to the sheep farmer from California. Over dinner at the construction camp, they shared their respective histories in Mexico and Australia. After dinner, the Brennans took their leave, Hanna suggesting another get-together in a few days so she might meet Thomas's wife, traveling with the sheep herd.

Lorenzo insisted they stop at Steve's supply station on the way home and fill him in on the progress of the McMillan ranch. Leaning against the counter were two strangers, immigrants by the layers of dust on their jackets and weary movements. They had come a long way.

"Boston, as a matter of fact," said the man whose extended belly kept him an arms-length away from the countertop. "We're trying to catch up to Osborn's wagon train."

"You missed him by only a week," said Steve, "Their party decided to start over in Prescott."

"That's fine," said the other man, scratching his curly beard beneath his chin. "We'll camp here for a few days and then continue to meet Justin."

Steve said, "That sounds like a plan. I suggest you circle your six wagons for tonight and be on the lookout for a red signpost flag tied to a dead, stripped pine tree tomorrow. That flag marks where you'll find fresh water."

Lorenzo and Hanna had been quietly eavesdropping, deciding to speak to Steve after the travelers left the supply station. Hanna, however, had an idea. "Sounds like you'll be spending the fourth of July in our valley. Why not make it a grand celebration, Steve? We could attend, and I'm sure Kyle and Sarah could be there. We met Mr. McMillan; he and those smaller sheep farmers would participate.

"The United States of America - 100 years, that's something. Don't you think so, Lorenzo?"

Everyone in the station agreed on contributions; baked goods, mutton for all, and a keg of Mckenna Whiskey Steve had saved for a special occasion.

***

The fledgling community came together at 1:00 pm on Jul 4th, 1876. A group of men spent the morning trimming a thirty-foot, ten-inch diameter Ponderosa pine, burying it in the soft soil near McMillan's corner post at Leroux Spring. One of the second Boston Party teenagers shinnied up to the top and attached Old Glory (now with thirty-seven stars along with the thirteen red and white stripes.)

Seven men stood before a solemn gathering around the pole, offering a rifle salute to commemorate the centennial. Thus, the community of Flagstaff was established.

The afternoon celebration included Indian wrestling, a shooting contest, and three-legged races. Thirty people enjoyed the festivities. Hanna met Mrs. McMillan, and the two women spent the rest of the day getting to know and like each other.

Lorenzo noticed the absence of Turk Corbin. Thomas indicated his foreman kept to himself on his time off and didn't like to be bothered with socializing.

The second Boston party moved south toward Prescott two weeks later, but five new sheep farmers stayed.

Steve Pembroke directed future wagon trains to camp down the Beale Road at Flagstaff, a cozy spot along the spring where they could find grass to feed their livestock and water to fill their barrels and canteens.

As the Brennans knew, the area's isolation posed no problem to the new sheep ranchers because wool did not spoil and could withstand the long, rough wagon journey to market in Denver, St Louis, Boston, and other cities in the east.

***

The whispers rolled along the entire length of Beale's Wagon Road in the Arizona territory like tumbleweeds in the desert: railroad construction would begin within the month. The railroad would cross the region by March '81.

Men left their wives at home and joined the rail gang. Chinese immigrants traveled east from San Francisco to pick up shovels and pickaxes to level the tie bed. Tent communities sprang up along the survey markers, and vendors began bringing in whiskey, beer, and desperate women.

The sheep ranchers from the community of Flagstaff met and strategized a lobbying effort for a station stop. They'd heard about a planned station in Winslow to the east and Williams to the west. Thomas McMillan was elected to approach the

Atlantic and Pacific Railroad management to secure a stop in Flagstaff.

On July 25, 1880, a woman stepped down from a chartered stagecoach out of Albuquerque. She stopped in at Pembroke's Supply Station and rang the bell on the counter. Steve Pembroke entered the warehouse, wondering how to assist the unusual solo traveler.

"I'm trying to locate the Brennan family," said the woman. She looked amazingly alert for having just traveled far on the dusty Beale Wagon Road.

"I can direct you to the Brennan's sheep ranch up the mountain there."

The woman pawed through her purse, pulling out a ragged envelope containing a nearly tattered letter. Carefully unfolding the letter, she scanned it and looked up. "Does Hanna Brennan live on the mountain?" she asked.

"You've got it. It's quite a hike up to the cabin," said Steve. "I could take you up there when I close up here if you don't mind riding side saddle in front of me on Taffy."

"Might I be able to pay Mrs. Brennan for room and board while I'm in the area?" the woman asked.

"Hanna is quite a force around here, vice president of the Sheepherders Association. Generous to a fault as well. You'd be welcome if you are an acquaintance of theirs."

"I believe Zachary, their son, worked for my father at one time, some years ago."

"Eli Blackstone, sure. He's one you don't forget. A relative of his?"

"I'm his daughter."

"It's near 4:00 pm. Give me a minute to close, and we'll head up.

As always, the knock on Hanna's front door startled her into dropping her stirring spoon.

"Just a second," Hanna yelled, "I'll be right there."

When Hanna opened the cabin door, Steve Pembroke stood beside a dark-skinned woman in a princess-style light gray suit. She wore what looked like an expensive straw bonnet encircled with a red velvet ribbon and adorned with a single feather.

"Hello, Hanna," said Steve. "I've brought you a boarder if you're willing. This here is Eliza Blackstone, daughter of Eli Blackstone. She's looking for Zachary. I told her he lived in San Francisco these days."

Hanna looked at Eliza, her dress, hair, and straight stature. Physically trim, with high cheekbones, a beauty. Hanna smiled. "Come in, come in. I'm Hanna, Zachary's mother. Please have a seat. It has been a long time since I've seen my son."

"I came to Arizona to learn more about my father," said Eliza. "I'm interested in his way of life out here. The circumstances of his passing. I spent four years at Oberlin College while Father came out west.

"I was quite young the last time I saw him. I know he worked for the Wells Fargo Stagecoach Co. In Ohio, he excelled as a blacksmith. During the war, he worked on special assignments for the North."

"You are welcome to stay here as long as you like. We have a small apartment with a bed in the barn where you can stay."

"Would you accept a five dollar-a-week stipend for your trouble?" asked Eliza.

"Heavens, no, your company will be enough. I get girl lonely up here. The conversation would be worth your weight in gold to me."

"I left my trunk down at the supply station."

"Don't worry. I'll send my husband down to fetch it. He'll be bringing the sheep in from the north pasture soon.

Eliza's interest in her father prompted Hanna to recall and explain the circumstances of Zachary's employment as a horse handler at the swing station.

"He must have been sixteen or seventeen at the time," said Hanna. "I worried over him for a month. Then Lorenzo and I traveled to the swing station and met your father. A gentle giant, he was. He and Zachary got along so well, and Zachary showed us all that he had learned.

"I haven't worried about my son since. It's been ten, eleven years since your father passed?"

"Twelve years this September," said Eliza. "One day, I'll meet your son. I have treasured the letter he sent to me."

The sound of uneven footsteps on the porch signaled Lorenzo's approach. The cabin door opened, and the tall man entered, using his shepherd's crook as a cane to help with his stiff leg. "Thought I heard voices," he said. "Who's our visitor, Hanna."

"Lorenzo, meet Eliza Blackstone. The daughter of Eli Blackstone. You know, from the swing station. Zachary's supervisor."

A brief flash of panic sent a flush to Lorenzo's cheeks.

The daughter.

How much does she know?

Should I warn her of Turk Corbin?

"Lorenzo," said Hanna, "Eliza needs the trunk she left at the Supply Station. I've asked her to stay with us for the time being in Kyle's old apartment above the barn."

"Certainly," said Lorenzo. "Just when I finish my tea. I'll attach the travois to the mule and haul it up."

Lorenzo kept his thoughts on Turk Corbin to himself. He didn't know all the circumstances; it had been long ago. He had not heard of any further indiscretions by Corbin. *Best to keep quiet.*

Hanna learned a great deal about her house guest in the following weeks. Eliza had a degree in accounting from Oberlin College. For the next eight years after college, Miss Blackstone was a junior and senior accountant for ever larger companies in Cincinnati. For the last four years, she has contracted as a consultant for the Standard Oil Company. When Rockefeller acquired a property, Eliza researched and audited the financials. She was able to amass a substantial amount of money to devote to understanding her father's Western allure.

On her trek across the New Mexico and Arizona territories, Eliza observed the activity along Beale Wagon Road and the Railroad survey markers and recognized a business opportunity. She hoped to take advantage of the future track and build a retail storefront specializing in women's fashion clothing and accessories. The women who moved west with their ambitious husbands would long for a decent gown, if for no other purpose than to attend church.

Ever the entrepreneur, Hanna encouraged Eliza to stake a claim in the fledgling Flagstaff community. Eliza's stay had put the idea of building her own boarding house a short distance from the tracks down the valley. In short, Hanna would develop the town. Thomas McMillan and herself owned all the property on the north side of the railroad survey. Hanna had spoken to Thomas about a land office and the layout of Flagstaff streets and residential and commercial lots. Hanna recognized what a huge benefit Eliza's expertise in business could provide to the community.

38 |Byline

Hanna opened the latest letter from Zachary, and an enclosed newspaper article fluttered onto the table. She read the editorial from the *Daily Alta California* on July 26.

> THE SHAME OF SAN FRANCISCO
> AND A PLEA FOR COMPASSION
> Zachary Brennan
>
> For three days, July 23, 24, and 25, San Francisco experienced its darkest time since the lawless days of looting in the aftermath of the Great Earthquake of October 21, '68.
> Since the Gold Rush, the city has not seen rampant disregard for human life and property.
> Backers held a rally in support of the plight of workers' rights among the unemployed of Pittsburgh in the vacant lot next to City Hall on July 23, as reported in this newspaper.
> Sponsored by the Workingmen's Party of the United States, the speakers at the rally advocated for peaceful discussion. The crowd was good-natured, the speakers poor, and the result for aiding their brethren was zero.
> Yet on the night of the 23rd, riots broke out and destroyed $100,000.00 worth of Chinese businesses. Four Chinese immigrants died.

> The ethnic violence was only halted through the combined efforts of the SFPD and the California state militia. They were joined by 1,000 civilian "Committee of Safety" members armed with hickory pickaxe handles.
> Citizens of San Francisco, to become a great city in the United States, we must rise above prejudice and hate. Jefferson wrote, and Lincoln echoed: We hold these truths to be self-evident, that all men are created equal, that they are endowed by their Creator with certain unalienable Rights, that among these are Life, Liberty, and the Pursuit of Happiness.
> Citizens of San Francisco consider the following definition of the word **pogrom** from Webster's Dictionary: "an act of organized cruel behavior or killing done to a large group of people because of their race or religion."
> We are better than that. We must be better than that.

Hanna reread the article in bed with Lorenzo that night before shutting off the last lantern. A tear threatened to stain the newsprint. "Our boy is quite a writer," said Hanna. "I believe we did something right by that boy."

"He's always been two steps ahead of me, Hanna," said Lorenzo. "He's a man now; I can see that. I don't worry about him. He's making his way."

Hanna showed the newspaper column to Eliza, who had come over from the apartment for breakfast.

"Your son is an impressive writer," said Eliza. "He sounds committed to San Francisco. Do you think he might visit someday?"

"I hope so, Eliza," Hanna said.

39 |Three Girl Gossip

The day in San Jose began to scorch by midmorning on the 5th of August 1880. The thermometer attached to the outside window of the church office read ninety-five degrees. After the first Unitarian Church of San Jose service, an ice cream social brought cool relief to the congregation.

Zachary excused himself from the company of the three young women gossiping in the rear of the community room. The large room in the Town Hall served as the congregation's sanctuary until the members could raise enough money to build a church. "Caroline," he interrupted, "I'll stand in line and bring you back ice cream and cake."

"Just ice cream for me, Zach; no cake, please," Caroline said.

The other two ladies ate their last bite of cake and handed their empty plates to Zach to cart back to the kitchen.

Olivia Halstead knuckled her waist with both hands. As tall as her friend Caroline and dressed in her best off-white taffeta hemmed dress, she watched Zach glide his tall frame through the crowd toward the kitchen. "Alright, Caroline," she said. "I want to know if you are ever going to hook that man," nodding in Zach's direction. The third woman in the group, Alice Coombs, nodded expectantly.

Caroline, taken aback, said, "Zach and I have been friends for years since the great earthquake. We ride together when he comes down on an assignment in San Jose.

"We enjoy each other's company."

"I should say," said Olivia. "He is so handsome."

"He is a good friend," Caroline reiterated.

"Nothing goes on between you two on those rides in the country?" pressed Olivia.

"I told you, he's a friend," Olivia said.

"I don't understand you, Caroline Wainwright. Those shoulders. Just look at him. He's one of the smartest and most ambitious men within fifty miles. And he is successful too."

"Yes, Zachary is all about his work. I don't think he thinks beyond his next story," Caroline said.

"Did you read his latest article?" said Alice. "I've heard he has received death threats."

Zachary appeared with cake and ice cream in one hand, just ice cream for Caroline in the other.

The social wound down. Zach swung up on Arrow and started back to San Francisco. He turned for one last look at Caroline. Her silhouette always flamed a fire within his chest. Even at this distance, he could imagine his hands grasping her slim waist and pulling her into his arms, her chin lifting even as her eyes lowered, searching for his lips.

The three women waved goodbye. Olivia turned once again to Caroline. "I'll be visiting my aunt in the city next March. I may visit the Alta California offices and suggest a society piece for Zachary to cover. You won't mind, Caroline, will you?"

Back in her room at the ranch, Caroline pondered Olivia and Zachary becoming a couple. She had never entertained the possibility of Zachary Brennan, the horse handler, as a suitor. They did not match; her father would never approve, as much as she, flushed hot, intimately yearning for him, secretly wanting him. Even more so as Olivia received his attention. She thought him very handsome. That was true. But her station, dowry, and background all made it impossible.

Yet, others saw Zachary as a man of substance, making a name for himself in San Francisco; no small feat. She would speak to her father.

Suddenly, Caroline panicked. *Am I too late?*

***

"Don't even think about taking up with that man," said Donald Wainwright, Caroline's father. "Zachary Brennan is trying to destroy everything I stand for and have built up in this county. I pay my workers to pick and mash grapes. If it weren't for our family, the coolies, and Mexicans would be begging by the side of the road."

"That is an exaggeration, Father," said Caroline. "Zach has nothing against you. He's told me how he admires you."

"You are fooling yourself, daughter. He endorsed the Workingmen's Party of the United States in that newspaper article. I'm telling you, he's a Marxist. This land will no longer be ours if they have their way."

Caroline put her hands behind her, clenching her fists but outwardly appearing calm, smiling sweetly at her father, sitting behind his desk. "Father, you must be wrong. Zachary Brennan is well respected in San Francisco."

Caroline had fought her whole life to find equal footing with her older brother in her father's eyes. As early as she could remember, she had tried to impress upon him her ability and desire to have a place of importance on the estate. As a rebellious teen, the patriarch had insisted Caroline attend Miss Porter's School in Connecticut. At finishing school, she learned how to sew fashionable clothes, including a split skirt for riding a horse astride like men.

The school's curriculum included chemistry, physiology, botany, geology, astronomy, and the more traditional Latin,

French, German, spelling, reading, arithmetic, trigonometry, and history. Caroline came home after two years, more determined to work alongside her father in the vineyard business. For a while, her efforts seemed to be succeeding. Yet Robert, her older brother, had attended a vintner school in France.

Robert and Caroline's father let her know that Robert, being the heir, would never consider sharing the responsibilities and profits of his rightful inheritance with his sister; unthinkable. Caroline would receive a generous dowry and must expect to marry well to establish her security. She remained hopeful, working through her mother to bend her father's will in her direction. She held off suitors for years, discussing possibilities with Zachary on their horse-riding excursions around San Jose.

She now realized how much Zachary respected her views and abilities. Her riding partner treated her as an equal. He could be counted on for sharing a life built on respect.

Don Wainwright relit his pipe, allowing his thoughts to conjure up multiple solutions to the problem of his stubborn and too-independent daughter. His carpenters had spent a month building and finishing his large cherrywood desk. The polished surface of the masterpiece reflected his image like a mirror.

Ultimately, the patriarch took an end run by trying a different tack. "Listen, Caroline," he said, "Let's compromise. Take your rides with your friend Zachary and ensure he holds to the values you profess so vocally.

"What about the church? Is he a faithful catholic?" Mr. Wainwright rarely attended Mass. Caroline attended the Unitarian service at city hall, withholding the fact of her attendance from her father.

Caroline recalled Zach mentioning his mother's Jewish heritage, but she kept quiet.

"You may want to bring up that crucial point."

“OK, Father.”

“Now, for my sake, I want you to accept an invitation from Randall Brookhaven for dinner. He’s in town this month, lining up suppliers and buyers for next season's orange crop. His family owns a large orchard estate north of LA. I met him, and he saw your picture on the piano. Unless I miss my guess, I predict you will like him. Do this for me, and I’ll agree to be cordial to Mr. Brennan.”

***

The reporter, concentrating on tightening the word count of his latest article, looked up at the sound of a second tap on his office door window. To Zachary's surprise, the door opened, and Olivia Halstead, Caroline’s closest friend, leaned in.

“Hello, Zachary,” Olivia said. “You really should have your name stenciled on the window. This is the third door I’ve opened trying to find you.”

“Usually, Amanda buzzes me when I have a visitor,” said Zachary.

“Oh, I breezed right by her. I have an event I want you to write up for the newspaper, but might you give me the nickel tour first?” said Olivia.

“Certainly, I don’t get many visitors,” said Zach. “I just need to drop off this copy to the editor, and I’ll show you around.”

“Maybe we could also go out to lunch, " Olivia said.

Olivia commented on the large, noisy presses, the swift paper transfer through the machines, and the smell of the ink. She skirted around oil, and ink drips like a professional ballet dancer, holding her dress tightly around her legs. She sighed audibly in relief when they finally left the building and headed for the Cliff House for lunch.

The restaurant, located close to the water, benefitted from the bay breeze, which made the warm day in March pleasant.

Olivia described the gala event to benefit the hospital in San Jose to be held the week before Easter, on Saturday, April 9th, 1881. She gave the details of the evening's agenda, the options for the meal, and the auction of decorated piñatas that the organizers hoped would raise thousands of dollars. Olivia helped Zach with the names and spellings of the more influential guests.

The maître d' sat the pair at a small two-top. The view out the window overlooked the bay. Ships jostled in their slips, and a large steamer sailed west. Olivia's dress swished underneath the table, gathering around Zachary's pants. He attempted to keep his legs discreetly tucked under his chair. On the other hand, Olivia seemed to have no qualms and continuously stretched her legs on either side of Zachary's legs. Zach felt her rubbing his leg with hers, even through the dress.

Olivia seemed more animated than when she stood in Caroline's shadow. She bubbled enthusiastically about the piñata she had constructed for the auction. She planned to attach real flowers to every square inch of the miniature unicorn. Olivia tended the flats of flowers every day, watering, weeding, and pruning the plants to keep them in shape. She proudly projected she would win the best of the show at the gala, attaching the flowers at the last minute.

When the gala conversation ran its course, Olivia switched to Zachary's reporting and asked at least twenty questions about the newspaper business and his job. She got some sense of his process, which impressed Zachary. She seemed genuinely interested and able to admire how an article came together for the paper.

When Zachary suggested he had to get back to work, Olivia turned the conversation again. "Zachary, you must come to the gala and cheer for my piñata. If you came down Saturday morning, you could stay in one of our guest rooms, and we could ride together in our carriage to the event."

"Will Caroline be submitting a piñata do you think?" asked Zach.

"No, Zachary, there will be no conflict of interest. The creative arts are not in her repertoire," said Olivia. "She'll be there, though, with men fawning at her heels."

Zach thought Olivia had gone too far, but she recovered quickly. "Don't take that the wrong way," she said. "Caroline is my best friend. I know her inside and out. You must know her pretty well. She can ride a horse like a cowboy. She bakes scrumptious cherry pies."

"Yes, we ride together often," Zach said.

"In the morning after the gala," said Olivia, "I hope we might go for a ride. I could use your expertise. I'm a real neophyte regarding horses, but willing to learn. What do you say?"

"I'll check with my managing editor, but I'm sure he'll give me the assignment.

Zachary awoke at sunrise on the 9th of April and packed a small valise for the weekend. Rather than subjecting his suitcoat to folding and wrinkling in the valise, he wore it unbuttoned. Yesterday's rain had cleared the air. If he hurried, the road would be less dusty as well.

He could have given Arrow his lead and let him find his way. He would have ended up at Caroline Wainwright's vineyard. Instead, he would head further south to Olivia Halstead's family estate. Arrow would turn twenty this year. An amazing horse. He was a tad slower in his old age but still, a rock when Zachary needed him.

When Zachary twisted the ringer at the side of the front door, Olivia flung the door open, reached up, and pecked at

Zachary's cheek, then yanked the bell pull, and within a minute, a servant appeared.

"Yang Sing," Olivia said to the oriental man who appeared in short order dressed in slacks and a white shirt. "Would you please notify the stable that Mr. Brennan's horse needs feed and a rubdown?"

Olivia turned to Zach. "I'll show you to your room."

Zachary followed Olivia up the grand staircase. She could hardly contain her excitement. He wondered if she had feared he might not show. For his part, Zach appreciated the attention. His assignments and deadlines at the paper precluded him from visiting Caroline or Olivia, for that matter, since last year's ice cream social.

"I'll be changing, Zachary," Olivia said, "so let's meet in the great hall at 6:00 pm. We'll arrive at the country club at about 6:30 pm for the buffet. The auction starts after dessert. I pushed for your favorite strawberry shortcake. See you in a bit."

Once in the assigned bedroom, Zachary rang for a servant. A Mexican man answered the ring, and Zach handed him his suit coat. He asked the man to brush out and spritz his outfit.

"Para quitar el barro, e espera a que esté seco, por favor, Juan."

"Si Señor," said Juan.

At 6:30 pm, Zachary helped Olivia into the buggy waiting on the circular drive in front of the four-column, two-story mansion. She hooked her arm in his, sitting so close he had to drive with only one hand on the reins.

The freshly washed and polished buggy looked like a king's carriage. The palomino pulled the cart with a decisive step, head forward and tail swishing. Arriving in front of the plaza, volunteers helped guests from their coaches and buggies and tended the horses. Olivia and Zachary crossed the plaza and entered the San Jose city hall. The building looked to Zachary like an imaginary King Arthur's castle, its battlement parapet encircling the building above the second-floor cornice.

The doorman announced the couple as they entered the crowded hall. Heads turned in their direction; the tall, dark-haired, striking man accompanied by Olivia, one of the local beauties and an event organizer.

Zachary quickly spotted Caroline in a breathtaking purple gown. He stood inches taller than the other men in the room. After stopping for greetings, Zach steered Olivia over to her best friend. Zachary desperately attempted discretion while gaping open-mouthed at the pale skin plunging into the vee of her gown. Suddenly his tongue seemed to swell, and he could only croak out, "Hello, Caroline."

Olivia, always the socialite, said, "Zachary, you know Caroline, of course. Let me introduce you to Randall Brookhaven, her beau.

"Pleased to meet you, Mr. Brookhaven." Zachary was not pleased. The man, dressed in an impeccable pin-stripe suit, had curly blond hair and an athletic stance.

"The name's Randall," the man said. "Glad to meet you as well. I understand you write for the *Daily Alta California.* We get your newspaper's weekly edition to keep track of the shipping lanes out of San Francisco."

Olivia interjected, "Randall runs an orange orchard north of Los Angeles. Two hundred acres, I believe."

"Closer to two thousand acres, Olivia," said Randall, "between our three locations."

Zachary noticed the connection between Caroline and Brookhaven. The evening had turned disastrous.

Both couples moved through the buffet line carrying their plates to the patio outside the crowded hall. Zachary still couldn't breathe. In all the years he had known Caroline, he had kept his distance, striving with every elevated position at the newspaper to feel eligible to move to a more equitable relationship and ask for her hand.

After one shake of Brookhaven's hand, he realized he would never achieve the status worthy of the most beautiful woman in his world.

The evening spoiled; he helped Olivia prepare her piñata, staying as far away as possible from the beauty in the purple gown.

The auction began. The piñatas were lined up on the cleared buffet tables, and the ten entries received oohs and aahs. Olivia's entry was seventh in the line, a multicolored unicorn adorned with tiny flowers from horn tip to tail. Caroline appeared at Zach's elbow as bidding began for the piñata to the right of Olivia's. Her scent gave her away, and Zach turned to her; Randall had vanished, at least for the moment.

Caroline leaned in close to Zach's shoulder. "When are we going riding, Zachary," she whispered. "You have ignored me for a year. I have missed you."

"I'm going riding with Olivia tomorrow," said Zachary. "She wants pointers. She is not an experienced rider."

"Let me know, Zachary," said Caroline, "when you are available for a real ride, won't you?"

"I will, Caroline," said Zach, "and soon. I'd say that your dress is stunning, befitting the most beautiful woman in the room."

"Why Zachary, you charmer, you better concentrate on your date. But thank you, you look very handsome tonight yourself. Please send me a note soon. I'll be waiting."

Just like that, Zachary's evening brightened.

The bidding began on Olivia's piñata. The bidding slowed at twenty-three dollars, and as the auctioneer raised his gavel, Zachary called out, "Thirty."

Eyes turned toward the tallest man in the room. But, the man in the grey top hat who had bid twenty-three dollars was not ready to give in. "Thirty-three."

The bidding war ended with Zach jumping to fifty dollars. A small fortune for a papier-mâché animal stuffed with candies. Zach's stomach had been turning since he started bidding. He had bought the unicorn to show Olivia he appreciated the invite. A chance to see Caroline dressed in a gown. Olivia was just as beautiful and displayed all her good qualities at the Gala. She just wasn't Caroline.

Had he impressed Caroline? That was the other reason he outbid everyone for Olivia's piñata. Harold Crenshaw had authorized forty dollars of the newspaper's money for a donation to the charity. Good advertising. The rest of the money would come from Zach's account, half of what he had saved.

Zachary did impress Olivia. When the auctioneer announced "Sold" and struck the gavel on the podium, Olivia ran into the audience and hugged Zachary tightly, kissing him ardently. "Thank you, Zach, thank you, thank you," she said, nearly crying joyfully.

Randall approached and shook Zach's hand, "good show, old man," he said. "Now, what are you going to do with a flowered Unicorn filled with candy."

"I have absolutely no idea," said Zach. "The Unitarians probably know of a needy family with a child's birthday approaching. Or I'll hang it up and whack it myself."

"Very generous of you, Zachary," said Caroline, giving him a quick peck.

"We better get going, Caroline," said Randall, "I have a long drive south yet this evening."

Everyone offered goodbyes, and the crowd dispersed. Back at Olivia's ranch, Zachary declined a glass of port. It had been a long day, and he had started early. Olivia hid her disappointment. She had hoped they would sit on the veranda and have two or three glasses of port.

The following morning, Zach dressed early and went to the stables to see Arrow. He fed his horse hay and mash, brushed him, and saddled him, waiting to cinch the saddle strap until after breakfast. Then Zachary looked over the stock in the corral and selected one of the lady's horses that he believed wouldn't be too much for Olivia to manage. The horse handler on duty mucking stalls agreed with Zach's choice. He clued Zach in on Olivia's riding expertise, or severe lack thereof.

Zach returned to the house, entering the dining room just as Olivia and her mother descended the grand staircase. Olivia wore a riding skirt.

Olivia's mother seemed as excited at the tall man devouring oatmeal and eggs as her daughter. Mrs. Halstead questioned Zach about his family and the Arizona territory. Olivia finally cut her off, standing and claiming to be ready for her lesson.

The stable hand steadied Olivia's horse at the mounting block. The leaping horn side saddle mystified Zach. He let Olivia struggle into the saddle as he couldn't determine how to assist without taking liberties.

The couple spent the first twenty minutes walking around the ranch house. Eventually, Zachary led the way toward the hills north of the corral. Zachary watched Olivia closely for the next hour, wary of her falling off. An experienced rider would look at ease riding side saddle, but Olivia hunched her back, swaying side to side as the horse walked along. Zach could hardly stand to watch. Of course, they couldn't stop for a rest. There would be no way for Olivia to remount without the mounting block back at the ranch.

Olivia smiled through what must have been an excruciating experience. Sweat soaked the high collar of her habit. Zach sweated as well, worrying about Olivia. He had no idea how to help her posture, sticking to basic reining directions. Eventually, Zach led both horses into a trot to give Olivia a sense of a real ride. Instead of gripping the leaping horn with her legs, she began to bounce out of the saddle. Zach immediately slowed back to a walk and turned back toward the ranch. He prayed she wouldn't fall the whole way back.

Zachary tied up both horses at the rail. The couple accepted glasses of lemonade from the kitchen staff and sat on the porch to cool down.

"You seem so comfortable when you ride, Zach," said Olivia. "I feel every bone and muscle in my body."

Zach sympathized, "I've been riding Arrow for over a decade. He knows which way I want to go before I do. You'll get the hang of it."

"I want to get better at riding, Zachary," she said. "You'll see. I'm going to practice. The next time we go riding, you'll see."

Olivia gathered the empty lemonade glasses and set off for the kitchen while Zach retrieved his valise from the upstairs bedroom.

Olivia stepped off the porch as Zach tied his valise behind the cantle. Arrow stomped, ready to leave, so Zachary mounted and leaned over to take Olivia's hand. She curtsied as he gently kissed her hand.

"Thank you, Olivia," said Zach. "This has been a memorable weekend. I'll write up a complimentary article for the paper. Look for it in the weekly edition. Our delivery wagon will pick up the Unicorn on Tuesday morning after delivering the San Jose subscriptions."

"Goodbye, Zach," said Olivia, "Thank you again for making our benefit such a success. I truly valued our time together. I hope you come calling again soon."

Zach turned Arrow toward San Francisco, relief washing over him in the cool breeze. Now he could concentrate on Caroline's words and his future with her.

40 |Harold Hedges His Bet

Two weeks after the gala, Harold Crenshaw walked into Zach's office, pulled up a side chair, and sat near Zach to slap him on the knee.

"Son, you are going to call me crazy," said Crenshaw, "but an opportunity has been presented to me that I can no longer ignore."

The reporter had never seen his boss so excited. Harold fidgeted in his chair, sputtering something about the snowmelt in Alaska. Zachary wondered if the man had decided to join the army, received another newspaper's offer, or had decided to run for mayor. "Spill it," Zach said, "Start at the beginning."

"I have been making plans for the past three weeks," said Harold. "I'm ready now except for one big detail involving you."

"Harold," said Zach, "say the word. You know I'll help any way I can."

Harold, encouraged by Zach's offer, proceeded. "I received a letter six weeks ago from a friend from my younger days of the gold rush.

"I spotted this man a beer in a saloon when he was about as down as a man could be. I ended up sponsoring his stake, and we became close. He was the most infectious dreamer I've ever known. Never found more than two pans of dust.

"That was over thirty years ago, but he never forgot that stake. He's up in the Silver Bow Basin in the southern tip of

Alaska and found enough gold to invite me to prospect the vein with him."

"Whoa there, Harold," said Zachary. "Surely you know the chances of you finding another vein are a thousand to one.

"My grandfather tried his hand at prospecting in '49. He left his daughter, my mother, an incredibly young woman at the time, to run our sheep ranch. Never came home. Died east of here without ever making it back to my mother. I never met the man myself."

Harold shook his head. "I've thought this thing through, Zach. I'm going to do it. I figure to go up there, spend one year looking and return…, luck or no luck. You're right. I don't want to become obsessed with the lifestyle."

"Who is this friend of yours?" said Zach.

"His name is Joseph Juneau. He's Canadian, and we've stayed in touch all these years. He has finally made a strike. He wrote of finding over a hundred pounds of gold ore; I'm the only one he has told of his good fortune."

I still don't understand why I am so important to your scheme," Zach said.

"Because I want to hedge my bet. I want something to return to, win or lose, while in Canada. I want you to take over as managing editor for the year I am gone."

Zachary leaned back in his chair, stunned.

"You think I could manage the operation?" he asked.

"Listen," said Crenshaw. "You've moved through each department from compositor to press maintenance to reporter and journalist. You know how the place works. The board respects you, and they've agreed to my recommendation.

"You're young, that's true. Thirty, right? But you're ready."

"You'll have to give me a day to think about it. I hate to give up on reporting. I love what I do." said Zachary.

"Split your time," said Harold. "Hire a hungry reporter but keep the juicy investigations for yourself. Then make sure everyone else is doing their jobs."

The next day Zachary agreed to the interim managing editor position. Harold left on a steamer heading up the coast to Alaska at the end of the week.

Understanding the management side of the business would entail a learning curve. Constant investigation and lead tracking pushed Zachary's weekly work schedule to sixty-plus hours. This left little time to write and polish his column. He advertised for a reporter, but no one applied. Instead, Zachary promoted one of the young compositors and hired a woman without experience to train as a replacement typesetter.

The commensurate salary kept Zach going. His bank account grew. Trying to get down to San Jose to visit Caroline became impossible in the short term, at least until he accomplished his new duties as managing editor.

Zachary wrote to Caroline four times, expressing his frustration in being unable to venture to San Jose, but by July, he could wait no longer. Zach immediately sent a wire to Caroline suggesting a riding date on July 24th. He received a telegram back; he would be welcome.

On the twenty-fourth, an hour before dawn, Zachary saddled Arrow and cantered out of the city, hoping to maximize his time with Caroline by arriving at the vineyard by 2:00 pm.

Caroline waved to him from the stables as he approached the ranch. She wore a new, long blue riding skirt over riding pants with straps under her boots to prevent the pant leg from riding up. Her waistcoat fit tight to her slender waist, but the sleeves ballooned a bit. The outfit was completed by a jaunting little velvet hat worn forward with a peacock feather wisping behind her.

From the mounting block, Caroline hopped right into her side saddle. She had arranged a picnic lunch. She asked Zach to pick up the picnic basket from the mounting block, then she tore ahead, riding at a cantor on her horse, Blackjack. Zachary scrambled, reached for the picnic basket, held it in his lap, turned Arrow, and galloped after Caroline.

After exiting the ranch gate, both riders let their horses slow to a walk.

"I try to read all your articles, Zach," said Caroline. "Unfortunately, my father studies them at length as well."

"Has he found fault with one of them?" asked Zachary. "Perhaps I could discuss my research on a particular subject with him. I strive to be impartial unless I specifically say I have a personal opinion."

"I'm afraid there would be too many articles for discussion," Caroline said.

"I could apologize for that if it would help. I want to think your father finds me acceptable."

"Father's opinion of acceptable is someone like Randall Brookhaven."

Zachary involuntarily shivered. He had two rivals. Randall Brookhaven, an orchard landowner, wealthy and local to California, and Caroline's father. Zachary had met Don Wainwright only twice, yet, he must have offended him with an article he wrote for the *Alta Daily California*. Zachary went quiet in the saddle. Caroline spoke no further about the obstacles to Zachary's ultimate goal. She expounded on the weather, the shadows the mountains threw across the prairie, and the deer they caught grazing by a lake.

Zach stayed attentive, absorbing her beauty, staving off the frost he felt for Mr. Wainwright and Mr. Brookhaven. Caroline seemed genuinely happy for his company. When they stopped by a stream for their picnic, Zachary lifted Caroline from her saddle and didn't let go.

"Caroline," said Zachary, unwilling to let her escape his grasp. "I've got to know if I am acceptable to you."

He leaned down, holding her shoulders, and kissed Caroline. He encircled her in his arms, crushing her to him as gently as he could stand.

Caroline reached up with a soft hand on his neck, holding him to her. Eventually, at the end of the kiss, Zachary watched her eyelids flutter open inches from his own.

"I guess I've answered my question," he said.

Caroline smiled, "It took you long enough to ask."

The couple regained their composure and spread the blanket. Caroline distributed the sandwiches and fruit while Zachary uncorked the bottle of Wainwright Reserve red and poured two glasses of wine.

On the second glass of wine, Zachary asked, "What's next for us, Caroline?"

"We'll have to win over my father. That may take time, darling. May I say that? May I call you my darling?"

Zachary nodded assent, his heart leaping again, "Whatever it takes," he said. After the last drop of wine, Caroline repacked the picnic basket, and they rose to fold the blanket. Zach tied the basket to the back of his cantle. Then he turned to face Caroline, drawing her into his arms for another kiss. They already seemed comfortable with how their bodies fit together and their shared heat.

"I've been in love with you for so many years, Caroline," said Zachary. "I'll work even harder now to win over your father."

"We'll both have to work at that," said Caroline. "I'll speak to Mama. She'll help."

"In the meantime, I will visit Olivia and let her know how we feel. I'm certain she had visions of a relationship beyond friendship."

"And I'll do the same with Randall as soon as we convince Father."

"I've been promoted to interim managing editor for a year in Harold Crenshaw's absence," said Zach.

"That's wonderful, Zachary," said Caroline. "I'll be sure to tell my father. It will help, I'm certain."

On the trail back to the vineyard, Zachary suggested a trip to a jeweler in San Francisco.

"I had another thought," said Zachary. "Why don't I draft an article about the vineyard, highlighting your father's start in the business and plans for future expansion? That gives me the excuse of seeing you during my research phase and allows me to find topics on which your father and I agree." Caroline thought the article was an excellent idea. The couple parted discreetly at the ranch, and Zach returned to San Francisco.

At two o'clock in the morning, Zachary stopped and unsaddled Arrow. He tied his companion to a tree branch to graze and spread the horse blanket under another tree a few feet from the road. Curled up to sleep in his suit coat, Zach felt more contented than he could have ever imagined, despite the chilly, star-filled night.

41 |One Last Ride

Ten days passed. On a cloudless California day, Zachary again set off for San Jose. He had no idea how he would tell Olivia about his newly discovered relationship with Caroline. Caroline had promised not to say anything to Olivia before Zach could speak to her in person.

When Zach arrived at Olivia's ranch, a late lunch was set out buffet style in the dining room. After loading his plate with potato salad, ham, blueberries, apple slices, cheese, and bread, Zachary poured a glass of wine. He carried his plate and drink to the veranda and sat on the porch swing next to Olivia.

"I can't wait to show you how far I've come since the last time we rode together," said Olivia. "I have practiced nearly every day."

The ache of embarrassment in the pit of Zachary's stomach strengthened. *She practiced for me*. "Riding is a skill that benefits a person forever," he said.

"I'll get us each a custard cup for dessert," Olivia said.

Zachary wasn't feeling up to dessert but ate every bite to be polite. It was delicious, and he complimented Olivia and the kitchen staff on an excellent meal.

"Let's go," said Olivia. She stood, dusting off the crumbs from the same riding outfit she had worn on their first excursion. She strode confidently to the mounting block where the stableboy held her horse at the ready. The handler helped her into the saddle. He handed her the reins and led the horse away from the mounting block.

Zachary noticed a marked improvement in Olivia's confidence. She led her horse around the yard, turning to the left and right, at one point backing her horse up ten yards. Her back straight, her riding impressive; she told Zach she had also tried one-foot-high jumps.

"My, you have the hang of it now," Zach said. "Your posture is good. Your reining is decisive, and your horse is responding quickly."

"Shall we go, Zachary?" said Olivia

The riders urged their mounts into a trot. Olivia kicked with her heels, and her horse began to cantor. Olivia appeared to Zach to still be in control. He admired her improved horsemanship. She looked as elegant as Caroline.

After an hour, Zach found a group of boulders that might provide Olivia with a means of remounting her horse. Zach pulled up Arrow and dismounted. He helped Olivia down. Olivia held on to Zach in a strange reversal of his earlier experience with Caroline.

Olivia didn't let go. Instead, she stretched on her toes until she could kiss Zach mightily on his lips. Then she buried her head in his chest.

"Zachary," she said, "I want you to like me, to want me. I practiced every day to not look clumsy. You do like me, don't you?"

"Of course I do, Olivia," said Zach, slipping away and turning his back to her. "It's just that…."

"What," whispered Olivia, "What is it, Zach?"

Zachary didn't want to hurt Olivia. She had tried so hard to impress and be attractive to him, to show her intelligence and willingness to do anything for him. *She's a great gal. Olivia's not Caroline.* Zach decided it was time to relieve the tension and his torture.

"Caroline and I are promised, one to the other."

Olivia stepped back, instantly angry. "Caroline told me you were just friends. She said that three times. Just friends."

"Things have changed," said Zachary.

"I don't believe you. I won't believe Caroline ever again," she shouted and turned away, crying. "I worked so hard. I've done everything right."

Zachary stood still as stone, both hands in the rear pockets of his dungarees. He had no idea how to comfort her or stop her sobbing. It was like trying to pick up the gun to help Eli. Frozen. *I'm the worst excuse of a man.*

Eventually, Olivia stopped crying. They both stood still in silence. Then Olivia turned toward her horse. "Let's go," she said.

Olivia refused to accept assistance onto her horse. She found an appropriate boulder and, in two tries, managed to get into her side saddle. She cantered off without a word to Zach. Olivia concentrated solely on her riding technique and getting home.

Neither spoke until Olivia pulled up on her reins and swung her horse around to face Zach. "When did this happen?" asked Olivia. "I want to know how much of a liar my best friend is."

"We met on the 24th," said Zach.

"The 24th of July?" asked Olivia.

"August," Zach replied, "Just a couple of weeks ago."

"Oh," said Olivia, coaxing her horse to turn around again.

When the riders arrived at the stable, Zachary stayed in his saddle. A stableboy helped Olivia to dismount. She began to walk toward the barn, not acknowledging Zachary.

Zach shrugged, "Goodbye, Olivia. I hope we continue as friends." When he received no response from Olivia, he turned Arrow toward the trail to San Francisco and rode off.

Olivia watched Zach canter away from the shadows in the barn. The pit of her stomach churned. She tried to be mad at Zachary, but the overriding sorrow of her dashed hopes only brought on tremendous sobbing and more tears. In her current state, she knew she couldn't face her mother, who had been equally hopeful for Olivia's prospects with Mr. Brennan.

Collecting herself and blowing her nose, Olivia called to the stableboy who helped her mount her horse. She rode in the opposite direction from Zach, not angry, just blank, no longer trying to smile or look pretty for Zachary Brennan.

In another half hour, Olivia had settled enough to face her mother and now craved her sympathies. Turning back toward the barn, Olivia's horse backed up a bit, trying to navigate the narrow space offered by the trail. That's when she heard the rattlesnake.

"Whoa," said Olivia, "Hold still."

The rattle sounded again, and Olivia panicked. Her horse absorbed her panic and stamped and whinnied, shaking its head.

"Steady, Girl," said Olivia, in a voice that clearly was not.

The horse became more excited and stomped backward, thrashing the snake dead.

The rattling stopped, and Olivia let out deep breaths in relief. She closed her eyes, bowed slightly, and crossed herself, forgetting about Zach, at least momentarily. *Not bad; no significant injury.* Even the horse had not suffered a snake bite.

The horse still seemed nervous. When Olivia nudged it forward with her heels, her mount jerked into a run, flying fast, leaving the trail to tear through the sparse brush in the basin, zigging and zagging to avoid bloodying its legs.

Olivia bounced in the saddle, unable to hold the leaping pommel with her legs. She spied a bog of cattails up ahead, thinking to fall off or jump away in that direction. She didn't, couldn't.

Now the horse and woman were beyond the cattails. A thicket and a large oak tree to the right had suffered a lightning strike. The horse headed that way. Just before the undergrowth, the horse stopped, planting her front hoofs and bucking with her hind legs.

Olivia flew over the withers, did a complete somersault, and landed near the oak tree.

***

The stableboy found Olivia three hours later after Mrs. Halstead requested that he hunt her down. He found her on her back. Dead. A sharp branch spike from a large fallen limb stuck through her right breast. Olivia's head was cranked at an impossible angle. The blood from the wound had solidified in the grass by her right side. The hostler galloped back to the ranch for help and informed the family.

***

Zachary set up a cold camp away from the road at the midway point to San Francisco and bedded down. The silence of the forest was a comfort.

***

The letter from Caroline informing Zachary of Olivia's death arrived four days later. Zachary felt shame and guilt after reading that Olivia's death had occurred on the afternoon of their ride and that she had been thrown from her horse. Weeping while he read, visions of tragedies settled once more on Zachary's shoulders:

- Jeremiah's blood: soaking his knee pants.
- Eli's blood: seeking the cracks in the floor around the heavy steel anvil.

- Olivia: dead like the others, her blood becoming sticky in the sun.

Zachary wrote a detailed letter to Caroline. His inability to save Olivia weighed Zachary down like leaden ankle shackles. Caroline wrote a love letter telling Zachary it would take time to get past Olivia's horrible death. She suggested that Zach's work might distract him from his hopelessness. If he could find a worthwhile cause to trumpet in his paper, it might help in a small way.

Caroline had informed her father of Zachary's promotion to managing editor of the Alta California Daily and Weekly newspaper editions. She assured Zachary that the prestige of the position had changed her father's attitude toward Zachary. The vineyard article would cement his conversion.

Zachary attended Olivia's funeral on Sunday, August 14th, 1881. Caroline and her family also attended. Zach wanted to take Caroline in his arms. Caroline offered a sympathetic kiss to his cheek, which drove him mad with longing. They both felt discretion should rule the day. Zachary did discuss briefly with Mr. Wainwright his idea for an article about the vineyard and wine brand. The Halsteads were polite to Zachary but did not wish to socialize. After offering his sympathies, Zachary retired to the back of the crowd. He left at the first tossing of dirt on the grave.

***

The article highlighting the Wainwright Vineyard appeared in the *Weekly Alta California* newspaper just before Thanksgiving. The feature included an interview with Donald Wainwright, master vintner, regarding his father's struggles in coming to California. Walter Wainright created the first

Wainwright Reserve Cabernet Sauvignon Wine. Starting with twenty plants at the New York docks, Walter had desperately protected the last three grapevine plants from a weeklong sandstorm while crossing the Mohave Desert.

The *New York Times* republished the professionally written article about a Western success story. So did the *Boston Daily Globe*.

The *Daily Alta California* editor visited Caroline Wainwright on Christmas Eve. When Zachary asked her father for Caroline's hand in marriage, her father gave Zachary a hearty clap on the shoulder, shaking his hand. In a private moment before dinner, Zachary took Caroline's hand in his and, with his other hand, reached into his suitcoat pocket and produced an engagement ring, slipping it on her hand as he asked her to marry him.

Over dinner, Caroline's mother, admiring the five diamond stone gold ring, asked Caroline about the couple's wedding plans.

"The sooner, the better," said Zachary.

Shirley Wainwright became quiet briefly, but Zach could envision the calculations she processed. "The soonest I can imagine would be an Easter celebration," she said. "Caroline, we'll discuss."

"Yes, we will, Mother," Caroline said. "We're both in our thirties now. I want a small affair. Zachary, do you think your parents will be able to attend?"

"I want you to meet them," said Zachary, "that's certain. I receive new rail track reports each month. The latest projection is that the Atlantic and Pacific Railroad won't complete the track through Flagstaff until the third quarter of next year.

"I propose we delay our honeymoon until we can take the train to Flagstaff in style. By coach, we would spend a month getting there and a month in return. By train, we could get there presumably in less than a week.

"I've located a brownstone walkup in the Nob Hill district to rent. We'll decide about a permanent home when Harold Crenshaw returns to the city."

"Zachary," said Donald, "You've been thinking and planning quite a bit."

"Yes, Father, Zach always seems to be working according to plan," said Caroline. "Arizona, what an adventure. I can't wait to meet your mother, Zach. You've told me so much about her and the schooling she gave you. The San Francisco Peaks. We'll go riding in the mountains when we get there."

Zachary ate the last bite of his piece of rhubarb pie. Caroline squeezed his leg with her left hand beneath the table. He looked over at her. She glowed. He put a hand on her thigh. *It won't be long now.*

***

On Easter, April 9th, 1882, Zachary Brennan and Caroline Wainwright stood before the San Jose Unitarian Minister reciting their vows. Per Zachary's wishes, the ceremony involved the bride's family and friends from the *Daily Alta California* staff. Since the Unitarians had no church structure, Mrs. Wainwright had acquired permission to hold the ceremony at Trinity Church in downtown San Jose. The warmth of the redwood structure added to the solemnity of the occasion.

The Wainwrights went all out in the planning of the reception. The vineyard employees set up a massive tent from the state fairgrounds. An orchestra played for the first hour, alternating between slower, two-step, and quicker polka music.

In a tailed tuxedo, Zachary set his top hat down on a table for the traditional first dance of the married couple. He came to the tent's center and joined Caroline in her Spanish-style wedding dress and mantilla.

"You take my breath away," whispered Zachary as they began their two-step. "I have loved you for so many years. I love you now more than ever. I'll always love you, beautiful girl."

"You have made me very happy, Zachary," said Caroline. "I believe in you. I worry you are inviting danger with your column. I'll try to be as brave."

Zachary laughed. "Believe me, Caroline, I've seen you on a horse, feeding poor, impoverished men and women, and at a rally for woman suffrage. You are far braver than me. I hope you never discover my true cowardice."

"Well, you dance divinely, husband. I suppose your mother taught you to dance as well."

"You'd be right, dear. Let's enjoy the dance. Tonight, I will be gentle but nervous. I will do my best."

"My darling, can't you gather how we'll be together as a couple based on how we fit and flow when we dance?"

"It is just that you are so beautiful, Caroline," said Zach.

"I won't break, Zach."

The music ended, but the couple continued to dance to their beat.

After the first orchestra left, a second band was set up in the tent. The band consisted of a fiddler, a banjo player, a guitarist, a piano player, and an accordion player. A caller used a megaphone to direct groups of eight couples in square dancing. The open bar featured Wainwright wine. After two glasses of Cab, the adults joined in.

At midnight, while the party continued, Zachary and Caroline quietly escaped in a buggy and drove to a hotel in town. For them, the night now began.

On May 10th, the owner of the livery where Zachary stabled Arrow asked Amanda, the receptionist at the Dailly Alta California building, to see Zachary. Amanda buzzed Zachary to the lobby.

"Mr. Ketchum," said Zachary, "What brings you down? I'm pretty certain I'm up to date with my payments."

"Nothing like that, Sir," said Ketchum. "Your horse died this morning. Knew it the minute I saw him on my morning round. I'm sorry. I'd guess he was pretty old by the look of his grey muzzle."

Zachary found a chair opposite the reception desk, sat down, and crossed his arms, swaying slightly. Finally, he found his voice.

"It happens," said Zachary. "He was quite old. He was my father's horse before he was mine. He was a companion, a friend, and the best damn cutting horse I've ever worked with."

"Do you wish to come over and see him off?" said Mr. Ketchum.

"No, thank you. Take care of the details, will you, Mr. Ketchum? I'll write to my father and let him know. Thanks for coming over."

42 |Editorial

Beginning in 1881, work crews out of Albuquerque progressed on the Atlantic and Pacific Western Division Railroad. Engineers conducted surveys to lay out the exact track location, and crews worked on the railroad bed, ties, and rails.

A Flagstaff town planning commission was formed and included the two dominant landowners in the area, Hanna Brennan and Thomas McMillan. The springs near McMillan's vast land holdings seemed a logical location for the town. Thomas and Hanna worked together sketching on paper streets and places for a future church, school, and, most importantly, a railroad station. Hanna proposed that Eliza Blackstone manage the land office (a tent near the train tracks.) She hired Wilbur Dawson, the surveyor, to stake out the streets and twenty-five-foot lots along Front Street.

The 250-foot-deep chasm at Cañon Diablo, fifty miles east of Flagstaff, required a substantial bridge. The first prefabricated trestle manufactured in the east and shipped to Cañon Diablo the first week in May was too short to span the poured foundations.

An order for a second bridge would cause a seven-month delay in crossing Cañon Diablo. Railroad workers squatted in the canyon, creating a raucous railroad town. Gambling houses, saloons, and whorehouses ruled the settlement. Within months unruly cowboys had killed four sheriffs trying to keep a semblance of peace. The lawmen were now buried on boot hill.

Nearby, the Wells Fargo Swing Station and Eli Blackstone's burial site turned to desert dust.

While waiting for the bridge, crews moved as far west as Flagstaff to prepare the track. The citizens of the growing community of Flagstaff, salivating over the prospects of the railroad, began constructing storefronts and homes along the main street near the springs and McMillan's ranch.

***

Hanna loved opening up letters from her son and sharing them with Eliza. Zachary continued to send her articles with his byline from the *Daily Alta California.* She received one such letter on May 6, 1882.

> **THE CHINESE EXCLUSION ACT BANS CHINESE IMMIGRANTS --CALIFORNIA DISREGARDS THE SPIRIT OF THE BILL OF RIGHTS**
> Zachary Brennan
> **Historical Context:** In a public ceremony in San Francisco in 1850, Mayor John W. Geary formally welcomed Chinese immigrants. By 1852, Chinese Californians comprised 20 percent of the state's newly arrived population. They joined that year's Fourth of July parade in San Francisco "on horseback and carriages, dressed in colorful silk and satin that dazzled the spectators."
> **Civil War Context:** In the early years after the Civil War, the U.S. officially committed to equal protection under the law and free

migration in 1868, adopting both the 14th Amendment and the Burlingame Treaty.

In 1879, California adopted a new Constitution that authorized the state government to determine which individuals were allowed to reside and banned the Chinese from employment by corporations and state, county, or municipal governments.

Current Affairs 1882: Three years later, China agreed to treaty revisions. Congress tried to exclude working-class Chinese laborers; Senator John F. Miller of California introduced a Chinese Exclusion Act that blocked the entry of Chinese laborers for twenty years. The bill passed the Senate and House by overwhelming margins. President Chester A. Arthur vetoed the bill and concluded the 20-year ban breached the renegotiated treaty of 1880. That treaty allowed only a "reasonable" suspension of immigration. Eastern newspapers praised Arthur's action, while the veto met widespread condemnation in California. Congress could not override the veto but passed a new bill reducing the immigration ban to ten years. The House of Representatives voted 201–37, with fifty-one abstentions, and the act passed. Although he objected to this denial of entry to Chinese laborers, President Arthur acceded to the compromise measure, signing the Chinese Exclusion Act into law on May 6, 1882.

March 4, 1882: Governor George C. Perkins declares a legal holiday to allow "one universal demonstration" to support the passage of the Chinese Exclusion Act.

The anti-Chinese demonstration in the afternoon in San Francisco was on a grand scale. The city's best citizens packed the meeting at Platt's Hall while 30,000 surged about the stands in Montgomery and Pine streets.

The day after the demonstration, the *Daily Alta California* reported, "Nearly all trade was suspended in this city to enable the business class to give the day to the grand anti-coolie demonstration."

U.S. authorities can now detain people of Chinese descent as they come through the port of San Francisco. The Exclusion Act supplies narrowly defined exemptions for ministers, diplomats, teachers, students, merchants, and those passing through the country on travel who need supporting documents and testimony of "at least one credible white witness."

Conclusion: White immigrants marched the original natives of this land onto reservations. We were the invaders. How can we claim the right to exclude immigrants from attaining a better life for themselves in this great land because of their skin color?

Answer: This correspondent maintains we cannot, **not in good conscience.**

43 |A New Insult

The sheep shorn, the fleeces washed and carded; the wool spinning could begin in a few days. He leaned against the pen rail, exhausted. Lorenzo's energy never matched Hanna's; she could still shear two sheep to his one. His leg had bothered him each day of the shearing. The steady throb of pain eased slightly in his leg if he kept his leg straight. As a consequence, Lorenzo rarely bent his knee.

The weather this May 10th turned warm early. Lorenzo limped toward the cabin. Halfway there, a piercing pain below his knee caused him to double over. He grasped the sheepherder's crook he used as a cane to keep from falling. This was something different. *Great, a new insult.*

Following her husband from the barn, Hanna saw Lorenzo grimace and helped him to the cabin. He made it as far as the rocker on the porch. Hanna fetched a chair from the dining table to function as an ottoman, and Lorenzo put his leg up as Hanna entered the cabin to prepare dinner.

Hanna came out on the porch fifteen minutes later to check on Lorenzo. His face looked flushed. Hanna gently squeezed his problem calf; she could tell it was swollen. She ordered her husband to take off his pants. The leg looked swollen and dark red from below the knee to the ankle. The pain had not subsided.

An hour passed, and Hanna became increasingly worried, but what was there to do? Blood was collecting in the lower part of the leg. Would blood flow out and relieve the pressure if she pricked the leg? Where would she puncture the skin? Should she cut a slit in his leg? Vertical? Crossways? Hanna couldn't decide. She entered the cabin and brought a cloth dipped in the water bucket. She laid the washrag on his forehead.

"That feels good," said Lorenzo.

Hanna examined the leg again. It felt hot and had turned a darker red. "I'm going to fetch another cloth and wrap your leg," said Hanna.

"That should help," Lorenzo said.

Hanna remembered the medical encyclopedia in her library collection. She retrieved her medical reference after she brought the second cooling cloth and wrapped it around her husband's leg.

After fifteen minutes of research, she discovered Lorenzo might be dealing with a blood clot in his leg. The accumulation affected the entire leg below the knee. Hanna read that in extreme cases, amputation may be the remedy of last resort. Otherwise, Hanna followed the text's recommended procedures using cool cloths and compression on the area.

Two hours passed. Lorenzo now accepted the pain and remained calm. He recalled lying on a cot in the field hospital at the Sacramento River in'47. He would live with the pain.

Then, as suddenly as the pain had arrived, his leg felt much better. The worst seemed to be over.

Five minutes later, however, Lorenzo began to gulp for air. He sucked air hard into his chest but still seemed out of breath. He called out for Hanna. She noticed his face and lips turning blue when she stepped onto the porch.

Lorenzo tried to speak between gasps, "Leg… better," he wheezed. "Can't…Can't… breathe."

"Oh Lorenzo, what can I do," cried Hanna. She clawed at the book, now looking for asthmatic symptoms or breathing difficulties.

Lorenzo suspected he might die. It was a terrible feeling. What would he leave undone? Hanna, fine. Zachary, fine. Sarah and Kyle, they'll take over the ranch. Then it came to him. "Hanna… Hanna… Get Eliza… Eliza… Got to warn her…."

"I'm not leaving your side. I can find something in the book to help," said Hanna.

"Go… Hanna, go… Got to tell Eliza…."

"Alright, my darling. I'll bring her," said Hanna.

Hanna gathered her skirt and ran as if Lorenzo's life depended on it, yelling for Eliza as loud as she could. Eliza heard her. She emerged from the barn on the run to meet Hanna.

The two women raced back to the cabin porch. Hanna looked at Lorenzo and screamed. Her partner for over thirty years would never hold her again. Eliza put her arms around her friend, and Hanna wept, her head buried in Eliza's chest.

***

The letter from Hanna announcing Lorenzo's passing landed on Zachary's desk on the 17th of May. Unable to focus on his writing, the managing editor met with various department heads and reporters for an hour. He put Horace Farnsworth, the social beat reporter, in charge. Horace would have Amanda's help in running the operation. Zachary would tell Horace how long he would be away the following day.

Zachary hurried home and showed the letter to Caroline. "We must go to your mother," said Caroline. "She sounds beside herself in the letter. Look at these incomplete sentences. She is distraught. She never writes this way."

"Yes, we're going to Flagstaff," said Zachary.

"But how, Zach," said Caroline, "you've said it will take a month to get there by stagecoach. The completion of the bridge across Cañon Diablo is months away. The train through central California to the Mohave Desert won't connect until next year."

"All that is true," said Zachary, "but there is another way. We can take the train from here to Los Angeles. That's a day's travel. From there, we can take the Southern Pacific train west to Yuma and Deming at the southern tip of the New Mexico territory. We'll transfer to the Atchison, Topeka, and Santa Fe train and travel to Albuquerque. We'll shift to the Atlantic and Pacific railroad heading west to the end of the line at Cañon Diablo. We'll have to take a stagecoach the fifty miles over to Flagstaff. I calculate two days by stagecoach, four days through the southern parts of the Arizona and New Mexico territories, and two days down to Los Angeles. That makes it an eight-day trip.

"Next year, or whenever the construction crews complete the tracks along the 35th parallel to Flagstaff, we can make the same trip in three long days. What do you say? Could we be ready to leave tomorrow?"

"I'll begin packing," said Caroline. "You go buy the tickets."

The couple boarded the train heading south at 7:00 a.m. for a 7:15 a.m. departure. Zach had purchased a first-class ticket so Caroline could while away the time watching the countryside. Zachary brought a book to read. *Ben-Hur: A Tale of the Christ*, by Lew Wallace, the Governor of the New Mexico Territory.

The train stopped at a cabin station just south of San Francisco. Caroline tugged on Zachary's suit coat. "Zachary, look who is boarding at this stop," she said.

Zachary looked at a crowd of Chinese coolies waiting to board the train. He estimated at least fifty Orientals. They wore conventional Western suits or traditional kimonos, or simple frocks.

"There is no way all those people can fit in that one railcar, Zachary," Caroline said.

"That is the only car they are allowed on," said Zach. "A sad state of affairs, I agree. I'll continue to write about such discrimination, though we lose circulation every time I do."

***

The Atlantic and Pacific train trip from Albuquerque to the end of the line at Cañon Diablo took over eight hours. At the end of the tracks, a sign attached high on a two-story claimed:

HOTEL – TWO BITS
STAGECOACH TICKET – FROM TEN CENTS

Stepping through the front door of the building, Zachary discovered that attached to the framed wooden storefront was a partitioned tent similar to the accommodations in Deming.

Zach asked about the stagecoach to Flagstaff and purchased tickets for the next day, departing at one o'clock. Then he asked about rental riding horses and received directions to the railroad stables four hundred feet back down the tracks.

Early in the morning, Zachary shook Caroline out of bed. He wanted to go for a ride before getting on the stagecoach.

Caroline did not see much in the terrain while traveling from Albuquerque to pique her interest. Desert most of the way. Indeed, nothing but desert as far as she could see here in this devil of a canyon. She decided riding would be a nice break and hurried into her riding habit.

Zachary fetched the horses he had rented and three water canteens for the ride. He knew how hot the ride might get, yet the morning would be the cool part of the day. The couple started along the canyon road down to the Beale Wagon Road, heading back to Albuquerque.

"This shouldn't take long, Caroline," said Zachary. "I want to see what's left of the swing station I worked at when I was fifteen."

Minutes later, Zach left the road and began to circle in the scrub, looking for the adobe building that had served as the blacksmith shop. After a half hour, he reined up and shrugged. "Guess it must be further east."

After five minutes of riding, he began circling again with the same result. Nothing.

"Alright," said Zach, "I may have to give up. I want to try it one last time. We'll head for the river. The Little Colorado River has changed course a bit over the years, but it is my best chance of finding what I'm looking for." Zachary rode off at a cantor until he came to the river. Caroline had no trouble riding alongside. Then he turned west, and five minutes later, he spotted a broken-down adobe wall about five feet tall.

The remnants of the grapevine he had planted were on the opposite side of the wall, crawling along the adobe like a thick spider web, sticking to it, and holding it up. The vine had a choke hold on the oak tree beside the wall. The tree had more than doubled in height. Too early for grapes, but the tiny clumps were already forming. After tying the horses to a tree branch, Zach scuffed around in the dust. He found nothing more than the broken wall.

"Zachary, what is this place?" asked Caroline. "Is this what you have been looking for?" She tried not to show her impatience with the desolate landscape.

Zach turned to her. "This is the place," he said. "I buried a man here."

"What," said Caroline, "Who? Were you sixteen? How did he die? I knew you worked at a stagecoach swing station, but you never said anything about burying anyone."

Zachary sat down on the broken corner of the wall and tugged at the grapevine. "My boss. A man named Eli Blackstone. He was a blacksmith. Ran the swing station. I was his apprentice and horse handler for the teams."

Then silence. Zachary didn't move, didn't speak, just sat still. Caroline had never seen her husband look pitiful, but that is what she saw now. Caroline went over to Zach and put her arm around his shoulders. "That's OK, Zach," she said, "You don't have to tell me. I can guess it was pretty bad."

"A stone-cold killer murdered him, Caroline. Shot him twice because of the color of his skin."

Now Caroline went silent. She left Zach's side and paced the small clearing, shaking her head and pondering what she had heard. Could this revelation explain Zach's outspoken articles in his newspaper? Striking out at injustice in memory of the man buried here. Why had he not told her of this tragedy? No wonder Olivia's death had hit him so hard.

She looked at her husband and felt sympathy and pride for the man she loved.

"I planted this grapevine as a monument to the man and for his daughter if she ever wishes to visit."

The visit to the broken-down adobe wall, seeing the grapevine clawing to survive, seemed like a tired reflection of the event that occurred so long ago. Zach worried Caroline would hear his heart thumping in his chest. He could barely swallow, nearly choking with emotion. Yet, he couldn't tell Caroline what his cowardice had caused.

The riders made it back to the stagecoach station in time to direct the loading of their trunks. One other man, a farm implement salesman, climbed into the coach.

Caroline had enough of the desert wind and drab. Zachary had returned to being easygoing and continued reading his book. The swing station in Walnut Creek, located about twenty miles from the canyon, allowed the three passengers to stretch their legs and visit the privy. The stagecoach pulled up to Pembroke's Supply station in Flagstaff around seven o'clock after Steve Pembroke had closed and gone home.

The stage driver helped Zachary carry the trunks onto the porch. The stagecoach went on with the remaining passenger, heading to Williams.

Zachary looked around, noting all the changes to his childhood valley. The railroad bed about one hundred feet south of the supply station looked ready for ties. Stakes were prominent in parallel rows running back east, to the west, and north. In the distance, Zachary could see buildings on the rise to the east in a neat row facing each other. Flagstaff looked like a town working on its future, planned, and progressing.

No one was around. Luckily, the full moon would light the trail up the mountain. Zachary offered Caroline a choice. Either they could hike up to Hanna's cabin together, or he would volunteer to go on up and saddle the mule and horse and come back for her.

The night was cool but not cold, and Caroline decided to go with Zachary.

Before starting up the trail, Zachary stopped at the walkway leading nowhere at the end of the supply station.

"My father owned a saloon. Built it right here when I was young. He built it; he burned it down," said Zachary.

Caroline, sensing another mystery, said, "Why did he burn it down? Was it an accident?"

"No," said Zachary, "We better get to the cabin. It is a hike. I'll tell you tomorrow."

"You better, Zachary Brennan. I can't believe how unaware I am of your Arizona past. I'll wait until tomorrow."

The couple, fighting exhaustion, climbed onto the cabin porch after the mountain hike, and Zachary knocked on the door. As always, Hanna, inside the cabin, jumped at the sound. "I'm coming," Hanna called out, detouring to the peg on the wall by the bed where she hung her robe.

She wrapped herself in the robe and poked straggling hair behind her ears. "Who is it?" she said.

Zachary kept quiet until she opened the door. "It's me, Mother," said Zach. "Your long-lost son."

Hanna threw both arms into the air and then leaped at her son, hugging him. Tears streamed down her cheeks.

"This is a surprise of a lifetime. I thought you might come, but I did not expect you to arrive so fast. Wait a minute. Who is this, my daughter-in-law?" Hanna embraced Caroline in a bear hug, fit for a mountain woman. Then she held Caroline at arm's length, her examination quick and complete. Then she hugged Caroline a second time.

"The look in his eyes tells me all I need to know about you, my dear. He loves you very much, doesn't he?"

"We were friends for years before I realized I loved him just as much as he loves me. I'm sure of it."

The three Brennans socialized for a half hour. Watching Caroline covering yawn after yawn, Zachary asked his mother for a nightgown for her. The couple visited the outhouse, said goodnight to Hanna, climbed the loft ladder, and fell upon the bed.

Zachary looked up at the logs framing the cabin's roof, as he had for all the years of his youth. Caroline lying close reminded him of Jeremiah, warm and breathing easily next to him. Chica would be lapping at his cheek. His heartache stabbed at him. Then Lorenzo slipped into his dream. The cold father of his younger years had finally understood their differences and warmed to Zachary's independence. He thought about how Lorenzo would have loved Caroline.

Jeremiah, look out for Father. Good hunting, you two.

44 |Grave Explanations

Zach and Caroline Brennan slept in until late morning, assisted by the quiet of the mountain cabin. The barn and the animals were too far away to disturb them. The sound of the creek burbling down the mountain behind the house acted like a rhythmic massage helping them both rest.

Eliza came over from the barn expecting breakfast. Hanna shooed her away to give her guests time to sleep in. The travelers rose in time for lunch, and afterward, Hanna asked about Zach's plans for the day.

"I want to show Caroline the ranch," said Zachary. "We'll go up to the high pasture and the valley. Mother, who's going to help you with the sheep now."

"I'll work that out. You know, Caroline," Hanna bragged. "Zachary ran the ranch for three years while my husband went to war. You have a very responsible husband."

"I agree with you," said Caroline. "Now he's running a newspaper operation, managing twenty-two employees and reporters. At thirty-one years old, that's quite another accomplishment. Hanna, you can continue to be proud of your son."

"Indeed, I am," said Hanna. "Caroline, his father told me months ago how proud he was that Zachary had such fiery independence. Son, he never worried about you making your way in the world."

"Let's get going, Caroline," said Zachary, standing ready.

Through the window, Hanna watched Eliza approach the cabin. Eliza knocked gently and opened the door, and walked into the room. "I could stand it no longer, Hanna," said Eliza. "I have been ready to meet your son for over a decade, and now here I am.

"Zachary Brennan, my name is Eliza Blackstone. I'm the…."

Zachary slapped his forehead, interrupting her. "You are Eli's daughter," he said.

"That I am," said Eliza, "pleased to meet you."

"Likewise," said Zachary, "This is my wife, Caroline. How long have you known my mother? How long have you been in Flagstaff?"

"Over two years," said Eliza. Your mother and I have been scheming business opportunities. I hope to start building in town soon. My tent store is getting old."

"I'm giving Caroline a tour of the property. I thought we'd start at the upper pasture. We'll have to catch each other up when I get back."

"Why don't I come with you?" said Eliza.

"Sure," Zach said. "Mother, how about you? Want to come along?"

"I've already been up there this morning while you were sleeping," said Hanna. "I'll stay here. I'm making scallop potatoes for supper."

Zachary, Caroline, and Eliza went directly to the barn and stopped at Eliza's apartment.

"This used to be where Kyle stayed," said Zach, "Kyle was Father's ranch hand. He married my sister, Sarah. They're coming over for dinner tonight. I can't wait to see her all grown up."

"They live a bit down the mountain and east," said Eliza. "Kyle will be in the upper pasture with half the sheep now. He has his stock of horses he trains as well."

The upper floor of the barn now had a definite woman's touch. The threesome walked along the spring creek up to the pasture. Zachary remembered every step as if he had never gone away.

As the threesome entered the upper meadow, a black and white border collie charged up, stopped, and barked a warning, keeping the sheep safe. Kyle yelled, "Gypsy, settle down. Hi Zach, been a while."

Zachary knelt and let Gypsy come to him for a big sniff. After two minutes, the dog begged for more scratches.

"Lorenzo's grave is with the others, Zach," said Kyle. "The headstone is probably still a couple of weeks away."

Zach walked directly over to the east corner of the meadow. A short fence separated the graveyard from the pasture. The fresh grave already sported wildflowers. Someone had scattered cut flowers around the head of the grave and beneath the headstones of the other two graves.

"The flowers are from Sarah, right?" said Zach.

"Sarah and your mom," said Kyle. "Hanna was up this morning already."

Caroline reached over, taking Zachary's hand in hers. "Tell me, Zachary," she said.

"Buried in this first grave is a man named Abelardo. He was our ranch hand. Don't know exactly how old he was when he died. I found him here with the sheep. Mother and I buried him, and I worked the ranch alone. He died the second year of the war."

"Was he a relative?" asked Caroline.

"No," said Zachary. "Just a Mexican ranchhand who felt like family to us. Taught me Spanish."

Caroline put an arm around Zach's waist. That would be Zachary's nature, calling a Mexican work hand part of the family. She could make out the headstone on the other grave beside Lorenzo's. It had weathered even more than the Mexican's headstone. "Jeremiah Brennan," she read. "I thought it might be your grandfather before I saw the dates."

"That's my older brother, Caroline," Zachary said. "He was thirteen, and I was eleven when he died."

Caroline fought an urge to get upset. *Another mystery.*

She needn't have worried. Eliza Blackstone spoke up, "No one ever talks about Jeremiah. I've been around the Brennan family for over a year and still don't know anything about Jeremiah."

Caroline looked over at Kyle. "Don't look at me," said Kyle. "It is as big a mystery to me as ever. I've tried to find out from Hanna, Lorenzo, and even Steve Pembroke at the supply station. Everyone always says Zachary will explain someday."

Caroline turned her husband to her and lifted his chin. He had gone instantly dark, as if that Cañon Diablo grapevine had reached up from the ground, entangled his ankles, anchoring him in place. "Is today that day, Zachary?" said Caroline.

"If you and Eliza take a seat on the bench over there by the tree," said Zachary. "I'll take a minute with my father and then tell you about Jeremiah. It's time."

Zachary stood beside the grave for a full two minutes. No solid thoughts of Lorenzo entered Zachary's mind, however. They had been so far apart for so long. Yet, before Zach had left for San Francisco, father and son had understood each other. Zachary was now sure of it. What was it Lorenzo had said? *No one is born brave.*

Zachary walked over to where Eliza and his wife waited patiently. Kyle leaned on his crook.

"Seems like a lifetime ago," Zachary began, "I was only eleven. Jeremiah, thirteen. I remember my brother's fascination with guns. Father gave him a rifle for his birthday, and Jeremiah practiced shooting every free moment.

"We were playing on the saloon's porch Lorenzo was so proud of. Built it himself. **Brennan's Last Chance Saloon.** Mother named it.

"Anyway, two men inside began to argue while we listened on the porch. We could tell they would pull their guns. Jeremiah went over to the window for a closer look. He just had to see that gun and could through the window.

"I should have yanked him back, but he was older and my hero. The two men drew and fired. The next thing I knew, my pants were sopping up… blood, so much blood. One man was dead. Jeremiah died.

"I should have done something. The gun spun out from the saloon doorway before me, and I… I just stared at it."

Caroline stood, rushed to Zachary, and hugged him. "Let's go back to the cabin, Zach," she said.

"You and Eliza go on down," said Zachary. "I'll help Kyle and Gypsy bring the sheep in." The tall man chuckled, feeling better. "For old times' sake," he said to Kyle.

Dinner that night brought all the Brennans together, along with Eliza Blackstone. Sarah stuck close to Kyle before and during dinner. She seemed reluctant to look at the stranger calling himself her brother.

Sarah gravitated to Caroline, who finally took Sarah by the hand, led her to where Zachary sat out on the porch, grabbed his hand, and clasped it to Sarah's

"This is your brother, Sarah," said Caroline, "and I am your sister-in-law. With the railroad's completion, we will visit at least annually and compensate for the years you have missed your brother. I promise."

"I'm sorry," said Sarah. "I'm just not used to having a brother. He's even bigger than I remember."

"Sarah," said Zachary, "May I hug you? I am so happy for you and Kyle. Thanks for being here all these years for Mother and Father."

Six people at the dinner table meant bumping elbows. Everyone pitched in during clean-up. Hanna directed Kyle and Zachary to move the table back next to the bed and set the chairs in a roomy circle around the stove.

Kyle invited Zachary and Caroline to Sarah's and his home on the morrow. Kyle wanted to show off his stock of horses.

"Kyle," said Zachary, "You're running two ranches now, the sheep and your horse enterprise. Seems like a handful, now that Father is gone."

"Used to it," said Kyle. "Lorenzo slowed down starting a year ago. He favored his leg daily, so Sarah and I helped out more."

Hanna had retrieved the medical encyclopedia and opened it to a bookmark. She quieted the rest of the conversations around the cabin and referred to the book on her lap. "I found a paragraph about embolisms the day after Lorenzo passed. I knew he had experienced a blood clot in his bad leg. The degradation of circulation in that leg over the years caused that.

"According to the book, what I thought was a breathing problem, in reality, was a chunk of the blood clot breaking off and lodging in his lung. His heart had to work so hard to pump blood to his organs that it gave out.

"Of course, all this is speculation, but it fits, I think."

"Do you have a plan for what is next, Mother," Zachary said.

"You and I always have a plan, Zachary," said Hanna. "Lorenzo and I made plans when we discovered the railroad construction had started.

"You've already seen some of the evidence of our plan."

"Hanna is the one that hired Wilbur Dawson, the surveyor, to lay out the town of Flagstaff," said Eliza. "I've already purchased one of the lots. I've contracted with Mr. Ayers to plane a sufficient amount of Ponderosa board feet to build a shop on Front Street. Mr. Ayers is hauling in a sawmill by rail and oxen. He plans to start cutting timber for railroad ties and building supplies by September."

"Eliza and I work together, Zachary," said Hanna. "I have reserved three of the choicest parcels next to Eliza's. I plan to move into town sometime next year and develop a hotel."

"What will you do with the cabin and the sheep," said Zachary.

Hanna smiled, "I've already spoken to Thomas McMillan about selling my stock to him. He can't wait to get a hold of my unusual wool bearers. I'll reserve a small herd for Kyle and Sarah if they want to manage sheep and horses. That's entirely up to them."

"And the land?" asked Zachary.

"I'll keep the land. Sell it off in ten-acre parcels as demand increases. The lots in town have already doubled in value, and that's nothing like what they'll be worth when the train goes to San Francisco.

"The hard part will be giving up on my blankets. But arthritis is making that too hard anymore. I can always manage a crew to make the blankets according to my designs if we return to a herd of thirty sheep.

"With Lorenzo's passing, I've made it a point to make out a will. The land is our family asset. If Eliza's predictions are accurate, and believe me, she knows her numbers. Sarah, both you and Zachary have nothing to worry about financially."

"No talk of that, Mother," said Sarah. "Kyle and I are doing well. Our horse breeding and training ranch make a respectable profit."

"Same here, Mother," said Zach. "I make an excellent salary at the newspaper. With the western population expansion, careers in journalism are in demand."

"You mustn't even give us a second thought, Mother Brennan," said Caroline. "My family owns the largest vineyard in San Jose, and wine never goes out of style."

"Enough of this talk," said Hanna. "Zachary, how about a cribbage tournament? I want to enjoy an evening with my son and daughter and their spouses. Lorenzo will be with us in spirit. I have a pie to divide for dessert later. Blackberry, his favorite."

Over the next two days, Zachary explored the valley and the survey markers for the lots and streets making up the fledgling community of Flagstaff Springs. He heard a great deal on the boardwalk of Hanna's counterpart in sheep ranching, Thomas McMillan. No one said an unkind word about him. Thomas and Hanna seemed to have mutual respect and a collective spirit of cooperation when developing the town.

Zachary never caught a whisper about Turk Corbin. Never gave him a thought. Corbin's work as foreman kept him on McMillan's sheep ranch away from town. McMillan now owned a thousand acres directly to the west of Hanna's property in and outside Flagstaff. Zachary incorrectly determined that Turk Corbin did not inhabit the Arizona territory.

Caroline and Zachary spent a second day with Sarah and Kyle and learned that Sarah would give birth in six months. While Kyle's ranch hand worked the sheep and horses, the foursome saddled horses and roamed the foothills of the magnificent San Francisco Peaks. Late spring is a glorious time of wildflowers and rejuvenated grasslands flourishing in the meadows sprinkled among the vast Ponderosa pine forest. Flagstaff's location over six thousand feet above the Pacific benefitted from both foothills and soaring mountain climates.

Caroline fell in love with the rugged Arizona area. The deserts that had dominated the vistas of the train trip were forgotten.

***

The next day Zachary knocked on Eliza's door of the barn apartment. He asked her to show the Brennan couple the lot she had chosen on Front Street and Hanna's stakes next door. He knew perfectly well which lot she had selected for her home/business, but the walk enabled them to get to know each other.

Eliza wanted to know everything Zach could remember about her father. Eliza and Caroline listened to Zachary's description of the intricacies of running a stagecoach swing station and blacksmith shop.

"Fair, demanding, strong, respectful, and expecting the reciprocal. That was your father," said Zachary.

Eliza patiently waited for Zachary to wind down. Zachary shook with emotion, describing his time as a horse handler and blacksmith's apprentice.

"He never looked down on my inexperience, never belittled me," said Zachary. "Even though I couldn't hold a candle to his formidable blacksmith skills, he instructed patiently, once, then he expected you to get the job done."

Eliza beamed, "That's how he was when I was little before my mother died. I loved him. He was my personal, huggable bear.

"Zachary, how did he die?" said Eliza

Zachary hesitated, closing his eyes and rubbing his chin, trying to choose the right words. "Quickly! It was swift. I do not believe he suffered long. That is all I'm prepared to say," he said, shaking with emotion.

"I understand," said Eliza. "He was a dear father, but I spent years away with my aunt. You must have known him even better than me, his daughter."

"I wouldn't say that, Eliza," said Zach. "Eli spoke of you about every day. A father couldn't have been prouder. I have known you since that time, even though we met days ago."

"Thank you, Zachary," said Eliza. "Your family has been so kind to me."

"Eliza, if I may ask," said Zachary, "how has the community received you here?"

"I'd have to say, I've been pleasantly surprised," said Eliza.

"I ask," ventured Zachary, "because I see so much discrimination in San Francisco, the Chinese, Indians, Mexican, people of color."

"Here in Flagstaff, my experience has been remarkable," said Eliza. "I guess everyone coming here is looking for a fresh start. It is a real community."

Caroline had been listening carefully. She surmised Zachary's hesitation at describing Eli's death tied into the anguish he displayed at the grapevine near Cañon Diablo. She decided to leave her questions to a time they were alone together.

Zachary looked visibly relieved. "Promise me, Eliza," he said. "If anything happens here that makes you uncomfortable, you must contact me immediately. I have gained influence with useful contacts due to my position at the *Daily Alta California*. I may be able to help."

Two days later, with all conversation exhausted, Zachary and Caroline packed their trunks, ready to leave. While Zachary packed, Hanna took Lorenzo's Paterson Colt repeater and holster from a peg on the bedroom wall, wrapped the belt around the holster and revolver, and set the bundle on the table.

Zachary spotted the gun when he descended the loft ladder. “Mother,” said Zachary, “What’s this.”

“Lorenzo never asked for anything,” said Hanna, “except a new wool blanket or coat every few years. The only things he collected were his firearms. I can manage his breech-loader rifle. Good for bear and wolf protection. I don’t even know how to load that gun.

“Consider taking it with you, Zachary. He would want you to have it, even if you never use it. In remembrance of him, take it with you, please.”

Zachary could see by the look in his mother’s eyes that an argument over the gun would cause his mother renewed heartache. The gun made him nervous, even hidden in the holster and wrapped with the belt. *I can get rid of the thing in San Francisco.*

“Ok, mother,” said Zachary. He returned the bundle to the loft and buried the gun and holster at the bottom of his trunk. He immediately went out to the well and washed his hands of the smell of the revolver and old holster.

When he returned to the cabin, he brought both trunks down from the loft and set them on the porch.

“Mother, I guess we’re ready,” Zachary said. “I’ve hitched the buckboard to take the trunks to the supply station.

“I don’t know when we will return, but it may be sooner than you think. You have inspired me, as always, Mother. The work you have done here to get this town started has caused me to think. Soon, Flagstaff may need a newspaper.”

“That would be wonderful,” said Hanna. “The council would welcome you, I’m certain.”

“Caroline and I have agreed,” said Zach. “We’d like to reserve the three parcels at the east end of Front Street. The ones with the three aspen trees. I can give you a deposit if you like.”

"Of course, we don't know when or if we will build there," said Caroline. "We'll have to see how the train shortens the trip here from San Jose and San Francisco."

Goodbyes were exchanged; Zachary loaded the trunks on the buckboard. After Caroline hugged Hanna, Zachary gave his mother a big hug and kiss. Hanna's eyes welled up, sad to see him leave again, excited that her son may someday soon come home for good.

***

On July 2nd, 1882, the first train passed over the Cañon Diablo trestle. On August $1^{st,}$ a train made it to Flagstaff. The entire community turned out to welcome passengers and congratulated the train crew.

Hanna moved forward with her plans. Masons completed the foundation for Eliza Blackstone's building and Hanna's new manor. These structures would be approximately three-quarters of a mile east of the springs, where several businesses had already purchased lots from Thomas McMillan. Hanna planned to pipe water from the springs to the east end of Front Street. She began consulting with engineers from Wilbur Dawson's office.

Mr. Ayers purchased a sawmill, took it to the end of the track, and transported it by ox team across the Little Colorado River and on to Flagstaff. He wasted no time establishing the Ayers Lumber Company, which provided the lumber for the railroad and board lumber for wood frame houses. Construction crews moved to town and began building Eliza's shop, Hanna's new home, and six other stores on the hill near the springs.

McMillan's lots were selling, and he began planning for a bank. Two saloons were under construction. A blacksmith from New Mexico came to town and set up a shop. Lyle Hampton built a silo and feed store a block north of Front Street. A cobbler worked out of a tent and found it challenging to keep up with all the shoe repairs needed by the railroad crews.

The month before the train arrived in Flagstaff, railroad executives visited Flagstaff. They determined an ideal location for the station on level ground three-quarters of a mile east of the springs. Business owners soon followed the station, displacing the town's commerce to Front Street of 'New Town,' near Eliza's and Hanna's property, while the houses remained in 'Old Town.' Hanna's property values shot up.

The railroad depot consisted of three box cars and a station platform on level ground, so the trains didn't have to start on a steep hillside. Sheep ranchers began using the railroad to transport wool. Cattle ranchers, drawn by the prospect of free or inexpensive land, realized they could now affordably ship their beef to the eastern market.

45 |Sit Still

Clear and cold, the moonlit night in the foothills near Williams, Arizona Territory, caused Turk to button his duster up to his neck. He needed to be more patient and wait for the farmer to return. This might be his easiest yet.

Whenever Turk came across a negro, he would look away while the feeling of spiders crawling up his arms eventually calmed. It all started when he turned thirteen. His mother, still lovely despite the copious amounts of Crow whiskey she consumed day and night, ordered Turk to get a job to support her habit.

Glennis Corbin's husband had left when Turk was eleven. Dan Corbin's inability to keep a job had been the source of many rants in the kitchen. He swore streaks about the tasks southern plantation owners gave to their slaves instead of hiring him to maintain and repair their ornate homes. When the rants ended one morning, and the house became quiet, it took young Turk a day and a half to understand that his father was gone for good. Glennis also blamed slaves for her predicament, and Turk couldn't agree with his parents more.

Turk had conflicting memories of his father. When Dan Corbin stayed sober and had a coin in his pocket, he and Turk occasionally fished for catfish in Atchafalaya Bayou or the Mississippi.

Turk learned to shoot while hunting raccoons with his father in the early hours of full moon nights. When Turk turned ten, Dan Corbin began playing mumbly-peg with his son. A game where players try to stick a knife in the ground as close to their foot as possible. Dan had played the game since his youth and usually won, even drunk. Turk stuck his foot with the knife in the match thrice while his father tipped his bottle for a guzzle and laughed.

After his father deserted him, Turk squeezed all the hurt and joy out of his consciousness. When he came across the elder Corbin's stiletto in a workbench drawer, Turk claimed it as his inheritance. From that point forward, he kept everything and everyone out. Turk had nothing, dreamed of nothing, and blamed everyone for his nothingness.

Turk didn't attend school, but one afternoon he came home early from his job as a janitor at the general store in Anguilla, Mississippi. The store owner closed early for a relative's funeral. When he entered his house, Turk heard what sounded like the dog jumping around on the bed in the room upstairs. When he rushed in, he saw a broad-shouldered, naked darky with fat rolls around his belly and back, flopping against his pale-skinned mother, her breasts bobbing to his rhythm. On the side table, he saw a one-quarter full bottle of Crow whiskey and two bits. A week later, Turk intercepted the man heading for his house again in the dark and stabbed him six times from behind with the stiletto. Turk never went back home. If he had returned, he might have killed his drunken whore of a mother.

When Mississippi joined the confederate states, Turk thought he had found a perfect way to find and kill negroes. It didn't work out that way. The other side shot back, so Turk deserted, ending up in jail. He escaped by killing the soldier that fell asleep on guard duty, and Turk headed for the New Mexico Territory.

Sure enough, the farmer driving his buggy home from Williams pulled into the barn, took care of his horse and rig, and entered the farmhouse. Turk immediately went up to the door and knocked. When the owner opened the door a crack, Turk pushed through, gun drawn, and ordered the man to sit in the armchair in the living room. Turk stood in front of him, not saying a word. Not necessary. This was Turk's actual occupation now, and his expertise was evident. He shot the man dead with a bullet to the center of the man's forehead.

Then Turk pulled up the other armchair and sat five feet before the man, watching blood soaking into the overstuffed headrest. Turk got comfortable, took an easy breath, and held still. Staring.

Still, as death, just like the thing in the other chair. *Is this what it is like?* No sound, indeed, no movement.

After minutes of focused harmony with the dead body, Turk used his inheritance to notch his gun handle, stood, offered his "Hallelujahs," and left. *One more down and out.*

46 |Interview of the Lawman

Zachary had his hands full at the newspaper, running an investigative reporting team that exposed police corruption and the 'Committee of Safety.' One of the reporters on the team began looking into shady methods for recruiting sailors to man the whaling ships working out of the bay. The practice of Shanghaiing sailors kidnapped from the boarding houses and saloons along the wharf caught Zack's attention. He organized a second reporting team to look into the situation.

In May '83, Nathan, the telegraph operator Zachary hired to listen for Associated Press dispatches distributed over the wire, stepped into Zachary's office.

"There was a murder yesterday in the Arizona territory," Nathan said, referring to his notes. "The crime was committed two miles outside the community of Williams. No witnesses, so there are no leads whatsoever. No motive has been determined.

"The man's name was Stubs Hawthorne, a negro farmer who worked twenty acres near the McMillan estate. Shot at close range.

"Thought you might be interested, Mr. Brennan, since Williams is near Flagstaff."

"Thanks for bringing it to my attention, Nathan," Zachary said. "I am interested. I'll check the California, Prescott, and Las Vegas newspapers for the next few days."

The event never appeared in any newspaper. Zachary thought about authoring an article but decided against it. He filed a copy of the dispatch in his Flagstaff file.

Returning to San Francisco from Flagstaff, Zach put the traumas of his youth and Olivia out of his mind. Living in California felt like living in a sanctuary. He lived a life free of the stigma that pricked his conscience.

This time, Zachary couldn't get Eliza out of his head. Lorenzo's revolver, hidden away, entered his dreams.

He woke up one night in a sweat. Laying close, Caroline looked at her husband, water beads running off his furrowed brow down the sides of his face. "What is it, Zach," she said. "You were shaking."

"It's the gun," said Zach.

"The gun is in the closet," said Caroline. "You can't even see it."

"I don't know. It haunts me, always has," said Zach.

"I can't imagine. Your brother's gone; all you can see is that gun."

"I'm at the end of my rope," said Zach. "I worry about Eliza. I'm worried you won't put up with me. You didn't know what you were getting into when you married me.

"I love you, Caroline."

"Zach, that's what matters. I love you as well. We have to beat this thing together," said Caroline.

"I have no idea how to do that," said Zachary.

Caroline smoothed out the sheets over her husband and snuggled into his chest. They were both quiet for a time. Caroline suddenly threw back the covers and sat up on the edge of the bed. "I think I might know a way," she said. "Something to try."

She left the bedroom for a minute and returned with the holstered gun and belt. She positioned the bedroom side chair next to Zach and hung the gun belt over the ear of the chair back.

"Maybe, it's like getting back on the horse," said Caroline. "We'll start with keeping it close by. When you manage that, you'll start holding the revolver, even fire it eventually." We'll step back if you panic or start having nightmares again."

Zach slept soundly that night and the next. Then the nightmare of the spinning gun returned. Caroline hugged him to quiet. After two weeks, Zach's closeness to the firearm no longer affected him.

Caroline then offered the gun for Zach to take for a brief five minutes before she turned down the lamp. Holding the gun for five minutes turned into ten, then fifteen minutes. Next, Zachary was required to handle the gun for fifteen minutes in the light and five minutes in the dark. Gradually, Zachary's powerlessness in the presence of a six-shooter began to ease.

The telegraph describing the negro man's murder in Williams, Arizona, gnawed at Zachary. Only thirty miles from Flagstaff and Eliza, the murder still seemed too coincidental in circumstantial evidence to the murder of Eli Blackstone. What if there were other underreported crimes in the territory?

One of his reporters stopped into Zachary's office on a Tuesday morning. Roy bragged about seeing Wyatt Earp walking through Portsmouth Square on his way to a faro game.

Intrigued, Zachary set out to meet Mr. Earp for advice on the Williams town murder. The newspaper or Zachary might hire Earp as a bounty hunter to find Turk Corbin or whoever committed these heinous murders and bring him to justice.

In a staff meeting, Zachary asked his reporting crew to be on the lookout for the famous gunman. He was not to be bothered, but if the man's favorite haunts could be determined, Zachary might write to him requesting an interview.

The reporter's efforts turned up a locale Earp frequented most days. Stanley's Ice Crème Shop on Mission Street. Zachary visited the store and sat on a stool at the far end of the bar. Wyatt Earp arrived shortly and settled on a seat in the center of the bar. He ordered a dish of vanilla.

Wyatt Earp looked to be six feet tall and athletic. Light lashes fringed his blue eyes, set beneath blonde eyebrows. His hair was yellow as gold. A heavy, tawny mustache shaded his firm mouth and swept below his strong, square chin. He wore a gray tailor-made suit, immaculate linen, and fashionable neckwear. Tan shoes.

He presented to Zachary a figure to catch a lady's eye.

Zach finished his dish of chocolate ice crème and left the store. The next day the newspaperman picked a seat two to the right of the corner stool. Wyatt again sat in the center seat. He favored vanilla ice crème. Earp ordered vanilla again. Zachary nursed his vanilla scoop, leaving the shop just before Earp finished his dish and left.

Two days later (Zach skipped ice crème for a day to not appear too obvious,) the editor chose the stool that would provide one empty seat between himself and Mr. Earp.

"I guess the vanilla here is about the best in the city," said Zachary.

"I like it," said Earp.

"I usually prefer chocolate, but the vanilla here is amazing," said Zach.

Wyatt Earp nodded.

As he finished the last lick in his bowl, Zachary turned to Earp, "My name is Zachary Brennan, Mr. Earp," he said. "I recognized you but wished to protect your privacy."

Earp nodded and tipped his bowler.

The next day Zachary came in after Mr. Earp and sat in the same seat he had occupied the day before. One empty seat over from Earp. Zachary set his hat crown side down on the stool to his left and ordered a dish of praline.

"Mr. Brennan," said Wyatt Earp, "What do you want?"

"Well," said Zachary, "If it is not too inconvenient, I'd…."

"Let me stop you there, Mr. Brennan," said Wyatt. "I know who you are. Editor of the *Daily Alta California,* right?"

"You've made inquiries about me, I see," said Zachary.

"Didn't need to. You are taller than me. I've read three of your articles. You're known."

"Well then, I apologize, Mr. Earp, for my not-so-subtle approach. I truly do not wish to bother you. I'll finish and let you enjoy your dish of vanilla."

Wyatt Earp smiled, cocked his head, took another bite, then said, "Might as well ask me your questions. These days I approve your copy or sue your newspaper if you print something I haven't approved."

"Fair enough," said Zach. "You've read my articles. I'm looking for the truth of Wyatt Earp and a little human interest. Tomorrow, let me buy your ice crème. We'll sit at a table for the interview. I promise to abide by your conditions."

Zachary sat at a table at the prescribed time and waited for Mr. Earp. He had no right to expect the man to keep the appointment, but at the top of the hour, Wyatt Earp came through the door and sat across from his interviewer. They both ordered vanilla.

For the next hour, Zachary asked questions, and Wyatt answered. Zachary learned of a 'down to earth,' no-nonsense man. For instance, Zachary asked if Wyatt practiced his draw.

"A fast draw is bullshit pulp fiction," Wyatt said. "I don't even strap on a holster most days. If I need a gun, I carry it. That way, the cowboy can see I am serious."

"What if the outlaw has a reputation?" asked Zachary.

"Well," said Earp. "I still have the advantage. They are either too young to know better or too drunk to react. I walk up, slap 'em, and clunk 'em over the head with my pistol."

Before the interview hour expired and the second dish of ice crème was eaten by both men, Zachary suggested he had enough material for an article.

"That's fine," said Earp. "I'll review what you write up tomorrow before I leave town. My girl and I are heading up to Eagle City, Idaho. I hear there may be a strike."

"One last question, Wyatt," said Zach. "Years ago, I saw a man shoot dead another man, a defenseless man. How would you go about getting justice in a case like that? Believe me, I am no hero with a gun like you."

"Zachary, what have I been trying to tell you? I ain't no hero. I do my job, just like you.

"To answer your question, if I were you, I'd send your territory deputy U.S. marshal after the man."

"This man has avoided prosecution for years," said Zachary.

"Then, you've got to do it yourself. Get the town council to back you with a warrant and take the outlaw into custody. Hold him for the district court or the Deputy U.S. Marshal. Turn him over eventually when the marshal shows up."

"I guess I can try. My hand still shakes if I'm holding a gun."

"You've got to keep concentrating on the job at hand, not the other possibilities. Start firing; none of this 'you draw first' to make it fair shit."

"I am glad I met you, Wyatt. It's been a real pleasure. Good luck in Idaho."

"Pleasure as well, Zachary. Whatever you do, I think you'll be OK. You're a straight shooter."

Zachary grimaced at Earp's final comment. Leaving the ice cream shop, he rode the new cable car on Union Street part way home, mulling Wyatt Earp's advice.

***

On June 27th, '83, Zach's office door opened to a man with a curly grey beard, sun squinting craggy eyes, wearing a beat-up slouch hat.

"I don't believe it," said Zachary. "Harold Crenshaw returned from the dead. It is damn good to see you. Just get back?"

"Actually," said Harold, "I've been back a week, Zachary. Keeping a low profile. Checking the lay of the land."

"I was beginning to think you were lost to us," said Zachary. "What's it been, two years, at least? I'm not complaining, but you said you'd be gone for only a year."

"I kind of did catch the fever," said Harold. "I had success in the vein we were working, but it seemed to continue deeper in the mountain, so I took more time to go after that next few feet and found more gold. That sequence happened three more times."

"What's your next move, Harold?" asked Zach.

"Shave and a haircut. I've held off on a bath. As you can see, I conducted my investigation in disguise.

"Got to tell you, I've been impressed with what I have found. From what I have heard, you are doing an excellent job moving the newspaper forward. Even got a couple of your articles the AP distributed to the newspaper in Anchorage. Fine work. The Board of Directors is pleased."

"Harold," said Zachary. "I hear a 'but' coming. I wouldn't consider continuing in this position now that you've returned. I knew it to be temporary all along."

"I guess maybe you've deduced the issue, Zachary," said Crenshaw. "I had a long discussion with Woodward, president of the board. They're impressed with your accomplishments, but you're just too controversial for their sensibilities. They hope you will stay as my lead reporter at your current salary. How does that sound, Zachary?"

"That will be fine, Harold. Investigative reporting and writing are what motivate me. Gets me up in the morning. I'm good at it. Let me talk things over with Caroline. You heard I'm married now. Anyway, I'll give you a definite answer tomorrow."

"One last thing, Zach," said Harold, handing Zachary an envelope. "Here's a bonus from the Board for stepping up in my absence and a check from me. You made my adventure possible, which has paid off for both of us."

That evening Zachary opened the envelope over dinner. "Let's see what the Board considers an adequate bonus," Zachary said while pouring more Wainwright wine into their glasses.

The check from the Alta California Co. checking account was for $3,000.00.

The check from Harold Crenshaw's account was for $10,000.00. The attached note stated:

> **Zachary, I hit it big, more than I can ever spend. Like you, the newspaper business is in my blood. Thank you for giving me a path back to what we do best.**
> **Sincerely, Harold**

Caroline raised her glass to toast her husband. After a clink and a drink, she said, "This changes things, doesn't it, darling."

"It seems so to me, my love," said Zach. "Added to what I've managed to save, we have the funds for setting up a newspaper in Flagstaff. We can build on the lots Mother has reserved for us. A genuinely delightful home. That's my dream, but what do you say? Could you manage a frontier town?"

"Zachary," said Caroline. "On our trip, I fell in love with your mountains, your people, Eliza, and the spirit of Flagstaff. I'm ready, and I know we can make it work. Add twenty acres in the foothills for horses, and I'm all in."

After learning of Zachary's plan to leave the company the next day, Harold called a staff meeting. While everyone huddled together in the lobby, the editor announced his return. Harold looked healthy, his hair trimmed, his beard gone, and he wore a new, expensive suit. He gave a short, impassioned speech about his excitement to drive the newspaper's mission forward.

After the speech, Harold announced Zachary Brennan's departure from the company, effective in two weeks. The employees quietly moaned, then extended applause erupted in recognition of the successful two years Zachary held the position of Managing Editor.

Zachary gave an even shorter speech than Harold's. Harold's return would allow Zach to return to his family homestead in Arizona to become the managing editor of a new local newspaper in Flagstaff, *The Flagstaff Flag.*

Later in the week, Zachary approached Harold with another idea. "Harold, I think you should consider buying a new rotary press. With the subscription increase over the last six months and increased outlying county circulation, we barely get enough copies of the Daily off the number one and two presses."

"Hmm. A third press might be in order. I'll check the numbers," said Harold.

"Instead," said Zachary, "sell the number two press to me for my paper in Flagstaff. One modern rotary press is equal to our two presses combined. I'd take the number two press off your hands for $550.00. I've checked, and that's a reasonable price for that old press. I know how to operate it and how to maintain it."

"As I say," said Harold, "I'll check the numbers. Sounds good, though."

"When you get your new press, I'll pay the same company that assembles it to dismantle the old press and crate it for shipment to Flagstaff."

Zachary spent a day moving his belongings out of Harold's office and two more days packing everything for shipment to Flagstaff. He authored his last article for the daily at the end of the week.

Having finished all his assignments and updating Harold on the outstanding investigations of the reporting teams, Zachary Brennan left the premises of the Alta California building.

Caroline and Zachary were ready to move to Arizona by the third week in July. Zachary sent a letter to his mother to expect them on the first train from San Francisco East to Flagstaff.

The rotary press manufacturer had sent a crew to dismantle the number two press and crate and label each piece. After the team had finished assembling the new rotary press, Zachary bought a copy of the Daily Alta California. The print seemed crisper and even from corner to corner of each sheet.

The Brennans waited for The Southern Pacific and the Atchison, Topeka, and Santa Fe trains to connect at Needles, California. Rumors suggested it would be any day now.

Zachary learned of a gunsmith shop on the corner of Powell and Pine: Paul Pinone: proprietor. Zachary felt uneasy just walking into the place. The small store had two ten-foot-long aisles, barely wide enough for one person. Racks in rows held rifles and shotguns upright. The store owner had aligned his available pistols for sale in a glass display case with a glass top. The small operation included an array of holsters on pegs behind the counter and a floor-to-ceiling open cupboard for ammunition. A sign over a door in the rear of the shop read: **Shooting Range**. Another door remained open for access to a firearm engraving workshop.

The bell attached to the front door brought the owner out from his back room. He had wispy grey hair and wore a headband with a magnifying lens for close engraving work. "How can I help you, sir?" said Mr. Pinone.

Zachary set a box on the counter and opened it. "I want to ensure this gun is in good working order," he said.

"For what purpose?" said Pinone.

"What do you mean?" Zachary said. "I guess to defend against outlaws or bears or other varmints."

"And how knowledgeable are you in firearms, sir?"

"No experience, to be honest. My father bought this gun a long time ago."

"Alright, that's where we'll start. This is a Paterson Colt repeater outfitted with a reloading lever and a capping window. Powder and ball ammunition.

"I'll tell you now that you'd never have time to reload if your five shots missed or winged a bear or an outlaw. I can oil it up and check it over for $1.50."

"What might be a better solution?" asked Zachary.

Mr. Pinone walked down the counter, opened one of the glass cabinet doors, and extracted a dull-steel gun with a polished mahogany grip.

"This here is your Colt SAA, Model P, Peacemaker with a five-and-a-half-inch barrel. Takes .45 caliber cartridge ammunition. No fuss, no muss. For a beginner, this is the way to go."

"How much does it cost?" said Zach.

"With your trade, $15.00, a holster is extra."

"Oh yes, I don't want anyone to think I'm some gunman. Any suggestions?"

Paul Pinone looked down the wall behind him at the holsters on pegs, grabbed one, went down to the ammunition cupboard, and brought back two cartridge boxes.

"This is a Texas shoulder holster. You wear it under your coat. Very discreet. Here are your cartridges. All told, you're looking at $23.25." Pinone reached into a drawer behind him and pulled out a bulletin, giving it to Zachary. "Study the instructions on this sheet. Especially the advice on keeping one chamber empty and the other safety features of the gun. Good hunting."

Zachary asked Mr. Pinone to put everything he had purchased in the box. Zach carried the box home and began to study the instructions.

47 |Flagstaff

Word of the final connection between the Southern Pacific railroad out of Mohave City and the Atlantic and Pacific railroad originating in Albuquerque spread rapidly. Businesses needing to transport freight east from California and west from the Arizona and New Mexico territories saw immediate cost savings. Passenger travel through the central latitudes of the United States became more feasible. Competition between multiple railroads crisscrossing the US drove travel costs down.

Zachary supervised loading his printing press crates and watched the train pull away from the Bayshore Yard, Brisbane. Zachary hoped Kyle had received his letter asking him to sign for the pallets when his shipment reached Flagstaff.

The Brennans boarded a passenger train heading for their new hometown two days later. The trip would take four days with stops and a connection change in Needles, California, where the SP and the A&P railroads connected. In May, to get to Flagstaff, the couple had traveled for eight days (sixteen days round trip.)

Zachary stepped off the train onto the station platform in Flagstaff. The significant changes to the town amazed him. Two months had elapsed since the Brennans left Flagstaff and returned to San Francisco. Buildings were under construction on the hill near the springs, and Eliza and Hanna's places were progressing.

The Brennans left their trunks at the depot and walked to Pembroke's Supply Station. Zachary borrowed the station's buckboard and team, drove back to the depot, loaded their chests, and proceeded up the mountain to Hanna's cabin.

The family spent a day telling stories of the events in town and news of San Francisco. At dinner, Zach announced his intentions. "I want to set up the printing press as quickly as possible and start publishing a newspaper. Caroline thought *The Flagstaff Flag* sounded like a great name."

"I can introduce you to Thomas McMillan," said Hanna. "He's renting out space in one of his storefronts on the hill. He has an office in town and spends time there every Wednesday, so tomorrow should work."

"Thanks, Mother," said Zachary. "I'll meet with him. If everything works out, I'll need Kyle's and Steve's help to move all the printing press crates. Any day, a coal load will arrive by train from San Francisco. I'll check with Mr. McMillan for an appropriate spot to pile it.

"That's a start. I want to build a newspaper office in 'New Town.' We brought plans for the home we want to build on the lots you reserved for us, Mother. We'll need to meet with the builders in town and get in line for a construction start.

I'll hammer alongside the builder for the next six months. The goal will be to get all our buildings enclosed before the heavy snow hits. Caroline and I are ready to dig in and help."

Zachary and Caroline unpacked their work clothes and took over the cabin loft. When builders finished Eliza's place in town, Eliza would move out of the barn apartment. Zach intended to move from the cabin to the barn while completing their own home in the valley.

Hanna accompanied Zach to Thomas McMillan's office, knocked on his office door in the lobby of one of the McMillan buildings, and Zach and Hanna entered.

After introducing the two men, Hanna begged off and left.

"I've heard a bit about you, Mr. Brennan," said McMillan. "Hanna is proud to bursting when it comes to you. She shares my big dreams for Flagstaff. That woman is a whirlwind of ideas and accomplishments, I tell you. Now she's talking about piping water down to new town."

"Nothing has ever stopped her, Mr. McMillan," said Zach.

"Please, not so formal. Thomas will do if I can call you Zachary."

"Zach or Zachary, I answer to either, both."

Over the next hour, the two men discussed Zach's plans for the newspaper and renting space until the construction crew completed his building.

Zach agreed to the fair rent of office space offered by McMillan. They shook on the deal, and Zachary stood to leave. The office door opened. A man shuffled in, his Stetson pulled low over his brows and looking down. Zachary didn't immediately recognize him.

"Zachary, this is my foreman, Turk Corbin," said Thomas. "Turk, meet Zachary Brennan. He's Hanna Brennan's son."

Turk turned toward Zachary briefly, said," Pleasure," and turned back to McMillan. "Boss, we need more feed for the north camp." Corbin hadn't recognized Zachary.

"Take care of it, Turk," said Thomas. "I'll be back tomorrow to check."

Without another word, Corbin turned on his heel and left the office. Zachary took a moment to recover from the shock of seeing Turk, the ghost from his past. Then Zach departed, thanking the rancher for the meeting.

Outside, Zachary walked over to the parcels where his home and office would be. He reflected on how small the disheveled Corbin now looked. So many years ago, and the man's appearance, if anything, had degraded even further.

Except for the well-worn gun belt strapped to his left thigh, Corbin appeared shaky to Zachary. That's what the gun was for. *Intimidation.*

The jolt of finding Turk Corbin right here in Flagstaff set off conflicting possibilities for Zachary.

On the one hand, Corbin and Eliza had existed near each other as long as Eliza had lived at Hanna's ranch. Zachary knew of nothing untoward that had happened. Turk would be busy managing the huge McMillan ranch, and Eliza spent much of her time corresponding with future clothing vendors. She lived up the mountain, out of sight.

Still, his plans suddenly seemed even more urgent.

Zach, Kyle, and Steve Pembroke, with block and tackle help, moved the printing press crates to the buckboard and then to the newly leased rental space. Zachary took over, spending the next weeks setting up the press.

The brand-new boiler and water reservoir tank arrived just a week after the railroad car carrying coal had rolled onto the branch track. Zachary spent another week transporting the coal shovel by shovelful to a discreet location behind the McMillan building.

48 |Investigation In Reverse

The Brennans settled into their new community. For four months, it seemed like everyone in town arose at dawn, and Zachary fit right in. By seven o'clock, the sound of hammers and saws competed with the buzz of the sawmill just outside of town. The rails were getting busier as more freight shipped out of California. Ten trains a day came roaring through at thirty-five miles per hour. Only two of them stopped in each direction. The conductors all indicated even more trains would whistle through next spring and summer.

Builder's construction crews worked at breakneck speed to enclose Zacks newspaper headquarters and his home at the edge of town before winter.

Zachary put together an issue of the Flagstaff Flag in October of '83. Zach resorted to the train schedules and building completion timetables to fill up two print pages.

He added a column introducing one of the new citizens of Flagstaff, Robert Cabreira. Mr. Cabreira arrived by train from Michigan, where he had graduated from the Michigan State Agricultural College. As a student, he studied horsemanship and farriery. While in college, he studied under Dr. Edward A. Grange, a pioneer in the field of veterinary science.

The article explained Robert's association with the American Veterinary Medical Association. A prominent local horse breeder Kyle Cantor coaxed Mr. Cabreira to move west and establish a practice in Flagstaff. Born in America,

Cabreira's parents were Colombian coffee brokers with offices in New York and Bogotá.

The obituary column described the accidental death of a carpenter who fell off the roof rafters of one of the new buildings in Old Town.

Mrs. Clarkston had died. At eighty-three, no one in town was qualified to declare a cause of death. Thirty-four of Evelyn's friends and relatives attended the funeral. Evelyn Clarkston was a well-liked and quiet lady. All of the Brennan clan paid their respects.

Eliza moved out of the barn apartment on the Brennan ranch on November 10th, '83. She occupied the upper floor of the newly completed Blackstone Clothing Store, which shared space with the Flagstaff Land Management office. Zachary helped with the move. In a private moment with Hanna, who helped pack Eliza's belongings, Zachary said, "Do you believe Eliza will be alright in town, Mother?"

"Why wouldn't she be," said Hanna. "Eliza is as much a part of the roots of this town as anyone."

"That's reassuring," said Zach.

"There was only the one incident that I've heard about."

"Oh," said Zach, "What happened?"

"At the time, Eliza told me you wanted to hear about such things. She asked me not to bother you or mention it to you."

"When was this, Mother, and what happened?"

Hanna busied herself folding clothes for the open trunk she was working to fill. Then she stopped to explain.

"Eliza was strolling down the walkway in Oldtown," said Hanna. "She had packages in both arms. Robert Cabreira, the veterinary, helped carry some of the packages. He turned into his office and loaded the packages he carried onto Eliza. After saying goodbye and thanking Robert profusely, she continued down the walkway. She came up to a man walking in the opposite direction. Eliza swears he shouldered her on purpose. The scoundrel knocked her down to the boardwalk and didn't apologize or help her. He looked back once with what Eliza described as an ugly smirk."

"Do you know who did this?" Zachary asked.

"Eliza described him as a thin man wearing a dark grey Stetson pulled tight and low on his forehead. Wore a gun, she said."

Zachary immediately thought of Turk Corbin. Zach had met everyone in and outside town: cowboys, farmers, cattlemen, lumberjacks, and sheep herders. Turk Corbin fits the description like no one else.

"Anyway, Zach," said Hanna. "You shouldn't worry. I asked that sweet man, Mr. Cabreira, to look in on Eliza occasionally, and he said he'd be glad to. We can keep Eliza safe between Robert, you, and I. Robert's already sweet on her."

Zachary and Caroline moved from the cabin loft to the barn apartment for the winter.

A snowstorm dropped eighteen inches on the town and two feet on the cabin in the mountain on Sunday, the 13th.

Zachary sat in a chair near the fireplace in the barn, feeding an occasional log to the fire.

In her nightgown, Caroline approached the chair from behind, putting her arms around her husband's neck. Then she moved around the chair to sit in Zach's lap for a kiss and a hug. The feel of Caroline's right breast and nipple through the cotton was distracting.

"What are you thinking, Zachary," said Caroline. "You're so quiet. Come to bed."

Zachary stood, picking up Caroline in his arms in one motion. "Tell you after," said Zachary. He took her to bed.

Later, Caroline, lying close, made circles with her finger on Zach's chest. She could tell her husband had again begun to concentrate on a problem, either with their new house, the newspaper building, or the newspaper itself.

"Alright," said Caroline, "let me help with whatever challenge you're working on. Talk it out. You're relaxed now, and your mind will set you right," said Caroline. "I can help."

"You've already helped, dear woman," said Zachary. "More than you can know. Much more than I deserve. I love you."

"I love you too, Zachary dear."

"Alright, but I warn you, what I'm about to tell you will be unpleasant. I've been working on a plan for a long, long time. Come back over to the hearth. The fire and light will keep us warm in the telling."

Zachary started his account the day Turk Corbin approached him at the swing station. The torturous retelling of the shooting of Eli and the spinning gun that Zach couldn't retrieve to prevent the murder of Eliza's father affected them both. "The grapevine, Eliza, your constant hints of worry for her," said Caroline. "This man Corbin. What could be wrong with him?" she said.

"We are all prejudiced, one way or another. His demons drive him to murder. Still bitter about the war? He would act the same way even without a war."

"You say you have a plan?"

"The man stays in the shadows. He doesn't socialize. It is like he stays hidden until he finds another victim."

"Even a woman? Would he dare?"

"So far, no, but who knows?

"I have this idea to conduct an investigative report in reverse. Smoke Turk Corbin out into the open. I conduct a human interest interview with the man, print the story, and see what reaction we get from the readers. If he tries to stay in the shadows and refuses the interview, I'll request stories from our readership illustrating his good character. Treat him like he's the most upstanding citizen working in the territory. Wait for someone to come forward to contradict such nonsense, hopefully with evidence, an eyewitness willing to testify against him. That and my testimony should stop him, even though Eli's murder happened so long ago."

"What about Eliza? Are you going to tell her what you're planning?" said Caroline.

"I don't think so," said Zachary. "It's just too hard. If we get results and the Deputy U.S. Marshal arrests Corbin, I'll tell her about Eli."

The next time Zachary met with Thomas McMillan, he explained his idea to highlight his foreman and the McMillan sheep ranch in next month's *Flagstaff Flag*. Thomas liked the idea. He sent a ranchhand to round up Turk. An hour later, Turk walked through the office door and fidgeted in a chair as Zachary proposed the article.

"I don't think so," said Turk, a smirk forming at the corner of his mouth. "No, I can't see it. Get someone else."

"Now, Turk," said McMillan. "This is an opportunity for both of us. Let's call it an assignment."

"Not going to happen, Boss."

"It will if I make it an order, Turk," said Thomas.

Zachary didn't want the article to explode in controversy for McMillan. "That's OK, Thomas," he said. "Turk isn't comfortable being in the limelight. I can still highlight the ranch without interviewing Mr. Corbin. Would that do?"

Corbin rose from his seat, crossed to the door, and left without saying anything to his boss or Zachary.

The article in the Flagstaff Flag covered the size of the McMillan holdings in acreage and sheep count. The McMillan real estate holdings in Flagstaff and Williams received most of the story. Still, Zachary sprinkled six mentions of the shy but highly competent foreman, Turk Corbin. Zachary described the man down to the notches on his walnut gun grip.

Zachary personally distributed his newspaper as far south as Prescott. The A & P train delivered copies to Albuquerque and Needles, California.

A man walked into the *Flagstaff Flag* office a week after distributing the special edition. He claimed Turk had murdered a negro man named Cornelius Tallin, who worked on his small milk farm north of Prescott.

When asked how Corbin had escaped prosecution, the man shrugged. "No one wanted to take it up," said the man. "We were in between deputy marshals at the time. I couldn't go after this man Corbin. I'm no shooter, and I had cows to tend. But it has bothered me to hell ever since. Four years ago. I'm certain the man you describe and Cornelius's killer are the same."

Agreeing to testify if Turk Corbin ever came to trial, Zachary had found the witness that could corroborate his testimony of Turk's violence.

That same afternoon, Zachary wrote a letter to U.S. Marshal Zan L. Tidball in Phoenix, describing the killing of Cornelius Tallin and Eli Blackstone. Zachary explained that witnesses were available for testimony and would identify Turk Corbin of Flagstaff, Arizona as the murderer. The culprit resided at the McMillan ranch near Flagstaff. Zach requested that a deputy journey to Flagstaff and arrest Corbin.

The construction crew finished Hanna's boarding house/hotel a month later. Hanna moved to her new home and immediately took in clients and travelers. No return letter from Marshal Tidball had arrived. Zachary assumed the arrest of Corbin would have to wait until spring for available manpower.

In the meantime, Zachary received two more letters from readers objecting to the references to Turk Corbin in the

McMillan ranch article that painted the man as an upstanding citizen. It simply was not true, the readers scoffed.

The heavy snows in January and February slowed construction in Flagstaff. Quiet blanketed the town as the inhabitants moved to indoor tasks; candle making, preserving fruits and vegetables, smoking deer meat, and drying herbs. The snow muffled the footfalls outside, so the opening of the door to the Newspaper's temporary headquarters surprised Zach.

Turk Corbin stood silhouetted in the open doorway. The man tromped over to Zachary, sitting at his desk. Ironically, Zach had been working on a follow-up article about the man standing before him. Turk, of course, hadn't bothered to stamp the snow off his boots. Instead, Corbin leaned over the desk, snow-melt dripping on Zach's notes.

"Who do you think you are, Brennan," said Turk. "You put my name in that fucking newspaper when I said I wanted no part of it."

Zachary stood. He looked down at the man. "You objected to being interviewed," said Zach. "In the newspaper, I printed what I obtained from alternate sources. Why are you upset? The article seemed very flattering, didn't it?"

"I have a right to my privacy," said Corbin. "If my name appears just once more in *The Flagstaff Flag,* you'll find this place turned into a pile of scrap metal."

Corbin turned and marched to the door, shaking snow and water off his duster and hat. He turned again to face Zachary, brushing back his overcoat behind the grip of his gun.

"You've been told!" Turk threatened. He turned again and left, not bothering to close the door, letting the snow drift inside.

***

Zachary heard a knock on the newspaper office's front door three days later. Zach opened the door and invited Thomas McMillan to join him at his desk. Zachary thought the man looked upset.

"Zachary," said Thomas. "I'm a man who has made it in this world by combining research with risk and hoping for a little luck. I've had to go with my gut feeling on occasion. I'm not much for asking for help."

"Go on, Thomas," said Zach, "I'll listen."

"This Corbin thing has gotten to me. He's been with me for five years now. He's a capable foreman. He worked the first four years diligently, and I had no complaints. Now I don't know.

"I received a letter yesterday from a man living outside Williams. He claims Turk shot and killed a negro neighbor of his last year. Saw him do it, or at least he thinks it was Turk. Same hat. He had the same strapped-down weapon on his left hip. Rode off after he did it; calm as you, please. The neighbor was too far away to identify Corbin, but Turk had buffaloed this man the day before on his porch, so the man got a good look at Turk at the time.

"I have to respond to this allegation. I believe in having friendly neighbors, not enemies. My question is: Do I stand by an employee of historically good standing?

"I will confront Turk with this letter. If I smell the truth, I'll cut him loose."

As Thomas spoke, Zachary opened his right-hand desk drawer and pulled out his thickening 'Turk Corbin' file. "You may want to peruse this dossier I've collected on Turk," said Zachary. "I'm an investigative reporter. I can tell you that the incident you have uncovered fits a pattern of behavior by Turk Corbin that is impossible to deny."

When Thomas finished looking over Zach's file, he sighed. "There is something else," said Thomas. "For the last nine months, I've noticed expenditures that don't make sense. Again, I have trusted my foreman with purchases and the distribution of supplies for years. I've been busy with real estate and the town's development. The information in these notes would indicate that I have made a mistake."

Zach sympathized with the older man. The two men talked about the town's progress, Hanna's waterpipe plans, the nature of sheep ranching, and Zachary's planned expansion of the newspaper.

"Thomas," said Zachary. "I know we haven't known each other long, but my mother and I have found you fair and honest.

"As we've been talking, I've thought of a way we can help you out. When I investigate, I always try to get at least two corroborating sources before I author my articles.

"You know our good friend, Eliza Blackstone?"

"Of course," said Thomas. "Doing an excellent job at the land management office. Smart lady."

"Did you know she once worked with Rockefeller on his business acquisitions back in Ohio?" Zachary asked.

McMillan shook his head.

"John D. Rockefeller of Standard Oil?' said Thomas.

Zachary continued, "If you would allow Eliza a week to review your books and receipts, I bet you will have answers about Turk Corbin.

The two men shook hands, and each went about their business. Thomas brought the books into the newspaper office the next day.

Eliza looked excited and determined when Zachary handed her the journals and a large box of receipts.

“Hopefully,” said Zachary, “you can complete your audit in two or three days so we can get the books back to Thomas before Turk Corbin gets wind of our investigation.”

“There is a lot here, Zachary,” said Eliza when Zachary approached her. “I’ll need to sort these receipts. They should be in separate folders ordered by date for easy cross-checking. I should be able to manage, though. You may need to check out suspicious receipts with vendors and customers.”

“I can do that,” Zachary said. “I’ll be your eyes and ears once you tell me what to look for. Do not even consider venturing over to McMillan’s office. Turk Corbin could show up any time, which would not be good.”

Within two days, Eliza found inconsistencies between receipts signed for by Corbin and the corresponding data in the journal. Instead of ten bags of corn grain indicated on a ticket, Corbin had entered a count of five in the journal.

“What do you think Turk did with the other half of these supplies?” Eliza asked Zachary.

Zachary shrugged, “No idea.”

Eliza called Zachary’s attention to five more large inconsistencies an hour later. “Turk couldn’t move this much grain, farm tools, and contraband without notice. One way would be to have a buyer take his share of the stores immediately as the vendor delivered the order to the ranch.”

“Turk could load the excess on a buckboard and drive to a storehouse somewhere,” said Zach. “I’ve heard enough about Turk’s movements to suggest that Williams might be a place to look west of here. It’s time for fieldwork. I’ll watch the McMillan ranch from up the mountain. If Turk goes anywhere in the buckboard, I’ll follow him.”

“The pattern didn’t start until about ten months ago,” Eliza said. “That might indicate Corbin is about to collect his spoils, make his money, and move on.”

"He's starting to make mistakes," said Zachary. "He's getting nervous. Operating more out in the open. He hates the attention he's gotten from my article, and now even Thomas doesn't trust him.

"I think you've done enough, Eliza. If I can follow Turk to his hideout or watch a buyer split a shipment with him, I'll publish our expose."

***

Kyle gifted Zachary with a gelding palomino named Pharoah the week the Brennans arrived from San Francisco. Caroline had chosen a chestnut quarter horse from Kyle's stock and promptly changed the mare's name from Daphne to Ginger. Zach insisted on paying top dollar. Hanna and Zachary worked on staking out twenty acres a short way into the foothills behind Zachary's double lot at the east end of Hanna's property. For now, Kyle boarded both horses.

Zachary informed Hanna about his letter to the U.S. Marshal, Eliza's audit of McMillan's financial expenditures, and his plan to further expose Turk Corbin's deeds. Zach borrowed Lorenzo's spyglass to observe the activity down on the McMillan ranch.

Since Hanna's property abutted the McMillan ranch, Zachary rode Pharoah into the San Francisco Peaks. He descended Humphrey's Peak on the west, finding a concealing group of boulders above the McMillan ranch outbuildings to set up camp. He constructed a tarp lean-to for shelter from the freezing nights and snowfall, which he shared with Pharoah.

Of the three horses Zachary had known, Pharoah seemed to need the most companionship. The horse constantly nuzzled Zachary and whinnied for his attention. The partnership between horse and rider would take time, but Zachary enjoyed the process.

For nine days in the middle of March '84, Zachary weathered the cold and the boredom of watching ranch hands come and go about their business. Sometimes Turk would seem to be barking orders from the porch, the crew standing before him. Today, a four-horse team wagon had pulled up, and with the help of the spyglass, Zachary watched Turk Corbin unload the large buckboard. He hefted sixteen sacks of something (Zachary couldn't make out what) into a shed. He worked alone at sunset.

Pharoah had a rough night, constantly nuzzling Zack as the wind blew snow in and around Zach's shelter and whistled through the trees and boulders. As a result, Zachary awoke and relieved himself long before dawn. Turned out to be fortuitous. Glancing at the ranch, Zachary saw a lit lantern on a post by the shed. Turk Corbin had hitched up a two-horse team to a buckboard, and Zachary watched him load eight bags from the previous day's shipment into the wagon and drive off.

Zachary broke camp calmly and started down the mountain, following the tracks of the buckboard, staying out of sight.

Once on Beale's Wagon Road, Turk had turned west toward Williams. At this hour, Turk's buckboard wheel ruts were the only tracks in the snow. Zachary followed. A mile before Williams, the furrows turned north.

Zachary dismounted and continued on foot. He was only interested in Corbin's destination and did not wish to meet with Turk. After a half-mile walk, Zachary spied a cabin with a small window and the glow of light within. Sure enough, Turk hefted the eight bags, one by one, into the shack. Using Lorenzo's glass, Zachary could see that the cabin contained everything from saddles, and farming tools, to feed supplies, ropes, shearing equipment, and fencing. Zachary returned to Pharoah and rode home, waking his wife just before breakfast.

"How about fixing oatmeal, toast, and coffee," said Zachary. "I'm starved."

Caroline stretched, yawned, and returned a hug from her husband. "Fine," she said. "While I'm fixing breakfast, you can read the letter that came two days ago from Phoenix.

The letter was from the U.S. Marshal's office. Tidball had assigned Deputy Leon Siddall to the Corbin case, expected to arrive in Flagstaff within a week.

Zachary read the essential points to Caroline. "That is great news." After breakfast, I'll need your help down at the paper. After typesetting this issue, you can help with the press and bundling. I'm confident that after reading the article, more will come forward to testify.

Caroline accompanied Zach down to the newspaper office, and while Zachary switched roles to a compositor, Caroline walked over to Eliza's shop. Eliza and Hanna were having tea. Caroline updated Hanna and Eliza on the results of Zachary's reconnaissance.

While Zachary worked on filling letters on his stick for transfer to the steel frame representing the front page of *The Flagstaff Flag*, Thomas McMillan knocked and entered.

"Got a minute?" said Thomas.

"Of course," said Zachary. "It isn't Wednesday. What brings you into town.?"

"Came to see you. I fired Turk Corbin this morning. He is no longer welcome at the ranch."

"Take a look at my page two notes," said Zach, handing over the description of the stolen goods in the cabin near Williams. "Deputy U.S. Marshal Siddall is on his way here from Phoenix. Should arrive in a day or two."

Thomas read the account of Zachary's surveillance.

"That bastard," said McMillan. "If I had known this, I would have locked him in a closet at the ranch. He could be anywhere by now."

Zachary thought momentarily, then said, "Who knows what he would have done if you had tried? I assume he's handy with that gun he wears. We should let the professional manage him."

"I agree," said Thomas. "But based on the evidence, the town council should issue a warrant for Turk's arrest. While you print your newspaper, I'll write the warrant, visit Hanna and the rest of the council, and gather signatures."

Light snow dusted the town beginning midafternoon. Caroline and Zachary had printed five hundred copies of *The Flagstaff Flag.* Bundles were prepared for the next train east to Cañon Diablo and Albuquerque, west to Williams, Needles, and on to San Francisco. The Prescott/Phoenix run would wait two days for the scheduled stagecoach.

The Brennans were exhausted from the physical printing press work and the tension of publishing the story. Zachary and Caroline were waiting for the coffee to cool when they heard a boy screaming in the street.

Zachary opened the front door just as a boy ran by.

"Hey there," shouted Zach. "Slow down. Your name is Jace Langley. Your dad's the new blacksmith. Take a breath and tell me what you're yelling about. Slowly, so I can understand you."

"Fire," said the boy. "Fire, Mr. Brennan. Fire, over at the McMillan building. The building next door is on fire too."

"Alright," said Zachary. "Run as fast as possible to the train depot and ring the station bell. Keep ringing it until people gather and tell them to bring buckets to the old town. We've got to put out that fire."

The boy ran off down the hill.

Zachary took off on the run for the McMillan building after grabbing two pails from a back closet. Caroline ran behind him, gathering her skirt and trying not to slip and fall in the slippery snow.

Residents of Old Town had already gathered, and the head of a bucket brigade originating at the springs sloshed water on the front of the burning building. Soon, Zachary heard the depot bell. More people arrived to help.

The snow became heavy, and the wind increased dramatically. The fire had crossed over to another building, and the McMillan building looked hopelessly lost to the fire.

Mr. Lopez, the bartender, came running up to Zachary, waving his arms wildly. "Mr. Brennan," he said. "The newspaper building is on fire."

"What," said Zach, "Which building?"

"Your building," said Lopez. "The printing press building."

Zach shook his head. "That makes no sense. The wind is blowing in the opposite direction from the newspaper."

Two buildings, including Thomas McMillan's office, were nearing the point of total loss. The fire raged on through a third building. The bucket brigade worked hard to contain the fire before it leaped to another structure. Zachary cajoled three men to run with him to the press building.

The south corner of the front of Zachary's office building had caught fire. Flames were already starting to lick the porch ceiling.

In despair, Zachary looked at the three men, trying to figure out a strategy. Zachary found two blankets and a tarp and distributed them to the men, who attempted to beat the fire.

An idea came to Zachary. He rushed inside the office, found a wrench, and uncoupled the fitting on the hose running from the water reservoir to the steam boiler. There was enough gravity pressure to spray the burning corner. One of the men used an ax to chop through the porch from the inside. The water from the boiler extinguished the fire. The printing press was saved. Zachary left one of the men guarding the building against further outbreaks while he ran back to the McMillan office building.

Five buildings had burned to the ground, but the fire had burned out. The acrid smell of smoke settled on the volunteers' clothes, and the ashes drifted to New Town. Three interior rooms in the McMillan building, including the accounting journals cabinet, escaped destruction. *The Flagstaff Flag* building had survived. People drifted to their homes. The Scofields went with Hanna to her boarding house; their belongings were lost.

Caroline and Zachary, exhausted, decided to stay at Hanna's for the night as well. A group of battle-weary volunteers gathered in the lobby. Thomas McMillan, unusually quiet, walked over to Zachary and handed him an envelope. "The warrant," he said softly, returned across the room, and sat down.

Jace Langley, the boy who had sounded the fire alarm, approached Zachary. "I saw him," he said.

Zachary's fatigue vanished. "What did you see," he said.

"I saw who started the fire."

Thomas rose again from his chair and joined the boy and the editor.

"Who did you see, my boy," said McMillan.

"It was your man, Mr. McMillan," said Jace. "I'm sorry, that man that hangs around with you sometimes. He's left-handed and wears his gun on that side, anyway."

Thomas and Zachary exchanged glances.

"Turk Corbin," said Zachary.

"The rat needs drowning," said Thomas, spitting mad.

Joseph Kardin, a baker, spoke, "Saw him ten minutes ago on horseback heading up the hill to Old Town."

Zachary stood, stuffed the warrant in his inside coat pocket, and called to Caroline, drinking tea in the kitchen with Hanna and Eliza. "I'm going back to the office. The Langley boy says Turk started the fire. It sounds like Turk is hanging around town. He may try to finish what he started this afternoon." Zachary led Caroline out onto Hanna's porch.

"What are you going to do?" asked Caroline.

"Arrest the son of a bitch if I can," Zach said.

"You can't do that. We've got to wait for the deputy marshal."

"If he starts another fire, we lose everything. I'm going."

Zachary kissed his wife and turned toward Old Town. Caroline tugged him back and hugged Zachary as tight as she could, trying to prevent him from leaving. He smelled of smoke. She felt the gun through his suit coat. She suddenly feared the firearm her husband carried.

Thomas McMillan came out to the porch. "Jim Udall said I could borrow his shotgun. I'll go to his house, get the shotgun, and meet you on the hill."

Zachary nodded, broke away from Caroline, and started down the street.

Hanna and Eliza joined Caroline on the porch. Caroline, in tears, revealed Zachary's plan to apprehend Turk Corbin.

"I'll get my rifle," said Hanna. "I can hit a running wolf at fifty feet."

Eliza looked perplexed. "Why is he going after Corbin?" she said. "You told me the deputy would take care of Corbin."

Caroline began to cry.

"Turk Corbin has tortured Zach's soul ever since Eli was killed," said Caroline. "He feels it is his fault your father died. He's written the whole thing down and put it in an article in the paper."

"How could it have been his fault,' said Eliza. "Caroline, tell us."

"He was there, Eliza. Watched the whole thing. Your father defended himself against that man and his six-shooter. Batted away the gun with the kiln poker and put that scar on Turk's hand."

Now Eliza began to cry. "Go on," she said.

"Turk had a pocket gun. He pulled it out and shot Eli twice in the chest. That's what Zachary saw. Zach might have been able to stop it. He couldn't pick up Turk's gun."

Hanna ran into the house, brought out her rifle and three wool wraps, one for each of them for warmth, and said, "Let's go."

The three women, at a fast clip, followed Zachary.

49 |Last Chapter

The long walk from Hanna's boarding house up the gentle rise to Old Town did not help Zach's nerves. He mulled Turk's options. Turk probably continued west of town toward Williams to cash in on his cabin of stolen goods.

Desperate from his first failed attempt at arson, Corbin could be relighting the McMillan building fire in the hope of destroying the ledgers that proved his misappropriations. Or the outlaw might turn Zach's printing press into scrap metal, revenge for Turk's name appearing in the newspaper.

The snow showers ended just as Zach crested the hill in Old Town. The clouds blew east. Open sky overtook Flagstaff. The sunset cast an orange glow on the charred building remains, enough light for Zachary to spot Turk. The man sloshed coal oil from a five-gallon can around the charred corner of the McMillan building. Before Zachary closed within shouting range, Turk tossed a match, and the Kerosene whooshed ten feet skyward. Billowing black smoke surrounded Corbin and his horse.

Turk emerged as the smoke drifted up and grabbed his horse's reins. Holding the reins in one hand, he used his free hand to pull the McMillan purchases ledger from a saddlebag and toss it into the hot center of the fire.

Like sentries, the charred bottom third of the porch posts framed the bonfire engulfing the corner of the burnt structure.

Turk Corbin manhandled his terrified horse. The horse continued to paw the ground and neigh, objecting to the cloud of choking smoke. Still holding the reins in his right hand, Turk smacked the horse in the jaw with his left hand. "Stop fussing," yelled Turk, turning and spitting part of his chew.

The horse reared, attempting to kick Corbin with its front legs. As it was, the horse burned the reins through Turk's bare left hand and instantly bolted toward New Town.

"Turk Corbin," shouted Zachary, now seventy feet away from the outlaw. "I have a warrant for your arrest. Better for you if you come peaceably."

"What's this bullshit, Paperman," said Turk, pulling his gun and firing at Zachary. On the same side of the street, Zack took cover behind a scorched open building door on his right.

Hiding behind the door, Zachary brooded over the bullet he had heard whiz by his left ear. He couldn't shake the closeness of his death out of his head. He shivered, cold sweat pouring down his back, yet his forehead burned as if feverish.

Off to his left, on the other side of the street, he saw Hanna, rifle in hand, take a position behind an outhouse about one hundred feet away from Corbin. *Could she be accurate at that distance? Could she fire the rifle; shoot Turk?*

Then Zachary noticed Eliza and Caroline peeking around the other corner of the outhouse. *What were they up to? What were they doing here?*

"Caroline," shouted Zachary, with a voice as shaky as his knees. "Go back, get out of here."

"You come with us," said Caroline. "Turk Corbin isn't worth it."

His wife made sense. What could he do against an accurate shooter? Zachary felt the gun against his sweating armpit. *I've never fired the gun. Shit, I can barely hold on to it.*

Zachary watched a desperate Turk looking this way and that for his best escape route. The fire behind him billowed higher and spread, smoke rising off of the shoulders of Corbin's duster as his sweat turned to steam.

Eliza stepped out from the outhouse cover and walked five feet toward the center of the street, a clear target but coaxing Corbin into the open, where Hanna would have a more precise shot. Zachary blinked. Amazing, unimaginable. Eli Blackstone came to mind. A man of action.

"You killed my father, Turk Corbin," Eliza said. "You are the scum of this earth, and your time has come."

Turk hesitated, desperate. "So, Paperman," he finally screamed. "You brought your negress with you for protection. I have no such compunction. Another notch." Laughing hysterically, Turk stood up from the burnt porch post he used for cover.

Hanna fired. Her shot hit the scarred post next to Turk, flinging wood chips in the air.

Zachary stepped out, drawing his gun from beneath his shoulder. He cocked the hammer so that a cartridge aligned with the barrel and sighted down it at Turk.

Turk fired his six-gun.

To his left, peripherally, Zach saw Eliza reel back, hit in the arm or side. Zachary pulled the trigger. The Peacemaker kicked back, hitting Zachary in the chin, and he wobbled back.

While Zach staggered, dizzy, Turk turned his gun toward Zachary and fired. A searing burn in his left side made Zach double over. Then he heard Caroline scream. "Zachary, Oh Zach!"

Zachary glanced up. The damn woman was running across the street toward him. Turk now took careful aim at Eliza, thinking Zach out of commission.

"I got another Negra in my sights," laughed Turk.

The smell of smoke was so strong Zach's vision blurred. He imagined blood bursting out the back of his falling brother,

Jeremiah, killed by an errant bullet. What if a bullet hits Caroline? *His love would be gone.*

Zachary straightened up, tears helping to clear his vision. Steeling his arm, he fired at Corbin. *Missed by a mile*. Unable to determine what danger Zach posed, Turk turned his attention back to Zach and fired. He was too quick; he missed as well. Zachary was doggedly moving toward Turk through the smoke. Each step was like walking through foot-deep mud.

Cock the Colt. *Think of the job, nothing else. Steady*. Zachary fired. Turk fell back, knicked in the shoulder by Zach's bullet.

Zachary stood just twenty-five feet away from the blackened posts, the wall of flame, and Corbin. Zach cocked the gun, but Turk was down and looked done. Zach's stomach turned, and he couldn't finish it.

Turk had fallen into a pool of kerosene leading to the mostly empty five-gallon can, yet he raised his gun toward Zachary. The fire flashed around Corbin, and the can exploded, the percussion flattening Zachary backward to the ground, engulfing Turk in bright orange flames. Corbin's scream ended after fifteen excruciating seconds like a sickening staccato laugh. Zach heard the breath wheeze out of the burnt badman and watched Turk's black blood pool in the slush.

Nothing for it. Turk Corbin; dead.

Hanna rushed forward, dropping her rifle and screaming, "Zachary… Son," she said. "My foolish boy." She hugged and kissed him five times on his face and neck.

Thomas approached with his shotgun, just arriving on the scene.

Zachary turned and hobbled back to his wife. Caroline helped Eliza and handed her off to the much stronger McMillan. Eliza suffered the same grazing wound on her left side as Zachary.

Zachary took Caroline in his arms. His hug squeezed the air from her lungs. Thankful they had both survived. He let up a bit for her to breathe and kissed her, eyes still streaming with smoky tears.

Having heard the commotion and gunfire in Old Town, the townsfolk arrived, took up buckets, and doused the fire in the corner of the McMillan building. Thomas McMillan took charge, organizing a burial detail and commandeering a buckboard to take Eliza and Zachary back to Hanna's place. Thomas helped Eliza into the buckboard, then gripped her shoulder. "Thank you again for your help," said Thomas.

"It has been a difficult day," said Eliza as she patted Zach's knee, sitting beside her. "It is in the past now. You agree, Zachary?"

"Yes, the past… Done," said Zachary. "Eliza, you amazed me today; you reminded me of your father."

Epilogue

By July 1884, construction crews had replaced the burned structures, erecting them in New Town, nearer the train station. Flagstaff no longer smelled of smoke. Hanna's water pipe initiative now provided Leroux Springs water to a water tower next to the depot. Hanna sold lots on the other side of the train tracks. The Flagstaff US Post Office opened for business next to the train depot. Zach carried Caroline over the threshold of their new home that month.

Hanna and Zachary Brennan, Thomas McMillan, A. E. Ayers (lumber,) Eliza Blackstone, and the Riordan brothers (cattlemen) formed the core of solid citizens for the town.

Flagstaff had a railroad, livestock, lumber, and service industries of merchants, cafes, hotels, and saloons. The town was set to become the largest city on the railroad line between Albuquerque and the west coast of the United States.

Eliza and Robert Cabreira became engaged to be married.

The Flagstaff Flag's circulation steadily grew, especially in the outlying small towns along the train route.

Zachary wrote to the Yavapai County sheriff, requesting a deputy to reside permanently in the area. Flagstaff townsfolk looked to Zachary as an unofficial lawman to settle minor disputes, a role Zachary disdained. He never carried his Colt SAA Peacemaker and never practiced shooting with it. He told folks he couldn't hit the side of a barn and wanted to keep it that way.

Author Request

Please rate and review FEAR OF THE GUN on Amazon USA
https://www.amazon.com/dp/B0BBTTYH6V
or on Amazon UK
https://www.amazon.co.uk/dp/B0BBTTYH6V

Please participate in the author's quick, four-question survey:
https://www.surveymonkey.com/r/6X8MQHL

Author's Blog and Website:
https://johngerts.weebly.com

www.ingramcontent.com/pod-product-compliance
Lightning Source LLC
Chambersburg PA
CBHW050844210726
48290CB00004B/1075
9781732603431